SPIDER'S WEB IN THE GREEN MOUNTAINS

A COOPER NORTH MYSTERY

by

Richard Wolkomir

ALSO BY RICHARD WOLKOMIR

WIL DEFT

(In a haunted forest in a spellbound land, one soul's afire—a novel of epic fantasy)

SINNABAR

(A New Jersey BMX biker vs. a dystopian wizardarchy—with two worlds at stake)

FRANKIE & JOHNNY, & NELLIE BLY

(Fifteen stories about what never was and never will be)

RIDERS OF THE DUST-GRAY STEPPE

(A Pleistocene western, and other dispatches from distant times and strange places—15 stories)

DOG DANCE OF SNIKIA

(A comic novella—if your dog's a genius, shouldn't you do what he says?)

THE BLUE CHAIR

(A mystery novella--In the quiet Vermont town, who strangled the student from Italy?)

JUNKYARD BANDICOOTS
& OTHER TALES OF THE WORLD'S ENDANGERED SPECIES

(With Joyce Rogers Wolkomir)

Richard Wolkomir is a long-time contributor of award-winning articles and essays to such magazines as Reader's Digest, Smithsonian, and National Geographic. Now he is writing mysteries, and also speculative novels and short fiction, with science fiction and fantasy stories appearing in a variety of literary journals.

Visit the author at www.richardjoycewolkomir.net

Author's website: www.richardjoycewolkomir.net

CHAPTER ONE

Rain.

Darkness.

A black motorcycle rumbles west on Hill Street, moving slowly because of the downpour.

And because its headlight is turned off.

Just before the stone arch, marking the entrance to Mt. Augustus College, the biker stops, stretches out a steadying leg, and twists in the saddle to stare at a house.

It is a large house, brick, built two centuries ago, Federal style.

Silhouetted in the living room's Palladian window, a woman reads a book.

Against the lamplight, she's just a tall shadow, but the biker knows her looks: gray-haired and lanky, almost gaunt. Cheekbones prominent. Penetrating gray eyes.

She looks like a gyrfalcon.

As the biker watches, she turns a page.

Gaze still fixed on the window, the biker reaches a hand into a long leather holster, affixed to the saddle, and—slowly— draws out a rifle.

Cooper North's window lit up—lightning flash—instantly followed by a thunder detonation. It sounded like a direct hit, but Cooper's reading lamp only flickered.

She remembered an old book's opening, often mocked: "It was a dark and stormy night…"

Gust-driven rain battered the window. Water gurgled in the big house's ornate gutters.

She thought, amused: nighttime storms don't foretell mayhem. Not actually. Maybe in old novels, but not in the real world. Not in Dill, Vermont.

She knew mayhem.

Thirty-six years as Allen County state's attorney—hundreds of prosecutions. Then Vermont's attorney general—hundreds more. Reckless endangerment. Manslaughter. Murder. But never a major felony on a stormy night.

Out on the street, the motorcyclist rests the rifle stock against a shoulder and squints through the telescopic sight.

Three months ago, after a stint on the state's Supreme Court, Cooper finally retired. She'd planned to read and watch birds, but that lasted for one Swedish mystery novel and one re-reading of *The Odyssey,* and one sunrise visit to Abner Park with binoculars. Then Mt. Augustus College telephoned.

"Coop, our new criminal justice program? Get it going for us, okay?"

She'd grumped about it, but only for show. Retirement already bored her.

Lightning again. Another thunder whack.

2

She put her thriller novel down on the side table and reached for her cane, laying it across her lap so she wouldn't need to grope for it if the power went out, and all the while she felt watched.

Henry.

He'd been at it two days now.

Thirty pounds of butterscotch-and-white Pembroke Welsh corgi. He sat on the living room carpet, studying her.

Rain blurs the scope, so the biker lowers the rifle and wipes the eyepiece with a handkerchief, then raises the rifle and aims again.

Last week, Cooper's nephew called from Boston to report a promotion, and a move to Brussels. Only thing is, he said, we can't take Henry. Then his wife got on the phone.

"Coop, it'll be so good for you, in that huge empty house—a dog for company!"

Two days ago they'd driven up from Boston and dropped Henry off. When the corgi realized they weren't coming back, his sharp brown eyes dulled. For an hour, he moped. Then he shook himself and methodically explored the house, room by room. That settled, he began surveillance of Cooper. Last night she'd awakened in the wee hours and there was Henry, sitting beside her bed, watching her sleep.

In her mind, Cooper heard her long-gone mother pronounce, in a sniffy voice: "Too clever by half!"

Yes, the dog's clever, Cooper thought. He's been exiled from Beacon Hill, so he needs to scout this new home, gauge this new person in his life, fit himself in.

Crosshairs on the woman's head, rock steady. Now squeeze....

Another lightning-thunder combo.

This time the lights did go black—startled, Cooper knocked her cane over, bending to grab it off the floor, in the dark.

Cracking glass.

A roar.

Receding, gone.

Now she heard only rain, and something ticked.

The lights flickered back on. Window shards glittered on the carpet. In the living-room's plaster wall, a puncture.

If she hadn't just then bent to fetch her cane, she'd have been shot in the head.

She snapped off the light. No point still being a lit-up target in the window. She sat in the dark, listening.

Tick. Tick....

It was the grandfather's clock, out by the stairs. It had kept time there for generations. Only now, though, did she notice its ticking.

Henry leaned against her leg, his fur warm, but she felt chilled. She thought about a vodka martini.

Fumbling on the side table in the dark, she grabbed the phone, and stared at the illuminated keys. Her house abutted Mt. Augustus College, so the campus cops were closest, and she keyed in their number.

4

After two rings a deep voice said: "Security."

She thought: "Mike Bolknor—it would be him."

Two minutes later a car skidded to a stop out front and a door slammed and her doorbell rang.

CHAPTER TWO

"Do you have enemies?" Bolknor asked.

Cooper shook her head. Who'd want to shoot her?

And should she have hired this man unseen?

She chaired the Campus Security Committee, and on the fall semester's first day, the former security chief dropped dead, of a cerebral hemorrhage. Cooper filled in, but they'd needed a replacement fast.

She thought: why, just when I've been shot at, am I worrying about this?

"I called the Dill PD," Bolknor told her. "Jurisdiction, right?"

He looked down at her, expressionless. Few men were tall enough to look down at her.

His application had stood out—forty-two years old, Army MP, then NYPD detective, seventeen years. Awards. Citations. Excellent references.

But why shuck a New York career for an obscure Vermont college?

"Dill PD'll dig the slug out of the wall, look for tire tracks," Bolknor said. "We'll watch the house here, keep eyes on you."

"For how long?" Cooper asked.

She thought: bodyguards? In Dill? Me?

Bolknor shrugged.

"Until we figure what's up," he said.

His New York inflection—too big-city for this small college in the Green Mountains?

Maybe too big generally. Street-tough big. Eyebrows a thick black bar. A heaviness, as if his insides were basalt. His words seemed to come up from deep silence. And that, with his size, could intimidate. Would he spook kids from hyper-protective homes? And could he handle rowdy students without going Flatbush Avenue on them?

She thought: why am I obsessing about this?

Then: it's to distract myself....

Because the shooter's still out there.....

And, yes, I'm frightened.

"It was a dark and stormy night," Cooper muttered.

Bolknor looked at her.

"Bulwer-Lytton?" he asked.

She nodded, thinking, well, that's a surprise.

Something touched her leg and she looked down, to see Henry looking up, brow furrowed, as if asking, you all right, friend? She swallowed a sob.

Shock, she realized. Trauma. Which infuriated her.

"I'll hunt that bastard down," she said.

Bolknor looked at her, but she couldn't read his expression.

"Probably no tire tracks, with this rain," he said.

He studied her, and even his gaze seemed heavy.

"Slug in the wall's not likely to offer much, either," he said.

He looked at her silently. It occurred to Cooper that he knew her—his putative new boss—no better than she knew him.

"So it's mostly up to you," he said.

She raised her eyebrows, unsure what he meant.

"Figure why," he said. "That's the only way we'll get to who."

He looked out the broken window, and so did Cooper, sixty-nine years old, but still with penetrating gray eyes. Through the broken pane, she heard rain pounding the slate walkway, and rumbling thunder, now distant. She thought she'd need to do something about that window, and her leg hurt more than usual, so maybe a new orthopedic shoe insert would help.

And somebody wants me dead!

A dark and stormy night.

Henry, sitting on the carpet, looked from Mike Bolknor to Cooper North, as if taking a reading, gauging what it all meant for Henry. Then he yawned, sticking out a long pink tongue. He lay down on the carpet, stretched out on his side, sighed, shut his eyes.

Almost immediately, Henry slept.

CHAPTER THREE

"Jeezum Crow!"

Cooper wished Tip LaPerle wouldn't use old Yankee euphemisms like that in front of Mike Bolknor, because she didn't want the new man from New York City dismissing Dill's police chief as a rube.

It was the next morning, a meeting in Cooper's office, above the campus-security headquarters, to coordinate the investigation. She couldn't read Bolknor, except that he wore a suit and tie, vaguely inappropriate in Vermont, where the sartorial norm was whatever, but she'd known Tip LaPerle most of his life, and she saw him bristling inside. He didn't like this big-city cop on his turf.

A memory bubbled up, from thirty years back: ten-year-old Tip LaPerle, like a sinewy kid goat, ready to butt, bursts into the Allen County State's Attorney's office. Oversized ears. Thatch of straw-colored hair. Blue eyes resolute.

"How do I become a policeman?"

If you knew what his father had been, and his mother, and his brothers....

Cooper sighed.

She thought: you need to be born here, in a small town like this, to grasp it.

You'd see the college, up on the hill, if you visited, and the cupolaed Victorians and brick federals, shaded by sugar maples. Downtown, you'd see Main Street's boutiques and eateries and indie-music cafes and bookstores. Farther down, where the hill bottomed out at the river, with railroad tracks alongside, you'd see Tenement Row, where Tip LaPerle grew up.

You wouldn't see the spider web.

That's how Cooper envisioned it: invisible strands crisscrossing Dill—feuds, affairs, business dealings, marriages, divorces, envies, jealousies, kindnesses....

Those strands interconnected everyone, and they stretched back through time, too, because lives here ran deep.

Cooper's own family came in colonial days, when the Dill brothers, Abner and Augustus, trekked up from Massachusetts to the Green Mountains wilderness, to start the sawmill that spawned granite quarries and other enterprises, and finally evolved into Dill Industries, the software corporation headquartered across Abner Park from Mt. Augustus College. Other families came down from Quebec, to blast granite out of the quarries. Stone carvers immigrated from Italy and Spain. And there were Sixties people, too. They'd come during Mt. Augustus College's love beads and "Hell No, We Won't Go" phase, and many stayed in Dill, opened music stores or artist supplies shops or organic food emporiums. Some, gray now, or bald, served on the city council, and took up such causes as turning empty lots into communal gardens.

Cooper looked at the two men sitting across from her desk. Mike Bolknor remained a puzzle, but she wanted him to understand that Tip LaPerle policed this town effectively, precisely because Tip understood the spider web, sensed its mutating strands. Tip knew Dill, down to its molecular level.

On the other hand, Tip might be just a tad impulsive.

Thinking about that, she pushed aside heaped paperwork to make space on her desk to rest her elbows, and suddenly—because last night's gunshot still unsettled her, since she normally wouldn't care—her office's mess shamed her.

Leaning towers of paper, books strewn on the floor, along with newspapers and magazines, and also Styrofoam coffee cups, some not-quite empty, on the desk a mulch of Newman's Own chocolate-chip cookie crumbs....

Her home was just the same.

She thought: "I'm Cooper North, and I'm a slob."

Which reminded her of the AA meetings she'd once needed to attend and she veered her thoughts away from that topic.

"I never saw the car," she said. "I only heard it—loud."

Something about that loudness nagged at her. No muffler?

"Jeezum," Tip said, shaking his head, looking at her.

She knew that meant, how could this happen, Coop? To you? And that he'd go after the shooter like a ferret.

11

Mike Bolknor sat mute in his chair, right ankle on left knee. She couldn't guess his thoughts. Even Henry the corgi, now sitting at Cooper's feet, after having crisscrossed the floor, snarking up crumbs, looked more involved in the meeting, bright eyes focusing on whoever spoke. She guessed Bolknor listened, professionally, but kept most of himself entombed in some deep-down internal vault.

"Coop, it's got to be somebody you put in jail," Tip said. "Got a grudge."

Cooper shrugged.

"Four decades, Tip," she said. "How many prosecutions? Two thousand?"

Mike Bolknor finally spoke: "Anything from the tech people?"

Cooper saw Tip stiffen.

"No tire tracks—rain, and it was all on pavement, anyway," Tip said. "Slug from the wall's a .30-06, hunting rifle, truckloads of them, just here in Allen County, so unless we find the weapon in somebody's gun rack, and match the slug to it…."

And now, Cooper thought, Mike Bolknor will say "told you so." Bolknor, however, didn't respond at all, not even with a facial expression.

Tip, though, suddenly glared at him.

"I suppose the NYPD's got super-techs, right?" he said. "Wizard out stuff from that slug our trooper lab in Waterbury couldn't get?"

Bolknor looked back blandly, and shrugged.

"Doubt it," he said

Cooper thought: Tip's lashing out because he's intimidated by the New York cop. And she felt embarrassed for him.

"I'll think about old cases," Cooper said. "But...."

Abruptly the door burst open—no knock—and a young woman rushed in, already talking.

"...so I'll need the files, all those case studies? From our evidence class?" she said. "That newspaper lady's coming again and...."

"Stacey—this is a meeting," Cooper said.

Now the woman noticed the two men, and she instantly got cute. It was subtle. A cocking of the head, so the blond hair cascaded down on that side, one hip slightly outthrust under her skirt, cornflower-blue eyes gone limpidly winsome. It was, Cooper thought, wryly, one of Stacey Gillibrand's talents, along with a genius for being annoying.

"Oh! You're talking about last night!" Stacey said. "I've got some ideas and...."

"Office hours," Cooper said, putting stone in her voice. "Come back then."

Stacey looked from Bolknor to LaPerle, eyes extremely blue. Then she looked at Cooper, did an eye roll, and shrugged.

"Okay," she said, giving the men an over-the-shoulder glance as she left the room.

Bolknor and LaPerle exchanged a look, eyebrows up, and Cooper thought maybe there was hope yet, for them to work together.

She shook her head, irritated.

"She's twenty-six, calls other students 'brats,'" Cooper said. "Divorced, been a law-office receptionist, now aims to become a superstar lawyer herself—if she starts playing Nancy Drew with you two, a little discouragement, please."

Bolknor and LaPerle both looked briefly wry, then serious again.

"Well, how about students then, with a grudge, like bad grades?" Bolknor asked. "Ticked off enough to take a shot?"

Cooper imagined Stacey Gillibrand shooting her. Motive: to take over Mt. Augustus College's Criminal Justice Program. That, however, was ridiculous, because it poured rain last night, and Stacey wouldn't risk soaking her hair-do.

"You're smiling, Coop," Tip said. "You think of something?"

Cooper shook her head, still smiling.

"Private joke," she said.

"Faculty?" Bolknor said. "Administrators? Step on any toes?"

"Everybody loves me," Cooper said.

"Dumped an old flame," Bolknor suggested, and Cooper laughed.

There'd been only one flame, at Harvard Law, where everyone, including the professors, cold shouldered her, because in that era women were unwelcome there, but one fellow student had welcomed her. They'd dated. Then polio struck and she was out a year. She'd come back with a lame leg and found her boyfriend married to somebody else. And later, in Vietnam, a sniper killed him. After that, there'd been one marriage proposal, which had mainly irritated her, but no more suitors, at least, none serious. Too tall. Too lame. And with gray eyes that looked right through you.

"Tip's probably right," Cooper said. "Somebody I sent to prison...."

They left it that Cooper would mull over old prosecutions. Mike Bolknor took the elevator down to campus security, to arrange a watch on Cooper's house. Tip LaPerle said he'd canvass Cooper's neighbors, see if anyone saw something.

Alone in her office, Cooper checked the Yellow Pages, then called a glazier. Next, she called her podiatrist, because of her aching leg. Maybe she needed a new shoe insert.

She put the phone down and something seemed wrong.

No Henry.

He slipped out, she thought. With Bolknor and LaPerle. She imagined him running through Dill on those short corgi legs.

Lost! Terrified! Alone!

She limped to the elevator, cane thumping on the floor, then impatiently rode down to Campus Security's offices on the first floor. She needed help to hunt for the dog.

Her dog.

Henry.

Three days, that's all I've known him, she thought. But if he got run over....

She barged into Mike Bolknor's corner office, and he looked up from the patrol schedules he was studying.

"Henry's gone," Cooper said.

She hoped she didn't sound hysterical. She'd always been calm. In court, nothing could shake her.

Bolknor studied her, then—with his chin—indicated she should look under his desk.

Henry lay there asleep, his snout resting on Bolknor's extra-large black-leather shoe.

Cooper thought: I'm a basket case.

She rode the elevator back up to her office, with Henry riding with her. She collapsed into her chair.

Once again she imagined a vodka martini in her hand, heard ice tinkling in the glass, felt the chill through her fingers. She thought about lighting up a Camel, inhaling its smoke into her lungs, feeling the bite.

She kept an unopened bottle of vodka in her desk drawer, alongside an unopened package of unfiltered cigarettes, each with a rubber band around it. When she needed to, she opened the drawer and thwacked both rubber bands. She did that now.

She thought: I've got to go watch birds.

Instead, she drove downtown and parked in front of The Percolator, her favorite Main Street coffee shop. Time for lunch.

CHAPTER FOUR

Cooper sat in a booth—enjoying a portabella-mushroom-and-red-pepper quiche, which she hadn't had to cook, a big plus—when Jack Abbott pushed open the door, scanned the room, spotted her, and barged toward her through the noontime crowd, grabbing the middle-aged waitress, June Winkel, by the shoulders to move her out of his way, ignoring her snarled curse, eyes fixed on Cooper.

"Hello, Jack," Cooper said, wearily, as he dropped into the seat facing her.

"Hey, I heard what happened last night, you getting shot at!"

Cooper waited, interested to see which way this would go. Sympathy? Something else?

"Wake-up call!" he said. "You finally ready to sell that monstrosity?"

Cooper sighed. This discussion inevitably ended with Abbott going into full cape-buffalo mode, telling her she was damned stupid, and Cooper figured she truly was stupid, if you defined the word as Jack Abbott did, meaning failure to do what he wanted.

"As I've previously mentioned, no," Cooper said.

"That's stupid!" Abbott said, raising a beefy arm and wiggling a thick finger to summon June Winkel, without looking in her direction.

"Why stupid?" Cooper asked.

"Because it costs what's in Fort Knox to heat it, and pay the property tax, and everything else, like keeping the grounds up, and now you're getting shot at in that damned thing, all alone!"

"No, now I have a Pembroke Welsh corgi living with me, named Henry," Cooper said.

"Crap," Abbott said. "You've got a will? Foist it off on that nephew of yours?"

"That's still to be decided," Cooper said.

"He's loaded," Abbott said. "He's got no interest in a big old house in this podunk."

"Jack, that house's been in my family over two centuries," Cooper said.

"Yeah, well like I've told you, it's perfect for a history museum, about the town here, Dill brothers and all that, which is what I want it for, and there'd be stuff about the Norths in there, so smarten up—ever consider a nice condo? No fuss?"

June Winkel showed up, gave Abbott a vinegary glower, and said: "What?"

"Coffee, black," Abbott said, eyes still fixed on Cooper, and June stomped off to fetch him his coffee, which Cooper could see she'd like to throw in his face.

It occurred to Cooper that Tip LaPerle and Jack Abbott both came out of Tenement Row, and both made something of themselves. Tip strove to separate from his thieving parents and brothers by becoming a cop, but Jack Abbott simply wanted to make money, which he'd done, wheeling and dealing, mostly in real estate. He now owned most of Tenement Row.

June Winkel brought Abbott's coffee and thumped it onto the table, sloshing a little, which caused Abbott to snarl: "Can't this place get decent help?" He said it to her back, though, because she'd already turned and walked away.

Abbott drank his coffee in three swigs, eyes constantly on Cooper. Even his graying brush cut seemed to bristle. Finally he slammed down the cup, pulled out his wallet, peeled off four singles from the thick wad inside, and slapped them down next to the empty cup as he got up.

"Damn it, Cooper, smarten up, will you?" he said.

Then he turned and barged out of the coffee shop.

Cooper watched him go. And she surprised herself, thinking: would Jack Abbott shoot at me?

To scare me out of the house? Or so I'd be dead before I could will the house away, so it would be up for grabs?

He'd been violent in his younger days, the toughest, meanest fighter in the tenements. He'd use his fists or a brick, snatched off the ground, whatever it took.

Was it him?

Cooper strongly doubted it. Wanted to doubt it.

But could she be sure?

Driving her black Volvo back up onto the Hill, for her podiatrist appointment, she felt deep-down

19

unsettled. And she wondered, were shoe inserts just an excuse for this visit with Dr. Drew Saunders?

Maybe.

She'd been shot at. Just now she'd fended off the real-estate bully. She needed a respite, so why not bask in an old friendship's warmth? Otherwise, it might be an iced Gray Goose Vodka, with an olive.

CHAPTER FIVE

"Off with your sneakers, Sweetcakes," Drew said, a syrupy remnant of South Carolina in his intonation, and Cooper dutifully removed her Nikes, thinking if anyone except Drew Saunders called her 'Sweetcakes,' she'd want to sock the condescending ass.

As Drew looked at her feet, she realized she wasn't just upset about the bullet through her window. It was also that she'd started suspecting Jack Abbott. He had the charm of a sledge hammer, but she'd known him for decades, couldn't believe he'd shoot at her. Did she delude herself? She'd thought she knew this town, and its people. But did she?

Maybe she didn't know Dill at all.

"How's Mona?" Cooper said, as Drew fingered her left foot's arch, a gentle touch.

Drew made his eyes impish and theatrically consulted his Rolex.

"At this second, Ms. Mona's holding court in our parlor," he said. "She's tasking the Dill Garden Club with her autumn edicts."

It was an old joke, in their circle, that Mona Dill Saunders had monarchal tendencies. Mona's mother started it, when Mona was six: "For that child, Queen of New England's too paltry—she demands Holy Global Empress!"

It stuck as a nickname, "Empress."

Which Mona always countered with a stern stare and an acerbic: "We are not amused!"

Actually, it did amuse her. For one thing, she was a benign monarch, as everyone knew. She believed imperiousness, in a good cause, was no vice, and her many causes were, in her opinion, all holy. Also, she knew her overbearing bluntness entertained her friends, because they understood she had a kind heart, if not a warm one, and fierce concern for her realm, which extended from Dill, and all of Allen County, to the entire state, necessitating frequent high-speed drives to the state capitol, in Montpelier, in her black Cadillac Escalade, to bully legislators into coughing up funds to save a threatened 1800s Quebec-border opera house, say, or a remote Northeast Kingdom bog, with its assorted amphibians, or to legislate support for alternative energy, Mona having put her money where her convictions lay, by populating an overgrown hayfield at a defunct old family farm with giant, slowly turning windmills.

Drew removed Cooper's orthopedic insert from her left shoe and scrutinized it.

"Where's the pain?" he said. "Foot? Lower leg? Knee? Upper leg?"

"Leg, all of it," Cooper said.

"Hmm," he said.

Cooper sat in his patient's chair, with her legs straight out, and he sat beside her on a low stool, eyes level with her feet, so she looked down on his bent head and noticed considerable gray now mixed with the gold, and a hint of incipient balding. Even so, Drew Saunders was still the same movie-star handsome man Mona Dill had brought home more than three decades ago, tall and slim, with amused eyes, her latest artwork find, after they'd met skiing at Stowe, where he'd just started as a junior partner in a podiatrist's practice. At the time, everyone thought Mona, fresh out of Skidmore, with an art-history degree, had fallen for a deep-south charmer infatuated mainly with her money, and yet here they were, still married, and Drew gave every sign of adoring her.

It comforted Cooper, thinking of these old things just now, friends she'd known so long, when somebody wanted to kill her.

Drew prodded her left foot's metatarsus.

That bullet!

She'd been settling into old age. She'd meant to rest and read and think and watch birds, until the college dragooned her into training future law officers and lawyers, and she'd been getting a little bored, anyway.

Then, the gunshot.

It seemed to tip her world.

She'd taken pride in being a prosecutor: when a crime stabbed the community, she cauterized the wound. Now she wondered if sending felons to prison merely embittered them, created a nighttime shooter. Did somebody hate her so much? An unsettling thought, and her mind veered away from it, back into the past.

"You came to town on that motorcycle," Cooper told Drew. "It was red, like a maraschino cherry."

Drew laughed.

"My faithful old Honda was judged an unseemly steed for the royal consort," he said. "Off with its head!"

He sat thinking, before he spoke again.

"Probably saved my life—nobody wore helmets back then."

"That first year, I remember, Jack Abbott took you hunting, along with some of his friends, thinking they'd have fun with the flatlander, but only you got a buck," Cooper said. "It got to be a running joke."

"My youthful heritage," he said, laying on the Dixie accent. "Why, back on the Saunders family plantation, Miss Coop, we all rode to the hounds!"

A joke, because his father had been a roofer in Charleston, his mother an assembly line worker, and he'd gone to the state university only because a wealthy old lady, whose lawn he mowed, and whose gardens he weeded, decided to pay the smart boy's way, as a charity, which everyone knew, because Drew told them about it, just as everyone knew Drew's deer-hunting days ended after that first year, Mona refusing to countenance "slaughtering quadrupedal innocents."

Drew had settled for opening a podiatry practice, for self-respect, even though their European excursions and luxury cars depended on Mona's heap of gold. He'd also started acting in the Dill Theater Guild's amateur productions, usually as the leading man, but never unwilling to play a fool or buffoon, either. There was golf, at the Dill Country Club, too, and a big sailboat on Lake Champlain, but Drew's hunting parka, and his Honda, vanished forever. Mona bought him a red Mustang convertible as a consolation, and he'd been driving sporty Mustangs ever since.

Cooper smiled.

She said: "Mona calls that period 'The Taming of the Drew!'"

Drew hung his head in pretend shame, then laughed.

"Okay, for that, Sweetcakes, you have to stand up," he said.

Cooper stood and he studied her feet with an analytical eye.

"It's the polio that hurts, not the orthopedic," he said. "But that insert's beat up, so I'll order a replacement, mainly to get my hands on all those Yankee dollars!"

Cooper sat back down and watched Drew scribble, feeling a wave of affection, for him, for Mona, for all the people she'd known so long in this town, and for Dill itself.

Drew finished writing and stared at the paperwork. Finally he looked up.

"Coop, the police went to all the houses on the Hill, about what happened, asking if we saw anything...."

She shrugged.

"Everyone's upset, and worried for you, and we'd like you to stay with us awhile, Mona and me...."

Cooper sighed. She'd been thinking she had nobody. Her brother had died three years ago, and his wife had died before that. Now their son, her nephew, was off in Belgium doing financial things. She lived alone in the big federal house, which Jack Abbott kept pestering her to sell, and sometimes she'd almost wondered if she should.

"Hell no," she thought. "I've lived up on the Hill in that house all my life, and I've got friends."

She reached over and touched Drew's shoulder.

"Thank you," she said. "But campus security's keeping an eye out, and I've got a corgi dog now—Henry wouldn't let anything happen to me."

CHAPTER SIX

Cooper awoke that night, and sat up in bed.

A noise?

Henry lay on the carpet beside the bed, sleeping undisturbed. Maybe she'd imagined something.

Faintly, through the window, closed against the late-September nighttime chill, she heard a barred owl call: "hoohoo-hoohoo." It sounded mournful, although the owl was just telling its mate, hunting elsewhere, in which of the college campus's maples it currently perched.

She'd once heard certain Native-Americans believed an owl calling your name meant you'd soon die.

"My name's not HooHoo," she thought.

Otherwise, she heard nothing except Henry breathing in his sleep.

"My nerves are shot," Cooper thought, ashamed, getting out of bed.

Her nightstand digital clock said 3:48 a.m., its numerals neon red.

Cooper sat on the bay window's built-in bench and half turned to look out at Hill Street, lit by the streetlamp out front, but also by the nearly full moon hanging just above the treetops. She knew the maples already had crimson and gold tinges, but she couldn't see the colors in the moonlight, only the dark leaves, nearly black.

No traffic moved along the street at this hour. She thought, look long enough, maybe you'll see a coyote prowl by, or a red fox, or a bobcat. So much of what's around you hides, she thought. You see only glimpses, and there's so much you'll never see at all, unless you accidentally look in the right direction, at the right moment.

Along the street, she saw houses like hers—large, built by people dead for centuries, dark, her neighbors asleep. She assumed they were. Even their Cadillacs and Lexuses and BMWs slept, in their ample garages, once carriage houses, when each house maintained a team.

Or were some people, like coyotes, roaming the small town's moonlit streets, preferring not to be seen?

"You're going nuts," she told herself.

And then she saw the car.

It was parked across the street, two houses down, toward Abner Park, under a large maple, in the shadow cast by the moon. She sensed the car was parked in that spot to take advantage of the tree's shadow, to hide. All her neighbors garaged their cars at night. And guests' cars would be locked up in the driveways.

Cooper felt fear ripple along her backbone.

Down under the tree, the car lit up, as the driver opened the door and got out. Then it darkened again, after he shut the door. She could just see him, standing by the car's hood, a large man, staring toward her house.

She had the feeling he wore a suit. As she watched, he stretched, and walked out of the tree's shadow.

Mike Bolknor.

"Does that man ever sleep?" she thought, irritated.

Immediately, she realized why Mike Bolknor parked there, in the shadows, and felt relieved, taken care of.

Even so, she still felt irritated.

To be watched over, like a child. To need to be watched over.

At that moment, the fear she'd been carrying like an ache, since the gunshot, left her.

Now she felt only quiet wrath, because of the nighttime gunshot, and she knew that anger would persist, until the wound to this community was cauterized.

And she thought: "Maybe Mike Bolknor doesn't sleep because he can't."

CHAPTER SEVEN

Cooper couldn't sleep, either, so early in the morning she called in a message to her office's answering service: she'd be in Abner Park, by the pond. She needed to think, but she'd be back in time for her evidence-analysis class. She left her cell phone number in case anyone absolutely needed to reach her.

She fetched her binoculars, and her jacket, because autumn was coming on. When she got to the front door, she found Henry waiting. Clearly he knew what a jacket meant.

"All right," Cooper told him, giving her voice a put-upon sound, when in fact it pleased her, to have Henry's company.

She snapped on the leash her nephew and his wife had left, but didn't need to pick it up: as soon as she opened the door, Henry bee-lined for her black Volvo, parked in the driveway, dragging his leash behind him. He ran around to stand staring at the passenger door, until Cooper opened it, and then he jumped in. Too short-legged to reach the seat, he leaped onto the floor, then clambered up onto the seat, twisting around to face the windshield. He seemed to grin.

Henry looked at Cooper, bright eyed, and barked once, meaning "Let's go!"

A pair of black ducks dipped along the pond's edge, bottoms up, stretching their necks down underwater, to nibble bottom-rooted pondweed. September was early for the fall migration, so Cooper knew she'd see no snow geese or Canada geese or solitary sandpipers or white-crowned sparrows heading south just yet, but it relaxed her to sit in one of the Adirondack chairs overlooking the pond, in the morning sunshine, and feel the day warming, while Henry sat beside her, apparently also watching birds.

Orange flashed in a shoreline maple and she raised her binoculars just in time: oriole. Then her cell phone rang.

"This Cooper North?"

A gravelly voice.

"Yes?"

"Your office said you're in the park, by the pond?"

"Yes, but who're....."

With a click, the call terminated.

Cooper sat staring at the now-dead phone in her hand. She didn't know the voice.

She tried to resume watching birds, saw a broad-winged hawk glide by, but kept thinking about the call, that maybe she shouldn't be alone in the park like this.

And then she heard a distant roar, coming toward her, its din mounting.

She'd heard that sound before.

Up on the drive, a big black Harley rounded the curve, and she saw the rider—wearing a Nazi-style helmet—stare down at her as he killed the engine and dismounted.

He wore biker denims and leathers, a huge burly man, unshaven. He pulled off his helmet and left it on the seat, releasing long blond hair, and started down the slope toward her, fast.

She waited, thinking: "What in the name of God is this?"

He half skidded down the hill in his heavy boots, with chains across the instep, and stopped in front of her. For one of the few times in her life, she felt small.

"Cooper North, right?" he said.

He extracted a paper from his leather jacket's pocket and glanced from a photo on the sheet to her, then refolded it and stuck it back in his pocket.

"Got something you need to know," he said.

"And you are?" she asked.

He looked at her, bristly face expressionless, then reached into his jeans' back pocket and fished out a wallet. He flipped it open and showed her a badge: DEA.

"You don't look governmental," Cooper said.

"Yeah, I work undercover," he said. "Right now it's just me operating around Dill here, so they texted me, said give you the word."

She looked at him, waiting.

"Guy named Sonny Rawston's out," he said.

She continued to look at him.

32

"Before my time here," the DEA agent said. "They just said this gentleman got out four years early—good behavior, maybe? Or somebody tugged on a string? He's been out eight days, but the office just found out, so they sent me to tell you."

"Appreciated," Cooper said. "But why the fuss?"

"In the penitentiary, over in New York, he made threats—seems to have a grievance with you," the agent said. "So they wanted you to know, which is all I know—they're steamed he got off early."

He put his wallet back in his pocket and climbed up the hill, digging in his boots' toes. He stuck the Nazi helmet back on his head, mounted the bike, started it with a roar. He gave Cooper a wave, then sped down the drive, his din waning after him until he was gone and the park was silent again.

Cooper leaned on her cane, looking up at the road, where the motorcycle had been. Henry looked, too, but quickly lost interest and began sniffing in the grass. Cooper tried to resume bird watching, but after a few moments gave it up. She drove back to the college and parked in the lot of the old brick Victorian that housed Campus Security on the first floor, her Criminal Justice Program on the second.

With Henry beside her, hurrying officiously on his short legs, she walked straight to Mike Bolknor's office, thumping her cane on the floor.

"Why DEA?" Bolknor asked.

"It was their case," Cooper said. "Six years ago, moving drugs down from Montreal, cocaine, heroin...."

Bolknor said nothing, just waited.

"He got ten, but they've let him loose four years early."

"You prosecuted?" Bolknor said.

Cooper wondered: when will I stop thinking of him as Bolknor, and think of him as Mike?

"It surprised me," she said. "Sonny came from a solid family here, father a mail carrier, mother a bank teller, and Sonny had been an honor student, president of the student council, wrestling team, all of that, and he graduated from the University of Vermont, too, business degree—I'd thought he was a manipulative kid, and Tip LaPerle brought him in a couple of times, shoplifting, marijuana, but we figured teenage high jinx and let it go."

Cooper thought: hair fiery red, eyes cold blue.

It was just surmise, impressions, but she wondered if certain criminals—Sonny Rawston being one—are born that way. By the time the jury handed down the guilty verdict, on the drug charge, Cooper had come to believe Sonny Rawston had a psychopath's lack of feeling for others and no sense of responsibility at all for his own actions. And she thought he got into drug dealing for thrills, and fooling authorities, and getting power over addicts, and getting people addicted, another feeling of power. Money, she thought, was secondary.

"So, in prison, he was threatening you?" Bolknor said.

Cooper shrugged.

"There's something else, though," she said. "When that DEA agent drove up, I realized it."

Bolknor waited.

34

"Motorcycle," Cooper said. "It wasn't a car with a bad muffler—whoever shot at me that night drove a motorcycle."

CHAPTER EIGHT

Henry came to Evidence-Analysis class.

So did the *Dill Chronicle*'s new cub reporter, a slightly plump young woman, smiley, black-rimmed glasses. She sat in back, digital recorder running, fingers tapping her laptop's keypad. Henry apparently liked her, because he plopped down beside her chair. Cooper liked her, too, but she wished Ariette Feenie would find something else to write about.

Why—in a series on the new criminal-justice program—did Ariette focus on just this class? And last week's story, the series' first, made the class seem aimed at identifying wrongful convictions, and fingering the truly guilty, when it was simply about how to handle evidence.

Cooper mostly blamed Stacey Gillibrand, who insisted on dominating discussions, as she was doing right now.

"...and as it's already been reported"—an approving nod to Ariette—"my particular interest, since I'll be a defense attorney, is where law officers erred in collecting evidence and evaluating it, and I'm digging into the Nub Duckins case, where that certainly happened!"

She paused to shuffle through her pages of notes, while a smattering of students turned up their eyes, payback for her eye-rolling during their own presentations. However, she didn't notice, because she kept her cornflower-blue gaze on Ariette Feenie.

"This is a case from eighteen years ago," Stacey said. "It was in Hart's Corners, where this old, slow-witted handyman and snowplow guy murdered a schoolteacher—supposedly!"

She stopped talking again to gaze meaningfully about the classroom, especially at the furiously typing reporter.

Cooper sighed. It wasn't in Allen County, not a case she'd prosecuted, so at least Stacey couldn't call her up for cross examination.

"I'm researching this—exhaustively—and …."

"That's good, Stacey," Cooper said. "Right now, let's hear what cases the other students have selected—so, Jerry?"

Stacey frowned, but sat down, as Jerry Shapiro stood, all five-and-a-half feet and one-hundred-thirty-six pounds of him. Long, curly black hair, a carefully trimmed black beard—he fixed his classmates with the sharp, amused gaze he planned to one day unleash on jurors.

"Back in Brooklyn, but—Hey—enough about me!" he began.

Cooper found herself thinking: he'll be an entertaining trial lawyer, and probably a good one.

His case, a town clerk who embezzled property tax receipts, turned on intricate auditing, which Jerry explained succinctly. He finished with: "So that, Boys and Girls, concludes math class for today."

Next up was Jerry's friend Chip Stack, who contemplated his loafers, then visibly forced his head up to stare at his classmates, like the proverbial headlight-transfixed deer, brown hair precisely trimmed, chinos and button-down-collar shirt perfectly pressed, prep school personified, except for stunned blue eyes, as if he'd just touched electrified barbed wire.

He'd shown Cooper a wallet photo of his home, in Bucks County, Pennsylvania, a sprawling mansion, on acres of meadow and forest. His father, a neurosurgeon, steeplechase rider, deep-sea fisherman, pilot, and one-time university star quarterback, had overwhelmed his son. Chip clung to just one ambition: to become a policeman.

Cooper had met the father at the semester's start, a brusque man, large and handsome. He towered over his son, who wasn't much bigger than Jerry Shapiro. Otherwise, the two young men were not twins—Jerry, with all that black hair, wired up, amused, and Chip, who stared at you, blinking, as if transfixed. Chip's father made no secret of his disappointment in his son's stature, and his career choice. Right now, Cooper guessed, as Chip stared at the class, he envisioned his father shaking his head in exasperation.

"Tell us about your case," Cooper prompted.

"This guy in town here, Sonny Rawston, smuggled drugs," Chip said. "He'd get them in Montreal, from biker gangs, and sneak them down Lake

Memphremagog, across the border into Vermont, in a motorboat, and then he'd sell them all around northern New England and down in New York—it was Professor North who got him convicted!"

Cooper thought: would Sonny Rawston shoot at me? She'd known him since he was a child....

"Evidence, Chip?" Cooper said.

"Well, the Border Patrol found a plastic barrel floating in Lake Memphremagog, with cocaine inside, which they guessed fell off a smuggler's boat, so they called in the DEA, who found a boat with cocaine traces, docked on the lake's Vermont side, in Newport, and they traced it to this Sonny Rawston, so the Dill police and Professor North, the prosecutor then, worked with the DEA, bugged Rawston's phone, and...I've got a lot more research to do."

"Good work, keep at it," Cooper said. "Now let's hear from Nikki Winkel."

Nikki bemused Cooper. So utterly different from her, yet—in some complicated way—a little like her.

Nikki, a Dill girl, shaped like a stick, wore ripped black jeans and red basketball high-tops and men's shirts with the sleeves cut off. She wore her dark hair shaved along the sides, spiky on top. She had a thin gold ring in one nostril. All of that would need to change, Cooper knew, if Nikki were to get what she craved—she'd applied for the new Criminal Justice Program as soon as it was announced, on her application saying she aimed to become a Vermont state's attorney. She hoped she'd get elected right here in Allen County, and her role model was Cooper North.

"What have you got?" Cooper asked her.

"My case was actually an acquittal, from two years ago," Nikki said. "Jack Abbott, owns those tenements down by the river? One of them caught fire, probably a drunken tenant smoking in bed, no smoke detectors, and a woman living there burned to death, so the state's attorney charged Abbott, criminal negligence."

Nikki paused to leaf through her notes, and Cooper thought how the tough-girl look must be a mask—father killed at the granite quarries in a freak TNT explosion, her mother, June Winkel, the waitress at The Percolator, struggling to raise three daughters alone, and behind the mother's stone face and vinegary voice, Cooper guessed, lay despair.

Nikki—bony, plain-faced—got her ripped jeans at the Salvation Army outlet. She'd cleaned houses after high-school classes, to eke out the family's income, and she looked after her younger sisters. Cooper saw in Nikki's defiant face no hope for anything without struggle. And in her eyes Cooper saw resignation, but fire, too, and realistic cynicism.

Cooper, behind the scenes, had persuaded Mt. Augustus to give Nikki Winkel a full scholarship. She still lived at home, looking after her sisters, and now clerked part-time at the Sweet Kumquat, a Main Street health-food store.

"Abbot's lawyer argued he did put in smoke alarms, but somebody took them down, probably to sell for drug money, and in court the state's attorney—who was not Professor North—couldn't prove that wasn't true, so Abbott got acquitted."

40

Nikki stared belligerently at the class, as if looking for an argument, but not getting any, she continued with her presentation.

"Next, I'm going to see if the prosecution missed any evidence that might have led to a negligence conviction, or, if there wasn't any to be had, why bring the case at all?"

Cooper glanced at her watch.

"Off you all go," she said. "Next time, remember, focus on evidence!"

She gave Ariette Feenie a meaningful glance.

"Gathering it, analyzing it—okay?"

By now Henry had padded up to sit beside her, and they both watched the students filing out, Jerry Shapiro and his friend, Chip Stack—energized mongoose and withdrawn tortoise, peering out from its shell, Cooper decided—and Nikki Winkel....

Cooper thought: this is good, this new work, these different students, their prospects before them, even Stacey Gillibrand, because the woman surely worked hard.

She's divorced, Cooper thought. She must feel alone, vulnerable. She wants to make something happen for herself, before that blond hair loses its sheen, and those blue eyes dull....

Even so, Stacey could be monumentally annoying—just now, instead of following her classmates out, she'd gathered up her pages of notes and hurried back to where the reporter was stuffing her laptop into her red backpack, and started talking animatedly, pointing to passages in her research. Cooper could see Ariette listening attentively. As she watched, Ariette reached into an outside pocket of her backpack and extracted a pen and steno pad, to jot notes.

Cooper had dealt with the press for decades, and wouldn't try telling a reporter what to write. Still, before this series got too distorted by Stacey's craving for publicity, she thought she might have a quiet word with Ariette, now walking out of the classroom, with Stacey still monologuing beside her.

After a moment, as Cooper stuffed her own paperwork into the manila envelope she used as a briefcase, Ariette walked back in, smiling. She bent down to pet Henry, who accepted the attention with royal condescension, then astonished disappointment, as Ariette stopped petting him to stand and frown.

"That shot at you, Professor North, that was terrible," she said, shaking her head in commiseration, but with a clear gleam of "hot story" in her eyes.

Uh-oh, Cooper thought. Here we go.

"Who do you think did the shooting?"

Cooper thought: dear child, you've yet to master Reporting 101—inducing an interviewee, on a sensitive subject, to babble.

"That's under investigation by the Dill police," Cooper said. "So you should put questions like that to Tip LaPerle."

Who'll tell you exactly nothing, Cooper thought. Because, right now, we have nothing

"Campus security, too," Cooper added. "If you want another source, try Mike Bolknor."

Ariette knew all that, of course. Cooper could see the young woman's earnest, good-natured face reflecting an internal struggle, trying to conjure up a question that would yield a juicy, career-advancing quote.

"Do you think it's someone from Dill?" she finally asked.

Cooper shrugged, turning her hands palms up.

She saw Ariette didn't know what else to ask, so Cooper asked a question of her own.

"About this series you're writing," she said. "Do you think it might get a bit distorted if it's focused on just one student?"

Ariette looked taken aback, but quickly rallied.

"Professor North, if Stacey Gillibrand's right, and that man got wrongfully jailed for murder all those years ago, that's the real big story here."

Cooper immediately realized the truth of that. Still....

"What if Stacey's wrong?" she asked.

Ariette said: "From what I've seen, I don't think she is."

So they left it there.

CHAPTER NINE

After the class, Cooper drove home, deciding to have lunch alone that day, just her and Henry. She poured a few kibbles into Henry's bowl, as a between-meals treat, but just a taste. Her nephew's wife had warned her that, given free rein at the food bowl, Henry would make himself tubby.

Cooper warmed up some kale soup, with a thick slice of crusty whole-grain bread, both from the Sweet Kumquat, her doctor having warned her many visits ago about LDL and HDL, and watch it!

While she ate she avoided thinking about bullets and bullies. She thought about goldfinches, and not seeing any all summer. They used to settle in her back garden like yellow sparks. Now, none. Another species getting scarce?

She heard a car stop out front and looked—Mike Bolknor, driving a campus-security Prius, arriving promptly at one, as arranged. She collected Henry and hurried out, so he wouldn't have to get out of the car and ring the bell.

She rode shotgun, periodically scanning the maple canopies, looking for goldfinches. She watched birds, she'd long understood, because of her leaden left leg, weighing her down—she liked seeing birds fly. Right now, though, she mostly thought about Chip Stack.

He'd come to her that morning, after the evidence class, because his father texted him, probably from the operating room, between brain surgeries: "Study medicine, like your sister! No gumption? At least be a lawyer! Don't shame us!"

Chip worried his father would stop paying his college tuition. If that happened, he'd work his way through, and he'd like a job with a police department, answering phones, whatever, a step toward his goal. To qualify he'd need some experience, and he'd asked if Cooper could help him.

Mike Bolknor, as usual, wasn't talking. So, between bird sightings, Cooper pondered Chip's problem. Simultaneously, she amused herself, watching Henry.

He'd started in the car's back seat, but he'd pushed his head up between the two front seats, then squirmed through, with considerable effort, and now sat on the floor at Cooper's feet, looking at her, clearly planning to climb up, so he could look out.

Just past Abner Park, at Dill Industries' glass-sided headquarters, they turned right, onto Slope Drive. As they started down, on their way to Dill's police station, Cooper broke the silence.

"I've got a student, plans to be a policeman," she said. "Would you take him on as an intern?"

"Hmm," Bolknor said.

"I could send him down to Tip, but I'd rather place him with you, if possible," Cooper said, hoping Bolknor wouldn't ask her why, because she really didn't know. Partly it was that interning with Campus Security might get Chip a part-time job there, handy to his classes. Convenience wasn't the entire reason, though. Cooper felt that fatherly disdain had shut Chip down, and that, somehow, Mike Bolknor could help him more than Tip LaPerle could, or would, a conclusion that surprised her, and perplexed her, because she still didn't understand Mike Bolknor's wiring.

"Why's he want to be a cop?" Bolknor asked.

Progress. The silent man spoke. But his question wasn't easy to answer.

"What about you?" Cooper said. "Why'd you become a cop?"

Silence.

Cooper waited.

"My father was NYPD," Bolknor finally said.

Another silence.

"Grandfather, before him," he added.

Cooper thought: ah, some information.

"Chip's father's a neurosurgeon," she said. "He doesn't think much of his son...."

Silence again.

It suddenly occurred to Cooper, looking sidewise at Bolknor's expressionless face, that this was a sad man, a depressed man.

Bolknor nodded, almost imperceptibly, so Chip's placement was resolved.

Henry now sat up and put his oddly large front paws on Cooper's seat. He stared up at her, apparently to gauge whether climbing up would earn him a rebuke, and Cooper waited, amused to see the dog calculating. Henry abruptly catapulted himself up and landed with his front half in Cooper's lap, and his hind legs scrabbling at the seat's edge, until he got solid footing. After a moment of testing the waters, he climbed fully into Cooper's lap—sending a sharp pain through her bad leg—and then turned so he could look out the windshield.

It irritated Cooper, the dog invading her space, using her as a perch, but then the stab in her left leg subsided into its normal dull ache. She stifled a sudden urge to kiss the top of Henry's head, thinking, Cooper North, I don't even know you anymore.

"Satisfied?" she asked the dog.

Clearly he was satisfied, staring out the windshield, bright eyes taking in the cars and pedestrians. Cooper watched, too, out of habit, scanning for familiar faces—many faces in Dill were familiar—and then she saw one.

"That's him, Sonny Rawston!" she told Bolknor. "See—red hair!"

Bolknor turned, took in a fortyish man on the sidewalk, average height, muscularly stocky, clean-cut, like an insurance agent, maybe, and then turned his eyes back to driving. In that moment, the man on the sidewalk recognized Cooper in the car, and smiled at her, close-mouthed, on just one side, but his blue eyes were icy. Still smiling, coldly staring, he slightly canted his head, and the gesture conveyed malice.

"Doesn't look like a druggie," Bolknor said, eyes on the road.

In the side mirror, Cooper saw Rawston staring after the receding Prius.

"I doubt he's ever used," Cooper said. "Wouldn't like losing control—I think he got his kicks hooking others, feeling the power."

Bolknor said nothing, turning the car left, off Slope Drive, onto Main Street. They passed The Percolator, and the Sweet Kumquat Natural Foods Store, then swerved into the alley flanking the Dill Police Station, and parked in the station's rear lot, in a slot labeled "Official Visitors."

"Sonny Rawston!"

Tip LaPerle sat behind his desk, shaking his head. He wore his uniform, but he'd laid the jacket across a chair, and Cooper noticed that at forty-one he still looked billy goat sinewy.

"Figured we'd finished with Rawston, at least for another four years," he said. "What about it, Coop? Sonny's our shooter?"

Cooper sat remembering that smile and nod Sonny just gave her. There'd been malice there. She had no doubt. Yet animosity, in itself, didn't rise to the level of actionable evidence. You couldn't indict a man for disliking you.

She sighed, and shrugged.

Mike Bolknor, who'd listened in silence, finally spoke: "DEA guy said he threatened you, in prison."

"Inmates brag," Cooper said. "Show off, how tough they are."

Yet, she didn't think bragging applied to Sonny Rawston.

She thought back to when they'd questioned him, in this office, and he'd sat in the chair Mike Bolknor now occupied, wearing chino trousers and loafers, with a light-blue dress shirt, red hair neatly trimmed, like a businessman, and his every response seemed to have a double meaning, or triple even, as if this were a game in which he expertly parried every question, making fools of his inquisitors, at least, in his own mind. He'd been cool and supremely confident, not a man with an impaired ego, needing to build himself up by bragging.

Except he'd been given ten years in prison. And when the jury foreman said "guilty as charged," and later, when the judge sentenced him, he'd stared icily at Cooper, and she'd felt that, in Sonny Rawston's mind, this was all the fault of Cooper North.

Bragging, though? Somehow she doubted it.

So why make threats against her, when the chances were good some prison rat would tell, hoping for reduced time?

Cooper thought: because he wanted word to get to me. He wanted to shake me. Because he likes manipulating people—it feels powerful. Would he try killing me, though?

"I think he's too cool-headed for a revenge shooting," Cooper said.

"Jail got to him, maybe?" Mike Bolknor suggested.

Cooper visualized what she'd just seen, the calculated malice in Rawston's smile, the ice in his eyes. Finally she shrugged.

"I don't know," she said.

Tip LaPerle slammed his hand onto his desk.

"All right, let's pull him in," he said. "Question the creep."

"No!" Cooper said.

Both men looked at her, LaPerle startled, Bolknor curious.

"Here's what'll happen," Cooper said, suddenly sure. "He'll have some alibi for the night of the shooting, maybe bogus, maybe not, and—he'll go straight to the press!"

She envisioned Sonny talking with Ariette Feenie, saying: I've served my time. I'm straight now. I just want to live quietly, but the police chief and former state's attorney, they've still got it in for me. I don't know why. They're stalking me! Harassing! Bullying! And how could Ariette resist, a cub reporter so eager for a big career-building story?

"I think that's what he wants," Cooper said. "To smear us with mud, especially me."

Both men sat back in their chairs, thinking. Tip LaPerle finally sighed.

"All right," he said. "We'll check into him, though, at least get where he's living—and, hey, what's he living on, got a job?"

"Uniforms probing around him…" Cooper said, dubious.

Dill's police department had no detective on its staff. So all investigations would be done by uniformed officers.

Another silent stretch. Henry wriggled out from under Cooper's chair, stretched, front lowered, tailless butt upraised. He yawned, hugely. Then he looked at them all in turn, seemingly pleased with himself, as if he'd added to the conversation.

"Here's a thought," Bolknor said, and Cooper saw Tip shoot him a quick glare, already annoyed at the interloper butting in.

"Cooper's probably right," Bolknor said, ignoring Tip's irritation. "Poking around officially, when we've got nothing on him, that might give him ammo, but there's another way."

Cooper and LaPerle waited.

"He gets investigated, but unofficially," Bolknor said. "Ordinary citizens walking around town, eyes open, here and there a discreet question…."

Cooper didn't like it. She saw what he was getting at, but it made her uncomfortable.

"They're just kids, for Pete's sake," she said.

She didn't have any better ideas, though.

"Yeah, well Coop and I know people in town," Tip said. "We'll be asking around, too."

Meaning, we know Dill and you don't, Mr. NYPD bigshot.

Cooper said: "Good idea, Tip, some discreet questions…."

"Yeah, do it nice," LaPerle said. "Wouldn't want to offend that garbage."

51

CHAPTER TEN

That evening, Henry noisily crunched kibble, then lapped half a bowl of water, dribbling it onto the kitchen floor. Cooper had what she called a "Sweet Kumquat Special," an organic frozen mushroom-and-broccoli pizza, heated in the oven, with a premixed salad of organic kale, spinach, and radicchio.

After dinner, as Cooper hand-washed the few dishes in the sink, she heard a roar, and felt herself go on high alert—a motorcycle, out front.

Abruptly, the engine shut down. Silence.

Cooper stood at the sink, thinking what to do. This early, with a hint of evening light still in the sky, Campus Security wouldn't be watching her house. She reached for the counter telephone, to call Mike Bolknor, but changed her mind.

No point bringing in the marines until she knew what was happening, so she dried her hands on a towel and hurried into the living room to look out the window at the street—parked at the curb, a big black Harley. No rider to be seen. Hill Street empty.

Cooper told herself: lots of motorcycles, world's full of them.

Still, why would somebody visiting a neighbor park at Cooper's house? And who'd be riding a Harley in this neighborhood anyway? And where'd the rider go?

She hurried into the library, cane thumping the hardwood floor, to look out the east-facing windows, toward Abner Park, Henry scrambling after her, excited by the hustle, thinking a new game must be afoot. Between her house and the neighbor's lay a stretch of lawn, then a row of lilacs, leaves already looking tired, with autumn coming on, and the neighbor's lawn beyond. She saw nobody.

Bad thought: had she forgotten to lock the back door? She hurried to the rear foyer, tried the door, and it was locked. Since the shooting, she'd become assiduous about that. She kept the basement's outside door locked, too.

Through the foyer window, she saw nobody lurking among the back garden's sunflowers and rose bushes.

West side? Toward the college?

She thumped her way to the dining room, to look out the window there, with Henry enthusiastically scrambling after her on his short legs.

It was just after seven, but in late September, at this hour the light faded fast. She could only dimly see the peony beds on this side, and the cedar hedge between her house and the campus

A man stood there.

He was on her side of the hedge, hands shoved into his trouser pockets, surveying her house.

She couldn't make him out well, a shadow in the fading light, but he seemed too thick to be Sonny Rawston, like a fire hydrant. She saw no rifle.

Cooper said: "Damn!"

She hurried to the front door, Henry at her heels. She threw open the door and burst out of the house, rushing around the side, cane's tip digging into the lawn at each step. She didn't know what she meant to do, except that she'd had it, feeling intimidated, frightened. Henry barked, thrilled to be in action, even if he didn't know what the action was, and the intruder turned to look at them.

Cooper cursed again, this time in exasperation.

"Jack Abbott!" she said. "What are you up to?"

Even in the dim light she could see Abbott's face flushing angry red. His buzz cut had grayed, but his Tenement Row temper hadn't moderated with all the years of real-estate deals, raking in money.

"Hell, get off your high horse," he said. "I'm checking the property line."

"And why, Mr. Abbott, would you be doing that?" Cooper said.

"Because," he said, "after I buy the place, I'll need to know."

Henry barked jubilantly, having a wonderful time. Cooper wished he'd sink his teeth into Jack Abbott's shin.

"I've told you, about three-thousand times, I'm not selling," Cooper said. "No means no!"

Abbott made a disgusted sound.

"And what're you doing with a motorcycle?" Cooper demanded.

"What I'm doing with the bike," Abbott said, "is my damned kid's home on leave from the Navy, and he took my Caddy for some damned date, and Beverly's got the Buick off with her buddies to something or other, quilting bee for all anyone tells me, maybe girls' night at the shooting range, and what I've got left to drive is Petty-Officer-Third-Class Abbott's Harley, so I'm driving it."

"How long has your son been home?" Cooper asked.

"Week and a half, so far," Abbott said. "And he's already on my nerves."

Cooper thought about that. A week and a half. Maybe this wasn't the first time Jack Abbott borrowed his son's Harley.

"I could have the papers ready tomorrow morning," Abbott said. "I'll give you appraisal plus fifteen-percent!"

"No," Cooper said, and Henry barked, as if for emphasis.

Abbott snorted, angry.

"Listen, you damned well better sell to me, and soon," he said. "You don't want getting shot in there, do you?"

"Is that a threat?" Cooper said.

"Damn it, I'm thinking what's best for you," Abbott said, and she could hear in his voice the effort to tamp down his anger.

It was nearly dark now, but she could make out Abbott glaring at her.

"Think about it!" he said.

He turned, started for the street, then stopped and twisted around to face her.

"Smarten up, Cooper!" he said.

She stood in the dark with Henry. After a moment she heard the motorcycle rumble to life, and saw its headlight shining.

Abbott roared away, leaving Cooper standing outside on her lawn.

Jack Abbott, she thought. Why are you so rabid to get my house?

And was it you?

CHAPTER ELEVEN

Late that night she awoke, looked out the window and saw a campus-security Prius parked across the street, in the big maple's shadow. She didn't know if it was Mike Bolknor watching over her, or one of his officers, but she felt reassured and went back to bed, falling asleep instantly. Henry, lying beside the bed, never awoke at all.

In the morning, in her college office, she held the start-up meeting of what Jerry Shapiro—apparently a Sherlock Holmes fan—dubbed the "Baker Street Irregulars."

"So we're going to tail this guy?" Chip Stack asked.

"Absolutely not," Cooper said. "If you do spot him, on the street, though, or wherever, just notice where he goes, who he talks to, what he does."

For one thing, she told them, did Sonny Rawston drive a motorcycle? Also, did he have a job? Otherwise, it was hard to see what he lived on. And exactly where was he living? His parents had retired to Arizona, so it wasn't even clear why he'd come back to Dill, or what he was doing here.

"Vows of silence, right?" Nikki Winkel asked.

"Not peep," Cooper said. "Especially don't tell Stacey Gillibrand, because she'll go off freelancing."

And she added: "Remember, there's no evidence against this man, so he's simply a citizen, like any of us— if he realizes we're snooping on him, he'll make trouble, okay?"

Nikki looked bored, but Cooper saw she took careful notes. Chip Stack looked beatified: chosen to do real police work! And on the same day Cooper told him he'd be interning with Campus Security. Jerry Shapiro, by contrast, looked amused. He'd spy diligently, Cooper knew, but there'd be jokes, and they started right off.

"I'm thinking trench coat," he now said. "And what about an accent? Albanian?"

Cooper ignored that and looked out her office window. Autumn's golds and reds already showed in the campus's maples, and students rushed to classes with their sneakers crunching fallen leaves, brown and dry. Many wore jackets, because late-September mornings in Vermont could already be frosty. Somehow the scene made Cooper sad.

She thought: it's the students, rushing. Because your life, when you looked back on it, from sixty or seventy decades out, was like a DVD fast-forwarding. Too fast. Better to stroll between classes, watch the season change. Except it's never entirely in your hands, is it?

She'd meant to finally rest, catch up on good books, think, watch birds. Yet, here she was, dealing with another attempted-homicide investigation, and this time the shooter's target was her. She sighed, and passed out mug shots of Sonny Rawston, supplied by Tip LaPerle.

Jerry and Chip stuffed their photos into their jacket pockets and left, while Nikki Winkel carefully slid her photo into her backpack. Cooper checked her wristwatch, because she was due for a get-together, at Mona Dill Saunders'.

Nikki bent to pet Henry, who'd been watching the meeting bright-eyed, then shrugged into her backpack. She started out, but turned.

"Jerry Shapiro's a joker, but he's got a razor brain," Nikki said. "Someday, when he's a defense attorney and I'm a prosecutor, maybe we'll fight it out in court—I'd enjoy that."

She started out again, turned again.

"Chip's sort of like clubbed with a two-by-four," she said. "I think he's getting better, though, slow, and he's a good soul."

And as Nikki Winkel left the room, Cooper thought: and you, little toughie, are razor sharp, too, and another good soul, even with that problem haircut, and you've got reason to be cynical—father dead, mother bitter, working since childhood, plain featured—but you're playing your hand, deft as you can, and, sister, I'm rooting for you.

Nikki was nothing like Cooper. Nothing at all, she thought. And yet...

CHAPTER TWELVE

Usually, if nothing prevented Cooper from attending one of Mona Saunders' afternoon socials, she made something up. One reason: she'd have to resist Mona's martini pitcher—while everyone else got tipsy, Cooper sipped Pellegrino. Also, party chitchat stupefied her. She'd come today, though, to glean information.

They'd fragmented into buzzing groups, in the vast parlor, its floor-to-ceiling windows looking out through the pillared front porch to Hill Street. Paintings, collected on Mona's annual European art expeditions, hung on the walls, mostly abstract squiggles and color splats, which baffled Cooper, and now Mona targeted Cooper with her most imperious stare and commanded: "Take my Beretta!"

Cooper shook her head.

"Take it," Mona insisted, squinting one eye shut, pretending to sight through her martini glass. "If that SOB tries it again, de-brain him."

Nessie Greffier tittered—"Cooper'd shoot her own knee!"

In high school, over fifty years ago, when they'd been classmates, Nessie had won many sharpshooting trophies. Back then, guns didn't interest Cooper, and they still didn't.

Nessie now colored her hair yellow, rather than letting it go gray, as Cooper had, and while Cooper tended, if anything, to be even leaner and ganglier than in high school, Nessie had plumped, but Cooper could still see the pretty, perky sixteen-year-old she'd been. And it occurred to her that, no matter how old you get, high school's always just yesterday.

Mona, rallying to Cooper's defense, after the knee-shooting barb, told Nessie: "Last night, at the range, you stunk!"

"I aced it, shooting the rifle!" Nessie protested. "I only missed with the pistol, because I'm still breaking it in—it's a Glock G42 .380 slimline!"

"It's cute," Beverly Abbott announced brightly, and Cooper found herself amused with these three, Mona and Beverly, both in their fifties, Nessie almost seventy, going off one evening each month to play Annie Oakley.

Bang, bang, she thought.

And then she forced away a grimace, as Nessie lifted the martini pitcher, because the vodka poured into Nessie's glass like icy liquid diamond. To distract herself, Cooper surveyed the tray of canapés—English crackers and Neufchatel, topped with caviar or anchovies or smoked salmon or crab. Cooper picked one with olives, which Mona imported from Naples, and focused on the saltiness, to take her mind away from the martini pitcher, as Nessie finished off her current glassful and poured herself another, spilling a little. After that, she fixed Cooper with a slightly cockeyed glare.

"S'you, I s'pose," she said, slurring.

Cooper looked at her, puzzled.

"S'you told them!" Nessie said. "The college—shoot down my realtor course!"

"What?" Cooper said.

She wondered, where did this come from?

Nessie took a big gulp of martini and then gestured wildly, spilling more.

"Cooper North says hop, everyone goes 'Whoopee!" Nessie said.

She'd meant to chide in fun, or pretend to, Cooper thought, but the vodka took over.

"They gave you that cops-and-lawyers course," Nessie said, waving her martini glass. "So now it's Cooper North, all over the papers, as usual...."

Cooper shook her head, annoyed. Also hurt. She turned away from Nessie, now wobbling in her high heels, to talk with Mona and Beverly.

Their topic was a new Main Street boutique, which didn't interest Cooper at all, so she pretended to listen, but kept mulling Nessie's attack, probably triggered by the *Dill Chronicle*'s article about the new criminal-justice program—basically pre-law. Cooper guessed Mt. Augustus rejected Nessie's how-to-sell-property idea as insufficiently academic, and now Nessie blamed Cooper.

"...and lots of designer things," Beverly was saying. "Gucci...."

"Barcelona again this fall?" Cooper asked Mona, hoping to erect a word rampart to repel any more Nessie attacks.

"In two days, I'm flying out of Logan, and then it'll be three weeks of trekking to galleries, yum!" Mona said, making a flourish with her martini glass.

Every autumn Mona jetted from Boston to Barcelona, where she maintained an apartment, and from there she traveled the continent. As she'd once explained: "To waste a Skidmore art degree, that'd be un-Yankee— especially when it cost Daddy so many hard-inherited shillings!"

"You and Drew," Beverly said. "Europe must be so romantic!"

Mona raised her martini glass and peered through it at the window.

"Drew Saunders does golf," she said. "He does amateur theater, he does tennis, he does skiing—he doesn't do art, that philistine, so Dr. Saunders must stay home and peer at people's feet."

"I wish Jack would take us over there," Beverly sighed. "He just does business, like now it's fake brains."

"Drew goes with me to Europe other times," Mona said, in defense of her annual solo art-buying expedition.

"Fake brains?" Cooper asked Beverly.

Beverly giggled.

"Oh, it's a Mt. Augustus whatchamacallit," she said. "AI something…."

She shrugged, indicating she'd reached her ken's outer edge.

Cooper thought: that's the new Artificial Intelligence Research Center the college's setting up, with Dill Industries, and what's Jack Abbott got to do with that?

Nessie now rejoined them, her martini glass overfilled and sloshing. Mona, nearly as tall as Cooper, looked down at Nessie, eyebrows haughtily arched.

"You drive here?" she demanded.

"Yup!" Nessie said, snorting as if she'd made a telling point.

"You're not driving home," Mona said.

Mona, as usual, looked svelte, in a posh black-velour dress, which Cooper knew would have some famous couturier's label affixed.

"I'll drive you home," Beverly Abbott said.

Nessie, wobbling on her heels, tried to focus on Beverly, but failed.

"Jack let me bring his Cadillac today," Beverly said.

She worshipped her husband for rescuing her from a Hart's Corners dairy farm, where her father and stepmother both worked her hard. And although Jack Abbott struck Cooper as a blunt instrument, she couldn't blame Beverly, who reminded Cooper of a tail-swishing golden retriever, brown eyes aglow with friendliness.

Mona meanwhile, continued staring down at Nessie.

"You drive that idiot motorcycle here?" she demanded, and Nessie wrinkled her brow, clearly unsure what she'd driven.

Cooper remembered Nessie rode with a motorcycle club, older people, who toured New England together, like an over-the-hill biker gang. She'd closed her real-estate agency, retired, and Cooper supposed she now cast about for things to occupy her time, probably why she'd wanted to teach a real-estate course, and maybe she needed a little extra income, too. Cooper still stung from Nessie's attack, but she also admired her old classmate, who had no schooling beyond high school, yet created a viable business for herself.

Nessie suddenly looked at Cooper, and her bleary gaze sharpened.

"Always lording it, back in school, so arrogant," Nessie said. "Oh, I'm a North, we're practically Dills, and I'm so smart, and you're all so stupid...."

Cooper felt stung again. In high school, tall and skinny, she'd never felt anything but awkward and unpopular. She wanted to tell Nessie, you were the pretty one, you were prom queen, you married the star quarterback....

"Class president," Nessie said, accusingly. "Student Council president, then all those bigshot jobs, picture always in the paper—I guess it slicks things for you, if your name's North, and doesn't have a 'La' in front of it, or a 'De' or a 'Du!'"

Cooper felt too stunned to respond. Beverly looked aghast, Mona disgusted.

It occurred to Cooper that Nessie's marriage ended in public pyrotechnics, because of his affairs, and inability to hold a job, and finally giving Nessie a black eye. She'd even changed her name back to Greffier. Cooper had admired her for picking herself up, taking classes in real estate, starting Greffier's Property Mart. It had been modestly successful, enough to support her, and let her retire comfortably.

"Didn't drive the Harley," Nessie suddenly announced to Mona. "Camaro!"

Cooper thought: all these decades, Nessie Greffier's hated me, and I never knew.

Beverly, visibly distressed, because people weren't getting along, although she didn't know exactly why, now tried to change the subject.

"That drug smuggler fellow?" she said. "He's back—yesterday I was in that shop, Appurtenances, buying Isotoner gloves, fawn colored, and Jack was waiting out on Main Street, because he hates shopping, and I saw him talking to that Sonny Rawston...well, talking...."

She trailed off, and Cooper guessed it was because Beverly liked niceness.

"They argued?" Cooper suggested.

"Jack yelled, all red-faced," Beverly said, looking at her shoes. "I asked him later, but he said forget it."

And what, Cooper wondered, does Jack Abbott have to do with Sonny Rawston?

"Oh, that Rawston boy!" Mona said. "Drew ran into Jack at the Percolator, and Jack said they'd let Sonny out of jail."

Mona looked thoughtful.

"Sonny Rawston," she said. "He did our lawn mowing, when he was in high school—whatever he said, even 'Hello,' seemed to have some innuendo, as if he were mocking you...."

Cooper thought: that's an apt observation.

Mona gazed into her martini glass, then shook her head, looked up, and said: "Drew told me he remembered when he used to drive over to Hart's Corners, because a housebound old farm lady there needed help with her diabetic feet—that was years ago—and one time he picked up Sonny, hitchhiking, and gave him a lift to the Corners...."

She glanced into her glass again, as if to refresh her memory.

"He asked the Rawston boy why he was going to Hart's Corners, and—this is what Drew told me—Sonny snapped, 'Stay out of my business!'"

They stood silently a moment.

"I really never liked that Sonny Rawston," Mona finally said.

And then Beverly, looking distressed, apparently feeling she'd introduced negativity into their discussion by mentioning Sonny Rawston, suddenly brightened and said: "It was old Mrs. Langley, I remember—that's who Drew helped with her feet!"

Beverly looked pleased, niceness restored, but Nessie suddenly paled.

She whispered: "Bathroom!"

And after Nessie rushed away, Cooper thought, in the morning, that woman should be sorry, for the things she said, except she probably won't remember saying them at all.

"Beverly," Cooper suddenly said, another thought coming to her. "Does Jack still hunt deer?"

Mona looked revving up for an anti-hunting snarl, but Beverly spoke first: "He's stacked all his rifles in the basement, getting dusty, because these days it's just business! Business! Business! I really wish we'd go to Europe, too! Even just Florida!"

People now began coming up to thank Mona, on their way out, and Cooper took the opportunity to wish Mona a glorious Barcelona trip—she could see Mona already had her mind and heart in Spain. Then she headed out to her Volvo, parked on Hill Street. She lived only seven houses away, but drove because her bad leg throbbed today.

She got into the car and started the engine, but then sat, gripping the steering wheel, thinking about motorcycles, and guns, and about what she'd seen in Nessie Greffier's eyes, when her old classmate glared at her.

She sighed, and shifted the car into Drive. She'd meant to go directly to her office, but now decided to stop home first—probably Henry would like to see her. And she guessed he'd like to go with her, to the office.

She thought: he wants friendly company.

CHAPTER THIRTEEN

As soon as Cooper opened her house's door, Henry marched out, as if by appointment, and walked to the Volvo's passenger side and stared pointedly at the car door. How he knew they'd be driving off mystified Cooper. She'd begun thinking he might be a genius dog. After just five days in Dill, he'd already assessed his new situation, judged Cooper acceptable, and appointed himself a full partner in their joint enterprise, whatever it might be.

Henry rode standing, back paws on the bucket seat, forepaws braced against the padded dashboard, sharp eyes taking in the students walking to classes, or basking on the lawns, heads back, eyes shut, absorbing the late-September sunshine. Every sugar-maple leaf glowed. At the Campus Security building, when Cooper got out of the car, the afternoon felt warm. Yet, she sensed an underlying chill, a subliminal foretaste of October. And, as she opened Henry's door, she heard geese.

She couldn't see them. They flew too high above the trees, but she visualized them in their inverted-vee formation, rushing across the sky. She thought: too early to fly south. Probably they headed westward, over the central spine of the Green Mountains, toward Lake Champlain, restless because the light was shifting, and they, too, sensed the coming chill. It excited them.

Cooper stood beside the car, head upturned, and Henry regarded her quizzically. She imagined a Canada goose looking down—Dill a toy town far below, mountains billowing everywhere, the Ira River a blue line, and all the world's air to fly in.

When the gabbling faded, Cooper limped toward the old brick Victorian, cane thumping. Henry rushed ahead up the stoop, stopped at the door, and looked back, impatient for her to open it.

On her way to the elevator, Cooper veered into Campus Security headquarters, and looked in at the corner office, where Mike Bolknor talked on his desk phone, while his new intern, Chip Stack, worked at a side table, leafing through paperwork. Cooper glanced over Chip's shoulder and saw it was last night's patrol reports.

"That's it, Chief," Bolknor said into the mouthpiece. "What we've got so far."

He put down the phone.

"That was Tip LaPerle," he told Cooper. "I was letting him know what Mr. Stack here dug up."

Chip kept scanning the patrol logs, but Cooper could see his back subtly straighten with pride. Good, she thought. Mike Bolknor gets it, this boy needs a male

70

authority's approval. Also good, Bolknor filling in Tip LaPerle. That would be the path to eventual amity, she hoped

"Tell her," Bolknor told Chip.

Immediately the younger man got up from his chair, beaming.

"Okay," Chip said. "After our Baker Street Irregulars meeting this morning, I walked downtown, thinking maybe I'd spot Sonny Rawston—I went into the Percolator, and there he was, sitting alone at a table drinking a latte, I think it was, anyway."

Chip ordered a black coffee and sat at a table off to the side, pretending to read a copy of the *Dill Chronicle* somebody left there, but watching Rawston out the corner of his eye. At one point Rawston's cellphone rang and he fished it out of his jacket pocket and put it to his ear.

"Rawston never said anything," Chip said. "He just listened, no expression on his face, like getting angry, or happy to get the call, just nothing, and then he hung up."

After that, Rawston left the coffee shop, and a minute later Chip followed him along Main Street. Rawston didn't hurry, but he wasn't casually strolling either, Chip said. He turned up Slope Drive, and so did Chip, keeping him in sight, but lagging far back.

"I figured if he noticed me, I'd just walk on up the Drive, a Mt. Augustus student heading for the campus, but he never even looked behind him."

Cooper remembered she'd told the students not to tail Rawston, just keep an eye on him. Still, it occurred to her that Chip Stack made a perfect tail: not tall, but not

71

tiny, either, nondescript brown hair, no memorable feature, like a Roman nose, clothes neat and preppy, a young man so easy to overlook, and forget.

"Professor North, what he did was walk along Hill Street right to your house," Chip said. "I was way back down the street, and I sat on somebody's stoop, like I lived there—he never looked back at me, anyway—and he really studied your house, and then he walked over to one side of the house, to look at that, then back, to look at the house's other side, kind of taking his time, like he was memorizing details, maybe doors, and windows."

Cooper exchanged a look with Mike Bolknor, and had the impression he drew the same conclusion she did, that Sonny wasn't trying to be subtle, sneaking a peek. In fact, the opposite, as if he hoped Cooper was home, and would see him out there.

"Then?" Cooper said.

"He walked straight to the Campus Security building, right here," Chip said. "I could see him standing at the door, but then he turned, as if he'd decided not to go in after all, and walked back down Hill Street."

After that, Chip had a class. He couldn't follow Rawston farther.

"Good work," Cooper told him, and Chip resumed studying the patrol reports, sitting up straight, radiating pride.

Mike Bolknor swiveled in his chair, to look at Cooper, leaning on her cane. Henry sat beside her feet, bright eyed, in his own mind, apparently, part of the team.

"Nothing we can do, so far," Bolknor said. "Rawston isn't breaking any laws."

He shrugged, palms up, and Cooper noticed for the first time that Mike Bolknor wore a wedding ring. She'd assumed he must be single, because in his application there'd been no mention of his marital status, and he'd never said anything about it. She thought to ask him, but changed her mind, thinking it would be intrusive, none of her business. Yet, she was concerned, because the man was now part of the college's administration, dealing with students, and she knew virtually nothing about him, except for his work with the New York Police Department.

"I totally forgot to ask," Cooper said. "You must have found a place to live?"

Bolknor looked at her, and she suspected he knew she was probing.

After a silence, he said: "I'm renting a place, on Maple Street."

That was on the campus's far side, running north from Hill Street, residential, mostly faculty homes.

"Somebody on sabbatical, letting out their house?" Cooper said.

Bolknor looked at her, and sighed, whether wearily, or sadly, she wasn't sure.

"No, just a couple of rooms," he said.

And the message, Cooper knew, was that Mike Bolknor lived alone.

He swiveled his chair around, so he faced his desk, ending the conversation. As he did, though, Cooper saw his face sag, as if it got heavy. Just a moment. Then the implacability returned.

"We'll be watching the house," he said.

He didn't turn around.

73

"At night," he said.

Cooper thought: I saw misery.

For the rest of the afternoon, Cooper brooded.

She sat at her computer, ostensibly going over professors' initial student assessments—strengths, career goals, suggested internships—but the print on the screen blurred and finally she stopped pretending to work. She sat back in her chair, drumming both hands' fingers on the armrests.

Nessie Greffier called her arrogant. Was it true? Was she arrogant? So much animosity! It hurt.

Mike Bolknor, meanwhile, remained a puzzle. She thought: the more I know him, the less I know him.

He guarded a secret. It wasn't some criminal offense or the like. She'd checked with his NYPD superiors, and they'd been genuinely dismayed over his self-banishment to the Vermont mountains. So why was the man here?

Another worry: sending students to spy on a convicted felon. She doubted Nikki Winkel and Chip Stack and Jerry Shapiro were in danger, but it still bothered her. Yet, she'd just seen Chip bask in Mike Bolknor's approval, for his surveillance work, maybe a highlight of his life.

And there was Sonny Rawston.

She guessed his game, to rattle her, but how far would Sonny take it?

Cooper sighed.

Her watch said 4:16, and the day had been long enough already. "Time to go read a book," she told

74

Henry, who seemed to understand, because he immediately got up and walked out the door, heading for the elevator.

A half hour after she got home, feeling too restless to read, Cooper decided to drive to Abner Park, so Henry could exercise. Also, she'd watch birds, active again now, after their midday siesta.

On her way out, Cooper grabbed her binoculars from the entryway table, and slung them from her neck. She locked the door, turned toward her car, parked in the driveway, and there, on the sidewalk—watching her, smirking—stood Sonny Rawston.

His loafers' toes stopped just shy of the sidewalk's edge, entirely on public space. Carefully on public space, Cooper thought. He wore tan chinos and a light green dress shirt, with a leather bombardier jacket, his red hair neatly trimmed. He stood looking at Cooper with no expression.

"Hi," he said. "It's been a lot of years."

Six years, Cooper thought. It should have been ten.

She walked down the driveway to confront him, Henry prancing along beside her on his short legs, and she made it a point to stop just shy of bumping into him. He didn't step back.

"What do you want, Sonny?" she asked.

He looked at her, without expression. Finally he sighed, theatrically.

"Getting shot at it!" he said. "Did that upset you?"

75

He shook his head, faking commiseration.

"What do you want, Sonny?" Cooper repeated.

"Were you scared?" he asked.

Cooper said nothing.

"I hope you're doing okay," he said, blandly. "After all we've been through together."

"That would be your trial, wouldn't it?" she said.

He looked down at Henry, sitting beside Cooper's sneaker.

"Do you like your little doggie?" he said.

Cooper said nothing. If she yelled at him, or looked afraid, he'd win.

"It'd be terrible, losing a beloved pet," he said. "Let's keep our fingers crossed."

She stifled an urge to jab with her cane, spear him in the gut.

"Go away, Sonny," she said. "There's nothing for you in Dill—go start a new life somewhere."

He looked amused.

"You're teaching at the college now," he said. "I'd love to meet some of your students."

She said nothing, didn't blink.

"Binoculars," he said, pointing at the pair hanging from Cooper's neck. "I bet you still go bird watching in Abner Park—say, aren't the best times for that early morning and early evening?"

She said nothing, and Sonny suddenly grinned. He tipped an imaginary hat, smirked, and walked off toward Abner Park, whistling.

Cooper watched him walk away along Hill Street. After a moment, she recognized the song he whistled. It was the old Bob Dylan anthem, "The Times They Are A-

Changin," and Cooper's mind lurched back to an afternoon when she was a Middlebury College junior, visiting home, and everywhere in Dill she heard banjos and guitars and harmonicas, and saw Jesus beards and pioneer frocks and long Joan Baez hair with flowers in it.

She thought: you weren't born then, Sonny. How do you know that song? And why whistle it now?

It occurred to her, all those years in prison, Sonny did research—he'd studied Cooper North.

Assiduously.

CHAPTER FOURTEEN

Cooper watched until Sonny Rawston dwindled into invisibility, far down Hill Street. Then she let Henry into her car and was just shutting the door when the phone in her pocket rang. It was the Campus Security building's work-study receptionist. He said Nikki Winkel had called, asking where to find Cooper.

"She's working a project for you, I guess," he said.

"I'm on my way to Abner Park right now," Cooper told him. "Tell her I'll be walking along the pond, with my dog, and after about an hour I'll be home."

"Okay," he said.

Certain flycatchers vexed Cooper.

She watched them sallying out from the pond-side maples, snagging ichneumon flies and bluebottles and craneflies, each bird smaller than a tennis ball, grayish-brown, with white wing bars and white eye-rings and a tiny pointed beak. Of this particular family, four species summered in the Green Mountains—Yellow-bellied flycatcher, least flycatcher, willow flycatcher, alder flycatcher—and she couldn't tell one from another.

Vexing.

Not that it really mattered.

What did matter was this September evening's serenity. An absence of Sonny Rawston, for one thing. And the sun, now low in the southwest, cast a honey-colored light over the park, and made the pond's still water look golden.

She'd hoped to see Arctic snow geese, flying southward over the Green Mountains, en route to their wintering havens, but none had come yet. Hooded mergansers dove in the pond, though, and mallards dipped, both leaving golden wakes. Dark stands of shoreline pine and balsam set off maples and beeches, already flaring crimson or amber. All the while, Henry snuffled in the underbrush. Periodically he'd pop his head out of the foliage, for a Cooper check—*You still there, friend?*—and then he'd disappear again, back to snuffling.

Cooper sighed. She'd heard outdoorsman friends say their hunting wasn't really about shooting deer or turkeys. It was an excuse to tramp in the woods. She had no desire to shoot anything, but she supposed her birdwatching was like that, less about identifying species than settling into a trance among the trees, listening to little lives scurry in fallen leaves.

At the moment, she thought, amused, her great problem was whether to sink into the sky-blue Adirondack chair, sited for pond watching, or the adjacent daffodil-yellow chair, or the snow-white chair. And then she heard a rumble.

Her stomach clenched.

79

It approached along Hill Street, getting louder. She guessed it had just passed the Dill Industries headquarters, coming this way. Where Hill Street ran through Abner Park, and briefly became Abner Park Drive, buried in trees, the rumble changed tone, but still came on, ever louder.

And then it was there: up on the Drive, a black motorcycle.

It stopped, just where the downhill path to the pond started, and Cooper looked up at the rider staring down at her—shoulder-length gray hair, a gray beard. He left his engine rumbling.

As Cooper watched, frozen, he reached down, to a long leather holster slung from the motorcycle's seat. He withdrew a rifle. He put it to his shoulder, and she saw him sighting down on her, peering through a telescopic sight.

She had nowhere to go.

This pond-side area was cleared, a broad swath of lawn. She couldn't hobble to the woods before he shot.

This is no way to die, she thought.

She flung herself into the blue Adirondack chair, the nearest chair, its high backrest facing the shooter up on the road, and she huddled down, making herself as small as she could. Whether the chair's thick wooden slats would stop a bullet, she didn't know.

She heard a gunshot, and simultaneously felt a jolt in the chair. She still breathed—the bullet hadn't gone through.

Now, she thought, he'll assume I'm dead, or shoot again, or come down the path, with that rifle, to make sure. And she had nowhere to go, because if she stood up and left the chair, she'd be instantly exposed.

Henry! What if he stopped snuffling in the underbrush, came out onto the lawn? Would he be shot? If she were gone, who'd care for Henry?

Another gunshot from the road, and this time the bullet burst through the chair's wooden slat, just left of her shoulder.

Now nothing, except her own heavy breathing.

He'll come, she thought. Down the path, with that rifle. And then he'd shoot her.

She thought: these are my last thoughts. And she realized her thoughts were of Henry, of what would happen to him.

"Hey!"

Up on the road, a woman's voice, yelling.

Then a second voice, male.

"We've called the cops, pal!"

She heard the motorcycle's engine rev, and she looked around the back of her Adirondack chair just as the rider u-turned and roared away, east on Hill Street, back the way he'd come.

Quickly, the roar faded, and was gone.

Henry popped out of the underbrush and looked at her, quizzical.

Up on the drive, Cooper saw two people, staring down at her.

Jerry Shapiro and Nikki Winkel.

And something occurred to Cooper. Just a vague impression, from long ago—but hadn't she seen that biker before?

Later, after the police cruiser skidded to a stop up on the road, and Tip LaPerle ran slipping down the path, and Jerry Shapiro and Nikki Winkel reported what they'd seen—yes, a black motorcycle, no license plate, rider with shoulder-length gray hair and a gray beard—they'd all gone back to the Campus Security building. When they told Mike Bolknor what happened, he grimaced. He looked, it seemed to Cooper, as if he'd been kicked in the stomach. She thought, Mike, it's not your fault! Instantly, though, his face lapsed back into inscrutability.

Cooper sank into one of the office's chairs. She looked for Henry, and saw him under Mike Bolknor's desk, asleep.

She sighed.

Jerry and Nikki had come looking for her because they'd scouted out where Sonny Rawston lived. Now, that seemed hardly to matter.

Things weren't clarifying. They were getting muddier.

Long gray hair, a gray beard?

Nobody she could think of.

Not their number-one suspect, Sonny Rawston.

Some stranger, then. Or somebody she'd prosecuted decades ago. Somebody who'd simmered for years, and now—on Medicare—decided to get revenge.

Putting criminals on trial had been her job. She believed most perpetrators understood that, but at least one did not, Sonny Rawston. He didn't blame his own criminality for his imprisonment. He blamed Cooper North. Maybe others shared that delusion.

Cooper wondered: are psychopaths commoner than we think? She'd prosecuted many of them, manipulators who took no responsibility for their own acts, who lacked all empathy for others. Surely, though, all psychopaths don't become criminals, Cooper thought. Many must live among us, piously passing the collection plate on Sundays, maybe, or selling us insurance, or bagging our groceries. They might even seem charming. Some may be our own relatives. And we never know, because they're so skilled at veiling their inner coldness.

And if she were gone, who'd look after Henry?

CHAPTER FIFTEEN

This post mortem of the shooting in the park was on life support. Nikki and Jerry had gone off to the cafeteria. Henry slept under the desk. Cooper and the police chief and the campus-security chief sat in Mike Bolknor's office, stumped.

Shoulder-length gray hair? Gray beard?

"Maybe this Rawston hired a hitman," Bolknor finally suggested.

Through the office window, Cooper watched students strolling toward the library on the lamp-lit campus walkways, or heading back to their dormitories after an evening course. They all wore jackets. Tonight was frosty.

Police cruisers now crisscrossed the town, looking for a black motorcycle, make unknown, lacking a license plate. Nobody in the room expected they'd find it. Once spotted by Nikki and Jerry, the shooter would have instantly gone to ground.

"Sonny? Hiring a hitman?" Cooper said. "It's possible...."

She doubted it, though. Sonny was too smart for that. A hired shooter could blackmail you, or turn evidence against you. Sonny had run his drug operation solo. She doubted he'd take on an accomplice now. Besides, what money could he possibly have to pay for the service?

"Shoulder-length gray hair, gray beard, no shooter types like that around here," Tip LaPerle said. "Not that we actually have any shooter types around here."

He sat thinking.

"Yeah, here's what," he said. "I'll get Corrections to give me a rundown on Rawston's jailbird associates, these last six years, see if any are currently out, matching our description."

He shrugged. All they had was hypotheticals, and straws to grasp. And hardly any straws.

"We dug a slug out of that chair you were sitting in," he said.

Another shrug.

"We'll see what that tells us, if anything," he said.

In the end, they decided to keep hunting for the motorcycle, and probing Sonny Rawston. After all, at Cooper's house, he'd issued veiled threats. What he'd said, written down, would look innocuous. It was how he said it, and you can't indict a man for intonations.

Clever man, Cooper thought. Too clever by half.

Cooper started out of the building, but stopped to answer a question from the work-study receptionist, at his post near the door: "Did your cousin ever reach you?"

"My cousin?" Cooper said.

"Well, he called, asking where to find you, said he was just in town for the afternoon, and I told him what you'd said, that you'd be in the park with your dog," the student told her.

Cooper looked at him, stunned. She had no living cousins.

She thought to ask what the man sounded like, but that would be pointless. He'd certainly disguised his voice. And trying to trace the call would be fruitless, because it would almost certainly have come from a cell phone, while the caller sat on his motorcycle, with a holstered rifle.

"Yes, he did find me," Cooper said.

That night she lay in bed, looking at the ceiling in the dark.

She knew post-traumatic stress kept her awake. Twice she'd been targeted.

Her mind kept disassembling the two attacks into pieces—motorcycle, shoulder-length gray hair and gray beard, brazenly shooting on a city street, then in a public park....

And there was Sonny Rawston. Those veiled threats. He must be part of this. She felt certain.

She sensed complexity, though. She'd learned to trust her impressions, and the feeling felt strong: this was nothing so simple as revenge. This was a jigsaw puzzle, with many pieces.

She tried to blank her mind, a technique she'd used before. Let your subconscious do the sorting and thinking. This time, though, staring at the ceiling in the dark, all she visualized was a spider.

It crouched, malignant, in the intricate web it had constructed. It stared at her ruby eyed.

With an exclamation of disgust, she threw off the covers and sat up on the bed's edge. Henry woke, too, and peered at her in the streetlamp light coming through the window, ready for whatever adventure might be afoot.

"Just an imbecile old woman," she told the dog, aloud. "Brain fog."

She got up and looked out at Hill Street. It was there, parked in the maple's shadow, as always, the Campus-Security Prius. She made out Mike Bolknor's large form, leaning against the fender, arms crossed over his chest, looking off into the night.

He didn't need to do this, she thought. He had officers patrolling all night. Any of them could watch her house.

It still irritated her, needing a babysitter. She did need one, though. And the Prius parked out in the dark reassured her.

She climbed back into bed. Again she visualized the ruby-eyed spider crouched in its web, but she pushed it aside, in disgust. A fabricated phantasmagoria. She'd decided to be done with fear.

Now she saw nothing. At some point, she drifted asleep.

CHAPTER SIXTEEN

Back on the campus next morning, at a meeting, Cooper thought about Nikki Winkel, and also about opulent office furniture.

She should be concentrating on what President Bentley Gardner was saying, this being a session of the President's Advisory Council, of which she was a member, but her attention wandered.

"...so I'd suggest a liaison group, to meet periodically with counterparts, at appropriate institutions—Middlebury, say, and Williams, and Bowdoin...."

Cooper didn't care. She liked Gardy. He was an old friend. Still, she didn't care.

She wasn't Nostradamus, but she could predict the liaison group's entire outcome: junkets. Plus, resume padding. Period. So she didn't care.

Yesterday, Nikki Winkel and Jerry Shapiro saved her life. She'd been shot at. Again. Now, here she sat, in the college's sumptuous Administrative Conference Suite, supposed to care about proposed inter-college gabfests.

"…and, next, we've had our endowment portfolio excoriated, for ecological incorrectness, as you know, if you read the student newspaper—well and good, but here comes reality, now, lifting its loathsome head, hissing "Investment returns!" So we need to…."

Cooper could see her reflection in the conference table. A Vermont crafter of luxurious corporate furnishings had hand-sanded its oak to glass smoothness, then brushed on many layers of costly resin, so that it seemed made of smoky quartz. And the room's armoire and side tables and chairs and wall panels matched. Portraits of former presidents and revered donors hung on the walls, wearing academic robes or tailored suits, gray or charcoal.

She'd never really noticed all this luxury before. She'd been born into it. She supposed her own portrait might someday go up on these walls, after her will was read, another revered donor. Would she, too, look smug?

She studied her reflection in the conference table, looking for smugness, but saw only a blurred face staring at her, as if from another dimension, a long, bony face. It occurred to her, for what this table cost, Nikki Winkel could fund all four years at Mt. Augustus College.

Was it true, what Nessie Greffier said? Had life been "slicked" for her, because her name was North? And was she arrogant?

Norths were bankers, since long ago, when Vermont was still an independent republic. Suppose, though, she'd been the daughter of factory workers. She guessed she'd sit less easy in this posh armchair, among these people marinated in importance. To her, they'd always been just acquaintances and friends, with the usual

89

human array of pluses and minuses, but would that less privileged Cooper, sitting here, feel like a shelter rescue among purebreds?

Another thought: what if I hadn't looked like a giraffe? What if I'd been as pretty as Nessie, and as popular? Wouldn't that, too, have "slicked" my way some?

She thought about Nikki Winkel, also no beauty, and impoverished. Two strikes against her. Yet, smart. Cooper had arranged a scholarship for Nikki. Would Nessie sneer, call it a kind of arrogance? Noblesse oblige?

"...and now, turning to the new Artificial Intelligence Research Center," Bentley Gardner said, "I've been talking with our Dill Industries partners about our little siting glitch, and...."

Cooper didn't understand artificial intelligence. Could a machine read "Macbeth?" Be moved by it? Enjoy it? Could a machine write "Macbeth?"

"In a nutshell," Gardy said, "Our new Brainlab— as dubbed by students—is set to be born, but where to put it?"

"Money?" somebody asked.

"Actually, we're awash in liquidity," Gardy said. "We've allocated funds of our own, Dill Industries' share quadruples ours, and Macchine Pensanti, our second corporate partner, over there in Turin, has its euros in the mix, so...."

Lots of money, he said. No place to build. Not a square foot left at the Dill Industries headquarters site. No empty lots left on campus, either. Yet, the new center needed to be close by, an easy walk from other college buildings.

"Luckily, a white knight's come forward, a local businessman," Gardy said. "He's promising to find campus-adjacent property where we can build and...."

Cooper woke up.

"Jack Abbott?" she said.

"Yes," Gardy said. "He's being quite accommodating and...."

A jigsaw-puzzle piece snapped into place.

Cooper's house, bulldozed, would make a reasonable site in itself. Out back, though, its grounds extended for nearly ten acres, all abutting the Mt. Augustus campus.

"History museum!" Cooper thought. "Liar!"

Millions for Jack Abbott, she figured. Many, many millions.

How far, she wondered, would he go to get her property?

He could guess she had it willed, probably to either her nephew or the college. He needed to buy it quickly, then, before she selfishly dropped dead of a heart attack or pneumonia.

So, she thought, he needs to buy it from me alive. And that means Jack Abbott wouldn't kill me.

Another thought came to her.

Scare me, though, into selling? Spook me out of my home?

Jack Abbott didn't have shoulder-length gray hair and a gray beard, but he could hire somebody who did.

Somebody to take potshots.

And just miss.

CHAPTER SEVENTEEN

It was satisfactorily nondescript, a mud-spattered blue Chevrolet Malibu, borrowed from the college's maintenance department. Cooper parked it in front of DeBouche's Gas 'n Groceries, at Main Street's eastern end, and now they sat in it, watching the house across the street.

Faded-gray clapboards. Two electric meters. Two mailboxes beside the front door, up on the sagging porch.

She'd figured her black Volvo would be too recognizable.

Ten minutes.

Jerry and Chip got out their smartphones and began clicking. Some game that meant nothing to Cooper. Nikki produced a notebook and pen and began working on an essay, for one of her classes. Cooper brooded.

Twenty minutes.

At last the house's front door opened, but it was just a white-haired senior citizen who stepped out onto the porch. Stooped, rheumy eyed, he looked the wreck of a man once large and sinewy. Painfully, he climbed down the steps, then stood at the curb, as if mustering strength.

Finally he trudged across Main Street to DeBouche's. As he limped into the store, Jerry Shapiro impulsively vaulted out of the Malibu's back seat in hot pursuit. Nikki Winkel, sitting in front, beside Cooper, muttered "Look, not up in the sky, it's a hummingbird, it's a Piper Cub, it's Superbrash!" She grinned, sardonically, but Cooper detected admiration. Meanwhile, in the back seat, Chip Stack looked dispirited, as if unhappy he hadn't thought of questioning the man. At least, it was action.

From the car, they watched through the store's large front window as Jerry made a show, inside, of picking up Cokes. At the register, while the old man paid for lottery tickets and hot dogs and a six-pack, the black-bearded younger man, eyes sharp, leaned nonchalantly against the counter and chatted him up.

When he got back to the car, Jerry reported the man was eighty-six. Wife died last year. Bone cancer, horrible, he'd said—"You won't see me going to mass anymore!" Worked all his days at the Abner Dill & Sons Granite Quarry, cutting stone, and now wheezed. Silicosis. Jerry finally edged in a question about his upstairs neighbor, and got a shrug.

"Naah, no job," the old man wheezed. "Guess not. Bugger don't talk. Got no social skills."

Now they sat in the car drinking Coke, except Cooper. At her age, if they sat here too long, the extra liquid would become an annoyance.

It was the upstairs apartment they'd staked out.

Yesterday, at the Slope Drive Laundromat, Jerry had fed quarters into a front-loader, and Nikki Winkel waited. They'd agreed: while Jerry's clothes sloshed, they'd critique each other's class presentations, but that got tabled because Sonny Rawston came in, with a laundry bag of his own.

While his clothes washed, then spun in a drier, they sat in a far corner, holding up magazines to hide their faces. When he finally scooped his clothes out, back into his laundry bag, they ignored Cooper's orders and followed him, risky, because—it occurred to Cooper—if he looked back, he might remember them from the laundromat, even with the face-covering magazines, a matched set of skinnies, wearing jeans, and Jerry's long black hair and black beard stood out, as did Nikki's hackles-up haircut and shirt with cutoff sleeves, but Sonny Rawston never looked back. At least, he never seemed to.

He walked down Slope Drive, then east along Main Street, past the downtown shops, to this house. They checked the doorbells' name tags: Hubert LeGrande downstairs, Sonny Rawston upstairs. After that they'd called the Campus Security receptionist, to ask where Cooper would be, and then walked back up to Abner Park to find her. They arrived just in time to see the gray-bearded biker taking aim, and shouted, "Hey!"

So they knew where Sonny Rawston lived. And, as of this morning, they knew more.

While Cooper attended her meeting, Chip Stack was withdrawing cash from the Dill National Bank's ATM, on Main Street. He heard a rumble and looked up to see a black motorcycle pass by. Sonny Rawston drove it.

It was that motorcycle they'd come to see.

94

Yesterday, in the park, Cooper had glimpsed the shooter's motorcycle. Jerry and Nikki got a closer look. Now they hoped to see if this bike was a match.

So far, no Sonny, no bike.

A few blocks farther east, Dill would fade into countryside, Main Street becoming County Road 12, winding through six miles of pine forest and hillside cow pastures, out to Hart's Corners, but not yet—this was Dill's East End, a neighborhood of weather-faded clapboard two-stories, built for granite workers in the 1920s, the quarries' heyday. Some quarrymen still lived here, but now most of the homeowners and renters clerked in shops, or shingled roofs, or drove delivery vans. Kids' tricycles and plastic action figures littered many of the yards, and there were basketball hoops nailed up on some of the electric poles.

"Here he comes," Nikki Winkel said, and they all heard the rumble.

Sonny Rawston drove up the street, U-turned the bike, and parked in front of the apartment house. He took off his helmet, looked up and down the street, and Cooper thought he looked at them, although she hid behind an AAA road map, as if she were studying it.

He walked up the steps, carrying his helmet. He closed the front door behind him.

All motorcycles looked the same to Cooper. Black motorcycles especially all looked the same.

She sighed, frustrated.

"Reconnaissance!" Jerry announced, and threw open his door and bolted out of the back seat before Cooper could say anything. Chip Stack got out of the

95

back on the other side and trotted beside Jerry across the street.

As they walked around the motorcycle, studying it, Chip pulled a pen and a small pad from his chino's back pocket. Cooper saw him scribble down the number of the license plate, a miniature of Vermont's green automobile plate.

Nikki Winkel, sitting beside Cooper, peered out the window and shook her head.

"It just looks like a black motorcycle to me," she said.

Chip and Jerry walked back across the street and got into the car.

"It's a Honda," Jerry said. "Old, I think, but in awesome shape, and there's something else."

"Look what's hanging from the saddle," Chip said.

Cooper peered, and this time she saw what she'd missed before: hung from the bike's black-leather seat was a black-leather rifle holster. No rifle in it now.

"That does it," Cooper said, folding up her map.

She'd just started the car when the apartment house's front door opened, and Sonny Rawston stepped out. He stood on the porch, and looked directly at them, sitting in the car, and grinned.

Cooper felt a spasm of embarrassment, caught spying.

She backed the car around in DeBouche's Gas 'n Groceries' little parking area. Then she drove back down Main Street, westward this time, heading for the police station.

Tip LaPerle put down the telephone.

"Sonny Rawston registered that bike with DMV just this morning," he reported. "Title's transferred to him from Specialty Sales, which is weird, because there's no trace of that company, not around here, anyway, not listed with the state tax people."

He stopped to drum his fingers on his desk, looking grumpy.

"Can't find any record of a sale, either, no sales tax, whatever—so maybe this company, if it even exists, donated this bike to our friend Sonny, right? Maybe it's a charity for needy ex-cons."

He looked even grumpier.

"Because he couldn't buy it, could he?" LaPerle said. "We've checked and this bird got out of the cooler with no savings, no bankroll at all, and you just heard his neighbor say no job."

"He's renting that apartment," Cooper said.

"That, too," LaPerle said. "So how's he pay rent? What's he living on? Vitamin-enriched air?"

"We still can't nail him," Cooper said. "I don't see anything illegal here—fishy, for sure, but being jobless and getting gifted with a bike isn't against the law—so we don't really have anything, yet."

"Yet," LaPerle said.

For the rest of the afternoon, Cooper felt preoccupied, and unsettled.

She dropped Nikki at her mother's rundown cottage, on a side lane off Slope Drive, and delivered Jerry and Chip to their dormitory, known to students as the Mt. Augustus Hilton. Then she drove back to her own house. She had four phone messages, two of them spams. Tip LaPerle had called to report on the bullet they dug out of her chair in the park: it matched the slug from her living room wall. Same .30-06 hunting rifle used in both attacks. She also had a call from Drew Saunders: Mona, in Barcelona, wanted him to tell Cooper for her, "Hola, buena amiga!" And, also, Cooper's new orthopedic shoe insert had arrived.

She took Henry walking in the back yard, then let him into the car and drove back to campus, where she found Mike Bolknor's corner office empty, so she scrawled a note: "Call me."

Riding up in the elevator, with Henry, everything felt askew, although she wasn't sure what "everything" was, except that she'd abased herself, getting caught skulking around Sonny Rawston's apartment. That grin he'd flashed at her had been a jeer. So this round, also, went to Sonny.

Except now they knew he drove the shooter's motorcycle, owned it. It had that rifle holster. Not proof of anything, not in court. Any biker could buy a rifle holster. Still, she had no doubts. This was the shooter's machine.

Yet, it was only this morning he got the bike licensed. And, yesterday, when Nikki and Jerry followed him home from the laundromat, there'd been no bike parked out front. Then they'd walked directly to the park, just in time to scare off the shooter.

Who couldn't have been Sonny. How could he get there ahead of them?

Unless he already had the motorcycle, maybe hidden out back. Maybe he'd used it for that first shooting, five days ago, that stormy night. Then, yesterday, he brought it out of hiding to take another shot.

Hadn't they said the bike the shooter rode, in the park, had no license plate? So he could have raced up to the park ahead of Jerry and Nikki, riding his new bike, as yet unlicensed, aimed and shot.

Except: Sonny Rawston didn't have shoulder-length gray hair and a gray beard.

So she felt preoccupied, and unsettled.

Her phone rang, Mike Bolknor. She told him what they'd found out.

"Hmm," he said.

And that was all.

That evening, with Henry's kibbles mostly gone from his dish, some of it strewn on the kitchen floor, since Henry was a slobby diner, and with a Newman's Own All-Natural Pepperoni Pizza baking in the oven, the time of day, once, when Cooper would be on her third vodka martini—she could almost feel the iced glass in her hand—just then the doorbell rang.

It took her a while to find her cane, and by the time she opened the door she saw a small boy on a bicycle pedaling away. On her stoop lay a package.

Its address label was typed. Just her name. No return.

Curious, she unwrapped it and found a cardboard box inside. She laid the box on her kitchen table and removed its lid.

She gasped.

This much malice! Who? To know me this well! And who would do this?

Inside the box, on its side, like some huge exotic gem, lay a bottle of Chivas Regal Scotch. Beside it lay a package of Camels.

There was a typed note—

"You've worked so hard! You've earned this!

"Scotch used to be your favorite, but then you switched to vodka, because you didn't really like vodka's taste and hoped it would help you quit. But wouldn't it be great, just once, to get some of that swell scotch taste again? Imagine it in your mouth, and sliding down!

"And how you loved Camels!

"Enough's enough—don't deprive yourself any longer!

An Admirer."

Cooper sank down into one of the kitchen-table chairs, staring into the open box in front of her. Her hands trembled.

Because she craved it.

She wanted to feel it on her tongue, that rich taste of expensive scotch, a little smoky. She wanted to feel it burn its way down her throat. And then would come the buzz, the easing of the thoughts always ricocheting inside her head, like tracer bullets, so that....

She sighed, tremulously, grabbed her cane, forced herself away from the box, lurched to the telephone.

"Campus Security, Mike Bolknor speaking."

"It's Cooper," she said, knowing she spoke so softly he might not hear.

"Please come—quickly!"

CHAPTER EIGHTEEN

She didn't explain why she'd needed him so quickly. He didn't ask. Somehow, he'd known to bring latex gloves stuffed into his jacket pocket, for handling evidence.

He examined the bottle of scotch, then the package of cigarettes. Finally he read the note. Cooper, watching, felt jittery and upset. She'd never told him about her alcohol addiction, in remission, but forever there, and now, reading the note, he'd know.

For something to do, she brewed coffee in the machine, a cup for each of them, French Roast. It wasn't scotch, but it was something.

"This'll give us zero," Bolknor predicted, laying the Chivas Regal bottle back in the box.

He peeled off his latex gloves and stuffed them back into his pocket.

"I'll send this down to the Dill PD, and Tip LaPerle can get it analyzed at the state lab, but we won't get anything," he said.

Fingerprints? Probably wore gloves, he said. Printer? Probably done in a library, or some other public place. Probably out of town. Ditto for buying the scotch and the cigarettes.

"No chance of tracing any of this," Bolknor said.

He shrugged.

Cooper handed over his cup of coffee and they both sat, resting their elbows on the kitchen table.

"Sonny Rawston?" Bolknor asked.

Cooper nodded.

"Probably," she said. "It fits."

Because, this afternoon, he'd caught her spying on him. So, a counterstrike.

And because, six years ago, she'd gotten him convicted, jailed. Not his own fault, couldn't have been—psychopaths never blame themselves. So she needed to be punished.

He wants me frightened, she thought. He wants me to squirm. He wants me to feel threatened and miserable.

Did he want her dead? Would he go so far?

But....

"I don't see how he could have known these things, about switching from scotch to vodka, especially," she told Bolknor. "I just don't see how."

He said nothing, drinking his coffee, letting her work it out.

Her friends knew, of course. She'd never made her drinking problem a secret. You couldn't keep a secret like that in Dill. They'd watched her struggle with it, unable to help except to sympathize and not condemn.

Nessie Greffier!

Cooper turned the possibility over in her mind. All these years, with Cooper never suspecting, Nessie had resented her....

And then there was Jack Abbott.

Not a friend, really. Beverly was, though, peripherally. And whatever Beverly heard or experienced, she'd tell Jack.

How far would Jack Abbott go? Cooper wondered. To rattle me, into selling my house.

She sighed.

"I keep coming back to Sonny Rawston," she said. "This is his style."

"Just about everything keeps coming back to Rawston," Bolknor said. "Except any kind of hard evidence."

"Too clever by half," Cooper said.

It occurred to her that Mike Bolknor had said nothing about her alcoholism, hadn't even looked surprised or shocked or bothered as he read the note. And now he sat there, drinking his coffee, face as impassive as ever.

Yet, she'd glimpsed sadness in that face. Depression even. And for the umpteenth time she wondered what Mike Bolknor kept secret. What had happened back there in New York?

She wanted to ask. He wouldn't answer, though. And he'd said nothing about her drinking. Not a word. So she'd, too, be a respecter of privacy and wouldn't probe.

Even though she really wanted to.

"Guess what?" Tip LaPerle said over the phone.

"I give up," Cooper said.

She'd just been watching the local-news wrap-up, ready for bed—still unsettled by this evening's malicious gift—when the telephone rang.

"That apartment Rawston's renting? It's one of Jack Abbott's," LaPerle said, and then muttered, "Why not just call the damned town Abbottville!"

Cooper heard the resentment. Tip LaPerle and Jack Abbott, both Tenement Row boys, had climbed up from River Street, down by the railroad tracks. Measured by money, though, Abbott had climbed far higher. And that, as old Vermonters might say, was a burr down Tip's britches.

Which brought up someone else.

Nessie Greffier.

There's a burr down her britches, too, Cooper thought. Me.

Nessie, she wondered—did you tell Sonny Rawston? About my switch from scotch to vodka?

She extinguished that thought. Remembering the bottle of Chivas Regal had already stirred her craving. And she knew of no tie between Nessie and Rawston. Except there could be a tie she didn't know about.

Jack Abbott, though. It now turned out, he definitely had a tie.

"I called up Mr. Money," Tip said. "I asked him how much rent Rawston was paying, and guess what?"

"What?" Cooper asked.

"He said, and I quote, 'Get a goddamned warrant, Tip, or get off my goddamned back!'"

"Hmm," Cooper said.

"Ain't that interesting?" Dill's police chief said.

Cooper went to bed, but lay looking at the ceiling. She heard Henry get up, walk around the bed, lie down again on the other side. He sighed. Maybe he sensed her uneasiness.

She got up to look out the window.

Campus Security's Prius hid under the usual maple. Too dark inside to see who sat in it, watching, whether Mike Bolknor or one of his men, but she felt protected. Also, irritated.

She steered her own ship. Always had. Now, though, this man, decades younger, whom she really didn't know, watched over her, and not just at night, either. He said nothing, but she felt he constantly watched, beyond his job's obligations, as if safeguarding her were entirely his responsibility, ten tons of it, even a compulsion.

Good!

That thought surprised her. Oddly, it didn't embarrass her.

I need help, and I want help. She confessed it to herself.

And she felt relieved.

Nothing moved outside, under the streetlamps, not even a foraging raccoon. Nothing she could see, anyway. Yet, something stirred in Dill—in five days, she'd been shot at twice, and she wondered about the next shot. Would that miss, too?

Fur brushed her leg and she looked down: Henry leaned against her shin, looking up. He felt warm.

106

"Are you my friend, Henry?" she asked, and immediately felt idiotic.

Henry yawned.

Out the window, the Prius's brake lights lit up, bright red, then went dark. Whoever sat in the car must have inadvertently pressed the brake pedal, maybe leaning over to reach a thermos of coffee. No more than that, but Cooper's anxiety boiled up.

Because the taillights looked like red eyes.

Spider eyes.

She'd visualized the spider before, squatting in its web, eyes like rubies. A message, she supposed, from her subconscious. She knew who the spider must be. Thought she did. No, she only guessed. And she balked at settling into certitude.

She thought: because of the spider's web!

She visualized its silk strands, stretching out, crisscrossing Dill, touching certain people, interconnecting them, but their figures were vague, as if she peered through mist, seeing only faceless specters.

She thought: No, it's not just someone who hates me, nothing so simple.

Henry howled.

Cooper started, astonished that so small a dog, broad-chested as he was, could make so deep and resonant a sound. He stared up at her, and she fancied he looked stern, and that she knew exactly what he was telling her: "Go to bed Cooper, so I can lie down again— I'm sleepy."

Laughing, she waggled an admonishing finger at the corgi.

"Henry, telepathy's hokum!" she said.

However, she got back into bed, and slept.

She awoke, and looked at her bedside clock. Seven a.m., October first.   Autumn's true start, Cooper had always thought.

This would be the sixth day, since that first shot, during the nighttime storm.

CHAPTER NINETEEN

It was a bright and tranquil morning.

Frost patched low spots on lawns, and the campus sugar maples now blazed amber, orange, scarlet. High overhead—too far up to see—Canada geese honked, and Cooper didn't want to go into the Campus Security Building. She wanted to stay outdoors.

She stood on the walkway, snug in her L.L. Bean down jacket, and thought about driving to Abner Park with Henry, to sit in one of the Adirondack chairs overlooking the pond and feel the morning slowly warm. She'd watch chipmunks scurry with puffed-out cheeks, stuffed with seeds to cache, and she'd let her thoughts wander, anything but gunshots.

She checked her wristwatch. Twenty minutes to Legal Reasoning Class.

She compromised and sat on one of the wooden benches flanking Campus Security's entrance, as Henry happily snuffled in the grass. A hint of smoke hung in the air, evoking Dill autumns decades ago, before leaf-burning restrictions, when smokiness marked October. Cooper thought: now it's wood stoves making this smoky tang, people all over Allen County firing them up, against the morning chill.

She wondered if Barcelona also got frosty, and guessed not so much. Mona Saunders must be having a high time, she thought, stalking Europe's galleries for canvasses with brushed-on blobs and dribbles, which reminded her she needed to pick up her new orthotic shoe insert. Also, did Henry need shots? Drew might be able to suggest a veterinarian, because he and Mona had a cat, an eccentric Siamese, an animal Cooper found inscrutable. Henry wanted, most of all, to be loved, and also to amuse himself, and to take in current events, using his sharp eyes and inquiring nose, and for good things to appear in his food dish, and—during lulls—to snooze, but what did cats want? Hard to know, and....

She heard a motorcycle.

She stiffened. Then she remembered this was Mt. Augustus College. She sat in front of the Campus Security Building. Nobody would shoot at her.

It swerved from Hill Street into the Campus Security parking lot and stopped in front of Cooper's bench. Sonny Rawston drove. Behind him, on the passenger saddle, sat Stacey Gillibrand, her arms wrapped around Rawston's waist.

Rawston stared at Cooper, face expressionless. Still staring, he pulled off his helmet, and the sunlight lit his red hair afire, but his eyes remained cold blue. Slowly, as if savoring this unexpected encounter, a bonus opportunity, he smiled, closed mouthed, all the while looking at Cooper.

Stacey dismounted and took off her helmet, attaching it behind Rawston's seat. She shook her head, to fix helmet matting, swirling her blond hair around her face, and all the while Rawston stared at Cooper, with that insinuating smile, and Cooper stared at the two of them, shocked by this pairing.

"Hi, Professor North," Stacey said brightly. "I'm all ready for Legal Reasoning!"

Rawston laughed, a mirthless sound.

"Hi from me, too," he said. "Professor North."

It sounded mocking.

"Say, would you believe it?" he said. "Stacey's my neighbor—so now I'm meeting your students!"

She wanted to stick her cane in his gloating eye.

He spoke again, sardonic: "Did you know, down at Dill Wine & Spirits—that's on Main Street, you probably remember—there's a sale on Chivas Regal?"

"Did you buy some?" Cooper asked.

Rawston shook his head, grinning.

"Never touch it," he said. "Personally.'"

Now she knew for sure: Rawston sent the liquor and cigarettes. And he wanted her to know it. No need for fingerprints. There'd be none anyway, and she doubted he'd bought them at Dill Wine & Spirits, either. As Mike Bolknor said, he'd go out of town for that, make it untraceable. What he wanted now was to send her to the local liquor store to see if he'd made a purchase, a goose chase, an embarrassment, so he could gloat. And maybe, if she visited the liquor store, seeing all those shelved bottles, she'd tumble off the wagon.

Too clever by half, she thought. And too nasty.

And who told him she'd switched from scotch to vodka? Somebody did.

His gaze shifted, almost imperceptibly, and he now stared, not at her, but past her. She half turned, and saw Mike Bolknor on the building's stoop, leaning against the doorframe, suit jacket strained across his chest, like a heavyweight prizefighter's. He said nothing, just leaned there, staring at Rawston without expression.

"Pleasure seeing you," Rawston told Cooper, chill eyed. "Stacey, I'll call you later."

He put his helmet back on, making it a point to do it slowly, and started the engine. He gave Cooper another closed-mouth smile, gaze like ice. Then the engine suddenly blatted and he drove off, Stacey and Cooper both watching him disappear down Hill Street, the bike's rumble fading away. And when Cooper turned again, Mike Bolknor no longer stood in the doorway, as if he'd never been there.

"Stacey, come up to my office, would you?" Cooper said. "Let's talk a few minutes, before class."

Once they were sitting in Cooper's office, Stacey inspected her nail polish—cornflower-blue, to match her eyes—while she waited to hear what her professor wanted, and Cooper didn't know what to say.

What's your relationship with Sonny Rawston? No. She had no right to probe Stacey's private life.

Watch out, Stacey—he's a psychopath, possibly dangerous. No. Warnings would probably backfire.

So she asked a neutral question: "You decided to live off campus?"

"Dorms, no thanks!" Stacey said, wrinkling her nose. "I'm twenty-six."

Yes, and you've been married and divorced, and you're making a new start, with stratospheric ambitions, Cooper thought. So, yes, dorm life would seem callow. And maybe the "brats," as Stacey called them, would judge her uncool, even shun her. Cooper wondered: was Stacey's high-handedness actually a bullet-proof vest? Also, she must face daunting college debt. And if that law degree never materializes? Cooper thought: all this blithe self-confidence—does it conceal anxiety? Insecurity? Self-doubt? Is it a Band-Aid?

"You're living on the East End?" Cooper said.

"Yup—rent free, for helping around the house, and I've got the whole upstairs," Stacey said. "Old lady's gimpy, can't leave the first floor, so she…oh…"

Stacey's blue eyes widened, but Cooper smiled, meaning "No offense taken."

"I can still lurch upstairs," Cooper said, ruefully shaking her head. "So that's lucky."

They sat looking at each other, while Cooper decided how to proceed, and settled on being circumspect, but direct.

"Have you known Sonny Rawston long?" she asked.

"Just since this morning," Stacey said. "He lives right next door!"

It troubled Cooper to see her face brighten.

Stacey, she remembered, came from Pittsburgh. So she'd arrived in Dill knowing nobody. Her classmates were younger. Now she'd met someone, possibly even a potential romantic interest.

"He's nice," Stacey announced. "I don't have a car at the moment, and he offered right away to drive me up here...."

Stacey suddenly frowned, and Cooper read her thought: could Mr. Nice actually be a predator? Cooper had told Henry telepathy was hokum, yet she knew Stacey was now reviewing everything Sonny Rawston had said, and his intonations, and his facial expressions, and body language. Stacey's forehead suddenly smoothed, and Cooper decoded that, too. Yes, he's really okay.

"That newspaper story?" Stacey said. "He'd read that, about how I'm looking into that schoolteacher's murder, in Hart's Corners? And he asked intelligent questions, really interested, and...."

"How's that going?" Cooper asked.

"It looks fishier and fishier," Stacey said. "Sonny volunteered to drive me over to Hart's Corners, to—you know—rummage around."

Cooper felt a chill. Stacey, off on that motorcycle with Rawston, alone with him, out among cow pastures and pine forests....

And what did he care about that old murder trial?

"Stacey," she said. "Did you know Sonny Rawston's just out of prison?"

Now the young woman scowled.

"That's the first thing he told me," Stacey said, defiant. "Totally up front, said he'd made a mistake, with drugs, but now he's turned around, so...."

Cooper wanted to tell her, run for your life, but dared not, knowing it would just push her further toward Rawston.

"Did he say his conviction wasn't for using drugs?" Cooper asked. "It was for selling them, a pusher?"

Stacey looked taken aback. Obviously he'd been vague about that. Then her mouth firmed, and she glared.

"What he did tell me was that you and the police chief here keep harassing him," she said. "That you don't want him making a new start!"

Cooper sighed. She'd guessed Rawston would put out this line, and it was effective. If she said Rawston's sole reason for returning to Dill was to punish Cooper North for getting him convicted, make her miserable, Stacey would dismiss it as an old woman's paranoia, proof she had it in for the man, who'd suffered six years in prison, paid for his mistakes, now deserved a second chance.

Stacey was the jury. Sonny Rawston was an astute attorney. He'd inserted a template in the jurors' minds. Now every witness's testimony would be mentally kneaded and shaped, so it fit into that template.

Cooper thought of the ruby-eyed spider, and its power, and her own weakness, and imperceptibly she shuddered. She kept her face placid, though, and her gaze mild.

"Oh well, here's what I actually wanted to ask you," Cooper said. "Have you, by any chance, noticed a man with shoulder-length gray hair and a gray beard in your neighborhood, possibly on a black motorcycle?"

Stacey, no friendliness in her gaze, shook her head.

"Anything else?" Stacey asked.

"No," Cooper said.

She watched the young woman get up and hurry out of the office, then sat staring at the empty doorway. After a moment, she squeezed shut her eyes. Abruptly, she slapped her hand against her desk, startling herself.

CHAPTER TWENTY

"There you go, Sweetcakes."

Drew Saunders finished fitting Cooper's new orthopedic insert into her Nike and handed it back to her. She slipped her foot into the sneaker and stood to try it out, while the podiatrist watched.

"Comfy?" he asked.

"It's fine," Cooper said, although, as she'd expected, it didn't actually ease her leg's ache.

"Glory be," Drew said. "That'll be twenty-two-thousand dollars, please, and fifty-six cents."

Cooper smiled, although she felt abysmal. Drew's office window looked out on a sunny October afternoon, the sky intensely blue, but Cooper's worrying made the day gloomy, as if black nimbostratus clouds covered the sun. She'd prosecuted Sonny Rawston, so she must be punished. Maybe he'd shot at her, or ordered it done—who was that gray-bearded biker, with shoulder-length gray hair? So far, no hard evidence linked Rawston to the shootings, but he'd certainly attacked her psychologically. He meant to inflict severe damage. Now he'd cozied up to Stacey Gillibrand, convinced her that Cooper harassed him. Would her other students fall for it? She hoped not, but she didn't underestimate Rawston. He was a formidable manipulator.

"Cheer up, Sweetcakes," Drew said, sensing her mood. "Twenty-two-thousand's just the standard price— for you, I'll take some off."

Cooper smiled again, weakly.

"Henry needs a veterinarian," she said.

They talked awhile, about the Saunders' cat, Chester, and various veterinarians they'd tried, until they found one who satisfied Mona's requirements, which Drew said were expertise, kindness, and forelock-tugging obeisance. Cooper borrowed a pen and a sheet from Drew's prescription pad and jotted down the clinic's name.

"Holding up?" Drew asked.

"I'm okay," Cooper said. "Upsetting as all this is."

"Well, think how we-all felt," Drew said, putting on his best drawl, "when that damn Yankee Sherman came a-marchin' and a-burnin' through!"

"Ah, the plantation—so sorry for your loss," Cooper said. "Heard from Mona?"

"Telephoned yesterday," Drew said. "She's loading up on neo-subjunctive hyper-realist-abstract canvases—ye gods and little fishes!"

He shrugged, a gesture of affectionate despair.

"Where'll she hang them?" he said. "I guess there's a couple of virgin wall spaces left, out there in the garage....."

"Have you talked to Sonny Rawston, since he got out?" Cooper abruptly asked.

For a moment Drew just looked at her, and she supposed he felt pity for an old woman, under attack, and that irritated her. You only pity the pitiful.

"We don't know how he's funding himself," Cooper said. "I thought he might have told you something."

Drew shook his head.

"He mowed our lawn, back in the long ago," he said, "I saw him in The Percolator, twice maybe, but I ignore him—he got sharp with me, years ago, and now I'm cranky."

"On the way to Hart's Corners?" Cooper said, remembering what Mona had told her.

Drew grimaced.

"Hitchhiking," he said. "I was seeing a patient in the Corners, back then, and I picked him up…."

He frowned, remembering.

"Just making polite chitchat, I asked what brought him to the Corners and he about bit my head off," Drew said. "Told me to keep my nose out of his affairs, so I dropped him where he asked, at the schoolhouse, and ever since I've obeyed orders and averted my nose."

"What would he be doing at the Hart's Corners schoolhouse?" Cooper asked.

Drew shrugged.

"I wouldn't know," he said. "And I certainly wouldn't ask."

Later that afternoon, Cooper took Henry to the vet. He didn't want to go.

He made that clear—when Cooper opened the Volvo's door, he didn't vault out. He wouldn't even get up.

He seemed, almost, to read the sign: "All Creatures Clinic—We Welcome Paws, Fins, and Feathers."

Henry sniffed.

Then he shut his eyes and pretended to sleep.

"Ridiculous!" Cooper told him.

She saw nothing scary, just a pleasant white-clapboard farmhouse, built in the early 1800s, before Allen County's hill farmers migrated west, to deeper soils, without rocks. Dill then ran streets through former pastures. Up went mansard-roofed Victorians and Carpenter Gothics. This old Cape, though, hung on, repurposed. Cedar hedges surrounded it, and giant sunflowers.

Cooper supposed Henry smelled a medicinal emanation, imperceptible to humans. Maybe some inept Boston vet crossed him, and now he hated them all.

"Up and at 'em, Henry," Cooper said.

Henry kept on pretending to sleep. "Come on," Cooper said, but he remained immobile. Finally, exasperated, she snapped: "Oh, for God's sake, Henry—man up!"

When the corgi showed no intention of manning up, Cooper, mumbling, snapped on his leash and tugged, which yielded only an impasse.

"Idiot!" she said.

She clasped her hands around his backside and pulled him—resisting—across the leather seat, forcing him to plop down out of the car. He stood on the driveway, looking cross, as Cooper open the car's rear door to fetch her cane.

"Let's go," she said, tugging on the leash.

Henry lay down on the blacktop and wouldn't look at Cooper, who tugged fruitlessly, except for straining Henry's neck in the direction of the clinic, while he took a keen interest, seemingly, in a bird feeder beside the driveway.

Cooper cursed.

She'd been shot at twice. She hunted the shooter, but through impenetrable fog. She could only guess who'd targeted her, or why. No evidence linked Sonny Rawston to the shootings, or to the biker with long gray hair and a gray beard. Rawston had coopted Stacey Gillibrand. Cooper feared the shooter would shoot again. She didn't know when. And now, this—a corgi using Mahatma Gandhi's tactics.

"Damn you, Henry!" she snarled, and immediately felt guilty.

She envisioned a grim-faced veterinarian emerging from the examining room with a diagnosis: cancer.

She'd watched that disease take her mother, the granite-willed New Englander she'd battled since childhood, and turned up her eyes over, and loved. Cancer shrank Bethany North to just skin-covered bones, oxygen tubes in her nostrils. Ever since, Cooper lived alone. She'd coped perfectly well, enjoying her own company. So it had seemed to her. Then into her house, on ludicrously short legs, strode this cocky dog.

He'd inveigled his way into her life. Not just a dog, she thought. Certainly not a pet. He was Henry.

"It's immunization shots," she told him, almost pleading. "They're good for you."

He still refused to look at her. And she, who'd always coolly handled complicated prosecutions, and every difficulty life presented, stared down the long driveway, toward Main Street, at a loss. Then, behind her, somebody spoke.

"Such a little drama queen!"

She turned to see a slim young woman in a white physician's jacket kneeling beside Henry, holding his head, and examining his eyes.

"Saw him through the window, snit attack, our little friend here," she told Cooper, finishing with Henry's eyes and now inspecting his teeth.

Cooper felt relief.

"That's Henry," she said. "He's here for a checkup, immunizations, whatever dogs get, but he's being ungracious."

"Uh-oh, Henry," the woman said, standing. "Don't make us use thumbscrews!"

Cooper had never seen so stunning a young woman—perfect white teeth against skin the color of dark mahogany, high cheekbones, lively black eyes, glossy black hair. Straightened, she guessed.

With a dazzling smile, the woman extended a hand to Cooper, who shook it.

"I'm Berry Randolph," she said. "It's brand new, and I do dote on the title, so I have to say, that's Doctor Randolph!"

She seemed so ingenuously pleased with her newly minted degree, and so amused with herself for being besotted with it, that Cooper had to suppress an urge to give her a hug. And, somewhere in her mind's hinterlands, she thought—"If only I'd looked like this, in high school, in college...."

Berry Randolph took Henry's leash and tugged. Henry rolled onto his back.

"Hah, passive resistance!" the vet said.

She laughed, showing those white teeth.

Now the veterinarian squatted down, got a grip on Henry, fore and aft, then hoisted him up and began marching toward the clinic. Henry, lying on his back, twisted his head to look back, past Dr. Randolph's supporting arm, and give Cooper an extremely dirty look.

Inside, a receptionist showed the vet a list of upcoming appointments, and it belatedly occurred to Cooper she should have made one, except that her mind currently seemed a writhing jumble of concerns, not least getting shot, and she'd come impulsively. By chance, though, a Siamese had just been cancelled.

Cooper filled out some forms, then followed Berry Randolph into an examining room, where the veterinarian placed Henry on a high table. He lay down with a peevish sigh.

"We can treat Henry a la carte," Dr. Randolph said. "Or we can do an annual plan, and for dogs we offer three levels—Chihuahua, Collie, or St. Bernard."

They ranged from basic, Chihuahua, which included standard immunizations and a once-a-year physical, to complete, St. Bernard, in which Henry could come in whenever he needed to, get whatever treatments or medications he required, with extras thrown in, from 24-hour home emergency visits to a GPS-tracker collar, monthly grooming and pedicures, and the services of a dog psychologist, should Henry ever seem depressed or anti-social. Cooper felt too roiled to evaluate the pros and cons. Also, she knew nothing about dogs. So she made the safest choice, opting for the expensive St. Bernard plan, money being the least of her problems, especially since she hardly ever bought anything except groceries.

She watched the veterinarian systematically feel all over Henry's body for lumps. Henry looked aggrieved. Cooper wryly turned up her eyes, believing he secretly enjoyed the attention. All the while, in her mind's back regions, she thought about Jack Abbott trying to bully her out of her house, and Nessie Greffier's hostility, secretly nurtured for decades. Mike Bolknor's reticence still troubled her. So did Tip LaPerle's resentment of Bolknor. And motorcycles and .30-06 rifles....

She thought: enough!

"Where's home, Dr. Randolph?" she asked.

That dazzling smile.

"Call me Berry," the vet said. "And you'll be Cooper, okay? Deal?"

"You know me?" Cooper said.

"I grew up over in Hart's Corners, sort of, and you've been in the newspapers and TV news as long as I can remember, with your picture...."

She opened a drawer and took out a stethoscope.

"Sort of?" Cooper said.

"Yup," Berry said, eavesdropping on Henry's inner thumps and wheezes.

She inserted a thermometer in Henry's rear end, which amused Cooper, who thought, "Take that, Mahatma!"

Berry, giving the thermometer time to work, leaned against the table and offered Cooper a vita sketch.

"So once upon a time there was a little girl in Harlem…."

She'd been the youngest of eight. Father killed in a robbery at the grocery store where he clerked, on 135th Street, just days after her birth. After that, her mother eked along, as a hotel maid, watching each of her children, in turn, out on the streets, slip into drug addiction and crime.

"She worried a lot about me," Berry said. "Because of what could happen to a girl as she got older…."

Especially a beautiful girl, Cooper thought. And once again she found herself wondering what her own life might have been, had she looked like Berry Randolph.

Finally, desperate, her mother enrolled Berry in the Fresh Air Program, and the little girl fetched up at a farm in Hart's Corners for the summer. It was a revelation, she told Cooper. All the trees. And the safe feeling. And, for a child who'd known only pigeons and rats, here were dogs and cats, and cows, too, and sheep.

Next summer, Berry enthusiastically returned to the Artie and Becca Woodruff farm in Hart's Corners. And the following summer, too. In August that year, word came that Berry's mother had been bitten in her sleep by a rat, and died with a high fever. Artie and Becca enthusiastically took Berry in permanently, as their foster child.

"After that, I was a Hart's Corners girl," Berry said, peering at the thermometer.

"Went to school there?" Cooper asked.

125

"Yup, a proud alumna of Hart's Corners Elementary, followed by Warner County Central," Berry said. "Soccer star, if I do say so, and let's not forget student council, and chess club!"

It occurred to Cooper, watching the vet withdraw three bottles of colored liquid and three disposable hypodermics from a drawer, that eighteen years ago she'd have been about nine.

"You must have been in second grade when that teacher was murdered," Cooper said.

Berry looked up from drawing one vial's contents into her hypodermic, and suddenly she looked dismal.

"Miss Langley—that was horrible," Berry said. "She was my teacher."

Cooper had a sudden thought.

"Did you ever see a red-haired man around then?" she asked. "He'd have been about twenty-three...."

Berry stood holding up her hypodermic needle, thinking.

"Nope," she said. "I don't remember any red-haired people in Hart's Corners, except Lucy Deveroux, who was in 4H with me, and her hair was more reddish-brown than actual red."

Even so, Cooper thought, Berry Randolph's now on my informant list. Because maybe Hart's Corners had something to do with the shootings. For one thing, Drew had driven a hitchhiking Sonny Rawston there, all those years ago. And why? Sonny wouldn't say. He'd have been just out of college then. Why hitch a ride to Hart's Corners, comprising a general store, and a lumber yard, and a smattering of vintage houses, mostly owned by commuters to Dill?

Berry injected Henry with a liquid, which he didn't seem to notice.

"Distemper," she said.

She opened another bottle and began filling a second hypodermic.

"Mildred Langley, when I was in school there, was a role model," she said. "It was because of her that I aimed for college."

That name, Langley, triggered a memory for Cooper.

"Related to an elderly lady?" she asked. "With a diabetic foot condition?"

"You must mean Erna Langley," Berry said, holding the hypodermic up against the light through the window, to make sure she'd drawn in enough serum.

"Old Mrs. Langley was Mildred's mother—did you know her?"

"No, but a good friend of mine's a podiatrist, and he used to treat her feet," Cooper said.

Berry looked away from her hypodermic.

"Dr. Saunders!" she said.

"You knew Drew?" Cooper said.

"I worshipped Dr. Drew Saunders!" Berry said. "We all idolized him—he was our very own movie star!"

Once or twice a week, she said, Drew would drive into Hart's Corners in his red Mustang convertible, wearing sunglasses, Hollywood handsome. Because the Langley farm was across the road from the Artie and Becca Woodruff farm, where Berry lived, she'd see the parked Mustang and excitedly telephone her friends in nearby country houses. They'd all rush to Berry's house and sit side-by-side on the fence, waiting for Drew to come out, after treating old Mrs. Langley, so they could see him and swoon.

It amused Cooper, because she had no doubt Drew Saunders knew why the little girls sat on that fence, like a row of birds, gazing intensely at the Langley house. Probably, she thought, drolly amused, he even posed a little for them.

Berry gave Henry his second injection.

"Heartworm," she said.

She went to work on the third hypodermic.

"You know what?" she said. "There was a red-headed man, now that I remember, because on the first day of school that year, Dr. Saunders dropped a red-headed man off at the school, on his way to old Mrs. Langley's."

Cooper got alert.

"What did the red-haired man do?" she asked.

"He walked into the classroom, and started talking to Miss Langley, up front at her desk," Berry said, mentally looking back into the past. "She was angry, I think."

"What did she say?" Cooper asked.

"Hmm, something about, I'm working and you shouldn't be here now," Berry said.

"And the red-haired man?" Cooper said.

"He shrugged, and they went outside to talk," Berry said. "And when Miss Langley came back in, she held a check, which she put in her purse, and then she went back to teaching us two plus two."

She gave Henry his third shot.

128

"Rabies," she said.

Over decades as a prosecutor, Cooper oversaw myriad cases. And now she felt that old investigative machinery in her head coming alive, gears meshing, flywheels beginning to spin.

She thought: Sonny Rawston, so smart, but you've left footprints!

Berry Randolph now pronounced Henry in perfect health. While she fitted the corgi with his new digitalized collar, and treated him with anti-flea and anti-tick preparations, just in case, and put together a Care Kit to go home with Henry, Cooper went out to the waiting room to pay for the St. Bernard Plan's annual fee. While she waited for the receptionist to return her Visa card, she noticed that now a white-haired man sat in one of the chairs, expression sour, a dachshund with a bandaged leg in his lap. Catching Cooper's eye, he shook his head, as if they shared some negative opinion.

"This used to be Dr. Pearson's clinic, been coming for decades," he said, frowning. "Don't know about these new people."

"I think Dr. Randolph's a wonder," Cooper told him.

"They're just two kids, you ask me," the man muttered, looking away.

"Here's your Visa card, Ms. North," the receptionist said, and, as Cooper turned to take it back, she noticed a framed photograph over the receptionist's desk, beside two framed diplomas. In the photograph, Berry Randolph wore a college graduate's robe and mortarboard, standing close beside a large, slightly pudgy man with curly dark hair and round, rimless glasses,

129

wearing a matching outfit, looking as if he'd just graduated from Teddy Bear U.

"That's Dr. Petracelli," the receptionist said. "He's Dr. Randolph's husband."

Just then Berry Randolph emerged from the examining room, with Henry straining against his leash, toward the door. She saw Cooper looking at the photograph and smiled.

"Tony," she said.

Momentarily, she gazed at the photograph, fondly.

"Hey, let me walk you out to the car," she said. "See if I can get Henry to finally like me."

Cooper opened the door and Henry charged out to freedom, tugging Berry along behind him.

"I'll be with you in a sec, Mr. Daley," she told the white-haired man in the chair, laughing as Henry tractored her out onto the porch.

Mr. Daley frowned pointedly at his watch.

"Tony Petracelli is my bright star," Berry said, as Cooper opened the Volvo's door and Henry clambered in. "We met in veterinary school, at Tufts—we both had scholarships."

He was, Cooper remembered, large, pudgy, and shambly. It occurred to her that Berry Randolph had evolved from the little girl who sat on a fence with her friends, swooning over glamorous Dr. Handsome.

"Tony's in Burlington today, doing a seminar at the University of Vermont, but we're partners here," Berry said. "And, when I have my troubles, he just steps in, and he does everything!"

"Troubles?" Cooper said.

Berry handed her Henry's leash, the other end still snapped onto his new collar.

"I have sickle-cell anemia," Berry said, and for the first time Cooper saw sadness behind the woman's eyes.

Cooper thought: she may not live so very long. She knows that. So does Tony Petracelli.

Impulsively, she bent over and hugged Berry.

She shut the Volvo's door, and Henry immediately got his forepaws up on the dashboard and began barking, which meant, let's go.

Cooper, though, thought of a final question. She leaned over Henry to ask it, through the open window.

"Berry, back there in Hart's Corners, did you ever notice a man with shoulder-length gray hair, and a gray beard, riding a motorcycle?"

Berry looked at her, thinking.

"Actually, yes," she said. "He used to come riding to the school once in a while, and Miss Langley would go out to talk to him."

"What color was the motorcycle?" Cooper asked.

"Black," she said.

"Thank you, Berry, for everything," she said.

Eighteen years ago, she thought. That biker already had gray hair.

Henry suddenly stretched out the window and licked Berry Randolph's face, making her smile. Cooper eyed the corgi sideways and snorted. Shaking her head, amused at Henry's newfound love for the vet, she shifted the Volvo into Drive, and started down the driveway.

Henry, with the dog equivalent of a grin, hind paws on the seat, forepaws on the dash, gazed out the windshield, and he gleefully barked at the world.

"Yeah," Cooper told him dryly. "Liberated at last, from that Chamber of Medical Horrors."

CHAPTER TWENTY-ONE

She awakened at six the next morning, feeling guilty. She didn't know why.

Later, as the machine brewed French Roast, she stared blankly out the kitchen window, at frost-stricken peonies, collapsed and limp-leaved. They needed to be cut away, to clear the beds for April's upthrusting red shoots, a childhood chore she'd shared with her brother.

Once they'd squabbled. Their father bought shiny new clippers, and her brother called dibs, leaving her with the tarnished old clippers, which seemed monstrously unfair.

She'd forgotten her precise sin—a bop on the fraternal head?—but not her mother's admonishment: "Someone's got something nice? That's nothing off you, Cooper, so be big!"

She thought about Nessie Greffier's envy of her career. It was ugly. Yet—and this was why she felt guilty—hadn't she yesterday felt a stab of envy for Dr. Berry Randolph's stunning good looks?

An hour later, she sat at her college desk, chin in her hands, still brooding, with fully inoculated Henry asleep at her feet.

"Professor North!"

Jerry Shapiro and Nikki Winkel rushed in. Nikki held a newspaper.

Cooper welcomed the interruption. She'd splayed out student essays on her desk to evaluate, but so far hadn't read any.

"Here's today's *Chronicle*, smokin' hot," Jerry said, pointing with a flourish at the paper Nikki held.

"Read all about it!" he said.

Pause for effect.

Then, punchline: "A new legal superstar! She streaks across the jurisprudential sky!"

Nikki made a disgusted face, but only because that's what cynical tough girls did. His clowning obviously amused her.

She held out the paper, and Cooper took it, noticing that Nikki had painted her fingernails black, and that she looked different in some other way, too. Henry emerged from under the desk and yawned at the visitors.

No, Cooper thought, as she spread the paper out on her desk. It hadn't been envy of Berry Randolph. Not really. More a "what if?" Would she, if she'd looked like Berry, have lived alone all these years? That thought surprised her—had she actually been lonely? She didn't think so. She'd had an extraordinarily full life, so many friends and colleagues, her days stimulating, with work that mattered. Sometimes, though, at night, alone in the big North house....

She shook it off and looked at the newspaper.

Spread out across page one's bottom third, under Ariette Feenie's by-line, was her second story on the new criminal-justice program. A photograph showed Stacey

Gillibrand, sitting at a table, apparently in her apartment, with her briefcase open, reams of documents and hand-scrawled notes spilling out. Stacey frowned over a document she held, blond hair fallen over one eye.

In 28-point boldface, the headline read: "Mt. Augustus College's New Pre-Law Program—One Student Takes It To A New Level."

Cooper read the story's opening:

"Eighteen years ago, in Hart's Corners, an aged handyman, convicted of murder, went to prison for life. Five years later, he died in his cell, of a heart attack.

"Was he guilty?

"Stacey Gillibrand, a pre-law student in Mt. Augustus College's new Criminal Justice Program, believes Nub Duckins was innocent, and she spends every evening in the Mt. Augustus College library, working to prove it.

"I'm inches from nailing this down," she says.

Cooper shook her head, exasperated.

She thought: Stacey, it's okay to try advancing your career, but this is damaging.

Cooper had persuaded Allen County attorneys and law-enforcement agencies to take on student interns. It had required effort, and diplomacy, calling in lots of IOUs. If students questioned their hosts' work, undermined it, those internships would dry up. Stacey Gillibrand was setting a bad precedent.

Cooper sighed.

Jerry, deadpan, asked: "So, in the movie, who'll play Stacey? I'm thinking...."

Nikki gave him a look.

Cooper thought: Nikki's done up her eyes.

Sable shadow on her lids. Mascaraed lashes. Black liner. It matched Nikki's newly black fingernails, and those ripped black jeans. She still wore a man's work shirt, though, with scissored-off sleeves, and over that a black-denim vest, with metal chains dangling from the pocket zippers.

Jerry wore a brown leather bombardier jacket, over a black t-shirt, his own black jeans looking fresh from some upscale men's store. His curly dark hair hung over his ears, but he neatly trimmed his mustache and beard.

Ms. Street, Cooper thought. And Mr. Hipster.

And she thought: something brewing here?

Pleased by that thought, because she wanted good things for Nikki, and she thought Jerry Shapiro might be a good thing, she almost smiled. Instead, she read more of the newspaper story.

"Professor Cooper North, who created the new department, pointedly asserts that the course in question is just one of many in the program, and that it aims solely to acquaint students with techniques for gathering and analyzing evidence.

"She says the course has nothing to do with reopening old cases, and that Ms. Gillibrand is acting entirely on her own.

"Stacey Gillibrand certainly agrees with that.

"'I've been digging up lots of evidence,' she says. 'I'm really close, just days away from proving somebody else bludgeoned the schoolteacher to death, not that simple-minded old man, Nub Duckins.'

"At this time...."

Fear washed over Cooper like a tsunami.

She stifled a gasp.

Reaching down, impulsively, she stroked Henry's head, as if the corgi needed solace, but it was Cooper seeking comfort, craving the dog's warmth.

Ariette Feenie had reported it clearly: Stacey Gillibrand sleuthed all on her own. So the internships were safe.

Cooper thought: what's terrifying me?

Henry suddenly howled.

She'd stopped petting him. He objected. So he'd howled. That was all, but it sounded like a banshee wail, and left her stricken.

Nikki and Jerry stared at her.

"An appointment," she muttered, reaching for her cane. "I just remembered."

She hurried out of the office, Henry scrambling after her, and rode the elevator down to the first floor, to Campus Security, where Chip Stack looked up from his computer to greet her, which she hardly noticed, rushing by and into Mike Bolknor's office.

He seemed, almost, to mirror Cooper, as she'd been when Nikki and Jerry burst into her office. He, too, sat at his desk, strewn with paperwork, patrol reports and equipment-order forms, reading none of it, staring out the window.

A partially disassembled Glock 22 lay to one side, along with containers of solvent and lubricant, a bore brush, patches, cotton swabs, and a cleaning rod. Beside the pistol lay a clip and a handful of .40-caliber rounds.

Most officers with whom Cooper worked had preferred the smaller Glock 19, considerably lighter and easier to carry concealed, but Bolknor was a large man.

As Cooper dropped into his visitor's chair, she watched him swim up, from great depth. He came up slowly, not quite surfacing.

"I need to talk with someone," Cooper said.

It astonished her, that Mike Bolknor would be that someone. In the old days, when an investigation snagged, she'd always reached for the telephone, dialed Tip LaPerle, hashed it over. Now, mystifying herself, she'd instinctively sought out this former NYPD cop, who mostly hid away in some psychic monk's cell, a sign scrawled on the door, "Keep Out."

"Did you see this morning's *Chronicle?*" she asked.

He nodded. Said nothing.

"I read it and panicked, and I don't know why," she said.

Absent-mindedly, he reached for his disassembled handgun, pulling it across the desk by its barrel, until it lay in front of him, not looking, his gaze still directed inward. An oil spot seeped onto a patrol report. He reached for his cleaning rod and began swabbing the barrel's innards, and it occurred to Cooper that, moments ago, in her office, she'd reached out just like this, only for Henry's warm head, needing solace, a friend, and it seemed to her sad, that a man would seek comfort in a Glock.

She thought: it's nothing to do with Mt. Augustus College. Whatever eats at him, it's locked away inside.

Bolknor sighed, and his eyes finally focused.

"Your panic attack—was it because that newspaper story hit on that old murder?" he asked Cooper. "In Hart's Corners?"

Probably, she thought.

Hart's Corners kept coming up. Yet, the connection, if there was one, wasn't all of it. Lots of things swirled in her mind.

She told Bolknor about the biker with shoulder-length gray hair and a gray beard, what Berry Randolph told her.

"Hart's Corners again," he said. "Eighteen years back."

"Not just that," she said.

She let her thoughts swirl.

In the park, the gray-haired biker shot at her. That was the second attack. And the first shooting, that stormy night, maybe that was him, too. Yet, what of Nessie Greffier, so resentful? Nessie, a sharpshooter, who rode a motorcycle. Jack Abbott, too. Avid for her property, a violent man, aggressive, with a basement full of hunting rifles. Riding his son's bike....

And then she imagined eyes.

They stared at her. Mocking. Cold.

"It's Sonny Rawston," she said.

She told herself: he's insane.

She'd prosecuted him. Now, for that, he meant to garrote her, certainly psychologically. Would he actually kill?

He'd coopted Stacey Gillibrand. He'd be driving her to Hart's Corners, on his motorcycle, tainting her mind with insinuations. He'd already convinced her that Cooper now harassed him, out of spite. Maybe he meant to turn all her students against her, one by one.

She'd once visualized a spider in its web, strands stretching out through Dill. It had to be him.

"It was Sonny's motorcycle that gray-haired biker drove, in the park, when he shot at me," Cooper said. "And where'd Sonny get it?"

"Rent, too," Bolknor said. "How's he pay that, and buy groceries?"

Cooper shook her head.

"He's unemployed," Bolknor said. "And he got out of jail flat broke, so where's he getting money?"

"That gray-haired biker?" Cooper suggested, and shrugged.

Murk obscured everything.

It surprised her, that Mike Bolknor had been thinking all this over. He hadn't seemed to be. She liked the feeling, that she didn't struggle alone. Now, at night, when she looked out her window, craving vodka, and saw the campus-security Prius parked under the maple, she no longer resented it, Bolknor keeping her guarded. And her yen for the drink ebbed.

"He frightens me!"

She'd blurted it out, aloud, then felt embarrassed. Cooper North was supposed to be bold.

Bolknor shook his head.

"He wants you sucker punched in the gut," he said.

It oddly pleased her, his speaking as he might to another cop, not making it nice for the old lady.

"So far he's got zero," Bolknor said. "So he'll step it up."

Cooper thought: exactly what frightens me.

"He'll trip," Bolknor said. "We'll get him."

Or I'll get shot, Cooper thought.

Something awful would happen. She felt it, a gnawing in her stomach.

Cooper rode the elevator back upstairs, with Henry, to fetch her jacket, and found herself thinking again about Berry Randolph. She knew little about sickle-cell disease, except its nastiness, but Berry must wake up every day, not knowing, will I have an attack today? How long will I live? And, every day, Tony Petracelli must wake up knowing what his wife faced. He'd known when he married her.

So it surely wasn't just a perfect nose and elegant cheekbones that attracted him. And she hadn't fallen for an Adonis. Cooper had seen his photograph.

Once, in Hart's Corners, little girls sat on a fence, in a row, swooning over handsome Drew Saunders. Berry had obviously matured into a different sense of what mattered. She supposed that something like sickle-cell disease could refine how you perceived the world.

"Someone's got something nice?" her mother admonished, so long ago. "That's nothing off you, Cooper, so be big!"

"Chew on that, Henry," she admonished the corgi, as she put on her jacket, but he just shot her an upward glance, roguish, she thought, and headed for the door.

A few minutes later, with Henry walking beside her, Cooper stepped out onto the Campus Security building's stoop and involuntarily stopped dead—Sonny Rawston sat on his parked motorcycle, one loafer braced against the stoop's bottom step.

On the top step perched Stacey Gillibrand, snickering at something Rawston said. She'd drawn up her knees under her skirt, and across her lap rested a crammed briefcase, which Cooper recognized from this morning's newspaper photograph.

"Speak of the devil," Rawston announced.

He looked sardonic.

"Like I said," he told Stacey. "Now she's got her storm troopers after me."

He turned his stare on Cooper.

"That's over the top, isn't it?" he said. "Even for you?"

Cooper raised her eyebrows.

"Bluecoats," he said. "Parked twenty-four-seven at the grocery store across the street, spying on me?"

Cooper shook her head.

"Stepping up the harassment?' he said.

Tone conversational. Gaze like ice.

Cooper thought: Tip LaPerle got frustrated. He's trying to flush Sonny out.

"I've got nothing to do with this," she said.

Stacey stared at Cooper, disgusted, as if Cooper blatantly lied. Sonny smirked. Then he looked pointedly down at Henry.

"Cute little fellow," he said.

He abruptly started his motorcycle, an obnoxious blat.

"Later," he told Stacey.

Then he roared off down the street, his noise dissipating behind him. Cooper hadn't noticed Stacey going inside, but when she looked, she stood alone on the stoop, except for Henry, beside her.

CHAPTER TWENTY-TWO

"We've gotta make this warty toad hop," Tip LaPerle told her over the telephone.

He sounded stubborn.

"Yeah, I know," he said. "We prod him, he gets testy in the papers, or something—what you said before."

Cooper didn't argue. She knew this mood.

"So, yeah, I got my guys parked across from that dirtbag, at DeBouche's Gas 'n Groceries, but guess what?" Tip said.

"What?" Cooper said.

"DeBouche—that's my Uncle Denis, my Mom's kid brother," Tip said. "We talked, turns out he's worried about robberies and burglaries, potential, so I've got my guys there, help out a citizen."

Cooper sighed.

"Community policing, okay?" he said.

She doubted "making the warty toad hop," by keeping him under continual surveillance, would make Sonny so jittery he'd slip up. More likely, he'd retaliate. Maybe he'd go to the newspaper. Maybe worse. On the

144

other hand, she knew from experience the pointlessness of arguing with a frustrated and irritated Tip LaPerle, so she let it drop.

"I called because I've learned something," she said.

She told him Dr. Berry Randolph remembered the biker with long gray hair and a gray beard—eighteen years ago, he'd stopped by the Hart's Corners school. So had Sonny Rawston, fresh out of college.

"That's the next county, not my jurisdiction," Tip said, thinking aloud. "State cops cover over there, but they're stretched super thin...."

"I could look into it," Cooper said. "Unofficially."

She told him about Jack Abbott bullying to get her property, so he could sell it back to the college at huge profit.

"That crud," LaPerle said, and muttered a curse.

No love lost between the two graduates of Tenement Row.

"I've been after him, about renting that apartment to Rawston, but he's a clam," LaPerle said. "I've got no leverage to pry him open, not yet, anyway."

They were both silent on the phone, contemplating their options. Or lack of options. Finally Tip muttered "Jeezum Crow!"

"You going tomorrow, to the mayor's shindig?" he asked. "In honor of his very own self?"

"I guess I have to—they listed me in the paper as a speaker," Cooper said. "See you there?"

"Yeah," LaPerle said. "We'll talk."

That October evening darkness came just after seven.

Cooper drew her living-room curtains, as she did every night now. No reason to be a klieg-lit target.

On the way home, she'd stopped at the Sweet Kumquat, to buy dinner, frozen Madras sambar. She'd also—on impulse—bought a special treat for Henry, organic hamburger. While her Indian meal cooked in the microwave, she watched him gobble up the ground sirloin, demonstrating his magical corgi powers to make food vanish from his bowl. Seeing his enjoyment pleased her, but she felt anxious, too.

Earlier, driving off the campus, she'd had a dismal thought, one she'd had before: what if the vet someday discovered Henry had cancer? She'd be alone again, in this old house. Too many empty rooms. Her footsteps echoing along the hallways. It would feel hollow. And cold.

So Henry got a deluxe dinner.

"Despite you being a lousy conversationalist," she admonished the dog.

He sat on the living room carpet, gazing up at her, eyes roguishly bright, as if he got the joke.

Cooper settled into her armchair to read. Tonight's selection was Emily Dickinson, because she felt an urge to revisit those poems, weightless as butterflies, but subtly complex, the world through a sensitive New Englander's astute eyes. She'd gotten as far as "Parting is all we know of heaven/And all we need of hell...."

An angry rumble.

Motorcycle.

146

It stopped in front of her house, growling in the dark.

Suddenly the engine revved into a blat, deafening, and Cooper dropped Emily Dickinson, staring at the drawn curtains, as the noise throttled back to a rumble.

Then it roared a second time.

As it subsided again, Cooper heard an angry curse. She got her cane and switched off her reading lamp and thumped to the front door in the dark. She cracked it open, just enough to peer out.

A streetlamp up the street shed some light, but dim. She made out the black shape of the motorcycle, bestrode by a thickset man wearing black, one boot braced on the curb, while a second large man stood planted in front of the bike, blocking it from going forward, and looming over the rider, who cursed him again.

She heard the looming man say something, his voice too low to make out the words, but she heard the yelled response: "Go to hell, jackass!"

Again the looming man spoke, a low tone, and this time the rider snapped down the bike's kickstand and jumped off the saddle, and something about his stance, head down like a bull, big fists out front, made Cooper know who it was. Who the other man was she guessed— he'd parked his Prius under the usual maple—and she started to yell out a warning, but not soon enough.

She watched, frozen, as the biker sent a huge fist flying toward the looming man's face, and Cooper had an awful feeling, except that, just slightly canting his head, the looming man let the blow whizz by and then, hardly seeming to move at all, left-jabbed the biker, knocking

147

him back, and then stepped into him, did something with his own leg, and the biker thudded onto his back on the pavement.

Cooper hurried out the door, Henry barking exuberantly after her. She got to the curb and saw what she'd never imagined she'd ever see: Jack Abbott lying supine, beaten, looking up stunned, as if he himself couldn't believe this happened. It had never happened before. He'd always been the big man standing, legs spread, looking down at someone he'd felled.

"Hell!" he said from the ground. "You've had Goddamned training!"

Cooper saw blood oozed from his nose, down the side of his face.

Mike Bolknor walked around him and inspected the motorcycle.

"No rifle holster, no rifle," he told Cooper, then, to the still supine Jack Abbott, "You carrying a handgun?"

No response, so Bolknor squatted down and patted Abbott down, without comment from the downed man.

"No handgun, either," he told Cooper.

After that they stood silently looking down at Abbott, except Henry, who trotted around the fallen man exuberantly, as if they were all playing an exciting game. Bolknor abruptly reached down and grabbed one of Abbott's wrists and pulled him to his feet, as if Abbott were child sized. Abbott looked down.

"Jack, what in God's name were you doing out here, revving that motorcycle, after everything that's happened?" Cooper demanded.

"Public street," Abbott mumbled.

Suddenly he pulled his chin up and glared at Bolknor.

"Assault and battery!" he said. "I'm getting you prosecuted."

"No you aren't," Cooper said. "I watched the whole thing and you punched first, so he was defending himself—don't be a jerk!"

Abbott looked down again.

"What were you doing, Jack?" Cooper demanded.

Silence.

Abruptly he cursed again, under his breath. He stepped to the motorcycle and swung a leg over and started the machine. He sat a moment, looking down, dripping blood from his nose, then started to drive off, only to immediately stop, staring back at Cooper.

"You think I'm a redneck bastard," he told her. "You think I'm only after money, and maybe you're right, but you didn't have to start out like I did…."

He sat that way, one leg stretched out, shoe braced against the pavement, looking down, silent. Then he raised his head to look at Cooper again, except the streetlight was too dim for her to see the expression in his eyes.

"You think I'm rich, and I'm just greedy, but you don't know what I'm up against," he said. "You don't know."

He revved the engine, drew in his bracing leg, and rolled off down the street. He drove slowly, and they watched him dwindle down Hill Street toward Abner Park, through alternating circles of lamplight and darkness, ever smaller, until he was gone.

"What do you make of that?" Bolknor asked.

"He wanted to scare me," Cooper said. "Spook me into selling my house—that's all."

And she thought: why is Jack Abbott so desperate?"

In the morning, Cooper took over a Critical Reasoning class from a professor who'd called in sick. Henry seemed bored with the subject, falling asleep beside Cooper's lectern and paying no attention at all. Cooper wondered if the students were equally uninterested, because Nikki Winkel passed a note to Jerry Shapiro, who scribbled something on it and passed it back, causing Nikki to smirk, and Cooper guessed this exchange did not focus on Critical Reasoning, except possibly at the third-grade level.

Chip Stack, meanwhile, politely listened, at least with half has brain, but he kept glancing down at printed pages he'd spread on his desk, which Cooper knew must be Campus Security Department work, from his internship, and she applied Critical Reasoning: his biological father kicks him in the psyche, so he seeks paternal approval elsewhere, namely Mike Bolknor.

Cooper thought: Okay. Still, you'd risk crossing your department head? Really? Because only God knows if vengeful lightning might smite your grades!

And if your professor calls in sick, Cooper thought, and somebody generously subs, at the last minute, unprepared, shouldn't you all at least pretend interest?

150

Only one student seemed fully engaged with the lecture, Stacey Gillibrand, frowning in thought, jotting in her notebook. Periodically, though, she shot Cooper a glare, which Cooper assumed expressed Stacey's induced belief that Cooper treated her new friend Sonny Rawston unfairly and spitefully, which Cooper feared would lead Stacey to a bad place.

"Let's talk about psychopaths," Cooper said.

Now drooping heads looked up.

You'll deal with them, often, she said, whether you're a police officer or attorney, because they're all around us. None has even a vestigial conscience, but very few kill, and the majority are not even violent, at least physically.

"More likely, they'll attack your mind," Cooper said, looking at Stacey.

Psychopaths, she said, regard other people as hassocks and garbage pails. They have no real feelings for others, only faked feelings, if it suits their purposes.

Still looking at Stacey.

Whatever happens, she said, it's somebody else's fault. And they are—she paused, making sure Stacey got the message—master manipulators.

Stacey now sat open-mouthed, staring at Cooper, who thought she saw uncertainty in the young woman's blue eyes, as if she were reviewing things said and done. Then those eyes hardened and Stacey abruptly stood, gathering up her books and papers, and fled the room.

Cooper stared after her, then—pretending to ignore the eruption—talked about ways to think about psychopathic behavior, and deal with it, whether you're a police officer interrogating a suspect or an attorney, defending a client who's possibly a weasel, or you're prosecuting that weasel.

"No matter what, you've got a bumpy, twisty road to navigate," she told the students. "So amp up your Critical Reasoning."

And then, to Cooper's relief, time was up and the class ended and she got ready to drive downtown, to the mayor's celebration of his New Dill Initiative, calling for sprucing up the commercial district with hanging baskets of petunias and faux gaslight streetlamps. He'd already pushed through a prohibition on tacking flyers onto telephone poles or slipping them under parked cars' windshield wipers, because it created litter and looked low class. He also planned a multi-story Main Street parking garage, inviting shoppers to come on down, even if it's raining or snowing. He wanted more town-gown cooperation, too, and he'd recruited Cooper to talk about the new Criminal Justice Program's student internships, which she guessed would excite the citizenry to the same extent her students got agog over her lecture on Critical Reasoning.

She told herself: One does one's duty.

She'd meant to take Henry with her to City Hall, figuring he could sleep on the podium while she talked, then provide a good excuse for her to leave quickly afterwards, but she changed her mind, realizing Henry might decide to trot down the steps into the audience, to meet and greet, and get attention.

So she drove him home. However, when she started out the door, he barked at her: you're leaving me here? Alone? Indoors? On a sunny October morning?

When she pointedly ignored the barking, he rolled onto his back with his four short legs in the air, a ploy he'd tried before, with excellent results. He looked at her upside down, winsome.

"Talk about master manipulators," Cooper muttered.

She decided to compromise and let him spend the next hour or so sniffing around the fenced-in back yard. First she made sure the gate was closed and latched, and the fence, buried in thick shrubbery, had no wriggle-holes underneath. Then she double-checked the gate. Yes, closed and latched.

"Take it or leave it," she told Henry, with a shrug.

He sat on the grass looking disappointed. In the few days he'd now lived with her, Cooper had learned to read Henry's mind. It was all in his eyes' expression, and how he angled his head, and his posture, and the tone of his barks. She'd also learned that Henry craved companionship.

"It's just an hour or two," she told him. "Buck up."

In the meeting room at City Hall, waiting to speak, Cooper noticed Beverly Abbott, but not Jack. She guessed he'd sent his wife as a stand-in, after yesterday's embarrassment, caught trying to scare Cooper, then floored by Mike Bolknor.

Cooper thought: trying to spook me out of my house? With motorcycle noise? You're smarter than that. Why so desperate?

Beverly chatted with Nessie Greffier, also scheduled to speak—her topic was attracting out-of-state retirees, to boost Dill's real-estate market—and Cooper saw her old high-school classmate surreptitiously glance at her. Or was it a glare? Nessie had been awful at Mona Dill Saunders' party. Did she wake up the next morning with a monster hangover, and remorse for speaking so nastily? Cooper decided to give Nessie a chance to apologize, and walked over.

"Oh, look," Nessie said. "Here's our own Clarence Darrow—deigning to let us bask in her aura!"

So, no repentance. Beverly froze, horrified. Nessie didn't even pretend to be joking now. She'd opened her inner cage door, let out fifty years of suppressed hostility. No stuffing those feelings back inside.

Cooper stared at her, started to say something, then shrugged and walked away. At the party she'd been hurt by Nessie's envious resentment, but now it left her blank. After high school, she supposed, Miss Popularity's glow faded, and seeing Cooper rack up accomplishments and honors, all those years, made her bitter.

Too bad, Cooper thought. Yes, she'd had a successful career, but she'd had her own disappointments—too tall and lanky, for instance, and maimed by polio—which apparently didn't register with Nessie.

"Someone's got something nice?" Cooper's mother had said. "That's nothing off you, Cooper, so be big!"

Cooper thought: be big, Nessie, but doubted it would happen. Nessie would have to marinate in her own poison.

She thought, not for the first time, Nessie's a crack shot. She rides a motorcycle. Would Nessie....

She pushed the thought away.

Tip LaPerle now spoke, reading from notes on cards. In line with the mayor's plans to brighten up Dill, he said, the police force would increase patrol-car washing to a twice-a-week routine, and if any of the cruisers got spattered, Tip said, they'd get washed "special." Also, the Dill Garden Club had offered to install and maintain window boxes at the police station, with chrysanthemums already on display for the fall.

Cooper suppressed a smile, seeing Tip struggle not to snarl. She could read his mind: "Mickey Mouse crap!"

Dill's new mayor, a retired Wall Street whizz, and a Mt. Augustus College alumnus, had retired to the Green Mountains, for the skiing and kayaking. Tip grumbled about "flat-landers" moving in, then trying to remake Vermont into Westchester County, or wherever they'd come from. Cooper nodded when he fulminated, but secretly thought the mayor's ideas were constructive. For instance, keeping winter's road salt washed off the patrol cars made sense.

Cooper spoke next—"...student interns... involvement with the community... fresh perspectives...." It bored even her, and she spoke exactly one minute, then left the podium, and the meeting room, and found the police chief waiting for her, on City Hall's front steps.

155

Main Street's maples still blazed orange and crimson and gold, although many leaves had already browned and fallen to the sidewalk. They stood a moment, silently, old friends, watching dead leaves twisting down through the air, which felt warm, for October.

"Tip," Cooper said, "this surveillance, it'll just antagonize him and...."

"To hell with that creep!" he said.

They stood silently again, watching the leaves.

"You got shot at twice," Tip suddenly said. "Don't tell me that sicko isn't involved, and when's the next shot?"

Cooper sighed.

"Mike Bolknor's got Campus Security watching my house," she reminded him.

She told him about last night.

"Yeah?" Tip said. "Bolknor whipped Abbott's butt?"

Cooper could tell that news brightened his day.

"There's another damned thing—Abbott!" he said. "Moneybags still won't tell me what rent he's charging Rawston, claims it's his God-given Constitutional right, or something, so what's he hiding?"

"Hmm," Cooper said.

Silence again, both watching dead leaves flutter down.

"I'm getting sick of this," Tip said. "Everything's frozen up on this shooting business, and—yeah—I'm keeping Rawston surveilled, maybe shake him loose, because lots of stuff don't make sense, like what's he living on, where's he getting money?"

Cooper stood silently, wondering how a scarlet leaf "knew" it was time to dry to brown, and fall. Autumn always invigorated her, the chill, the change. It also saddened her. Soon water would freeze in Dill's backyard birdbaths, and the mountains and valleys would turn white.

"Hart's Corners, that's involved, too," she said. "Somehow."

"Big ball of yarn," LaPerle said. "You can't figure where to pull, to start it coming apart."

To herself, Cooper thought: more like a spider's web, with its strands crisscrossing the town. And who's the spider?

On her way home, Cooper stopped at the Sweet Kumquat to buy Henry more organic hamburger. He needs extra protein, she told herself.

She knew she lied. She'd bought the treat out of guilt, for leaving him alone.

When she walked in the front door, she didn't hear the expected bark of greeting, or the scrabble of corgi paws on the hardwood floor. Mad at me, she wondered? Then, relieved, she remembered she'd left him in the back yard.

Just a momentary memory lapse, but it bothered her. If you forget something at age thirty, so what? Nearing seventy, though, you worry, you can't help it, even if you know it's nothing, that your mind's still perfectly sharp.

She put Henry's hamburger, wrapped in white butcher's paper, into the refrigerator. Then she checked her week's calendar, which she kept affixed to the refrigerator door with magnets. No classes this afternoon, no appointments. So, she could go back to the office. Grade essays. Work on next semester's class schedules. Look over applications from prospective students.

Or she could take Henry to Abner Park.

An easy choice—today might be autumn's last sunny, warm day. You never knew. A cold rain could come anytime, with a whipping wind to strip limbs of their leaves. For now, though, the park's sugar maples would be at their maximum scarlet, the birches and beeches rich gold.

Henry would like it, she thought. He'd amuse himself making fallen leaves fly up. He'd rummage in the bushes and briefly disappear under spruces, barking for fun. Yes, good times for Henry, she thought. And then, wryly, mocking herself: so he'll forgive me!

She shook her head at that neediness.

Henry had joined her household only days ago, but just now, driving home, she'd looked forward to Henry's company. What did the college kids call it? Hanging out?

Doesn't even play Scrabble, she thought, and went to the back door to fetch him.

She stopped on the slate patio, not immediately seeing the dog.

"Henry?" she called.

No response.

She called again, then scanned the yard, inch by inch, suddenly terrified she'd see a white-and-butterscotch body, lying on its side. Stroke. Coyote attack. Stray bullet from some idiot target shooting in his back yard.

158

She didn't see him.

Something like a cavern opened up inside her, a vast hollowness.

She started around the yard's periphery, as fast as she could limp, cane's tip digging in, stooping to peer under the shrubbery along the fence, to see if he lay in there, or if she'd missed an opening under the fence, when she'd looked earlier.

Nothing.

Then she saw the gate—open.

She'd left it closed. Latched. She'd double checked it. How could a small dog unlatch it?

She imagined him, desperate to get out and find her, jumping up, hitting the latch with his nose, or a flailing paw. It was too high, though. And the bolt had a knob on it. You grasped the knob with thumb and forefinger, then twisted it out of locked position. It didn't twist easily. Then you pulled on the knob, to slide the bolt from its socket, and the bolt didn't slide easily, either. Henry couldn't have done any of that.

On the grass lay a steak.

She'd missed it before, lying beside an old hand pump, a remnant of Norths from two centuries ago. It lay in the pump's shadow, which was why she'd initially missed it. It looked like a fresh Porterhouse, or maybe T-bone. Cooper wasn't much of a carnivore and didn't know meats well.

She fought the urge to sink to the grass and howl.

Instead, she stared at the gate, eyes wide. Abruptly, she lashed out with her cane, whacking the gate so hard it swung shut. She glared at it, as if about to strike

159

again, but then her expression changed, slowly hardening, to something like dry ice.

She thought: how'd they guess I wouldn't be here?

Instantly she knew: the *Dill Chronicle* had announced this morning's meeting. It had given the meeting's times. And it had listed her as a speaker.

Public knowledge, then. She wouldn't be home. And they'd assume she wouldn't bring the dog to a meeting.

How'd they know, though, that she'd leave the dog in the back yard?

Answer: they didn't.

They'd assume Henry would be left alone in the house. They wouldn't try the front door, where they might be seen. They'd make their way around here, meaning to pry open the back door. Easily done, with a crowbar.

Then, for them, good luck: Henry stood in the back yard, watching them. They'd brought the steak to lure him into their hands in the house, but it would work just as well in the yard. And, for all his exceptional intelligence, Cooper knew, Henry could not resist a steak.

So, while Henry sniffed the meat, snap a leash on him—you could buy a leash in any pet store, or at a Walmart. Then you'd lead him away. He'd probably resist, planting his paws, but he was a small dog. Not hard to pull along, against his will.

Then, into your waiting car, and away.

"Bastard," Cooper muttered.

She stood, staring at the vacant yard, the unlatched gate.

Abruptly, she spun around and hurried into the house. She grabbed her jacket off the chair where she'd left it, and her keys off the table. Then, cane thumping, she lurched out the front door, to her parked Volvo.

On the way downtown, she forced herself not to jam down the gas pedal, not to slap the horn, to blare slower cars out of her way.

Should've called Mike Bolknor, she thought, turning left on Main Street. No time for that, though.

She drove past the Dill Police Station and didn't stop. No time for that, either.

Farther down Main Street, she slammed on her brakes, just shy of DeBouche's Gas 'n Groceries, and parked at the curb, askew. A Dill Police Department patrol car sat in the store's out-front parking area, and she thought about fetching the cop—not visible, probably in the store, enjoying a gratis cup of coffee—but then, knowing the cop could do nothing, without a warrant, she hurried across the street and up the porch steps of the two-story house with faded-gray clapboards, noticing the black motorcycle parked out front.

Something not right made her stop, staring at the bike. What? A blank. She shook her head angrily and pulled open the door. A short hallway. On the right, the door to the ground-floor apartment. To the left, stairs.

She charged upwards, listening to the sounds of her own two feet and cane—shuffle, shuffle, thump; shuffle, shuffle, thump.

At the top, another short hallway, leading to what? Storage room? In front of her, the door to the upstairs apartment, voices murmuring behind it.

She pounded her fist on the door, and kept pounding.

Finally—her fist upraised to pound again—the door opened, and Sonny Rawston stared at her. Slowly, his mouth twisted into a wry smile. He surveyed her, triumphant.

"Why, it's our Ms. North!" he said, glancing behind him. "Look, she's come to visit!"

Over his shoulder she saw Stacey Gillibrand sitting at a table, holding a coffee cup, looking toward her, uncomprehending. Another cup rested on the table, and a plate of ginger snaps.

"So nice of you to drop by," Sonny said.

"Cut the damned crap!" Cooper said. "Where's my dog?"

Sonny looked back at Stacey, making sure she took all this in. Then he turned back to Cooper, amused.

"Your little doggie ran away?" he said.

Cooper nearly smashed her cane across his smug face.

"Where is he?" she demanded.

"Well, if I see him, I'll let you know," Sonny said. "What about putting up 'lost doggie' fliers around town?"

"I said cut the crap," Cooper told him. "I know damned well you took the dog—probably you've got him caged up in here somewhere."

Sonny looked back at Stacey, as if astonished by the assault.

"Seen a little doggie in here?" he asked.

"No!" Stacey said, and she glared at Cooper.

Sonny now leaned against the door jamb, head cocked to one side, eyeing Cooper judiciously.

162

"How about this," he said. "I'll let you in—no warrant required!—and you can search every room, under the bed, whatever."

Cooper glared at him, knowing this wouldn't go well.

"Search away," he said. "But if, by some tiny chance, there's no little doggie here, you make a nice apology."

He looked at Cooper, waiting.

She pushed past him into the apartment, knowing she wouldn't find Henry there.

She scanned the kitchen, and the dining area—no place to hide a dog. Next she barged into the bathroom. Sink, toilet, bathtub-shower. Again, no place to hide a dog. She returned to the living room. Two well-used armchairs and a small television. No hiding place. Finally, feeling futile, she lurched into his bedroom, cane thumping on the hardwood floor.

Bed. Closet. Chest of drawers.

In the closet, three extra shirts and a pair of jeans and pair of chino slacks hanging up, and a lightweight jacket and a winter parka. In the chest of drawers, underwear and socks. On top, a chipped cereal bowl holding a freebie ballpoint pen from Dill's Sizzlin' Sicilian Pizza Parlor and a half-empty bottle of artificial-tears eye drops and a key and three peppermint lifesavers in their cellophane wrappers. On an overhead shelf lay a gray sweater, thrown up there and crumpled.

No dog anywhere. No place for a dog. Cooper knew she wouldn't find Henry, but she'd hoped to spot some clue to where Rawston hid him. She'd found nothing, though, just Rawston's meager possessions. She guessed cups and plates and utensils and pots and frypans came with the apartment, along with the furniture and the tv. More a military field station than a home. Everything sparse and orderly, under control.

"Where've you got the dog?" she demanded.

"Oh, for God's sake," Stacey suddenly shouted. "Just leave him alone!"

Cooper stared at Stacey. Had she helped Rawston steal Henry? No, she decided. He can delude Stacey, but I just don't believe she'd turn criminal for him.

"Stacey," she demanded. "Have you seen him ride off today?"

"Absolutely not!" Stacey said.

Sonny looked on, enjoying himself.

"He's never been out of your sight, off on his motorcycle?" Cooper said. "Say just before lunch time?"

She saw Stacey's glare waver. It lasted a split second. Then she shook her head, as if at an outrage.

"I said so, didn't I?" she said.

Yes, and now you're lying, Cooper thought. You probably haven't even been here that long, but he's persuaded you I'm harassing him, so you're refusing to admit you don't really know where he's been and when.

"Are you sure?" Cooper said.

Confusion momentarily fogged Stacey's gaze. Cooper knew that look. In trials, she'd often seen witnesses waver like that, hesitate. And then, because they feared the defendant, or because they remained loyal to a false narrative, even in the face of contrary facts, they went ahead—with fierce conviction—and perjured themselves.

Cooper turned to stare at Sonny. He gazed back, calm, confident. He radiated triumph. She supposed he'd wanted to engineer just this scenario, but it worked out better than he'd supposed, because here was Stacey to witness—Cooper bursting in, attacking Rawston in a spiteful rage, hurling accusations. Hadn't he said she was out to get him?

And a bonus: he'd now humiliated Cooper. Made her look a fool.

"Don't hurt that dog," she told him. "Remember that!"

She pushed past him, out the door.

"What about my apology?" he told her back.

She started down the stairs, then stopped. What was at the end of the corridor? She spun around on the stairs, stepped back up to the floor, then hurried down the corridor to the door at the end. Locked? No, the handle turned. Inside, a vacuum cleaner, a bucket, a mop, a broom, a dustpan. No dog.

Cooper stood looking at it all and exhaled, unaware she'd been holding her breath. She'd let her hopes rise.

Slower now, she turned. Rawston stood in his open doorway, leaning against the jamb, gaze sardonic. She cursed and clumped past him, down the stairs, then out the front door, desperate for fresh air.

She stood on the porch, shoulders slumped.

Across the street, a white-haired man stepped out of the convenience store. Cooper paid no attention. Leaning on her cane, she stared at Rawston's parked motorcycle. What bothered her about it?

On the opposite curb, the white-haired man gazed wearily at the street, as if gathering strength for a journey. Cooper remembered him, the retired granite worker from the downstairs apartment. He finally started forward, trudging across the macadam. Wincing, he climbed the steps to the porch, where Cooper stood, staring at the motorcycle. He looked at her, rheumy eyed, once a large and strong quarryman, now stooped and wheezing, his lungs damaged by a lifetime of inhaled granite dust.

"You're that prosecutor lady," he said. "I've voted for you."

"I'm looking for a lost dog," she told him. "Have you seen one, or heard barking, out here, or maybe upstairs?"

He stood looking past Cooper, at nothing in particular.

"Had a dog myself, once," he finally said. "Beagle—run off into the woods, on some scent, I guess."

He looked vacant.

"Jules," he said.

"Jules?" Cooper said.

"Yeah, named him after my Uncle Jules," he said. "Had a beagle look to him, that uncle."

More vacant staring.

"Never came back out of the woods," he said. "My wife, cried for a week—now she's gone, too—don't mind saying I cried some, too."

Cooper wasn't sure if he'd wept for the lost dog, or his lost wife, or both. Some part of her wanted to weep, too, helplessly, because she'd stupidly left Henry unattended in the yard. Because he might now be dead.

166

Or in pain. Or terrified. And because, when she finally parked the Volvo in her driveway, and unlocked the front door, and walked into her house, it would be empty.

"Didn't hear any barking," the old man said.

"What about your upstairs neighbor," Cooper said. "Hear him drive off on that motorcycle?"

He looked at her, bleary eyed.

"I was having my second cup of coffee…."

Cooper waited.

"This an investigation?" the man said. "Cop car's been parked over at the store, couple of days now, I think."

"Yes, it's a criminal investigation," Cooper said, grimly.

"So, second cup of coffee, that would be about eight-thirty, around in there, heard him roar off," the old man said. "Can't have a conversation, not with that fellow…."

"When did he come back?" Cooper asked.

"Heard that bike of his about a half hour later, say nine," he said.

Cooper thought: I hadn't left yet for the meeting. So it wasn't Sonny after all? Maybe he was just giving Stacey a ride to the college, or buzzing off to buy butter or something.

And then: would Nessie Greffier do something like this? Or Jack Abbott? She couldn't imagine it. Not their style. This was Sonny Rawston's style.

"Thanks for the information," Cooper said, her voice sounding dull.

She started down the stairs, to the street. She knew the old man watched her go.

"Course, he went out again," he said.

She spun around, stared at him.

"Yeah, I'm sure I heard that bike start up again," he said.

"What time?" Cooper said.

"Would've been, let's see…."

He stood looking into space.

"Got hungry, fried up a couple eggs…."

Cooper waited.

"About ten, I'd guess," he said. "There abouts."

"And when did he come back?" Cooper asked.

"Let's see," he said. "Yeah, I heard the bike rumble in, shut down, and him going up the steps, talking, probably that girl from next door with him, so…."

Cooper waited.

"Maybe a half hour ago," he said.

"Thank you," Cooper said. "You've been a great help."

He looked at her, and the small part of her mind not focused on Henry registered that he regretted their conversation's end, because now his loneliness would resume.

And mine, Cooper thought.

"I'm pro-cop," the old man said behind her, as she started down the steps.

"'Protect and serve!'" he said.

Cooper watched him trudge into the house. Then, at the curb, she stopped, staring at Rawston's parked motorcycle. When she'd first seen it, something struck her as wrong. But what? Dust coated it. Otherwise, just another black motorcycle.

168

"Damn," she said.

She crossed the street and walked into DeBouche's Gas 'n Groceries.

As she'd expected, the officer—Eddie Pike, newest member of the force, no more than twenty-two—leaned against the counter, a paper cup of coffee in one hand, a half-eaten chocolate-chip cookie in the other, while the store's clerk on duty, a slim girl with glistening black hair and a blouse tight over a large bosom, leaned against her side of the counter, laughing over something Eddie had just said, her merriment excessive, in Cooper's opinion, because Eddie Pike wasn't notable for his wit.

"Hi, Ms. North," he said, partially showing off for the girl, Cooper knew—see, I know Dill's big shots!

You've been here all morning?" Cooper asked. "Watching Rawston?"

"Like a hawk," Eddie said, and the girl giggled.

"See him ride off on that motorcycle?" Cooper asked.

Officer Pike pulled off his uniform hat and ran a hand through his blond crewcut. He looked out the window, blue-eyed. He seemed to contemplate the question, but Cooper knew he didn't know what to answer, because he'd hardly kept a watch on Rawston at all. He'd spent the morning here in the store, flirting with the clerk and drinking free coffee.

She sighed.

"I don't suppose either one of you heard a dog barking out there?" she asked.

Both looked at her, blank eyed, and simultaneously shook their heads.

Cooper sighed again.

169

She turned and walked out the door and stood on the store's stoop, staring across the street at Rawston's motorcycle. She felt like sinking down, to sit on the stoop, stay there, never going back to her empty home at all.

It occurred to her, dully, what bothered her about the motorcycle. It was that Sonny couldn't have taken Henry.

How could he scoop up the dog, cage him in a pet crate, then carry him off on that bike? She tried to imagine him rumbling through town, a large mesh crate balanced in front of him, a barking dog inside, holding onto the teetering crate while he steered the bike.

No, that couldn't be.

A borrowed car? Stacey had none. Rawston had no other friends. Tip had found out that much.

Rented a car? He'd have had to drive his motorcycle to Montpelier, thirty miles away, driven back in a rented car, snatched Henry, hidden him somewhere, driven back to the capital, turned in the rental car, biked back to Dill.

Impossible. Not in the time available.

Rented a car yesterday, or before? No, because then he wouldn't have his motorcycle. And his downstairs neighbor just said he'd heard him riding it. And surely even Ed Pike, gabbing in the store, would have glanced out the front window from time to time, noticed the motorcycle gone, seen a rental car parked there.

That left two possibilities.

Rawston killed Henry at the house, carried off his body, and dumped it. Into the river, maybe.

Or the dog snatcher wasn't Sonny Rawston.

170

CHAPTER TWENTY-THREE

She couldn't go home.

She drove to the campus, took the elevator up to her office, then opened the drawer in her desk. She stood looking down at what lay inside—an unopened bottle of vodka and an unopened package of Camels. Each had a rubber band around it.

After staring into the drawer a while, she suddenly reached for the vodka bottle, but stopped. She stood with her hand poised an inch above the bottle. Abruptly, with a shudder, she pulled her arm back.

She stared a while longer into the drawer. Finally she sighed. She reached into the drawer again and grasped the rubber band around the vodka bottle between thumb and forefinger. She pulled it back, held it stretched out a moment, then let it snap. She did the same with the rubber band around the package of cigarettes.

She sighed again, then slowly closed the drawer. After that, she sank into her desk chair and stared at the wall, slumped.

Finally she got up and walked to the elevator, descending to the first floor. She walked into the Campus Security offices, where Chip Stack, busily interning, worked at a large wall map of the campus, bristling with tacks with tiny spherical heads, some red, some green, some blue. Chip, checking a printout, was rearranging the tacks on the map.

"We're going to install a new bunch of security cameras," he told Cooper.

She registered his pleasure, at doing police work, even if at the clerical level, but she felt too drained to say anything.

"Is Mike Bolknor around?" she asked.

"Went to Montpelier, for the afternoon," Chip said. "To a meeting about left-over military equipment and…."

"Alone, or with Chief LaPerle?" Cooper asked.

Chip told her the two men drove to Montpelier together. He started to explain about the map and colored tacks, but she'd already turned and he spoke to her back as she walked out of the room.

Mike Bolknor and Tip LaPerle sat with Cooper in her office. They'd just gotten back from the state capital, from their meeting on military surplus, and Cooper guessed the conversation in the Dill PD patrol car they'd shared never got beyond night-vision goggles and Kevlar vests.

Bolknor, sunk into his internal vault, gazed at an invisible spot on the wall, and LaPerle looked ready to bite.

"Rawston!" Cooper said.

She slammed her fist onto her desk.

"He damned well did it!"

After a silent moment, LaPerle spoke.

"Warrant? Search his apartment?"

"I already searched it," Cooper said.

"Probably couldn't get a warrant anyway," Tip said. "Not for a lost dog, and we've got no evidence."

More sitting in silence.

"I'll send the guys around, talk to your neighbors," Tip finally said. "Maybe someone heard his bike, or saw it parked out there."

Cooper guessed no neighbors would've been home. They'd be in their offices, at Dill Industries' headquarters, across Abner Park, or they'd be wielding scalpels at the Allen County Regional Medical Center, or they'd be in their downtown law offices, fine-tuning contracts. In any event, their Victorians were big and thick walled. Inside, in the kitchen, say, you wouldn't hear a bomb explode out on the street. Besides, cleaning services mostly worked mornings, their vacuums roaring.

She knew Tip had no illusions about that, but he wanted to help.

"Eddie Pike see anything?" he asked.

"Coffee cup," Cooper said. "Pretty clerk behind the counter."

Tip grunted.

"Rawston's a goddamned eel!" he said.

Cooper sighed.

"You grab him, get slime," he said. "Wriggles away."

Cooper shook away an image of Rawston knifing Henry. Or striking with a crowbar.

Toss the dog's body into the river?

Or would she find Henry thrown onto her doorstep, fur bloody?

She rested her elbows on her desk and put her head in her hands.

"Maybe the dog's alive," Bolknor said.

Cooper looked up at him, face bleak.

"He might use the dog, somehow, to torture you," he said.

Cooper thought: send me packages in the mail? A paw? Then another paw? A head?

"So where could he keep the dog hidden?" Bolknor said.

Cooper thought: in Stacey Gillibrand's apartment?

No, it was the same as she'd concluded before. Warp her thinking, yes. But he couldn't turn Stacey criminal. Cooper felt sure. And the dog would bark. Henry was an enthusiastic barker. If the dog was alive, he'd be hidden where nobody could hear.

"His motorcycle had dust all over it," she said.

"Dirt roads," Tip said.

Cooper raised her hands, palms up, and shrugged. They all knew why.

Dirt roads radiated out from Dill in all directions, a network of them. Some streets started out paved, in town, but ultimately turned to dirt. Some of the paved roads got dusty, too.

"He's got no property, no friends to lend him a house," Cooper said, wearily. "So where's he hiding Henry?"

174

She sighed.

Bolknor had resumed looking at the wall. LaPerle stared at his hands. Cooper finally spoke, quietly.

"Would that jackass even feed my dog?"

Cooper drove home, but only slowed in front of the house, forcing herself to look at the front stoop.

Nothing thrown there. No dog body.

She couldn't bring herself to go into the empty house, so she drove on downtown and parked on Main Street. She sat in the car looking at the storefronts, realizing only belatedly that she'd parked in front of Dill Wine & Spirits. She sat slumped in the seat, staring at the store's display window, an artful arrangement of bottles— clarets and zinfandels and Kentucky bourbons and Russian vodkas and brandies and amaretto.

After a while she reached for her cane.

She opened the Volvo's door, not feeling under her own control, as if somebody far off sat at a screen, looking through her eyes, twisting knobs and moving levers, making her walk to the liquor store's door.

A human drone.

She stood on the sidewalk, staring through the glass door into the store.

She thought: no.

Not this.

Against her will, her hand reached out. It grasped the handle and pushed the door open. She walked in.

Tony Cittadino stood behind the counter, looking at her, surprised.

Until a few years ago, she'd been a regular customer. Tony frowned, making it clear—this upset him, Cooper North back in his store.

"For Christ's sake, Cooper...."

"No, it's okay, Tony," she said. "I've got some guests coming, and they'll...you know."

Lies already, she thought.

"Cooper, I don't want to sell you any of this stuff," Tony said. "This isn't good."

"No, it's okay, Tony," she said. "It's not for me."

A few minutes later she walked out with a bottle of single-malt scotch in a brown paper bag, and she felt Tony's unhappy, disapproving eyes on her through the front window, all the way to her car.

"I'm not really going to drink this," she told herself. "This is just a test."

That made her feel better. With the bottle in its bag lying on the passenger seat, Henry's seat, she backed out of the parking slot and started driving down Main Street, past the police station, its windows now fitted with window boxes, courtesy of the Dill Garden Club, displaying chrysanthemums, red and yellow.

"That's nice," Cooper thought. "Mickey Mouse, but nice."

Tip couldn't help, she thought. No case here.

Just a lost dog.

She avoided looking at the bottle in its bag, lying on the seat. She felt it, though, a magnetic pull.

Farther down Main Street she saw DeBouche's Gas 'n Groceries already lit up, because evening was coming on fast. A patrol car sat in the parking lot, and Cooper made out an officer sitting inside.

Not Eddie Pike, she thought. Not out there like this, doing what he's paid for.

If the rookie cop had done his duty, maintaining surveillance, would he have seen Sonny Rawston with the dog?

Probably not, Cooper thought. She'd already decided Rawston couldn't have carried the dog off on his bike. Still, if he'd actually watched, Officer Pike might have seen *something*.

She chose a street at random and followed it out of town.

Dill's houses gave way to roadside pastures, slanting up to ridges lined with pines and firs, dark against the still silver sky, and then she turned off onto a dirt road, going nowhere in particular, windows in the houses and old farms she passed now just beginning to light up yellow, white smoke wisping from chimneys, and she felt winter's onset as a coldness in her bones.

CHAPTER TWENTY-FOUR

Cooper woke up the next morning with a pounding head and no memory of last night. She lay in bed, and moaned, heavy with a familiar shame.

For decades she'd awakened like this. Nauseated. Aching. Insects seeming to crawl under her skin.

Finally, in the past few years, she'd freed herself, a triumph of the will. And now....

She'd had an AA partner she could telephone, but Anne died. Cirrhosis of the liver. It had shocked Cooper into finally quitting, and she'd stayed sober until last night.

She lay looking at the ceiling.

If only Mona Dill Saunders were back from Spain. She'd once babysat Mona, but their sixteen-year age difference meant nothing now. She could talk with Mona. Mona had iron in her.

Cooper cursed and sat up on the edge of the bed, staring at a spot on the floor, beside the bay window. Henry's spot.

Finally she got up and showered and tried to make herself look okay, but she couldn't meet her own gaze in the mirror. She made coffee, all she could tolerate for breakfast, and sat at the table, staring at Henry's food dish and water dish, both white plastic, side by side on the floor, feeling as if her brain had gone numb.

Great strategy, she told herself. Fight back by going limp. Lie on the floor.

Abruptly she pulled on her quilted jacket, and stuffed gloves into the pockets, and hurried out of the house, not locking the door behind her, perversely, because what did it matter anymore?

Halfway to the car she turned around. She climbed back up the stoop's two slate steps and locked the door.

At the college, she sat at her desk, thinking about the vodka bottle in her drawer. If she had a small glass of it, or two, she'd feel better. Hair of the dog. Easily done.

But—she thought this, staring at the still unopened drawer—that would be unethical. That unopened bottle in the drawer wasn't for drinking. It was for not drinking. So, opening it would be a moral lapse. Better to go down to Dill Wine & Spirits, and buy a new bottle there. Another single-malt scotch. Her favorite.

No.

She imagined Tony Cittadino, behind his counter, staring at her, black eyes sorrowful. Worried for her. And deeply disapproving.

She thought: mind your own business, Tony.

Irritating, his judging her. He had no right.

A plan occurred to her. Later, she'd go for a pleasant ride eastward, on back roads, taking in the denuding maples and ashes and beeches, many with black branches already stark against the sky, looking like neurons. She'd rattle across an old covered bridge she liked, over the Connecticut River into New Hampshire, and she'd buy something at a package store there, where nobody knew her. No nosing into her private life.

Abruptly her face sagged.

God!

It's starting again.

She didn't know what to do.

She did nothing.

Elbows on her desk, she buried her forehead in her palms.

She imagined Dr. Berry Randolph waking up this morning. Maybe sickle cell would strike today. No knowing. Yet, she'd drive to the veterinary clinic with cheer, even joy. Cooper had seen that in her.

No help there. Thinking of Berry Randolph's courage, she didn't rally. Instead, she loathed herself more, as a coward, a weakling. And thinking of the veterinary clinic....

Was he suffering?

Dead?

And somebody wanted to shoot her.

She yanked open her desk drawer and stared down at the unopened bottle of vodka.

It was that nothing led anywhere. She could get no purchase on all of this, the shootings, the taking of her dog. Every path meandered and then faded out.

A knock on the door.

She sat frozen. After a moment, she slid the drawer shut.

"Come in."

Her voice sounded like a frog croak.

Chip Stack came in.

He sat in one of the visitors' chairs and shot a look at her. She'd seen people look at her that way before, during her drinking years, taking in the bloodshot eyes and the pasty face and the pained expression. If any asked, Cooper had always said, flu trying to get me.

Chip didn't ask, though, and she sensed underlying excitement. However, he didn't get to it directly.

"I wanted to tell you I got a car," he said.

She looked at him, wondering why this mattered when she felt so awful.

"It's just a used Honda Civic," he said. "Eight years old, but in pretty good shape."

She gave him, she knew, only a blank stare, but she couldn't help it.

For some reason, she found herself thinking: all those drinking years, I did my job. Didn't I? I did it well. Nobody ever questioned that.

It gave her some small uptick.

She could see her blankness made Chip uneasy, but he soldiered on.

"Anyway," he said. "I wanted you to know, I can do more surveillance now, if you need it, also Jerry Shapiro and Nikki Winkel—we all drive."

"That's good, Chip," she said.

Her voice still sounded like a croak.

"Thanks," she said.

She waited for him to go.

He continued sitting, and it suddenly occurred to her she mattered to this young man. She helped him toward the police career he wanted. At least, he believed she did.

Annoying!

Yet, she'd agreed to come out of retirement, take on this college job. And she'd always handled responsibility.

Just not now.

She thought: leave me alone.

Followed by another surge of self-loathing.

That's it, she thought? Curl up on the floor? Let Sonny Rawston kick you into a lump?

"Actually," Chip said, "I already used the car, for surveillance."

At last we get to it, Cooper thought. She tried to look interested.

"Yesterday afternoon, after I bought the car, I took it for a drive," Chip said. "So, I was going east on Main Street, when I saw Sonny Rawston coming towards me on his motorcycle, bundled up against the cold."

Cooper continued trying to look interested.

"I guess he was coming from his apartment," Chip said.

Cooper nodded, all the encouragement she could muster.

"I backed around in the alley alongside the hardware store," Chip said. "Then I tailed along behind him."

So what, Cooper thought. Off to the supermarket to buy eggs?

"He turned right up Slope Drive," Chip said. "Then he turned left off that, onto Starke Lane."

Yes, a nice residential street, Cooper thought. Mostly older two stories, a few Fifties ranch houses, and only a few of them, as yet, converted into apartments and condos.

"He pulled into the driveway of a house, just before Starke Lane bends around to the south, down the hill, back to Main Street," Chip said.

Chip had parked down the street, and made a show of getting out and lifting the car's hood and examining the engine, as if he had a problem. Sonny Rawston got off his motorcycle and sauntered up to the house carrying an envelope and rang the bell. After a few moments the door opened and he went in.

Chip waited. After about ten minutes Rawston came out and got on his motorcycle, without the envelope. He drove back along Starke Lane, barely glancing at Chip.

"It looked like he was headed back to his apartment," Chip said. "Anyway, I had to get back up to campus, for a class."

They sat looking at each other, Cooper wondering who Sonny Rawston would be seeing. Tip LaPerle's officers had checked around, and found he had no friends in Dill. Actually, he now had one, Stacey Gillibrand, but she didn't live on Starke Lane. And a ten-minute stop didn't sound like visiting an old buddy.

"One-thirty-two Starke Lane," Chip said. "That was the house."

After Chip left, Cooper didn't know what to do, except she felt imprisoned in her office. So she got her jacket back on and rode the elevator down to the first floor.

She walked past Campus Security's glass door, not looking in, for fear she'd see Mike Bolknor there, talking to one of his officers, or to Chip, maybe, and she'd catch his eye and then get into a conversation. She had nothing to say. So she hurried out the front door and to her Volvo.

Cooper started to open the passenger door for Henry, then cursed, and slammed the door shut again. She got into the driver's seat and snapped in the seatbelt, only from habit, and drove out of the Campus Security parking lot. She didn't want to go home. She didn't want to go anywhere in particular.

Except over to New Hampshire.

It'll get worse, she thought. It'll get harder and harder to stop.

If Mona Saunders were here, she'd talk with her. Mona would say: For Pete's sake, Coop—stop sniveling and get a goddamned grip.

Maybe she'd get a goddamned grip.

Mona, however, wasn't here.

Cooper drove slowly along Hill Street, feeling New Hampshire's magnetic pull. Fighting it, she turned right, down Slope Drive, then right again on Starke Lane.

A pleasant street, she thought. Houses here were smaller than Hill Street's behemoths, like hers, but well-kept, cozy behind cedar hedges and rose bushes and lilacs. Maples shaded the street in summer, but most had now lost their leaves, letting in the wan autumn sunlight.

Absent mindedly, she kept an eye on the house numbers—one-twenty-eight, one-thirty....

She braked, suddenly, in front of number one-thirty-two.

A house from the nineteen-twenties, Cape-Cod style, its clapboards painted brown. Cooper sat in her Volvo, stopped in the middle of the street, staring.

It was Nessie Greffier's house.

Cooper didn't like how Tip LaPerle looked at her.

She'd driven here directly from Starke Lane, and stomped into his office. Ever since he'd peered at her face, looking unhappy.

"Flu's after me," she said.

She could see he didn't buy it.

"Let's focus on the issue here," she said. "Sonny Rawston visiting Nessie Greffier—that smells."

"Could be some reason," Tip said. "Coop, you're looking like you did when...."

"I'm looking to get my dog back," she said. "Rawston? Nessie?"

Tip shrugged.

"Nessie Greffier hates me, I told you that, since high school," Cooper said. "Maybe he got her to hide my dog."

Tip stared at his desk. When he looked up, he shook his head.

"I can't just go search her house," he said.

He shrugged again.

"You know that," he said.

She exhaled in exasperation.

"What you could do is ask some questions around there," Cooper said.

Tip stared into space a while, then looked at her and nodded.

"Okay, like, good evening, Starke Lane taxpayers," Tip said. "We're hunting a lost dog, and we wonder if you've heard any barking around here, maybe seen or heard motorcycles...."

"Exactly," Cooper said. "And when they ring Nessie Greffier's doorbell, especially, it'll be sharp eyes, right? And perked-up ears?"

Tip looked pained.

"Even if it's Eddie Pike!" Cooper said.

She knew he'd have dressed the rookie cop down by now, for failing to adequately surveil Rawston's apartment house.

"I'm wondering, that envelope Rawston brought her," Tip said.

"Good question," Cooper said.

"Coop, I really don't like how you're looking," Tip said.

She lurched to her feet.

186

"Keep me posted," she said, already halfway out the door.

Outside, on the police station's stoop, she stopped and exhaled, as if she'd been holding her breath all that time.

She looked at the chrysanthemums in the window boxes, but hardly saw them. Then she walked slowly to her Volvo and drove towards home.

On Slope Drive, though, she abruptly swerved into a driveway, then out again, reversing direction, now driving back the way she'd come, down the hill. She turned left on Main Street, then right on Foundry Street, downhill again. She turned left on River Street and drove past Tenement Row, heading east.

Beyond the Dill town line, she knew, River Street became a county road, blacktop all the way to the Connecticut River. You crossed on an old covered bridge. At the bridge's midpoint, you left Vermont and drove into New Hampshire.

CHAPTER TWENTY-FIVE

Next morning, Cooper stood on the Campus Security Building's stoop, head pounding. She was supposed to speak to the Criminal Law I class, a guest lecture, but had no will to do it. So she stood on the stoop, looking at the door handle.

"Professor North?"

She turned, and saw Stacey Gillibrand hurrying up the steps, wearing her red backpack.

"That man you asked about?" Stacey said. "Shoulder-length gray hair, gray beard?"

Cooper managed a nod.

She felt nauseated.

"I've seen him," Stacey said. "It's sort of creepy."

Cooper waited, looking at the young woman through a haze of headache and nausea, wanting to bolt, to go where nobody was, lie down with a chilled washcloth over her forehead, but also wanting to hear. Very much wanting to hear.

"I saw him right on campus," Stacey said.

Cooper looked away from Stacey's blond hair. It seemed too bright. It hurt her head.

"Outside the library," Stacey said.

Every evening, Stacey said, she worked in a library carrel, scrutinizing case records from eighteen years ago—the bludgeoned Hart's Corners schoolteacher, Mildred Langley.

"It absolutely wasn't that old handyman!" Stacey said. "Nub Duckins got wrongfully convicted!"

She shook her head, outraged.

"Somebody else did it!"

She glared, as if defying a justice-blocking mob.

Because she felt so ill, Cooper thought: Oh, for God's sake, little girl, let it rest.

"I'm proving it!" Stacey said.

Every day after classes, she said, she worked in her carrel, poring over police reports and court records and newspaper stories. At six-thirty, she stowed her papers and left the library, to walk home for supper, and then study.

Three nights ago, as she left the library, she saw the gray-haired man sitting on a bench on the library's slate patio. She paid no attention, but then she happened to glance back and saw him watching her walk away. He checked his wristwatch, as if he had an appointment.

"It's just that you mentioned a man like that," Stacey said. "And he's been sitting on that bench three nights now, and every time he checks his wristwatch."

Cooper thought: why didn't you tell me before?

And she thought: is it me he's waiting for? Because he knows campus security watches my house every night? Because he assumes I'll eventually use the

189

library, probably in the evening? Suppertime, campus temporarily deserted, already dark—perfect for another shot.

She shook off the thought.

"We'll look into this," she told Stacey. "Definitely."

Stacey nodded, and started toward the door. She stopped, staring at the door, then turned.

"Professor North—your dog...."

"Yes?" Cooper said.

Stacey started to speak, then frowned.

"Oh, nothing," she said, shaking her head, as if to dispel unwanted thoughts, and walked into the building.

As soon as the Criminal Law I class ended, Cooper rushed out the door, as if she had an appointment. Actually, she dreaded getting waylaid by students with questions. She didn't want to talk. She wanted to go home and lie down.

She'd bought three bottles of single-malt scotch in New Hampshire. She had two unopened bottles and one bottle still a quarter full.

She promised herself: I won't drink any of it now.

As she walked up to her door, though, she felt the liquor's draw. Then she saw a manila mailer lying on the stoop. She picked it up, saw it had no postage, no return address. It had just one printed word: "North."

She laid it on the kitchen table and stared at it, while she brewed coffee.

He'd have worn gloves. She had no doubt. There'd be no fingerprints.

She sipped coffee, then blew on it, because it was too hot. All the while she stared at the mailer.

Don't open it, she thought. Don't read it. Don't see what he's sent. Burn it in the fireplace.

She opened it.

Inside she found a color photograph, the right size to frame and stand on your piano. It showed a metal-mesh crate. Inside the crate lay Henry, looking out.

His bright eyes were dulled, sad.

Cooper stared at the photograph a while. Finally she laid it carefully on the table, as if it might shatter.

She looked into the manila mailer and saw a piece of paper, with text printed on it. She pulled it out and read it.

"Hey there, Ms. North—

"Want your little doggie back? Before it's too late?

"Here's what you have to do.

"On the day after tomorrow—so you'll have time to think about it, and what could happen to that little doggie—you'll get stagger-around drunk. At noon, you'll go to City Hall and stand on the steps, probably wobbling, and you'll make an announcement—

"'I, Cooper North, am a stuffed shirt, who likes to throw her weight around, and ruin other people's lives when they never did anything to me, and I'm a slobbering drunk, just as you see me now!'

"Don't worry, there'll be an audience for your performance, because a circular will be distributed around town, announcing the fascinating event.

"If you don't do it, you'll periodically receive photos to keep you posted. You'll be able to watch your little doggie slowly starve.

"Looking forward to seeing you at City Hall."

Cooper sat a long time, head down, photograph in one hand, note in the other.

After a while she got up and struggled back into her jacket. She took her gloves from the pockets and put them on and walked out the front door. She inserted her key in the door's lock and turned it, carefully, as if everything depended on that door being securely locked.

She stood looking at the locked door, still holding her keys, and sighed, because she knew locking the liquor bottles in the house didn't mean she wouldn't get to them eventually. And locking the picture of Henry in the house didn't mean it wasn't etched into her memory, along with the accompanying printed note, because she could recite its every word.

Slowly, she drove downtown to the police station and parked in the lot behind the building, in one of the "visitor" spaces. She didn't get out. She sat staring through the windshield at the station's back door.

Abruptly, she restarted the Volvo's engine.

To tell Tip LaPerle about the photograph and the note would be too humiliating. Especially the note. And, if she did tell him, he'd rampage. She knew him well. He'd haul in Sonny Rawston with no evidence, and that would lead to serious trouble. She couldn't let him damage himself.

And if she did tell him, and he did what she knew he'd do, one option would be crossed off—she wouldn't be able to obey the note and get drunk and stand on the City Hall steps at the appointed hour and shame herself in front of the town where she'd lived all her life, in front of people who respected her.

Henry would starve.

Slowly, she drove out of the parking lot, back onto Main Street.

If only Mona Dill Saunders were here. But she wasn't.

She thought about talking it over with her Baker Street Irregulars. Nikki Winkel? She shook her head.

Using students as a crutch? Had she really come to this?

She drove hardly aware of her sneaker on the gas pedal, her hands on the wheel. She turned right, up Slope Drive, then left on Hill Street. She drove through Abner Park noticing the maples had now lost most of their leaves. Their limbs, stark against the sky, looked like bones.

A crow, perched on a branch, cocked its head, pointing one eye down, so it could watch her drive beneath it.

She passed her home, not looking at it. It seemed hostile territory.

It was only as she drove onto the campus, and then into the Campus Security Building's parking lot, that she realized whose advice she'd come seeking, whose thoughts she wanted to hear.

Mike Bolknor wasn't in. He'd gone home for lunch, Chip Stack said.

While he talked to Cooper, he worked on the wall-mounted campus map he'd shown her once before, glancing from the map to a printout he held in one hand.

New camera installations, Cooper remembered.

She didn't care.

Chip's gaze moved from the printout to the map, which showed every campus street and building. He marked a spot by resting a fingertip on it, a dormitory's rear entrance, then rechecked the printout. He pushed in a green-headed pin. More scrutiny of the printout. He fingered a different spot on the map. This time he pushed in a red-headed pin.

Cooper doubted Mike Bolknor required his new intern to spend his every spare minute on the job here, sticking in pins.

"Maple Street, isn't it?" Cooper asked. "Where he lives?"

"Number twenty-five, apartment one," Chip said, still pushing in pins. "It's just off the campus, and he usually walks home for lunch."

He said it as a classical Athenian might say, "And here, in this temple, dwells the god Apollo, radiant with light."

"Thanks," Cooper muttered, and left.

She didn't feel like telephoning. Or like walking, either, no matter how close the apartment was, because her left leg throbbed, in time with the throb in her forehead. It would be rude to just knock on his door, unannounced. Normally she'd never do that.

She didn't care.

She got in her car and drove west on Hill Street, one campus block, then turned right on Maple Street. She parked on the other side of the street from number twenty-five, a well-kept Victorian, painted salmon, with green trim, hiding behind a front-yard spruce.

She climbed out of the driver's seat and leaned in to get her cane, where she'd laid it across the passenger seat—Henry' s seat—and then limped across the street to the house and up the steps to the porch.

Two mailboxes beside the door indicated two tenants. She opened the door and stepped into an anteroom, with a stairway leading up. A dark oak door on her left had a sign: "Apartment One."

Beneath the sign, a metal frame offered the tenant a spot to slip in his business card, or a paper rectangle with his name, but the frame was empty.

Cooper knocked.

No sound came from the apartment, only silence.

It disturbed her, as if there'd been a death.

She sighed and walked back outside and crossed the street and got into her car. She sat in a funk, not knowing what to do.

And then she saw Mike Bolknor walking toward her on the opposite sidewalk. He walked with his hands in his trouser pockets, head down, heavy shoulders hunched under his suit jacket. She had the feeling that instead of lunch he'd walked, going nowhere special, just walked.

He stopped in front of the house and looked up, as if surprised to be there, not even sure where he was. His heavy black eyebrows seemed collapsed, his eyes stricken. He looked as if he'd been staring into hell.

195

He shambled up the porch steps, his large black shoes scuffing on the wooden treads. He opened the door and disappeared inside.

Cooper sat in the car looking at the porch.

After a while, she started the car and drove slowly away.

She drove home, and sat at her kitchen table, staring at the quarter-full bottle of scotch.

Just a dog, she told herself. Henry's just a dog.

She'd never had pets. Her father boarded his Morgan horses at an old farm, out on the Snowville Road, one of the Dill family's many properties, and when Cooper and her brother ardently petitioned for a puppy, their mother snorted.

"No livestock!"

Vinegary, yes, a New Englander's scorn of sentimental anthropomorphism. But faked. Even at eight years old Cooper sensed that. And she knew what Bethany North hid—pets would die. Pain, grief. Her children must be shielded. And so must she.

Cooper thought: No, he's not just a dog. He's Henry.

She reached for the scotch bottle, then pulled back her hand.

He'd gotten her drinking again. That's what he'd wanted. That's what he got. No crime, no possible legal action, just as he'd planned. Now he held Henry over her head.

Abase yourself in public.

Or I'll starve your dog.

196

He'll die slowly. I'll send you photographs. You'll see.

She knew Sonny Rawston took the dog. No doubt at all—the blackmail note said "your little doggie." Rawston's terminology. Because he wanted her to know. Not triable proof, though. She could do nothing.

Just as he wanted.

She reached for the bottle, and the telephone buzzed.

"Professor North?"

"Yes?" she said, disappointed by the voice.

She'd thought it might be Mike Bolknor.

"It's Stacey Gillibrand, and I…."

"Yes, Stacey?"

"Your dog…."

"Yes Stacey?"

Silence. Cooper waited. Finally the woman spoke again.

"What color was its fur—I saw the dog, in your office, but I forget."

"White," Cooper said. "And butterscotch."

An indrawn breath.

"On his sweater sleeve!"

"Yes?"

Silence again.

Cooper heard Stacey breathing, then finally speak.

"Damn!"

Breathing again.

"He better tell me."

Said almost in a whisper. Then, a shout.

"He better!"

"Stacey...."

She spoke to a dial tone.

Cooper didn't know what else to do so she finished off the quarter-bottle of scotch. Then she fell asleep on the living room sofa.

She awoke to clarity.

She sat up on the sofa and stared out the window, through the phalanx of curbside maple trees, at Hill Street. No black motorcycle had stopped out there, in the morning light, its red-headed driver turned to leer at her in the window, but even so....

He'd made his demand.

Get drunk. Stand, wobbling, on city hall's steps. Announce your unworthiness to your assembled fellow citizens.

Do that, he'd said, and save your little doggie.

She couldn't. She'd known all along she couldn't.

Too much New England vinegar in her. Too much Bethany North.

She couldn't do it even to save Henry.

Not only that. Rawston had no truth in him. If she obeyed him, maybe he'd return the dog—dead, on her doorstep. Got back your little doggie, right? As per our agreement? More likely, he'd simply think up new humiliations to force her to perform.

So she wouldn't do it. Couldn't do it.

What she could do—fiercely—was fight.

And he'd erred.

When she'd awakened this morning, achy headed, mouth tasting as if she'd eaten garbage, she'd imagined Rawston, in his apartment, exulting. She'd sent him to prison, so she must be abased. Now he'd made it happen. He was puppet master! Horse breaker!

In his elation, though, he'd slipped up. He didn't vet his plan, not down to its molecular level.

Just one small mistake. Maybe it wouldn't save the dog. Even so, he'd feel the counter-stroke, know they were onto him. Rattled, he might reveal a clue to where he'd hidden Henry. And if she proved it, that he'd stolen the dog, there'd be an indictment. A trial. And, given his record, jail.

Finally, she could do something.

She saw the emptied scotch bottle lying on the carpet, beside the sofa, where she'd dropped it. She leaned down, gripped it by the neck, and carried it to the kitchen recycling bin.

I'm not going down this road, she thought.

Not again.

Her father had been a drinker. And his father before him. They'd both kept it under control. Bankers. Successful. Yet, all those emptied liquor bottles. As a child, Cooper had resented seeing her father drunk in the evening, smelling of whiskey, felt shamed by it, but then, later in life, the urge had come upon her, too, and she couldn't resist.

She thought: I can resist now.

She pulled on her jacket and grabbed the manila envelope containing Henry's photograph and Rawston's note, and pulled the two unopened bottles of scotch out

199

of the kitchen cabinet. Then she marched out to the car—envelope tucked under one arm, a bottle clenched in each hand—and dropped everything onto the passenger's seat, and walked back up the stoop, cane stabbing the walkway's slates, because she'd left the house's door ajar.

Now she shut it. And locked it.

After that, she drove onto the campus, past the Hiram North Gymnasium and the Dill Industries Nanotechnology Laboratory, and the Audrey Topper Liberal Arts Classroom Center, too fast, and stopped behind the cafeteria, next to the dumpster. She got out and walked around the car and pulled opened the passenger door. She grabbed one scotch bottle's neck, turned, and stared at the dumpster. Then, abruptly, she lofted the bottle up and over the dumpster's side. Inside, it thudded. She grasped the other bottle, stood a moment, then tossed it, too, over the side. This one hit something hard inside, and cracked.

She stood looking at nothing in particular. Then she made a sound like a snarl and got into the car again. She drove back through the campus, still too fast, and down Slope Drive to Main Street, and turned left.

At the Dill Police Station, she parked in a visitor slot, facing the building's windowless brick backside. She got out of the car, threw open the station's door, and surged through, left hand gripping the manila envelope, right hand wielding her cane as if it were a cudgel, whacking the tile floor. It sounded like pistol shots, and Eddie Pike, manning the desk, jerked up his head, startled.

Chief's in his office, he told her. In a meeting.

So Cooper took a seat where she could watch the rookie officer pretend to busy himself with paperwork, mainly for her benefit, she guessed. Probably, when Eddie got scolded for failing to keep a steady watch on Rawston, her name came up.

She waited, the manila envelope resting on her lap.

She thought about Stacey Gillibrand's call—clearly Stacey saw Henry's fur on Rawston's sweater sleeve. So he'd duped her, claiming he hadn't taken the dog. She'd believed him. Now she knew, and it enraged her. Would she switch sides, though? Say what she knew? Cooper wasn't sure. Stacey made no secret of believing Cooper persecuted Rawston. So maybe she'd confront him, shout at him, then let it pass. Or maybe, if they were lucky, she'd threaten to tell, unless he gave back the dog, and that would finally rattle him.

Cooper thought: let her stew. Try this first. If it fizzles, then lean on Stacey Gillibrand.

Five minutes later, Tip's door opened and he stepped out, about to say something to Eddie Pike, but then he saw Cooper sitting on the visitors' bench.

"Coop?" he said.

"I've got something," she said.

"Jeezum Crow," he said. "Why didn't you come on in?"

He shot a dark look at Eddie Pike.

"Eddie suggested that," Cooper lied, "but I decided to wait."

She saw Eddie look at her with gratitude.

"Well, what's up?" LaPerle said, holding open his office door for her.

Mike Bolknor sat inside. A large sheet of paper lay across Tip's desk—a map of the Mt. Augustus College campus—which they'd clearly been going over.

"Our new security cameras," Bolknor told her. "Thought we'd coordinate."

His voice, expressionless, as usual, didn't hint at what she'd seen in front of his apartment house, the face of a man who'd looked into hell. She sensed it, though, underneath, deep despair.

It occurred to her that Tip LaPerle seemed less resentful of Bolknor. And credit for that, she realized, went to the Campus Security chief. He'd been working at it quietly, must have been, like right now, making it a point to coordinate with Tip, on the beefed-up new campus video-surveillance system.

Good, she thought. Let's coordinate. Let's all get along.

She showed them the manila envelope with its one-word address: "North." Then she opened it and pulled out the photograph of Henry in his cage and the note. She laid them on the table.

Tip picked up the photograph and studied it. Bolknor read the note, expressionless, then handed it to Tip, and looked at the photograph.

Tip abruptly threw down the note and slammed his fist onto his desk.

"Bastard!" he said.

She could see him mentally getting out his handcuffs.

"Tip, remember that ordinance the mayor pushed through?" Cooper said. "No circulars tacked onto telephone poles? Slipped under windshield wipers?"

She could see Tip thinking.

"Too much litter," he said. "Doesn't look good, right? Public nuisance."

They sat looking at each other. Out the corner of her eye, Cooper saw Mike Bolknor eyeing them both, puzzled. Suddenly, though, he grabbed the note off the desk and reread it, then nodded.

Coordination, Cooper thought.

Later that day, after Tip's officers began returning from street patrol, Cooper felt a guilty pang, because the perps they brought in—caught red handed tacking circulars to telephone poles and sliding them under car windshield wipers—were seven boy scouts and their troop leader.

All seven boys and their scoutmaster, Emmet Monaghan, stood in a row against the wall, in their scout uniforms, feet shuffling, eyes darting around.

"Jeezum Crow!" Tip shouted. "City ordinances, Emmet—they get published, don't they? Right in the *Chronicle!*"

Here we go, Cooper thought. Tip LaPerle in full kick-up-dirt-with-your-hooves mode, because he's got Sonny Rawston smoldering in his brain, but these are just kids, for Pete's sake, and Emmet Monaghan, and you're scaring the pants off them.

Emmet, scarecrow thin, nearly bald, with a few wisps of gray hair, stood looking at his shoes. He'd been in Mona's class at school, and Cooper had vaguely known him, small-town fashion, most of his life. He hadn't actually been picked on, except by his father, a burly garbage truck driver, who despised his puny son as an affront to his own bull-moose gametes, but nobody had noticed Emmet much in school, so he'd been disregarded and invited to nothing. Afterwards he'd worked at Dill Hardware, as a clerk, all the while taking night courses at Community College of Vermont, earning an associate's degree in accounting, and ever since he'd worked in Dill Industries' payroll department. Emmet volunteered for all sorts of community projects, like the Boy Scouts, and still never received much notice or thanks.

"Tip, do you mind if I ask Emmet a few questions?" Cooper said mildly.

Dill's police chief shot her a suddenly sheepish look, an expression she knew from her days as Allen County state's attorney. It meant he'd suddenly realized he'd rampaged into a china shop, bellowing, and needed Cooper to extricate him, before the floor got littered with broken plates and vases.

"Yeah, and don't worry, Emmet, okay?" he said. "Nobody's getting the chair here."

And that, Cooper thought, is as close as Tip LaPerle ever gets to making nice. She turned to look at Emmet Monaghan, and smiled.

"We need your help, Emmet, that's all," she said. "You and your scouts."

She could see eight sets of scared eyes looking at her with hope. No jail time for them?

"Somebody's trying to commit a hoax, a fraud," she said. "It's whoever's behind those fliers."

Emmet, on autopilot, reached into his pocket and pulled out one of the circulars, crumpled up. He straightened it out and stared at it, as if his fate depended on what it said.

"Can I have a look?" Cooper asked, holding out her hand, and Emmet gave her the flier, cautiously, the way you might hand over a live grenade.

For the benefit of Bolknor and LaPerle, she read it aloud:

"To All Citizens of Dill, Vermont—

"Ms. Cooper North, former state's attorney and attorney general and supreme court judge, wishes to share with everybody in town an important message about herself and her character.

"Please gather in front of City Hall tomorrow at one a.m. and Ms. North will appear on the steps and tell you all what she wishes to say.

"Be there—you'll be talking about it for years."

Cooper handed it to Tip LaPerle, who scanned it, and handed it to Mike Bolknor, who glanced at it, then laid it on LaPerle's desk, atop the heap of circulars the patrol officers had confiscated from the scouts and retrieved from telephone poles and windshield wipers. Cooper saw Emmet Monaghan's left eyelid beginning to twitch.

"I thought it was you," he said, giving Cooper a pleading look. "Wanting us to hand these out."

He said he'd received a telephone call, a man's voice, asking: would the Scouts be interested in distributing public-service notices around town? If you do it, he said, there'll be a two-hundred-dollar donation for the troop.

205

"It would fund our camporee," Emmet said. "It's next June."

And then, voice sounding in pain: "Do we have to give it back?"

Cooper told him no, and for the first time he looked almost relaxed. He said he'd found the heap of circulars to distribute on his doorstep, along with the money, in cash, in an envelope.   On the envelope somebody had written: "To the Dill Boy Scout troop, from Cooper North, for services to be rendered."

"It just seemed okay," Emmet said. "I thought it was you."

"That voice on the telephone," Cooper said. "Recognize it?"

Emmet shook his head, chagrinned.

"He had a sort of accent," he said. "I don't know what, just sort of funny."

Disguising his voice, Cooper thought.

"Anything else?" Cooper asked.

Emmet shook his head, eyes plaintive. He clearly wanted to help, but could think of nothing to offer.

"Mr. Monaghan?"

Mike Bolknor suddenly speaking. Cooper could see Emmet looking apprehensive again. Big man, deep voice, scary.

"Over the telephone, did you hear any background noise? Any sounds?"

Emmet scrunched up his face, to show he was thinking. Then he unscrunched.

"Yes!"

They all looked at him.

"A dog barked," he said.

Cooper felt a stab of relief. At least Henry was still alive.

"Also, a sort of grinding sound, kind of far off," Emmet said. "Or maybe it was more like a whooshing."

"Did it sound like water, then?" Bolknor asked. "Maybe like a waterfall?"

Emmet stood vacant eyed, remembering the sound. Then his eyes focused again.

"No, not like that," he said. "I don't know what it was."

Tip LaPerle's patrolmen reported they'd removed all the circulars the scouts had posted. So not much damage done on that score.

"What the hell's that grinding sound supposed to be?" Tip asked, after the scouts left, but got only shrugs.

Cooper thought they'd made less progress than she'd hoped. And she doubted they could coax any more out of Emmet Monaghan and his troop.

"Ideas?" she said.

"Yes." Bolknor said. "Where'd this jobless guy, just out of the penitentiary, get two-hundred dollars in cash?"

No answers to that.

"Where'd he print up those circulars?" LaPerle asked. "Maybe get him that way?"

Cooper said she doubted it. Almost surely he used some public computer and printer out of town, probably out of the county. There wouldn't be fingerprints, either. Not when he could buy latex dishwashing gloves at any convenience store.

Nobody argued that.

All right, Cooper thought. Stacey Gillibrand, you're up next.

CHAPTER TWENTY-SIX

That afternoon she taught an Evidence Analysis Class on polygraph tests. She'd planned to corner Stacey afterwards, but Jerry Shapiro and Chip Stack got to Cooper first.

Stack: "Lie detectors, they're okay in all courts?"

Shapiro: "Seriously? Spike a graph line, get sent to Sing-Sing?"

They had other questions: What if you pop tranquilizers before getting wired up? What if you're just naturally stressed? Can you be forced to get polygraphed?

Cooper thought, good. Future cops and lawyers, actively interested in their trades' tools. So she couldn't shoo them away. While she answered their questions, though, she saw Stacey slip out of the classroom, glancing back over her shoulder as she hurried out the door. It looked to Cooper as if the woman meant to avoid talking with her about yesterday's telephone call.

Cooper thought: all right, Missy. We'll talk later—your pal Sonny's got my dog. Probably he's starving that dog, and snapping photos with his cell phone, to prove it. And you know he's doing it. So, yes, we'll talk.

And then she thought: watch out! I'll drive down and thump a ladder against your house. I'll climb up and smash your window with my cane. I'll burst into your apartment, and then, Sweetie, you bet you'll to talk to me. Here I come.

Thinking that made her feel better.

Or I'll wire you up to a polygraph!

Still, in her mind, she heard the grandfather's clock by her house's staircase. Tick, tick, tick....

How must Henry be feeling, caged, in a strange place, alone, hungry?

She thought about calling Berry Randolph, at the All Creatures Clinic, to ask how long a dog of Henry's size could survive without food. She decided to wait, though, not sure she really wanted to know. Also, letting information out might muddle the investigation. Just now Sonny Rawston would be digesting Cooper's refusal to play his game, and she didn't want to disturb his digestion

She wondered, though: did she partly want to call Berry because Mona Dill Saunders wasn't here? Did she want a stand-in confidante, someone she liked and respected?

That annoyed her.

Later, at home, she thought about lie-detector tests.

Not about vodka martinis. Not about single-malt scotch.

She told herself, wryly: congratulations!

She immediately recoiled, because praising herself for not thinking about liquor was, in itself, thinking about liquor, a stealth thought, and she knew where it might lead.

This would be hard, walking this stony road, twisting like a snake. She knew, because she'd walked it before, and lurched off. Not this time, though. She felt her will tightening. No more stumbles.

So she resumed thinking about lie-detector tests.

She'd like to summon a Vermont State Police polygraph expert from Waterbury. She wished she still had the authority. She'd like to wire up certain people, ask targeted questions, then see what happened to their pulse and blood pressure and respiratory rate and sweatiness.

Sonny Rawston.

Did you shoot at me? Hire someone else to shoot at me?

Who's that biker with shoulder-length gray hair and a gray beard? Your creature?

Where's my dog? Stacey saw his fur on your sweater sleeve. Is he in your apartment building? Some other building in town? She'd keep naming possible hiding spots, until she named the right one, and he denied it, and the graph lines spiked.

And how do you support yourself, with no job and no money in the bank?

Jack Abbott.

Why flat-out refuse to tell Tip LaPerle what rent you're charging Rawston? Are you two in cahoots on something? And you're after my property, for the college's new AI Research Center. You'd make millions. Would you shoot me for it? Actually?

Nessie Greffier.

Do you truly hate me enough to blow me away?

And why'd you get a visit from Sonny Rawston?

Cooper shook her head.

Polygraphs had their limits. For one, psychopaths can trick them. They can lie coolly, triggering no graph spikes. They feel no stress lying. No guilt. They feel no guilt about anything.

Mike Bolknor.

You, too, colleague.

No polygraph, but please say why you're so depressed. Tell the truth. I want to work with you and trust you. I worry that something made you run away from New York, maybe something you did. So I need to know.

She sighed.

Then she threw a frozen Thai dinner into the microwave and loaded a tumbler with ice cubes, from the refrigerator, and poured it full of water.

Adam's ale, on the rocks.

As she ate, alone at her kitchen table, a sudden gust rattled her window, and something scraped. Lilac twigs, she realized, rubbing against the house's bricks, in the wind. Abruptly, rain spattered the window over the sink.

She thought: another dark and stormy night.

At six-thirty she watched the local news on tv, hardly paying attention, feeling tense. It's the storm, she told herself. And because I'm not finding Henry. Stacey had slipped away from her, after class, so she needed to drive down there, confront the woman. Do it tonight, she told herself. I'll drive down around eight, when she's back in her apartment, studying.

On the screen, Dill's mayor appeared wearing a Santa Claus hat, to make an announcement: we're planning a Merry Dill Christmas! There'll be promotions, like rides along Main Street in sleighs, drawn by Percherons! He smiled enthusiastically into the camera. We'll make Dill the go-to place for Christmas shopping! And we'll attract tourists, too! Come on up from New York and Boston! Celebrate with us! An old-fashioned New England Christmas!

Cooper raised an ironical eyebrow. Mentally, she admonished the mayor's hoped-for winter tourists: wear long johns! Bring battery heated socks! Don't forget snowshoes!

Next, a perky meteorologist, faking a concerned frown, admonished viewers to stay inside if they could, because it was near freezing outside, raining, mixed with sleet. She pretended to shiver. And then a notice flashed: "Breaking News."

Abruptly the screen showed police cars drawn up at odd angles, under trees, both Dill PD and Campus Security. Now the camera focused in on a newswoman, wearing earmuffs and a raincoat, and speaking into a hand-held microphone.

"We've just learned there's been an incident on the Mt. Augustus College campus, although the police are giving no information just yet!"

Tip LaPerle appeared on camera, looking grim.

"We'll issue a report shortly."

Reporter again: "We'll be back when we know more—now, we return to our regularly scheduled newscast."

213

Cooper muted the sound and sat staring at the television screen, trying to guess where on campus the patrol cars had congregated. No lecture halls appeared on the screen, or laboratories or dorms, just lots of trees.

It's the Arbor, she thought.

That was just beyond the library, where a descendent of Augustus Dill planted specimen trees, a hundred-fifty years ago, a living exhibit, just about every species of northeastern tree. A walkway wound through the Arbor, starting at the library and ending on Hill Street, at the campus entrance. When Franklin Dill Witherall opened the Arbor, he announced it was to be a place "where professors and students might peacefully ambulate, while contemplating nature and all of Creation," but modern students dubbed it "the Witherall Amour Preserve." It had streetlights, but widely spaced.

Her telephone rang.

"Cooper—it's Mike Bolknor."

He used a cell phone, she guessed. His voice sounded hollow.

"We're just past the library," he said. "You should be here."

CHAPTER TWENTY-SEVEN

Cooper parked her Volvo behind the last cruiser in the line of patrol cars and turned off the engine, freezing the windshield wipers in mid swipe. As she got out, a gust drove cold rain against her face, mixed with stinging sleet.

Luckily, she'd heard the tv weather report and she'd swathed herself, sweater, parka, slicker. She pulled her cane out of the passenger side, then reached back in and grabbed a neon-yellow Paddington Bear rain hat and put that on, not caring that she looked faintly ludicrous.

Far up the line of cruisers, she saw a crowd of officers, one a head above all the others. Mike Bolknor. She started forward, carefully, because of the sleet on the sidewalk, and because she suddenly guessed what she'd see, and dreaded it.

She glimpsed yellow crime-scene tape up ahead, but couldn't see anything else, because of all the blue uniforms milling around, while a photographer snapped flash pictures from various angles. As she shouldered her way through to the front, a siren wailed and a State Police van from Waterbury pulled in and double parked. After a moment its two front doors swung open and the rear doors slid back and four crime-lab technicians got out, three men and a woman, each automatically looking up to see the source of the rain and sleet pelting them, as if it were unexpected, even though they'd just driven across half the state listening to the wipers clack.

Cooper realized she'd forgotten to wear boots. Her sneakers had already soaked through.

She made her way to Mike Bolknor, at the front of the crowd, and stood beside him. He didn't look at her, and said nothing. He stood staring at the ground, rain running down his face, and she, too, stared at the patch of ground, enclosed by the crime-scene tape.

Her stomach lurched. Not because she'd never before seen a body, seen blood. Hardly that.

As state's attorney, on every serious case, she'd routinely worked closely with the police. She'd always arrived at the crime scene, whatever the hour, worked with the troopers or Tip LaPerle on strategies for collecting evidence.

It was different with the man currently serving as Allen County State's Attorney. He worked hands off— don't get involved until the police finish investigating, then evaluate their evidence, decide if prosecution is viable.

Privately, she thought he was lazy, but she never mentioned it to Tip LaPerle or anyone else. Allen County kept reelecting him, so she had nothing to say.

Still, she'd never worked that way. So she'd seen crime scenes, hundreds of them, and bodies.

But this time she knew the victim.

She heard Bolknor mutter to himself: "Campus Security!"

It sounded like a curse.

"Don't be a jerk," Cooper snapped.

They stood silently then, staring down. Bolknor, one handed, wiped rain from his eyes.

Tip LaPerle sloshed up beside them, wearing just his soaked uniform, looking chilled.

"Jeezum Crow," he said.

She lay on her back.

Cooper thought: no, Campus Security didn't drop this ball. Not you, Mike. It was me. I let this happen.

Lights set up by the police made everything stark—the rain-soaked fallen leaves, the walkway's slates, the body.

A bullet wound in her forehead seeped blood.

It ran down her face, into her blond hair, which lay spread out around her head, wet and lank. Blood had pooled on the slates, but the bleeding had already almost stopped, with no pumping heart to ooze it out of the body, and the rain had already diluted the blood, turning it from red to pale rose.

Her cornflower blue-eyes stared straight up into the rain. Raindrops fell on those eyes, and sleet, but they didn't blink.

Cooper supposed the shooter had lurked up ahead, and the force of the bullet to her forehead toppled her backwards.

She'd been wearing her red knapsack, but that had been pulled out from under her, off to one side, opened, its books and printouts strewn on the ground.

Somebody went through that stuff, Cooper thought. What did they take?

A memory: Stacey, standing up in class, expounding her certainty about a wrongful prosecution, eighteen years ago, in Hart's Corners. Those blue eyes intense with conviction, but even so she'd tossed her head, to swirl the blond hair, looking cute. Needing to be admired. Most eyes in the class turned up at the grandstanding, and Stacey ignored them, argued on. Because it wasn't grandstanding after all. Not entirely.

She meant to right a miscarriage of the judicial system. More than anything, that's what she'd wanted.

Cooper thought: and I dismissed her as self-adoring twerp.

There'd been so much life in this one. And will. And hope. And need to prove her worth. And she irritated me.

I chose to be annoyed.

And that made me stupid.

Her body seemed a wax dummy, empty inside. Stacey Gillibrand was gone.

"Jeezum," Tip LaPerle said. "Anybody got ideas?"

"Yes!" Cooper said. "Let's get to Sonny Rawston, right now."

They rode downtown together in Tip LaPerle's patrol car, Cooper riding shotgun and Mike Bolknor sitting in back, filling up the space and looking so grim he was scary. Cooper's slicker dripped rainwater onto the seat and LaPerle's uniform smelled like wet dog and everything in the car felt cold and damp.

Cooper sighed and watched the wipers thwack rain and slush off the windshield, sounding like her house's old grandfather's clock, beside the stairs, ticking.

LaPerle turned left off Slope Drive, onto Main Street. Cooper wished he'd switch on the siren, giving voice to a sound inside her, a silent wail.

Tip said: "By the way, penitentiary people finally reported—remember? Rawston's prison buddies? Gray beard, long gray hair? Shooter for hire?"

Nobody said anything.

"Well, nada," LaPerle said. "Nothing. Nobody like that."

Silence again as the car moved slowly along Main Street, the pavement glistening with rain and accumulating slush. At the apartment house where Rawston lived, the police chief muttered, "Oh, hell," and abruptly made an illegal U-turn and parked in front of the house, facing back toward the center of town, behind Rawston's motorcycle. It hardly mattered, because theirs was the only car moving along the street tonight.

As they headed for the house's porch steps, Mike Bolknor put his hand on the motorcycle's engine.

"Warm," he said.

Inside the house, Cooper held up a hand, for them to stop, and then knocked on the downstairs neighbor's door, with its hand-scrawled card tacked to the doorframe: "Hubert LeGrande." They waited in silence.

Finally, the door opened, and the retired quarryman stood blinking at them, rheumy eyed, in a threadbare bathrobe. He wheezed, from silicosis.

He looked from Cooper to the police chief, in his blue uniform, soaked with rain, and then at the big man, in a dark suit, grim, standing behind them both, then back to Cooper.

"Sorry to bother you again, Mr. LeGrande," Cooper said. "Do you mind answering a question about your neighbor upstairs?"

LeGrande shrugged, glancing again at the police chief. Cooper could see new interest in his eyes. This was police business. Better than tv and a couple of beers and a fried-up sausage from the convenience store across the street. Cooper could smell the after-odor of his sausage-and-beer dinner, wafting through the apartment's open door.

"We're wondering if you've heard anything from your neighbor today, especially this evening?" Cooper asked.

LeGrande blinked at them.

"This about what's been on the tv?" he said. "Somebody at the college, getting shot like that?"

"Just routine questions," Cooper said. "Have you heard him going in or out tonight?"

LeGrande's eyes looked at each of them, finally resting on Mike Bolknor.

"Who's that big guy there?" he said.

"Mr. Bolknor heads up Campus Security, at the college," Cooper said. "Now, if…."

"Had a cousin that big," LeGrande said. "Six-five, something like that—got run over by a freight locomotive, working the trains, loading up cars, and...."

"Sorry to hear that," Cooper said. "Now, about your neighbor...."

"Getting too damned cold for that motorcycle he drives," LeGrande said. "Guess that's all he's got, though."

Cooper suppressed impatience

"About his comings and goings," she said. "Have you…"

"Roared off this morning," LeGrande said. "You'd think they'd make them put mufflers on those things...."

He shot an accusing look at Tip LaPerle.

"Came roaring back a couple hours later, something like that, before lunch, anyway, went clumping up the stairs."

Cooper thought: off to visit the dog? She hoped so. Maybe even to feed him.

She sighed.

LeGrande stood looking at them, his eyes red and irritated. Cooper thought he'd told them all he had to say, but then he spoke again.

"Damned noisy that thing."

Silence. More staring. And then LeGrande offered a final observation, as if he'd been saving it up.

"Went out one more time," he said.

He stood looking at them, wheezing.

"About dark," he said.

Cooper looked back at LaPerle and Bolknor, making sure they registered it: Rawston had driven off on his motorcycle, just before Stacey Gillibrand got shot.

"Got back about an hour ago," LeGrande said. "Around when the local news finished up, or maybe just after they started the big news, you know, out of the network, terrorists and all that."

Cooper thought: Rawston rode off on his bike just before Stacey's murder. And just after the shooting, he came back here.

She glanced again at Bolknor and LaPerle. Then she turned back to the downstairs neighbor.

"If you think of anything else, call Chief LaPerle, at the police station, okay?"

"Yeah, sure," he said.

They turned and started up the stairs. Cooper led, followed by LaPerle. Bolknor's shoes sounded heavy on the treads. Halfway up the stairs, Cooper turned and saw Hubert LeGrande still in the doorway, watching them. She started to turn around, but then LeGrande spoke.

"Just that other thing," he said.

He sounded distant, standing at the bottom of the stairway.

"Just that blond woman came over, from next door," LeGrande said.

Cooper could see he parceled out his information on purpose, a little at a time. It added interest to his lonely day. She looked at him, waiting.

"About three o'clock, maybe, or four, I don't know," LeGrande said.

He stood blinking up at them, where they stood on the stairs.

222

They waited.

He grimaced, wetting his lips with his tongue, looking up. Finally he spoke again.

"They had a doozy of an argument," he said.

"Rawston yelled at her?" Cooper said, unconsciously raising her voice, to talk down the stairs.

"Nope," he said. "Could hardly hear him—it was her doing all the yelling."

"Did it sound as if he hit her?" Cooper asked.

More staring up, blinking.

"Nope," he said. "Just her yelling, really ticked off about something—and then I heard the door slam, and her rushing down the stairs and out the front door."

"Anything else, after that?" Cooper asked.

"Nope," he said.

They stood looking down at him, from halfway up the stairs.

"Thank you," Cooper said, giving Bolknor and LaPerle a glance.

LeGrande nodded and watched them walk up, blinking, and Cooper had the feeling he wished he could dredge up something else to tell them. It was entertaining.

Sonny Rawston opened the door as soon as they knocked, as if he'd been waiting for them. Probably saw the patrol car park out front, Cooper guessed.

"What's the harassment du jour?" he said.

He said it straight-faced, as if asking a waiter about the evening's specials, sincerely interested.

"Questions," Tip LaPerle said. "May we come in?"

Cooper saw Rawston hesitate, probably ready to demand to see a warrant. Then, almost imperceptibly, he shrugged, and looked wry.

He thinks this is going to be fun, Cooper thought. He thinks he's going to talk us into a corner, and leave us humiliated.

"That dog again?" he asked.

He shook his head at Cooper, making a sad face.

Cooper thought: as if my concern for Henry shows I'm unbalanced. And he feels sympathy for the batty old lady.

Rawston stepped aside from the doorway and gestured with his arm, a theatrical flourish, ushering them in.

Cooper thought: welcome to my humble abode, Three Stooges, come in and amuse me with tomfoolery.

He's in control, Cooper thought. That's what he believes.

Rawston pulled out a chair from the kitchen table and sat. He didn't offer them chairs, so they continued to stand.

"Want to search the apartment, all over again, for your little doggie?" he asked Cooper, and she saw cold amusement in his blue eyes.

Nobody answered him, so he leaned back in his chair, waiting.

Tip LaPerle glanced at Cooper, and Cooper glanced back, one eyebrow raised, a signal they'd evolved long ago, meaning the Dill police chief should handle the questioning, at least for now. They hadn't worked it out overtly. It just arose, shortly after Tip became police chief, and they'd used it for years. And this was Tip LaPerle's turf.

"You rode off on your motorcycle tonight, around dark, six or thereabouts," Tip said. "Where'd you go?"

Rawston stared at him, as if dumbfounded by the question. Pretending to be, anyway. Or maybe not pretending. Cooper couldn't tell.

"Why are you hectoring a citizen?" Rawston said.

"We're requesting your help with an investigation," LaPerle said.

Rawston looked at the three of them in silence. They waited. Finally LaPerle spoke again.

"So you won't say where you went?"

"What's that supposed to mean?" Rawston said.

"That you seem to be hiding something," LaPerle said.

Silence again. Cooper could see Rawston considering it, turning it over in his mind.

"I went to look at used cars," he said.

"Which dealership?" LaPerle asked.

"None," Rawston said.

They waited.

"Everything's closed up, it turned out," Rawston said. "And it's raining, and it's getting too cold for the bike, so I came back."

"You didn't hear the weather report on tv?" LaPerle asked.

"I hardly ever watch tv," Rawston said. "How about you, Chief? Big tube fan?"

"So, used-car shopping," LaPerle said. "Anybody who can verify that?"

225

Rawston turned up his palms, and sighed, as if it were one pointless question beyond endurance.

"I verify it myself," he said. "Gentleman's word."

"What about Stacey Gillibrand," LaPerle said. "Could she verify where you went?"

"How would she know?" Rawston said.

Cooper couldn't read his expression.

"Is this still about that dog?" Rawston said.

"You and Stacey argued earlier this afternoon," LaPerle said. "Was that about the dog?"

Rawston looked stony. Cooper sensed his mental gears turning.

"Nah," he said. "She asked me to help her write some class paper, and I said I wouldn't."

He still looked blank, but behind that Cooper sensed triumph. He'd sidestepped them, quickly figured out how.

"Because that would be cheating, wouldn't it?" he said, piously. "I couldn't do that, you know, and then she blew up—Women! Right?"

They all stared at him.

"She tell you something different?" he asked.

Cooper suddenly spoke: "We need to look at your sweaters."

Rawston's gaze hardened.

"That's just a bit intrusive, isn't it?" he said.

"You don't want us to examine your sweaters' sleeves?" Cooper said. "You have some reason?"

"My reason is I'm sick of being hassled by you people," Rawston said.

226

Cooper said: "Stacey yelled at you this afternoon—did she threaten to tell the police she found my dog's fur on your sweater's sleeve?"

Rawston stared at her, silent, but hate in his eyes, and anger.

"How do you have enough money to buy a new car?" Tip LaPerle asked. "Even a used one?"

"That's between me and my chief financial officer," Rawston said. "Privileged information."

"How'd you get that motorcycle?" Tip asked.

No response, except a stony stare.

"There's a rifle holster attached to that bike's saddle," LaPerle said. "Where's the rifle?"

"That holster just came with the machine," Rawston said. "I don't do guns."

"How are you paying for this apartment?" LaPerle said.

"Privileged," Rawston said. "I want you all out."

"You're a person of interest in a murder investigation," LaPerle said.

For the first time Rawston looked unsure.

"As far as we know, you were the last person to see her alive," LaPerle said. "And you argued—she yelled at you."

Rawston stared at them.

"Stacey?" he said.

He looked stunned, but Cooper couldn't tell if it was real or a good acting job. Finally, he spoke, his face so tight his voice sounded like a hiss.

"Get a warrant."

And, as they walked out, he added: "Watch out— I'll sue for harassment."

227

They stood on the apartment house's front porch, looking across the street at DeBouche's Gas 'n Groceries. Fluorescent light shining out the front window gave the parking lot's rain-soaked macadam a spectral sheen. No cars in the lot tonight.

Through the window they could see the clerk sitting at the counter, reading a magazine, in the unnatural light. She looked lonely

Sleet no longer fell, and the rain had abated. Just a cold drizzle now.

"Black-ice weather," LaPerle muttered. "They never think about that, drive like nutballs."

No cars passed, though. It seemed like a deserted town.

"First thing when we get back, I'll check what was in Stacey's backpack," Cooper said. "Whatever the shooter didn't take."

"What's he looking for?" Tip asked.

Cooper suddenly cursed.

"What?" Tip said.

"Her apartment!" Cooper said, already halfway down the porch steps.

After a moment, LaPerle and Bolknor clomped down the steps after her and followed her to the house next door.

Cooper pressed the doorbell button, and they waited.

After a while a stooped woman, her white hair clipped short, shapeless in a powder-blue sweat suit, opened the door and stood looking up at them, through silver-rimmed bifocals. Her red-rimmed eyes made Cooper think she'd been weeping, as the woman glanced at Bolknor, then stared at Tip LaPerle's uniform.

"You're the police chief," she said.

She stood off kilter, and Cooper saw that her right leg twisted inward. Cooper's left leg mostly felt like lead, because of her youthful bout with polio, but this woman's situation seemed much worse. Arthritis, Cooper guessed. Not just in that right knee. Shoulders, too, from the way she hunched. Probably in her elbows. And she kept her fingers clenched, the knuckles painfully enlarged. Her blue eyes, though, remained sharp, although red.

"I know why you're here," she said.

"Would you allow us to look at your tenant's apartment?" Tip asked.

"They didn't say who it was, on the television," she said. "They showed her, though, lying there on the ground, getting rained on, and it was the clothes she wore, when she left here this morning, and that red backpack of hers, and I cried, because she was a good girl—I hope she didn't suffer."

"Yes, a good girl," Cooper heard herself say. "She died instantly, no pain."

"Why?" the woman asked.

"We're trying to find out," Cooper said, and started to introduce herself, but the woman interrupted.

"I read the papers and I know who you are," she said. "I watch the tv news."

"This man directs Campus Security at the college," Cooper said, putting a hand on Mike Bolknor's arm. "We need to look at Stacey's rooms."

"I'm Marjorie Olson and I'm eighty-four years old and my husband and I never had kids, although we wanted to, and he's long gone," she said. "Stacey brought energy to this home, and hope, and decency, and I wished she'd been my daughter."

Mrs. Olson's eyes focused far off, and her lower lip trembled. Cooper feared she would cry.

"Are you all right?" Cooper asked, as mildly as she could.

Mrs. Olson looked down, stopping the tremble in her lower lip. Then she looked up at Cooper.

"Like this evening," she said. "I went over to DeBouche's for tea and a dozen eggs for tomorrow's breakfast—every morning I make breakfast and Stacey helps and we eat together—but I left the front door wide open, I do things like that, now, and didn't notice until I got back from the store, and if Stacey was still with me she'd have taken care of that and never mentioned it to me."

Again the unfocused look towards something far away.

"She'd gotten to be friends with that Sonny Rawston next door," she said. "His parents were alright, but he was a sly boots, even as a little boy, and I told Stacey...."

She sighed.

"Go up there and look," she said. "You won't be bothering that poor girl now."

And, as the three of them started up the stairs, they heard Mrs. Olson down below in the foyer tell them: "I haven't been up there in a long time, because of my leg, so don't mind any dust please."

As they reached the top of the stairs, from down below, they heard a near whisper: "That poor girl."

Stacey's apartment turned out to be the small house's entire second story—bedroom, bathroom, second bedroom, which Stacey used as a study room. They stopped at the top of the stairs looking from room to room.

"Jeezum!" Tip said.

Skirts flung onto the floor. Slacks. Sweaters. Cardboard boxes emptied of the papers they'd held, now strewn across the carpet. Drawers left open, or completely pulled out and thrown on the floor. Sofa cushions pulled off and thrown on the floor. A thorough ransacking.

Mike Bolknor, eyes on the chaos, reached into his suit jacket's pocket and extracted three pairs of latex gloves. As he handed them around, Cooper saw irritation in Tip LaPerle's face and she guessed why: they'd all been suddenly summoned to the crime scene, but only the big-city cop anticipated handling evidence. And he hadn't brought gloves just for himself. He'd thought of that, too.

Or maybe he always carried gloves, just in case.

It miffed Tip. He accepted the gloves, though.

They each pulled on the gloves while gazing fixedly at the devastation.

It looked as if a hungry bear had ransacked the rooms. Blouses and jeans hung from opened drawers. Beside the dresser, in heaps, lay bras and bikini briefs, in black and in fruit colors, grape, lime, lemon, strawberry. It angered Cooper, seeing Stacey's undergarments exposed like this. Strangers weren't supposed to see these.

Her closet had been emptied, too, and coats and jackets lay twisted on the carpet and across the bed, the sleeves at odd angles. It looked like carnage. Even her bathroom had been searched, perfumed soaps and scent bottles and bottles of eye drops and aspirin swept out of the medicine cabinet and jumbled in the sink, and on the tiles. Cooper saw a prescription bottle of lorazepam, 1 mg., a common drug for easing anxiety and stress.

"Poor Stacey," she thought.

She picked the bottle up and studied it—it had been prescribed by a physician in Stacey's home city, Pittsburgh, and Cooper pulled out the pen and small pad she routinely kept in a pocket and wrote down the doctor's name and telephone number.

Stacey's office had gotten the full savagery of the search. Books strewn on the floor, computer printouts and scrawled notes scattered like stripped-off leaves after a windstorm.

Cooper picked up one piece of paper: a page from an essay on tort reform, for one of Stacey's classes. Clearly not what the searcher sought.

"All we've got here's what didn't get taken," Cooper said.

"Question is, what got took?" Tip said.

Bolknor said nothing.

Neither did Cooper.

She knew what the shooter was after. Now that it was too late.

She thought: Stacey annoyed me, and that made me stupid.

232

On the way out, they told Marjorie Olson what had happened upstairs in her house, and she looked stunned.

"It must have happened when I went across the street," she said. "And I forgot to shut the door."

"Lucky," Mike Bolknor said.

Startled, the white-haired woman stared at him.

"If you'd been there, you might be dead, too," he said.

CHAPTER TWENTY-EIGHT

A half hour later, they sat in Mike Bolknor's office, thinking what to do next.

In the adjacent room, Chip Stack—called in from his dormitory—studied archived video feeds from the new campus surveillance system. Chip had arrived suppressing jubilation.

Cooper thought: it's because Mike Bolknor asked for his help, something his father never did.

When they'd told Chip who'd been shot, however, he'd jerked back, as if from an electrical shock, and stared wide-eyed. For now, they'd said, please keep mum. And he would, Cooper had no doubt. He wouldn't even tell his pals, Jerry Shapiro and Nikki Winkel.

He's steady, she thought. Reliable. He'll be a good cop.

They'd already discussed how long to keep silent, because reporters, particularly Ariette Feenie, from the *Dill Chronicle*, would be scratching at the door. They decided to go public soon, at least partially, hoping tips would come in. First, though, they needed to notify the dead woman's relatives, and that might take time.

Stacey had been living in Pittsburgh, they knew. Who her relatives were, or where they lived, they didn't know. They didn't even know if Gillibrand was Stacey's last name by birth, or the name of her ex-husband. They had no information about her life.

Cooper thought: Stacey, I hardly knew you. And for that—not bothering to know her students—the professor gets D-minus.

Bolknor had assigned one of his officers to check the college's admissions records, but that required getting the dean of admissions to rouse himself from the tv and drive to the campus in what was now a cold drizzle. So far, no word on that front.

Cooper had the name of Stacey's doctor, from the lorazepam bottle they'd found in her bathroom, another possible source of information, but it was too late to reach his office tonight. They'd have to call tomorrow.

I never warned her, Cooper thought. Not straight out.

She slapped her hand against her chair's armrest.

I only warned her in code, tried to, at least, a classroom talk about psychopaths. I just assumed she'd grasp it was a warning about Sonny Rawston. Maybe she got it, but shrugged it off, because Sonny had already convinced her I harassed him.

If I'd only spoken directly....

Tip LaPerle interrupted her reverie.

"So what have we got?"

"It wasn't a random shooting," Cooper said.

"We don't know that," Tip said. "Not for sure."

"I got targeted twice, now my student's dead," Cooper said. "Not likely to be coincidence."

"Her backpack tell us anything?" Mike Bolknor asked. "All that stuff pulled out and left on the ground?"

His voice sounded like it came up from a well.

Cooper wondered: why do you keep blaming yourself, Mike? It's not you who failed this girl.

"Crime lab people gave us a list," she said. "Mostly class papers and quizzes, a Principals of Basic Law textbook, no personal letters....That was about it."

"It's like her apartment," Tip said. "We know what got left, not what got took."

"Well, that tells us something," Bolknor said.

They both looked at him.

"Somebody wanted Cooper dead," he said. "And then they wanted Stacey Gillibrand dead."

He sat looking at his hands. Large hands, Cooper thought. She imagined they could inflict damage.

"It was different with Stacey, though," Bolknor said.

He kept looking at his hands.

"They went through her backpack, ransacked her apartment," he said. "Nobody searched Cooper's house."

Now he flexed his hands, as if he wanted to do something with them.

"So they just wanted Cooper dead," he said. "They wanted Stacey dead, too, but they also searched her stuff—she had something they wanted."

"Or something they didn't want anyone else to see," Cooper said.

Bolknor looked at her.

"Right," he said. "Maybe that."

He spread his hands, inviting further thoughts, but Cooper's only thought was: I'm jumping to conclusions. Maybe it was Sonny Rawston, Probably it was. Maybe not, though.

Chip Stack burst through the open door.

"You've got to see this!" he said.

Chip sat at a large computer screen. He'd summoned up feeds from the four cameras set up around the library, and divided his screen into four frames, one for each camera. At first, all four frames remained blank, the campus deserted, with no motion to activate the cameras, not even a squirrel. Abruptly, one frame lit up.

It showed the front of the library and its surroundings, in black, white, and gray. In the cones of light from streetlamps, rain and sleet streaked down. Everything looked dismal.

"Watch this," Chip said.

A man walked in from the right. He carried a long package.

"Freeze it," Bolknor said.

Chip clicked the mouse and motion stopped on the screen.

"Can you blow it up?" Bolknor said.

More clicks and the camera seemed to dolly in, the miniaturized man growing, although the focus got fuzzier. Still, they could make him out.

Gray beard. Gray hair down to his shoulders.

Tallish, slim build.

His package looked to be a canvas carry case, for a rifle.

"Anybody recognize him?" Bolknor asked.

LaPerle shook his head.

Cooper said: "Something...."

"You know that creep?" LaPerle said.

Cooper said: "It's just that...."

She thought.

"I saw him when he shot at me, in the park," she said. "Maybe, though, I saw him once before, too, long ago, possibly just a face in a crowd, or maybe it's my imagination, or maybe he just reminds me of some movie character."

"Yeah," LaPerle said. "Eye-witness testimony, used to be the gold standard, now...."

"Start it moving again," Bolknor told Chip.

Another click.

Now the man stopped in front of the library. He stared at the building's glass door and granite stoop and steps, glistening in the rain. He checked his wristwatch. He looked at the library again, then turned, and walked off the screen, purposeful, heading toward Hill Street, into the Arbor. He looked like a tiny man in a miniature world where all was gray.

In the screen's upper-right corner, a digital readout noted today's date and gave the time—6:22 p.m.

Now the screen grayed out.

"No motion, so the camera turned off," Chip said. "It'll come on again if something moves."

"Do we have cameras down along the trail through the Arbor?" Bolknor asked.

"Not yet," Chip said.

Another screen lit up—an image of a Campus Security patrol car, moving slowly along the library's

238

flank, then turning toward the campus's central quadrangle. Again the screen blanked.

Abruptly, the original screen brightened again, a view of the library's glass door, and a shape moving behind it. Now the door swung open and a woman stepped out, toting a backpack by its straps.

"Stacey!" Chip said.

In the screen's upper right corner, the readout said "6:32 p.m."

They watched as Stacey paused on the library steps, looking up at the rain. Miniaturized, at a distance, she looked like a doll, small and easily broken.

Cooper thought: why didn't I ever notice how fragile she was?

Stacey wore a shiny slicker over jeans and a thick turtleneck sweater. As they watched, she shrugged into her backpack, letting it rest on the back of her slicker. They knew the backpack to be bright red, but on the screen it looked gray. They knew her jeans were blue, her sweater buff, her slicker yellow, because they'd seen her lying dead on the ground, but on the screen it all looked gray.

She looked up at the sky again. Then she began walking, toward the frame's left side, into the Arbor. She walked briskly, as if eager to get home, where it would be dry and warm, out of the rain and sleet.

Cooper thought: you never got home.

Again the frame blanked.

Cooper saw Chip staring at the empty screen, stunned. And she thought, yes, that's how it can look, Chip, the last moments of a life, perfectly normal.

Bolknor's telephone rang and he glanced at the Caller ID readout.

"*Dill Chronicle*," he said.

Cooper picked up the telephone and gave her name.

Ariette Feeney's voice in her ear.

"We're working on tomorrow morning's paper," she said, excited. "So there was a shooting up there, yes? And who was that?"

Over the phone line, Cooper heard the reporter's computer keys clack.

"We can't release the name until we've notified the family," Cooper said.

"Then what details can you give us now?" Ariette asked.

"Somebody unknown shot a woman this evening, on the Mt. Augustus College campus," Cooper said. "She came out of the library at 6:32 p.m. and walked into the Arbor, where apparently the killer waited for her, and shot her, probably with a rifle."

Clack, clack, clack.

"A student or a professor or a member of the college staff?"

"Student," Cooper said.

Clack, clack, clack.

"Was this some kind of sex crime?"

"Apparently not," Cooper said.

"Who's investigating?"

"Campus Security officers, Dill Police Department, with technical assistance from the State Police Crime Lab."

"What else can you tell us?"

"Right now, nothing."

"Professor North, this is a small town, and you've been shot at twice, and now there's been a murder—don't you think the public has a right to know what's happening?"

Clack, clack clack.

Cooper thought: Good Lord, haven't you done enough damage, Ariette?

And then: I even like Ariette.

"Anything at all?" Ariette said.

"Nothing more right now," Cooper said, and she slammed the handset down into its receptacle.

LaPerle and Bolknor looked at her, startled by the vehemence.

"I'm going home," Cooper said. "I'm going to think about this shooting, and about my dog."

And, later, lying in bed in the dark, she glanced at Henry's sleeping spot, on the floor by the window, then resolutely looked back up at the ceiling. She wondered if he was in distress, or in pain, and then put that thought out of her mind because there was no action she could take, other than to brood.

She'd looked out a half hour ago and seen the Campus Security car parked under the usual maple. It might have been Mike Bolknor sitting inside, but she couldn't tell. She disliked that Prius parking out there, because of the reason for its parking there, and because she despised being dependent, but it reassured her, too. She knew that.

She thought about her anger toward Ariette Feenie, a young woman simply doing her job and trying to advance in her career. Cooper had once been a young woman doing her job, trying to make a mark. Even so, when she thought of Ariette, she smoldered, and all the while she knew it wasn't really Ariette who angered her.

People moved across her mental screen.

Sonny Rawston, so snide and confident. He'd taken her dog. Of that she had no doubt. He'd given up his plan to use the dog as blackmail, to force her to humiliate herself, but maybe he still held Henry captive. Or maybe he'd killed the dog. It was him, though. He'd taken Henry.

Stacey had seen the corgi's fur on Rawston's sweater sleeve. He'd probably burned the sweater by now. Stacey had confronted him about that sleeve. She'd yelled at him. And, maybe, for knowing he'd taken the dog, she'd been shot.

Maybe.

Except they'd seen the killer on the surveillance video, and he wasn't a red-headed youngish man who could be your insurance agent. Gray beard and shoulder-length gray hair. A biker, maybe. Or an aging rock star, from a group that disbanded way back. Or maybe he looked like somebody she'd once seen, but couldn't remember.

Surely the gray-haired man shot Stacey. Almost certainly. Did he shoot on his own, though? Or following somebody's orders?

Jack Abbott walked across her mental screen, and then off, followed by Nessie Greffier. Both, somehow, connected to Sonny Rawston. Maybe all three were

242

interconnected, a triumvirate. Or maybe they just seemed connected, an optical illusion.

She hadn't been shot at for revenge. She knew that now.

Once more the image of a spider came into her mind. It lurked over the town, ruby eyed, its web crisscrossing Dill. That spider watched her, but she couldn't watch the spider, because she didn't know who that spider was. Not yet.

She glanced out the window again, at the parked Prius, on guard.

Go away, Mike, she thought. Get some sleep. No reason to park there every night, not now.

And she thought: no, it's not really you making me angry, Ariette. It's me, for keeping my eyes shut, and letting that girl be killed.

Early the next morning, when she arrived on campus, she found Mike Bolknor already there. He stood on the Campus Security building's granite stoop, leaning back against the building's bricks, drinking coffee from a paper cup, waiting for her.

Now last night's rain and sleet were gone, and the sky seemed swept clean, autumn blue. A wind from the west, off the distant Adirondacks and Lake Champlain, swirled brown maple leaves across the campus lawn.

"Crime lab people got the bullet that killed her," Bolknor said. "It was a .30-06, from the same rifle that shot at you, both times."

She nodded, not surprised.

"No footprints, so he must have been careful, stayed to the stone pathway," Bolknor said. "We got the girl's admission records, and we have a next of kin."

Cooper nodded. It would fall to her, she had no doubt, to make the call. She didn't relish it.

"She put a note with her application," Bolknor said. "She said, 'I'm twenty-six, and requiring me to name my mother is outrageous!'"

Cooper supposed it was, in a way.

Bolknor handed her a slip of paper on which he'd written the Pittsburgh telephone number of Stacey's mother, Trudy Baker. Gillibrand turned out to be her ex-husband's name. It surprised Cooper that Stacey hadn't insisted on retaining her own name. Maybe she didn't want to be Stacey Baker. No father around, it seemed.

"All right," Cooper said.

She took the paper up to her office and sat looking at the telephone, working up the resolve to make the call.

It wasn't as if she hadn't made scores of calls like this before. So she punched in the numbers.

"Yeah?"

"Is this Trudy Baker?"

"In the flesh."

"Are you Stacey Gillibrand's mother?"

Silence.

Then: "What the hell's she done now?"

"Mrs. Baker, I have bad news."

"Yeah? What else is new?"

244

"I'm sure you know Stacey's been a student at Mt. Augustus College, in the Criminal Justice Program...."

"Miss Bigshot Lawyer, yeah, anything to act like she's better than us, but here's what—debt up over her hairline, with that college stuff, because she married that pervert, who finally ditched her, and Miss Smartypants didn't get two cents because the jerk couldn't spell W O R K!"

"Mrs. Baker, I'm Cooper North, and I direct Stacey's program...."

"So pin a rose on your nose."

"Mrs. Baker, I'm trying to tell you that your daughter is dead."

Silence.

Then: "So how the hell'd that happen?"

"She was shot—a murder."

Silence.

"Mrs. Baker...."

"Well, she'd always find a way, wouldn't she?"

"Find a way?"

"To get attention!"

"Mrs. Baker, there's the question of returning her body to you and...."

"What do I want with her body?"

"Mrs. Baker, we...."

"Cremate her, okay? Then scatter her wherever you want, okay? Because I've had enough trouble with that one, all her life, lecturing me, for God's sake, how to raise my own damned kids...."

Silence.

And then Trudy Baker hung up.

Cooper stared at the dead telephone receiver in her hand.

After a while she called the number on Stacey's prescription bottle, her doctor's office, and got a phone tree. After working her way through myriad possibilities ("If you wish to renew a prescription press…"), Cooper heard "to talk to a member of the staff please stay on the line," and she listened to an innocuous cover of the Beatles' *Hey, Jude*, until somebody finally answered the phone.

An older man's voice: "Kind Hands Clinic, receptionist's off today, this is Harvey Clocker, physician's assistant, can't help with foreign policy, but if you've got a cough, sneeze, or aching toe, give me a try."

Cooper told him who she was, and asked a question.

"Yes, I've known Stacey since she was a little girl, but we can't give out information…."

"Stacey's dead," Cooper said. "Murdered."

"My God!"

Cooper gave him details of the shooting, and said they needed help with the investigation.

"Of course," he said. "That poor girl."

"Your clinic prescribed lorazepam for her?"

"Yes, to help her sleep," he said. "It's a relaxant, a mild sedative."

"I just spoke with Stacey's mother…."

"That would be her stepmother—and, with Trudy, who wouldn't need lorazepam?"

246

"We've only known Stacey a few weeks, here at the college," Cooper said. "What can you tell me about her?"

"Quite a bit," Clocker said, and he began to talk.

He said Stacey first visited the clinic as a thirteen-year-old, bringing a ten-year-old brother, actually half-brother, bleeding from a bicycle spill. She'd opened a purse wadded with dollar bills to show she could pay. Baby-sitting money, she said. And doing chores for neighbors, like dog walking. She'd brought the injured boy to the clinic because Trudy Baker wouldn't, saying if he broke himself, he could damn well fix himself.

"You've heard about wicked stepmothers?" Clocker said. "Well, even the kids she'd given birth to got burned."

Stacey's birth mother had died of breast cancer, when Stacey was three, and shortly after that her father, a carpenter, married Trudy, whom he'd met because she clerked at a hardware store he patronized. They had three sons, including the injured bicycle rider, and then Stacey's father, an Army reservist, got called up.

"Roadside bomb in Iraq, blew him apart," Clocker said. "Which irritated Trudy—she'd bring the kids in for shots, because the schools required it, and she'd complain about Baker 'leaving her in the lurch,' and she'd say, 'So poke the brats and make them cry,' and then she'd laugh—raising three sons, plus Stacey, who wasn't her own, let's say she didn't rise to the occasion."

Clocker said he'd watched Stacey grow up. She'd come to the clinic for the flu, and for soccer injuries, but sometimes just to talk with him, about problems with Trudy, trouble at school, boyfriends....

247

"I guess she appointed me her grandfather," he said. "You may have noticed that she could be flirty, especially with older men, and that was because she'd lost her father—she craved the love, not getting any from Trudy."

He said Stacey's main character trait was crusader: "I guess she'd seen so much injustice at home that she hated it, couldn't tolerate it."

Trudy doted on one boy, he said, and treated the other two, and Stacey, as if they were vermin infesting her house. Stacey constantly stood up for herself, but even more she defended her two scorned half-brothers, which enraged Trudy.

"So the house was a war zone, and right after her high school graduation—she invited me and my wife to attend, which was good, because Trudy didn't bother to show up—anyway, maybe a week later, she married this Gillibrand kid."

Stacey's new husband had been a high-school classmate, a thin, sensitive boy who wrote poetry and read it at local poetry slams. He'd been bullied a bit in school.

"Probably that was the attraction," Clocker said. "Stacey had that urge to help victims."

Gillibrand attended college, while Stacey supported them both, as a clothing store saleswoman, Clocker said.

"Then one day he announced he'd found his life's true love, who turned out to be another guy, and that was the end of that," he said.

Stacey decided she wanted to be an attorney.

"Stand up for the poor and forgotten," Clocker said.

She took Community College courses and, meanwhile, worked in a law office as a receptionist, saving her money and learning what she could, by asking questions. Finally she'd enrolled at Mt. Augustus, in the Criminal Justice Program.

"And then she got shot," Cooper muttered.

"And then she got shot," Clocker echoed.

Silence for a moment.

"I've got to get off the line," Clocker said. "Patients are coming in, and—to tell the truth—I've got some tears."

Later that morning, Tip LaPerle telephoned.

Cooper picked him up at the police station. Then she drove the Volvo east, along Main Street, with Tip riding shotgun, a folded paper sticking out of his uniform's jacket pocket.

Cooper braked at DeBouche's Gas 'n Groceries, backed the car into the store's lot, then drove out and parked across the street, in front of Sonny Rawston's apartment house.

"No bike," Cooper said. "It's usually parked here."

LaPerle said; "Crap!"

They walked inside and started up the stairs, Tip taking two treads at a time, Cooper lagging, her cane thumping on the boards. Tip knew to ignore Cooper's limp and forge ahead. Get chivalrous and she'd snarl.

He pounded a fist on Rawston's door.

No response except empty silence. He pounded the door again, louder.

"Police," he announced. "Open up."

No response.

"He isn't in there," Cooper said.

LaPerle cursed.

He pulled a phone out of his pocket and got up a list of numbers, chose one, and tapped it. He turned on the speakerphone, and Cooper heard the ringing.

"Who the hell's this?"

Jack Abbott's voice.

"Tip LaPerle, police business."

"Who gave you my cell number?"

"God did," Tip said. "We're at Sonny Rawston's apartment."

Silence.

Then: "So what?"

"So I've got a warrant in my pocket to search his place, and your tenant's not home, so I need you to give me a key."

"Go find Rawston, damn it—get the key from him."

"This is a murder investigation."

Silence.

"Obstructing the police, Abbott, that's indictable!"

Under-the-breath cursing.

"All right, LaPerle, just stand there, like a good little boy, and I'll come along."

"Better be righteously speedy," Tip said, but Abbott had already killed the connection.

While they waited, Cooper told LaPerle about her telephone conversations that morning, what she'd learned about Stacey Gillibrand.

"Hmm," Tip said.

"I didn't get Stacey right," Cooper said.

"What about her ex-husband," Tip said. "Maybe he came after her, some kook reason, traced her up here, took his shot."

"I checked," Cooper said. "He died a year ago, a sleeping pill overdose, maybe an accident."

They stood silent, thinking.

"Besides," she said. "That wouldn't explain those two shots at me."

Both stood silently, looking at the closed door. Then Cooper spoke again.

"These shootings weren't about revenge."

"Yeah," LaPerle said. "I figured…."

"You see where this leads."

LaPerle sighed.

"Thing is, that's off my turf, so…."

Downstairs the front door opened, then slammed, and footsteps thudded up the stairs, and Jack Abbott stomped onto the second-floor landing, red-faced with anger.

He thrust a hand into his trouser pocket and came out with a key, which he suddenly hurled, meaning for it to clatter onto the floor, but Tip deftly caught it. For a moment, the two men glared at each other, but then LaPerle grinned.

"Thank you, Mr. Abbott," he said. "Please join us—maybe we'll have questions."

He unlocked the door and opened it and looked inside and whistled, surprised. He stepped aside so Cooper and Abbott could look in. Abbott cursed.

They walked into an emptied apartment.

Cooper walked directly to the bedroom, opened the closet door, saw nothing inside except hangers. No sweater with dog fur on its sleeve.

He'd made the bed before he left.

No trace of Sonny Rawston remained. No clothes in the closet. No unwashed dishes in the sink.

"He's on the run," Tip said.

Cooper shook her head, puzzled.

"It's like when he snatched Henry," she said. "How'd he carry off his stuff on a motorcycle?"

"Did he leave owing you rent, Jack?" Tip asked.

"No."

"How much did you charge him?"

Abbott snorted, angry.

"I don't have to tell you that."

"Yes you do," Tip said. "Murder investigation? Refusing to cooperate?"

"It's slipped my mind."

"Did I mention this is a murder investigation?"

"I didn't murder anyone, damn it."

"You're withholding evidence."

Silence.

"Why, Jack?"

Abbott refused to look at him, mouth set, his face furious red. Beneath the anger, Cooper detected what? Fear? Anxiety? Even panic? Jack Abbott suddenly seemed to her like a wild boar, cornered by yapping dogs. He'd stay mum, certainly right now. And if Abbott would talk to anyone, it wouldn't be to Tip LaPerle, his fellow graduate of the riverside tenements, who'd risen to esteem and authority in Dill, while Jack Abbott merely got rich.

"Jack, I looked through here before," Cooper said. "On top of the bedroom chest of drawers he had an old cereal bowl, gone now, but it had odds and ends inside, including an old skeleton key—do you know what that opened?"

"How the hell would I know?" he said.

He whirled and started for the door.

"Hey, I'm not done with you," Tip shouted.

Cooper held up a hand, meaning, "Cool down, Tip."

She followed Abbott out the door and stood behind him, before he started down the stairs.

"You'll have to tell us what's going on," she told the back of his neck, which could have been a bull's.

He stopped on the stairs.

"You'll have to," she said.

"Who's that guy you work with, that big guy?" Abbott asked, not turning around.

"Mike Bolknor," Cooper said.

"Yeah, him," Abbott said. "Maybe."

Then he charged down the stairs and she listened to his heavy footsteps and then the slamming of the front door.

They drove back to the police station and secluded themselves in the chief's office, where Tip surprised Cooper—he reached for his telephone and called Mike Bolknor at the college.

"You'd better be here for this," he'd said.

Cooper thought: peace overture!

253

Fifteen minutes later the three of them sat figuring what to do.

"First thing is, find that crudball," Tip said. "I already sent out an APB—troopers, other towns, Border Patrol—look for a redhead on a black bike."

Bolknor shook his head.

Cooper saw Tip immediately glare, feeling contradicted, and she thought: no more peace overture.

She loved her friend Tip LaPerle, who'd burst into her office so many decades ago, still a small boy from the riverside tenements, afire to become a cop, an officer of the law, the maximum distance he could imagine from his family. And she wanted to tell him now: Tip, don't get prickly, thinking this New York detective scorns you, because I've watched, and that's not what he's about at all.

Bolknor shook his head again.

"Rawston's gone to ground," he said. "He's hiding someplace close."

LaPerle, scowling, silent, waited to hear how that got figured.

"He's a smart guy, right?" Bolknor said. "He'll expect an APB, and knows he'd get grabbed, trying to bike his way out of this, so he's hiding—that's his best bet."

Tip nodded, grudgingly.

"Okay, we'll hunt," he said. "Except he's probably got that damned bike in a shed somewhere, but he'll need groceries or something, so maybe somebody'll see it, or hear it—a motorcyclist's going to stand out, this late into October."

Cooper thought: peace again?

As they talked over steps to take, Tip jotted down a list of what else needed to be checked out.

How does Rawston fund himself?

If he's just got a motorcycle, how'd he transport a Welsh corgi, not to mention all his stuff from the apartment? Did he have an accomplice with a car?

Still unsolved, and key to the case—who was the gray-bearded biker with the beard, the actual shooter? Did he work for Rawston?

"Let's not forget Rawston visiting Nessie Greffier," Cooper said. "There's been a murder now, and a suspect's on the run, so we have every right to question her."

LaPerle shook his head at Cooper.

"Thing is, she's an upstanding citizen and all that, so my guys in blue knock on her door, patrol car parked out front, that'll get the neighbors buzzing, you know how it goes."

"All right," Cooper said. "I'll handle Nessie myself."

She watched as LaPerle added to his list, while Mike Bolknor sat slouched in his chair, staring at his shoes, looking gloomy.

"I guess we're agreed?" Cooper said. "On what this is about?"

Bolknor shrugged.

"That eighteen-year old murder," he said.

Cooper thought: he looks like a street tough, but he's got eyes, and he thinks. He just doesn't say much.

Bolknor said: "Newspaper stories, they stirred it up."

Cooper nodded. She held up her index finger.

"*Chronicle* story number one," she said. "It sounds like I'm going to get my students digging into that old Hart's Corners case—and right away I get shot at, then shot at again."

Bolknor held up two fingers.

"Second story," he said. "Now we're told it's just Stacey Gillibrand looking into that old case, all by herself—and she's shot."

They fell into silence again, thinking.

"That's trooper turf over there," Tip said. "If I go asking around in Hart's Corners, they'll get their panties knotted up, so we'll need to bring them in...."

Cooper shook her head.

They're undermanned, she said. They'd go at this half-hearted, and they'd need to poke around here in Dill, too—your domain, Tip, right?—and even up on the campus. They'd be starting from zero, and they might actually slow us down.

"So let us do the poking," Cooper said. "Mike and I, we'll go dig."

"Hart's Corners, that's over in Warner County," Tip said. "They'll be snippy, getting their old case questioned."

Cooper made a disgusted sound.

"Emerson Clough's ready to retire," she said. "Which he should have done twenty years ago, as a public service—I'll handle that human hot-air balloon."

Then, for Bolknor's benefit: "He's state's attorney, next county over."

Tip, grinning, scribbled a new item onto his list.

"How do you spell 'balloon?'" he asked.

That afternoon, in evidence class, Cooper discussed DNA techniques, but the students fidgeted, glancing at the classroom's one empty chair.

Stacey Gillibrand's chair.

Her body lay wrapped in black plastic, in a cooler.

Murdered.

It bewildered the students. And they felt guilty, for turning up their eyes at her.

Showboat, they'd labeled her. Attention grabber. She'd played the age card, too, the grownup among toddlers, particularly annoying because partly true. Also, blond and pretty—so it just follows—you're an airhead, okay?

Cooper thought: I'm no better. I branded her a pest, and that's all I saw. A pest. I never looked past that, didn't bother.

She was so alone. I sensed it, but disregarded it. And the sadness in that blond head, the worry.

Stacey needed tranquilizers, couldn't sleep, because she'd bet everything on a law degree. To finance it, staggering loans. An inner fury drove her to make that wager—she'd seen so much injustice, to her siblings, to herself. It didn't crush her. It made her a crusader. She meant to fight wrongs, and her sword would be the law.

"Damn!"

Cooper slapped her lecture notes onto her desk.

It sounded like a shot, and slouching students jerked upright in their seats.

"To hell with DNA right now," Cooper said.

She glared around the classroom. Widened eyes stared back.

"Let's talk about a 30:06 slug," Cooper said. "Bursting through her skull, into her brain."

She'd been angry with Ariette Feenie, for writing the articles that started the shootings, but it was really Cooper North who angered her. She'd never warned Stacey about Sonny Rawston, not directly. Then that gray-bearded man lurked outside the library, and she'd misread that. Now her student lay dead.

An image suddenly swarmed into Cooper's mind: ice cubes tinkling in a glass of tawny single-malt scotch. She could taste its smoky bite. With a curse, she pushed the thought over the edge of a mental cliff, into oblivion.

Too late to help Stacey now, she thought, but her killer's still out there.

And she thought: we'll burn you at the stake!

"This is evidence class," she told the students. "Let's talk about evidence."

She told them what ballistics said about the slug that killed Stacey, that it came from the same rifle that shot twice at Cooper. She told them about the mystery shooter, with shoulder-length gray hair and a gray beard, and about how Sonny Rawston preyed on Stacey's loneliness, and on her sympathy for the mistreated. Now he'd gone into hiding.

"Let's make it a wiki-investigation," she told them. "Like Wikipedia, on the Web, anyone can contribute—for starters, report motorcycle sightings, especially if the rider's got red hair."

Another thing, she said, is that the killer ransacked Stacey's apartment and rifled through her knapsack. We can guess why. Any stray papers blowing around, grab them and bring them here.

"That's enough," Cooper said. "I'm too upset to teach anymore today, go study or something."

She watched the students file out, usually boisterous after a class, this time somber. Nikki Winkel stayed behind.

"That killer searching Stacey's rooms?" Nikki said. "Looking in her backpack, for whatever she'd dug up on Hart's Corners?"

Cooper waited

Nikki said: "Well, he didn't find anything."

"Why do you say that?" Cooper asked.

"Because she never took her Hart's Corners stuff home," Nikki said. "We got talking once, at the library, and she told me—she kept it all in a library locker."

Cooper must have looked puzzled, because Nikki shrugged.

"That's where she did her research," she said. "At the library, like using the microfilm machines to check old newspaper stories, and court records."

Nikki had on new blue jeans today, instead of ripped black Levis. They looked crisp from K-Mart. She'd traded her de-sleeved man's shirt for a woman's white blouse, maybe borrowed from her mother. She still wore her dark hair shaved along the sides and spiked on top, and that thin gold nose ring, but today she'd toned it down from her usual all-out Visigoth. She'd even switched from black eye shadow and liner to blue, with fingernails to match.

Cooper suppressed a smile.

She thought: this is Nikki's idea of dressing up. She's showing respect for her murdered classmate.

An hour later, after getting a pass-key to the lockers from the librarian, Cooper sat in a library carrel, looking at Stacey Gillibrand's weeks of work, retrieved from her locker. Cooper had heaped it all on the carrel's built-in desk—microfiched copies of old news stories, mostly from the *Warner County Weekly Courier,* some from the daily *Dill Chronicle,* photocopies of court proceedings, printouts of state police reports....

So much information, she thought, so laboriously gathered. Every evening Stacey dug out more information, studied it, then—at six-thirty, probably too weary to do more—crammed it into her library locker, along with all she'd collected other days, and shrugged into her parka.

From the library she'd walk along the Arbor's winding path to Hill Street. Then, night after night, she'd walk past Cooper's house, in the dark.

As if watching a movie, Cooper visualized Stacey's trek.

Just before the Dill Industries complex, she'd turn right on Slope Drive, down the steep hill to Main Street. Turn left. Maybe she'd look into shop windows as she passed, boutiques displaying overpriced jackets and slacks and blouses, or a store devoted solely to fancy olive oils and another to imported French and Belgian chocolates. She'd walk block after block, past the police station, thinking about the Duckins case, probably, and her debts, and how someday, when she'd finally become a lawyer, she could go into the boutiques, buy some nice things, and maybe sometimes thinking about Trudy Baker, in

Pittsburgh, not happy thoughts, until she finally climbed the stairs to her apartment, where she lived alone.

No more.

Cooper thought: we should treasure our sentience. It's so fragile.

She began reading through the mound of paperwork, page by page.

Stacey had highlighted passages and names with a yellow marking pen, so that Cooper could follow the young woman's thinking, and she saw the pattern of those thoughts, and how they pointed relentlessly toward a conclusion.

Cooper thought: how did the prosecutor miss all this eighteen years ago? And the public defender, appointed to the Nub Duckins case by the court, since the old handyman had no money—how did he miss it?

Stacey hadn't missed it. And she'd been building the case for Nub Duckins' innocence, right up to that final dreary evening, when the gray-bearded man with shoulder-length gray hair hid along the Arbor path, waiting in the rain. He'd watched Stacey walking toward him, eager to be home. He'd raised his rifle, braced it against his shoulder, aimed. Then he'd pulled the trigger, sending a .30:06 slug through Stacey's skull, into her brain.

Cooper stared at the mound of marked up paperwork. And she thought—too late!—what a superb lawyer this young woman would have become.

She sat back in her chair, and sighed. She thought how she'd blinded herself, convinced the gunman targeted only her, wanting revenge for some long-ago prosecution. They'd all assumed that, but revenge had nothing to do with it. Neither did Cooper North.

Stacey had told her about leaving the library, several nights in a row, and seeing the gray-bearded man waiting outside, checking his watch. Cooper silently berated herself now. She'd been so sure that she herself was the target, she'd missed the obvious. It was Stacey the shooter now stalked. Ariette Feenie had corrected her first story, making it clear that Stacey—and she alone— was digging into the eighteen-year-old murder in Hart's Corners.

He'd watched to make certain. Every evening Stacey left the library at six-thirty.

He could count on it.

At that hour, the campus was virtually deserted, students in the dining halls, faculty mostly gone home. He'd probably checked the Campus Security patrols, too, knew where they'd be driving at that hour. A good time to park at some innocuous spot, car or motorcycle, then walk past the library, carrying a rifle in a canvas tote case.

I could have saved her, Cooper told herself.

She suddenly imagined the chilled stem of an iced martini glass between her fingers.

She cursed.

CHAPTER TWENTY-NINE

Later that afternoon, under a gray autumnal sky, Mike Bolknor drove a Campus Security Prius east on Main Street, with Cooper in the passenger seat, in a grim mood, pensively eyeing downtown's shops—The Percolator, Sweet Kumquat Natural Foods....

She remembered how drab this street once looked.

A hundred-fifty years of New England weather had dulled the buildings' bricks. Wind-blown dust and pollen had grimed them.

Nobody noticed.

Then new people moved in, up from the cities, keen to pep things up. They replaced old plain-Jane stores—Village Dry Cleaners, Barton's Appliances—with boutiques and bistros. Out came pressure washers and paint rollers. And the town council, energized with newcomers, passed an ordinance: every Main Street business had to put up a funky new-style wooden sign, hand-carved and colored, and Cooper, eyeing the new signs, had to admit they livened the town.

Harmony Hank's Musicorium, All Things Doggy, Olio d'Oliva....

Mona Dill Saunders described Main Street's bright new zeitgeist, approvingly, as "perky-quirky."

Now you could buy sesame-multigrain bagels on Main Street, or samosas, or sashimi, or cheddar-cheese-and-Vermont-organic-bacon crepes.

You couldn't get your shoes re-soled, though. Peterson's Shoe Repair had died along with old Orville Peterson. Anyway, everyone now wore running shoes, including Cooper.

She thought: survival of the commercial fittest, but still....

They drove by Appurtenances, the recently opened clothing store, and she stared, bemused, at its artful window display of designer suits and skinny jeans on black-wire mannequins, striking bizarre postures.

She thought: we're supposed to contort ourselves?

They passed more foodie cafes, brew pubs, indie-band nightspots....

At the town's edge, they drove by a circa-1900 cow barn transformed into the Blue Heifer, a new restaurant, featuring tiny portions and weighty prices, where you dined at tables made of old pickle barrels and your maple-syrup wine or sparkling cider arrived in a Mason jar, once used for putting up peach or blackberry preserves. Mona and Drew Saunders frequently urged Cooper to join them here, but mostly she wouldn't, because the pseudo-rusticana reminded her of Gertrude Stein's famous pronouncement, "There is no there there," and it annoyed her.

She thought: this isn't the town where I grew up.

Her sniffy tone sounded like her mother.

Even so, that former Dill didn't strive to be smart.

And nobody got shot.

Stacey Gillibrand—whose mother didn't want her—would be cremated.

They'd have some sort of ceremony, students and professors. They'd scatter her ashes, probably in the Arbor, where she'd been murdered.

No, this isn't the town where I grew up, Cooper thought.

And then, surprising herself, she thought: so what?

Yes, the town had changed. Too many young people tried heroin now. Homeless panhandlers now drifted in.

Interstates, Cooper thought. They connected Dill to Montreal, Boston, New York. Just a few hours' drive now. Great for drug dealers. When she'd started as a prosecutor, the only drug criminals were joint-smoking Hippies and LSD trippers. That seemed innocent now.

Even so, she thought, Dill's roots still went deep, down through the thin mountain soil, into the granite bedrock's crevices.

She thought: the new stores didn't murder Stacey Gillibrand. Neither did funky signs. Something alien killed her, some malevolence. It snuck into Dill, and it bided here.

Don't blame the town, she thought.

Besides, she liked Dill's modernized bookstores. You could check out a possible purchase while relaxing at a café-style table, with a cup of herb tea, or even a grilled bleu-cheese-and-bosc-pear sandwich, if you missed lunch. And she appreciated Dill's enlarged and upgraded library, with computer terminals for Googling, and evening seminars, maybe on the 1700s Independent Republic of Vermont, when Ethan Allen waged guerrilla war against New York, or a how-to session, Mastering Your New Smart TV. And she liked how the town required cell-phone towers to hide in church steeples.

Cooper sighed.

Sometimes—she had to admit it—she did enjoy a gourmet meal, with good friends, without needing a day-long Amtrak ride to Penn Station.

Even so....

She glanced at Mike Bolknor, wanting to ask if he, too, ever felt like an endangered species, in an evolving ecosystem, but he drove scowling, thick black eyebrows almost meeting over his nose. So she said nothing. Besides, he was decades younger, and his memories were of New York, buildings razed, new skyscrapers rising, neighborhoods in flux, like Times Square transformed overnight from seedy to Disneyland.

She knew Tip LaPerle instinctively understood Dill, but she doubted Mike Bolknor did. Certainly not yet. He looked through the Prius's windshield and saw eateries and boutiques. Cooper did, too, but she also saw what used to be.

Just past the Blue Heifer, the road curved north, Main Street becoming County Route 12, and it twisted among hills, as it had since its packed-dirt days, before Cooper's time, when Percherons pulled hay wagons.

266

As a child, she'd ridden along here on Sunday afternoons, in her parents' Lincoln, sharing the back seat with her brother, as they drove to the Hart's Corners general store to stock up on huge wheels of Crowley cheese, or jugs of dark-amber maple syrup. They'd driven out here, too, for Warner County's annual fall-foliage festival, in the Hart's Corners Community Hall, a traditional New England boiled dinner. Cooper wondered if they still served up those heaping plates of corned beef and fresh-from-the-farm turnips. Probably they did, she thought, but she just didn't care for it now, the steamed-up room, the hearty conviviality, too much to eat. And she thought, wryly, no, you can't keep them down on the farm, not once they've seen Harvard Law.

A word came into her mind: "palimpsest." Where had she heard that?

She looked out the window again, at old hillside farmhouses. They still had their attached barns, so farmers could do the milking on sub-zero January mornings, without needing to go outdoors. Now, though, the barns might serve as two-car garages. And the doctors and professors who today owned these farmhouses had painted the clapboards fresh white, black on the shutters, with tax-deduction Herefords grazing in carefully fenced pastures. Some hilltops, offering Green Mountains views, had sprouted new homes architected to mimic those traditional Vermont farmhouses, minus the barns, but super-insulated, with energy-efficient picture windows and rooftop solar panels and satellite disks.

Here and there stood ramshackle dwellings, eccentrically turreted, windows mismatched, unpainted vertical-plank siding weathered gray—they dated back to the communes-and-love-beads Sixties, built by back-to-the-earth immigrants, from Boston and New York, in Rumpelstiltskin style.

Cooper muttered: "Where are the snows of yesteryear?"

And Mike Bolknor, who'd been driving in a dark trance, responded, as if automatically, maybe not even knowing he spoke aloud: "Francois Villon."

Cooper wanted to ask how a New York cop came to know a line written by a Medieval French poet, but she suppressed the urge. She doubted Bolknor would answer.

What does this man brood about, Cooper wondered.

As they left Allen County, driving into Warner County, the gentrification ended. Here, the old farmhouses looked decrepit, rusting tractors in front of sagging barns. Every so often, they passed a weathered mobile home, once for hired hands, now for whoever couldn't afford rent in town.

Warner County had stayed agricultural, right to the sad end, when traditional dairy farms went nearly extinct in this part of the Green Mountains, herds sold off, unused pastures now scrubby with juvenile pines and spruces. It saddened Cooper, the passing of this hill-farm way of life, even though she'd been raised in town, a banker's daughter. And it had been grueling work, bulk milk selling for a corporate-determined pittance.

Palimpsest.

Now she remembered: Mona, just back from Europe one year, had adoringly unrolled an ancient parchment she'd bought, for Cooper to appreciate the medieval monks' tiny drawings of unicorns and fantastical lions. Some of the hand lettering still looked sharp, but other sections seemed blurred.

"It's a palimpsest," Mona said. "Parchment cost a lot, so they'd take an old manuscript, erase it, write over it, and make a new manuscript, except you can still see the old stuff underneath—like looking back through time."

Like this ride along County Route 12, Cooper thought. Or Main Street in Dill. You see what's new, but the old is still there, underneath. Look hard, and you see it.

A palimpsest.

She thought: what's past isn't really gone. And, sometimes….

They drove into Hart's Corners, much smaller than Dill, and hardly changed, Market Street looking as it had for decades.

Merchants here, along with carpenters and butchers, once served hill farmers, who came into Hart's Corners to stock up on Bag Balm for their cows, at Hardy's General Store, and maybe buy new Wellington boots. Hardy's remained, but now selling crusty fresh-baked organic breads and the *New York Times* to Warner County's new-wave organic farmers, trying to make a go of it, growing basil and oregano, or yams, corn, and radishes, or herding goats for artisanal cheese. Even so, except for the new-model SUVs parked along Market Street, and walkers with eyes fixated on their smart phones, Hart's Corners was a Brigadoon. Its houses and buildings looked as they always had.

Cooper told Mike Bolknor where to turn off Market Street. Still looking out the window, at the unchanged town, she thought: this could be eighteen years ago. This could be the day somebody axed a schoolteacher to death.

Nub Duckins got convicted.

Stacey Gillibrand didn't believe he did it.

Something else happened that day. She'd convinced herself. And, whatever it was, she'd stirred it, agitated it, so that it came skittering up through the years. And it killed her.

Nub Duckins didn't shoot Stacey Gillibrand. He'd died in prison.

"That driveway, over there," Cooper told Bolknor.

They turned down a long drive through a spruce-balsam copse, finally stopping under the Clough ancestral home's pillared portico. Cooper gritted her teeth as she rang the doorbell, exasperated in advance.

"I'll talk to him," she told Bolknor. "I've done it before, God knows."

Emerson Clough opened the door, a man as tall as Cooper, and equally gaunt, with close-trimmed hair the color of iron and a long, sculpted face, which always reminded her of an over-bred Great Dane.

She pushed aside the thought, as she'd pushed it aside many times before, that she and Emerson, if you squinted, looked just a bit alike.

Clough surveyed Cooper, leaning on her cane, and raised his gray eyebrows, ironical, amused.

That's right, Cooper thought. I'm a rhesus monkey. I do antics.

270

She wondered if keeping eyebrows up that long hurt.

"*Hic est domina legis!*" Clough said.

Cooper visibly stifled the urge to tell him to stuff it.

"What an acute observation, Emerson," she said. "Yes, here's the lady lawyer."

Clough glanced at Mike Bolknor, who seemed too big for his suit, although it fit, a briefcase under one arm. Then he asked Cooper a question.

"*Tua magnus simia?*"

Cooper thought: good, say it in Latin, so you don't get punched.

It meant: "Your great ape?"

Bolknor's expression remained as baleful as usual.

Clough made a sound like a snicker, pleased with himself, as if his insult in a dead language had conquered and dominated the man. He glanced at Cooper, to see if she appreciated his sally, but got only a glare.

He laughed.

Then—with a magisterial arm wave—he ushered them both into the house's formal living room, furnished with Victorian tables and sofas and Tiffany lamps, the detritus of many generations of Cloughs.

Cooper wondered if all Cloughs had been self-admiring stuffed shirts. Maybe something in the genes.

A colonial grist mill started them off, Cooper knew. It evolved into a feed-supply warehouse, where farmers bought food for their livestock, and those early Cloughs wangled a railway spur through Hart's Corners—train crews hoisted up towering tin tubes, containing conveyor belts, to cascade tons of grain and mash into

271

the Clough warehouse's two-story bins. Then the emptied cars loaded up with Warner County's cheeses and potatoes and corn and wool and maple syrup, for transport to Boston and New York, farmers paying to use the Cloughs' track-side loading platform. Cloughs also bred Clydesdales and Percherons, for farm work, ultimately moving on to sell tractors and pick-up trucks.

As the farms died, so did Clough enterprises, Cooper knew. Driving into town, they'd passed the feed warehouse, boarded up now, a ruin, the railroad tracks rusted, with goldenrod and thistle growing between the ties. Warner County paid its state's attorney little, and nobody wanted to run against a Clough, anyway, so Emerson effectively had the job for life. Besides, there wasn't much work, the county's hamlets and depopulated hillsides so lacking in crime that the state's attorney now worked alone, the voters having eliminated the assistant state's attorney position a decade ago.

In any event, Emerson Clough inherited a hefty portfolio, everyone knew, stocks, bonds, annuities, and real-estate holdings, which kept the sole surviving Clough in Cadillacs and Savile-Row suits.

Clough settled into a leather-upholstered armchair—folding like a jackknife—and pointed to the armchair he'd chosen for Cooper, less luxuriantly stuffed than his own, and to a straight-backed wooden chair for Mike Bolknor, too small for the man.

After that, ignoring Bolknor, he regarded Cooper.

"Well, well, Coop," he said. "How long's it been?"

Four decades, she thought.

She looked out his living-room window at the house's surrounding spruces and firs. October winds had blown sugar-maple leaves into the needles, where they hung like Christmas-tree ornaments, red and gold.

Cooper didn't want to look at Emerson Clough.

Finally, though, she did.

"As I said on the phone, we're here about your Nub Duckins case," she said.

She thought: actually, your only case. Only consequential case, anyway. In decades.

Once the county provided him with an office. These days, he worked out of his home.

Clough stared at her. Then he steepled his fingers and sighed and pronounced: *"Quid fodere mortuis?"*

Showing off, Cooper thought. Mainly to himself. And teaching Mike Bolknor his blue-collar limitations.

"The dead?" Cooper said. "Why dig it up? Because what's buried here got a young woman's brains blown out."

Clough threw up a long bony hand, in wordless dismissal.

"Coed, wasn't it?" he said.

Cooper looked away again, thinking: no, she wasn't a "coed" and an "it." What happened won't go away, just because you don't like the implications. She was Stacey Gillibrand. A grown woman. With fears and hopes and worries and a nasty mother and a bright future as a crusading attorney, and a college professor who misjudged her.

"She dug into Mildred Langley's murder," Cooper said. "It got her killed."

273

Emerson sighed, as if simple-minded peasants had come pestering the duke, complaining of imaginary werewolves.

"Still vaulting into surmise, are we?" he said. "Just like when you arrived here, green as pasture grass?"

Again the amused raised eyebrows.

She'd been twenty-six then. He'd been thirty-eight, and assumed his twelve extra years granted him seigniorial license to lord it over the newbie, just out of law school. This had been her first job, Warner County's assistant state's attorney, under Emerson Clough. That position no longer existed, but those "vaults into surmise" had won cases—Warner County had cases back then—and started her on her career's upward trajectory. And maybe, it occurred to her, that rankled him.

She'd known him since childhood, because their families moved in overlapping circles. She'd thought him a stuck-up prig.

When she came to work with him, though, excited to finally be practicing law, determined to do some good, and she saw him grown up, he'd seemed urbane. And handsome.

Half a year later, he'd suggested they get married.

"Matched breeding, yes?" he'd said. "And caliber?"

He'd assured her: "No need to worry about that gimpy leg."

She'd declined.

By then, after the snide slights, and the aristocratic airs, and the offhand slurs against Jews and Blacks and French Canadians, not to mention the "Neanderthals," his term for all who worked with their hands, she'd returned to her original assessment. Emerson Clough was, in fact, an insufferable prig.

Besides, she'd discovered, as a prosecutor, he was inept.

"We've read the Duckins trial transcripts," Cooper said. "Why did testimony about an alibi get disregarded?"

Clough shook his head, eyebrows raised again, as if importuned by the village idiot.

"Alibi?" he said. "Nub Duckins whacked Mildred Langley with an axe, he did it down in the school's basement, his janitor's lair—his own axe, by the way—for chopping firewood, to burn in the basement's wood stove, and his fingerprints were all over the axe handle."

He gave Cooper a disdainful stare, but she shook her head.

"It was his axe," she said. "So his fingerprints would naturally be on it."

"No other fingerprints on it," Clough said. "Just that primate's."

He raised his eyebrows.

Then he said: "*Quod loquitur, se ad!*"

Cooper thought: he actually believes saying it in Latin makes it true.

"No," she said. "That fact does not speak for itself."

She squelched rising anger.

"A murderer might wear gloves," she said. "Then there'd be only the janitor's prints on the axe, the innocent janitor."

Clough eyed her blankly, as if he hadn't heard what she just said.

"Mike, could I see the transcripts?" Cooper asked, and then saw he'd already extracted them from the briefcase, and turned to the pages she needed, and now held them out to her.

She'd thought he sat there brooding, paying no attention. She'd been wrong.

She scanned the transcript.

"Here's where Duckins' friend gets called to the stand, Perley Mack," she said, eyes on the transcript. "I'll read it."

"Defense: We've heard testimony that Mildred Langley was murdered that Friday evening between five-thirty and seven-thirty—Mr. Mack, do you know where Nub Duckins was at that time?

Witness: Hell yeah, we was both out back of my place, out of town there, having some cold ones.

Defense: That whole time?

Witness: Ayuh.

Defense: Your witness, Mr. Clough.

Prosecutor: What do you do for work, Mr. Mack?

Witness: Do some house painting, do some shingling, help out up at the Singleton Farm, with the spring sugaring, little of this, little of that....

Prosecutor: Very little of this, isn't it, Mr. Mack? And very little of that? Is it fair to say you mostly drink beer and loiter around Hart's Corners?

Witness: I dunno, Emerson, can't say I ever saw you with a Budweiser in your hand, but ain't you mostly loitering, up in that big house there? Hell, ever since we was all in school you....

Prosecutor: Objection!

Judge: Jury, ignore that. Witness will confine himself to answering questions.

Prosecutor: Thank you, Your Honor. Tell us, Mr. Mack, do you have a criminal record?

Witness: Yeah, I got tagged a couple times, but....

Prosecutor: What for, Mr. Mack?

Witness: Nothing much. Got a DWI. Troopers gave me grief over that damned chainsaw thing, which I just borrowed anyway, 'cause Pokey Harris left it lying in his backyard and he wasn't around to ask him to use it, and mine blew a gear or something in it....

Prosecutor: Quite a few things like that, Mr. Mack? Let's see here—failure to pay child support? Drunk and disorderly?

Witness: I ain't a saint.

Prosecutor: Mr. Mack, have you ever lied?

Witness: Stretched it a little? Who hasn't? Like you come in, midnight, maybe, and your wife says....

Prosecutor: So we've established you're a liar. Is Nub Duckins your friend?

Witness: Sure, he's a little dim, old Nub, but he's a good egg.

Prosecutor: Would you tell a lie to protect a friend?

Witness: Depends.

Prosecutor: Thank you, Mr. Mack.

Cooper put down the transcript and stared at Emerson Clough.

"You're obviously leading the witness, making unfounded insinuations...."

Clough sighed, theatrically, looked at the ceiling, then shook his head.

"I prosecute," he said. "That's my job, get convictions."

Cooper thought: no, your job's getting justice done, and railroading innocent people isn't justice. However, she couldn't rearrange Emerson Clough's neurons, so she said something else.

"Why didn't the public defender object to your questioning?"

Clough laughed.

"He didn't have a clue," he said. "Just hatched from some third-rate, never-heard-of law school, tried one feeble objection and John Banton—presiding— chewed him out for it, and after that he mostly shut up."

Remembering, he snickered.

"Wasn't Banton your cousin?" Cooper asked.

Clough shrugged.

Cooper said: "Nowhere in these transcripts is there even a mention of motive—why would Nub Duckins kill this woman with an axe?"

Clough looked blankly at her.

"Who knows?" he finally said. "You can't read a tiny mind like that—maybe he lusted for her and she denied him, or maybe he just got drunk and crazy."

"That's a lot of maybes," Cooper said.

Clough shrugged again.

Cooper leafed through the transcript pages.

"Here's where Nub Duckins took the stand," she said, and she read the passage.

278

Defense: Mr. Duckins, where were you on that Friday night, between five-thirty and seven-thirty?

Defendant: I was out to Perley Mack's trailer, visiting, you know, and I remember we talked about deer hunting and....

Defense: Mr. Duckins, what reason could you have for murdering Mildred Langley?"

(Defendant dabs at eyes with handkerchief)

Defense: Why are you crying, Mr. Duckins?

Defendant: Because I ain't never hurt nobody, and I loved Mildred, ever since she was little, such a cute and smart little thing, I always thought, when I used to do some hired-man work at her folks' farm, and then she grew up to be a teacher, and she was always nice to me, and she helped me get the job at the school....

(Defendant continues weeping, finally dries eyes with handkerchief)

Defense: Mr. Duckins, in the past few months, did you ever see people hanging around Mildred Langley, people you knew or didn't know, who might have had bad intentions toward her?

Defendant: Everyone liked Mildred! She was nice!

Defense: Yes, but people coming around?

(Defendant frowns, thinking)

Defense: Mr. Duckins?

Defendant: Well, there was that red-headed fellow come around a few times, but I already told you about him, didn't I?

Defense: Yes, we discussed all this, Mr. Duckins, you and I, between us, but now it's time to tell the court.

Defendant: Well, like I told you, this red-headed young fellow came around, and I heard Mildred tell him he shouldn't be coming while she was teaching, but he just sort of shrugged, like, and they went outside and talked....

Defense: Others?

Defendant: Used to see this guy come around on a motorcycle, after school got over, when Mildred was up there alone, grading papers, I guess, and she'd always tell me, real nice, that there wasn't any need for me to keep on working and that I should go home and enjoy the evening, because she was like that, and....

Defense: What did this motorcycle driver look like?

Defendant: Had hair down to his shoulders, like one of those Hippies, and a beard, but I don't think he was a Hippie, because of being old, all gray, you know?

Defense: Did this man and Mildred Langley seem to get along?

Defendant: She always seemed really glad to see him, sort of lit up, so I could tell they were good friends.

Defense: Anybody else come around?

Defendant: Just that big guy from Dill, who got married to Beverly, who was Bill and Agnes Carmichael's daughter, from that farm out there, except Agnes was just Beverly's stepmom, and he'd always come around town here whenever somebody died and their property got up for sale, might be a farm, or a store, and I saw him talking sharp to Mildred a few times, about acreage he said the Langleys didn't need, I think, since they'd stopped dairying, but I don't think she sold him any, even though I heard him yelling about it once from all the way down in the basement.

Defense: So there were people coming around who weren't part of the school?

Defendant: Yeah, a few did.

Defense: Thank you, Mr. Duckins.

Defendant: And that woman, too, out from Dill.

Defense: That's someone we hadn't discussed, Mr. Duckins—who was she?

Defendant: Pretty lady, yellow hair, came out a few times, sometimes along with that big guy, like they were in it together, both talking at Mildred, and not so nice, either, I didn't think.

Defense: Your witness, Mr. Clough.

Prosecutor: No questions at this time.

Cooper laid the transcript on her lap and stared at Emerson Clough. He stared back, eyebrows raised. Finally, she spoke.

"Emerson, did you look into these people coming around the school, like this gray-haired biker, for instance?"

Clough threw up a hand, dismissive.

"Just malarkey the Neanderthals threw up," he said. "To save Duckins' hide."

"Did you talk to the kids in Mildred Langley's class," Cooper said. "To see if they saw anything?"

Clough exhaled, as if finally exasperated with the conversation.

"They were just kids, Cooper," he said. "All kids know is they like lollipops."

Cooper stared at him.

"Anyway," he said, "the investigator we used, part-time, he herniated a disc, couldn't get around much, finally retired to Florida, as I recall...."

"Emerson," she said. "Why did you ignore Perley Mack's testimony, that Nub Duckins was at his house, while the murder was committed?"

Clough pressed his fingertips together and frowned.

"Perley Mack never knew his place, which is down among the microbes," he said. "In elementary school...."

He stopped speaking in mid-sentence and sat looking irritated.

Cooper knew that Emerson Clough had attended Hart's Corners Elementary, until his parents switched him to a Massachusetts boarding school. In her parents' social circles, it was laid to complaints about bullying— Emerson was the bully.

Cooper and her brother had both gone through Dill's public school system. She'd once overheard her mother suggest private school for Cooper and her brother, where the curriculum might be more challenging, and her father snorted: "Upper-class ghettos!" He'd been drunk, which was usual in the evening. Not my kids, he'd said. I don't want them turned into little snots.

He'd attended a prep school himself, and then gone on to Princeton. After that, he'd enlisted in the Marines, as a private.

"Semper fi!" he'd told Cooper's mother. "That's where I got educated!"

Cooper, sitting in Emerson Clough's parlor, with all its antiques, suddenly stood.

"Emerson," she said. "What you did to Nub Duckins was criminal."

"I prosecuted," he said.

He glared at Cooper, and she could see a knot working in his jaw.

"I did my job," he said.

A vein in his forehead pulsed.

"And all these years," he said, teeth gritted. "It wasn't me preening—newspapers, tv—vulgar!"

He stayed seated, still glaring, as Cooper spun around and walked out of the parlor, cane banging against the floorboards. Mike Bolknor followed her. At the door, Bolknor stopped and looked back. For the first time since they'd arrived, he spoke to Emerson Clough, his voice low, with a sharp edge.

"*Cooper est leaena!*" he said.

Back in their car, Cooper turned to look at Bolknor, as he drove down the driveway.

"Where'd you learn Latin?" she asked.

He didn't respond until he turned the car out of the driveway, onto the side street, and then it was just a word.

"Jesuits."

When they got back to Market Street, at the town's center, Cooper spoke again.

"Thank you," she said.

Bolknor shrugged.

What he'd said to Emerson Clough pleased Cooper. It greatly pleased her.

"*Cooper est leaena.*"

"Cooper is a lioness."

Cooper directed Bolknor off Market Street, down a side lane, and they drove a block past small clapboard houses, then a second block of weedy fields, where Guernseys once grazed, virtually in town, to the short lane's end, at a wood-framed building, painted muddy yellow, with a sign over the double door: "Hart's Corners Elementary School."

School was out for the day, with the sky—this late in October—already darkening.

Cooper thought: if this was eighteen years ago, in just an hour from now, or two, when it's night, in this little schoolhouse's basement, someone will cleave Mildred Langley's head with an axe.

They got out of the Prius and stood looking at the school, which had a playground on one side, with swings and a slide. There also was a wooden merry-go-round, each seat fronted by a steel push-bar, so the riders, pushing and pulling together, could make the merry-go-round spin.

Cooper envisioned little Berry Randolph on that whirling merry-go-round, along with schoolmates, all pushing and pulling and shrieking. It brightened her mood a little, an antidote, partial, at least, to Emerson Clough, who'd sent an innocent man to jail, and maybe knew it all along, and didn't care.

Stacey Gillibrand had figured it out. She meant to exonerate Nub Duckins. She meant to find the real murderer. Cooper never took her seriously, never really talked with her, never asked what she'd found about the man who'd died in prison. And now Cooper thought: sin of omission.

She stood, frowning. Mike Bolknor, meanwhile, standing beside her, gazed back down the lane, at the overgrown empty lots bordering the school.

"Nobody to see what happened here," he said.

"Nobody," Cooper said.

"A car could park here," he said. "Or a motorcycle…."

Cooper pointed to the forest of mixed maples and pines behind the school. Bolknor nodded. No witnesses on that side, either, except red squirrels and porcupines.

A basement window glowed. Cooper had telephoned before they left Dill, asking the current janitor to wait for them.

They opened the schoolhouse's door, left unlocked for them, and walked into a hallway, lined with classrooms lit only by the fading daylight through their windows, each with miniature desks lined up, facing the big desk in front. Kids' artwork covered the walls, mostly of flowers, in crayon, or watercolors, colored red or gold or violet, but some pupils had created misshapen dogs and cats, or little houses beside pine trees, with stick-figure moms and dads and children.

Cooper smelled chalk dust and the aroma produced by crowded-together kids, a wet-jacket smell.

That scent pervaded Mildred Langley's days.

Cooper had studied newspaper photographs of her. Dark hair, parted on the left, down to her shoulders. Eyes wideset in a thin face. A slender woman, intense, attractive, but not voluptuous. Yet, somehow—was it the mouth?—Cooper saw something sensuous in Mildred

285

Langley, and in her eyes, dark blue, she saw something like desperation. Maybe she'd felt stifled, growing up on the Langleys' dairy farm, in out-of-the-way Hart's Corners. Yet, after college, she'd returned here to teach, and Cooper guessed why.

Her mother, she thought. Mildred's widowed diabetic mother. There was no one else to care for Erna Langley, hardly able to walk. Only Mildred.

She'd enjoyed teaching, and her pupils. Cooper gleaned that from what Berry Randolph told her. Yet, she'd been a young woman. Maybe she wanted more. Romance? Potential husbands would be scarce in Hart's Corners. Suitable ones, at least.

Thinking these things, Cooper heard Emerson Clough's snide voice: "Still vaulting into surmise, are we?"

And she thought, yes, I'm still vaulting.

And now it came to her, vividly, how the teacher's last evening must have gone, eighteen years ago.

In her empty classroom, Mildred Langley sits at her desk.

Night is coming on.

Students have left. So have the five other teachers.

Mildred is not alone, though—down in the basement, in the janitor's workshop, Nub Duckins is splitting firewood into stove kindling. It is late autumn now, and cold, especially the nights. She hears the axe blade chopping into wood.

She wishes to be alone. She must be alone.

Purposefully, she walks downstairs. Duckins stops his chopping, and looks at her, with the watery eyes of an old hound, adoring its beloved young mistress.

She tells him: You go on home now, Nub. You enjoy your evening.

He leaves thinking how nice Mildred Langley is to him.

You go on home now, Nub. You enjoy your evening.

Through a front window, she watches him trudge down the lane, toward the town's center. A bristle-faced man, in his sixties, short and pudgy, flecked with wood chips, simple. She watches until he is gone.

Then she returns to her desk. To pass the time, she grades papers.

She waits.

Cooper called: "Hello?"

Her own voice, in the schoolhouse's silence, startled her.

Footsteps clumped up the stairs from the basement, and the current janitor appeared, a wiry twenty-something, hair buzzed down to black dots, earlobes gold-studded, the letters "M.C." tattooed on his left cheek.

"Hey, I'm Johnny Fandozzi," he said, accent pure Boston. "What's happening?"

Cooper thought: he's nothing like Nub Duckins.

She'd studied the former janitor's photographs in Stacey Gillibrand's cache of newspaper clips. His attorney had cleaned him up for the trial, his sparse gray hair wetted down and neatly combed, stubbly face shaved. He wore an obviously new suit, cheap, just bought from a discount outlet. His attorney surely insisted on it. He looked uncomfortable in his suit. Normally he'd have worn heavy work trousers, Cooper guessed. And a flannel shirt, grimed with chainsaw oil and sawdust.

A weak man's mouth. Simplicity in his eyes, and sadness. As a boy, a pupil in this school—she somehow knew this—he'd been bullied. And it suddenly occurred to her, with absolute certainty, just who did that bullying.

And this trial, she thought, continued what began in elementary school, Emerson Clough's bullying of Nub Duckins. Clough had a mean streak. She'd seen it. And what activated it, she knew, was his victim's helplessness.

In the courtroom photos, Duckins sat frozen, wide-eyed. His young attorney, sitting beside him, looked just as terrified.

Emerson Clough didn't appear in these photographs, but Cooper could easily imagine him in the courtroom, tall and lean and patrician, cruel eyes staring coldly at Nub Duckins, voice superior, edged with scorn.

"Hey, let's do the grand tour," Johnny Fandozzi said. "Wow, checking out an old murder, like on tv, right?"

They followed him, footsteps echoing in the empty hallway, and looked into the six classrooms, one for each grade, all identical except that, as the grade levels went up, the kids' artworks on the walls got more sophisticated.

Mildred Langley had taught second grade. Her old classroom, when they stopped to examine it, looked like

288

all the others. After eighteen years, no trace remained of Miss Langley.

Cooper imagined that last day of Mildred Langley's life. Little Berry Randolph would have been sitting in this room, at one of the small desks. Maybe she'd be working on a crayon drawing, possibly a dog, wanting to make it as lifelike as she could, because she loved animals, and she craved Miss Langley's praise.

Imagining the dog Berry drew, Cooper suddenly grimaced.

Henry.

She shook the thought away.

"So, okay, here's the back door," Fandozzi told them, opening it up.

Outside stood a shed, for the school's lawnmower and leaf rakes and hedge clippers. A Honda Civic, multiply dented, its blue paint faded, seemed to squat in front of the shed. Instead of green Vermont plates, it had Massachusetts plates, red on white.

"Yeah," Fandozzi said, looking at his plates. "Like, maybe I'll go back to Boston, you know?"

Cooper asked why he'd come to Hart's Corners and he looked down and shook his head and muttered: "Marie Cappabianco."

Then he pointed to the basement door.

Looking morose now, he led them downstairs, as if into a cave, out of what daylight remained. Here all the light came from sixty-watt bulbs hung from the ceiling.

Fandozzi waved a hand to indicate the boiler that occupied half the basement, its pipes like a giant octopus's arms, carrying steam up to the classroom radiators. A fuse box on one wall sprouted thick black wires in every direction.

Cooper thought: this is Hart's Corners, where nothing changes.

Steam radiators? When had she last seen them? Or a fuse box? It was all circuit breakers now, except here. She supposed the old Yankees overseeing the school's budget spent no extra dimes, and she imagined some retired hill farmer, face wind-reddened, regarding her with shrewd eyes, pronouncing: "Steam's kept 'em warm, good hundred years, so might's well leave it— ayuh!"

Fandozzi, now lost in melancholy, stood staring at the basement's other half, which had a workbench and an equipment cabinet and a peg-board displaying saws and hammers and screwdrivers and wooden shelves holding used paint cans. Off to one side, beside an old iron woodstove, with its tin exhaust pipe leading to an exposed-brick chimney built into the wall, sprawled a pile of split firewood and a thick wooden chopping block, with an axe stuck into it. Against one wall stood a worn sofa, opened into an unmade bed, and a hot plate on an off-kilter table beside unopened cans of Campbell's baked beans and Chef Boyardee spaghetti, and a battered pot, and an opened loaf of store-brand bread, half gone.

"Do you live here, Johnny," Cooper asked.

"Yeah, they pay crap, so I get to camp here, part of the deal," he said. "Don't tell—it's embarrassing."

"Did you put in the sofa bed?" Bolknor asked.

"Naah, that's an old-timer," Fandozzi said. "See, back in the day, on super cold nights, janitors slept over,

290

to feed firewood into the boiler and stove—boiler burns oil, now."

Cooper glanced at Bolknor, and saw he'd registered it, too. Eighteen years ago, that night Mildred Langley died, this sofa bed was here.

Cooper asked: "Mike, those reports, in the briefcase...."

Bolknor pulled out two files. He handed the coroner's report to Cooper and began reading the state-police crime scene report himself.

Johnny Fandozzi flopped down on his rumpled bed and lay supine, staring morosely at the ceiling.

Bolknor abruptly looked up from the crime-scene report. He stared at the shelves holding paint cans, then at the concrete floor.

"Something?" Cooper asked.

"They found her blood on that shelf's wood," he said.

He walked over and inspected the shelf boards closely.

"Here's a dent in the wood," he said. "About head level, for a woman not too tall."

Cooper leafed through the coroner's report, stopped to read a passage, then looked up.

"Right," she said. "Mildred had a secondary wound at the back of her head, not from the axe."

Bolknor looked down at the concrete floor at his feet.

"Her body lay here," he said. "In a pool of her blood, from her gashed-open head."

Cooper studied the coroner's reports.

"Whoever swung the axe, chopped into the back of the head," she said. "And that killed her."

They stood looking down, staring at the spot on the floor where the teacher's body had lain. Cooper finally spoke.

"So that's clear, then."

Bolknor nodded.

"Murderer first slammed her backwards into the shelving," he said.

Cooper scanned the papers in her hand again.

"Right," she said. "That made that secondary wound on her head."

They stared again at the floor. Johnny Fandozzi got up and sat at the sofa bed's edge, also gazing at the floor, but clearly puzzled. It was just concrete, Mildred Langley's blood long-ago washed off.

Cooper said: "So, first, the murderer slammed her head against the shelves, knocking her senseless, probably, and she fell down prone on the floor."

Bolknor said: "Right, then our murderer checked her and she still lived, so he grabbed Nub Duckins' axe and finished the job."

"Wearing gloves," Cooper said.

Johnny Fandozzi moaned and flopped back down on the bed, both hands over his face.

"Hey, I bet this teacher had a guy, you know?" he said. "And she told him uh-uh, and he went firecrackers!"

He moaned again.

Cooper glanced at Bolknor.

"Could be," he said.

"What else could it be?" Cooper said.

Bolknor shrugged.

Johnny Fandozzi still lay on the bed, hands over his face. Cooper looked at him a while, and finally spoke.

"So her name's Marie?"

"Marie Cappabianco," he said, through his hands.

"Want to talk about it?" Cooper asked.

As it turned out, Fandozzi had been waiting for the opportunity to tell his story, because he immediately sat up and launched into it.

"So, we're in high school, back in the North End, me and Marie," he said. "Way tight, except her folks didn't like me so much."

For one thing, Marie's father taught economics at Boston University and her mother directed a nonprofit low-income advocacy agency, while Johnny Fandozzi's father drove a department-store delivery van and his mother looked after the little Fandozzis, of which there were nine. Beyond that, Marie earned A grades in everything, while Johnny focused on basketball and track.

"Okay, so my grades weren't so hot," he said, morosely.

Marie took Advanced Placement courses in digital technology. He racked up athletic trophies and basked in his fellow students' adulation.

"I was like a star, you know?" he said. "Like I'd get named in the newspapers, and sometimes I'd be on the tv, making baskets? So I kind of focused on all that, you know?"

What he'd do after high school didn't enter his thoughts. His athletic stardom filled his brain. Besides, it went without saying—Marie would be Mrs. Johnny Fandozzi and they'd still live in the North End, so he could hang out with his old buddies, and there'd be little Johnnies and Maries.

Then they graduated.

Marie Cappabianco enrolled in Mt. Augustus College, in its highly rated program in software engineering, which included a hands-on internship at Dill Industries. He stayed back in the North End, looking for work, with no luck. And after a month Marie stopped responding to his texts and didn't answer her cell phone. Finally he'd driven up to Vermont and found her dormitory on campus.

"It just won't work, Johnny," she told him. "High school's over."

He admitted he'd cried.

He'd lurched around the campus, trying to think how to win her back. In the library, he saw a bulletin-board notice: "Janitor wanted, Hart's Corners Elementary School."

Now he told Cooper and Bolknor: "Maybe she'll shake out of it," he said, looking dismal. "Like, we need to be together."

Cooper doubted Marie Cappabianco would see it that way, but she didn't say so. She wanted to say, Johnny, go back to Boston, get on with your life, but she didn't. She thought about her return to Harvard Law School, after polio, to find her former boyfriend married to another woman.

"Does she have a new boyfriend, in college?" Cooper asked.

Johnny shot her a startled look, as if he'd never thought about that.

"Who knows?" he said, gloomy.

Cooper looked at his glum face, branded with Marie Cappabianco's initials, tattooed on his cheek.

"What if Marie did have a new boyfriend?" she said. "Would you be so angry you might attack her?"

Cooper looked meaningfully at the axe stuck in the chopping block.

Johnny looked at the axe, and shuddered.

"No, I'd just feel worse," he said. "Man, like way worse!"

He lay back down on the bed, looking at the ceiling.

"And if I did go bozo like that, it'd be disaster city in here," he said. "Paint cans all over the floor, tools thrown around, and that axe would've whopped everything, like this bed and the table and the boiler—like an H-bomb going off in here."

He lay still, staring morosely upwards.

"But I wouldn't," he said.

Back in the car, Cooper looked out the window as they drove past the empty lots where cows formerly grazed. She said nothing and Mike Bolknor said nothing.

They drove past the next block's small houses, into the town's center, and Bolknor turned left on Market Street, heading back toward Dill.

Cars and SUVs and pickup trucks drove along the street, residents heading home after work, or out to buy something for supper. A few people still walked along the sidewalk, wearing thick sweaters or jackets. Heavy parkas wouldn't be coming out until after Christmas, along with fleece-lined boots, when temperatures on some days

295

would sink toward zero, but a hint of that coming winter already chilled the late-October evening.

"Stop!" Cooper shouted.

Bolknor instantly pulled to the curb. He turned to look at Cooper, but she'd already thrown open the door, grabbing her cane on the way out. She surged up the sidewalk, back the way they'd come, nearly at a run, cane whapping the sidewalk's concrete.

"Henry!" she called.

Up ahead, a woman walking a dog on a leash, startled, stopped and turned to see who yelled, and the dog turned, too. It was a Pembroke Welsh corgi, its fur white and butterscotch, and it stared at Cooper with interest as she lurched up the sidewalk.

"Henry!" Cooper said again.

"I'm sorry," the dog walker said, puzzled. "This is Jennifer."

Cooper stopped and stared down at the dog, who looked up at her, as if eager to make a new friend. Cooper suddenly shook her head and groaned.

"My mistake," she muttered.

She turned and limped back to the car. She eased herself inside and shut the door. Mike Bolknor shifted out of "Park" into "Drive," and the Prius started rolling ahead, back to Dill.

Cooper said nothing. Neither did Bolknor.

CHAPTER THIRTY

At eight-thirty the next morning, they met in Tip LaPerle's office.

Cooper barely listened as Mike Bolknor reported on their Hart's Corners visit—she stared out the window, brooding over Henry.

Hungry? Hurt? Dead?

She remembered an admonishment, from long ago: "Nothing to do about it!"

And, silently, she shouted at the admonisher: "Go to hell!"

Because you could do something. Maybe. If you tried.

"Cooper, if they're nasty, it's on them, so pay no attention."

Even back then, in fifth grade, she'd wanted to shout: "Go to hell!"

She hadn't known the words, though. And one didn't speak like that to one's mother.

Tip was saying: "...so, yeah, Rawston visited that teacher, but he's gone poof, so..."

He leaned back in his chair, glowering.

Cooper thought: Tip's got his teeth gritted again. It's because he couldn't investigate in Hart's Corners. That's trooper turf, and they'd get their fur up, so Mike Bolknor got to do it.

Tip couldn't afford to rile the state cops. Cooper understood. Dill PD had no detective. So they relied on State Police investigators. Troopers were stretched thin, and if Tip needed one of their people....

Cooper sighed.

She wished Tip would drop the simmering animosity toward Bolknor. He'd seem warming to the man, almost, but then he'd turn surly again. And she wished Bolknor would be more forthcoming. His dark silence distressed her. Sometimes it scared her. What happened, back there in New York, she wondered? What terrible thing?

"Okay, no Rawston, so let's hammer the others," Tip said. "Like Jack Abbott."

He sat up.

"I'll haul him in," he said. "Just thinking about it, I get all tingly."

Cooper shook her head.

"He'll never talk to you, Tip, and you know that," she said. "He'd rather get the electric chair."

His face stiffened. After a moment, though, he spread his arms, palms up, ceding the point.

Cooper suppressed a smile. They'd worked together for years, when she'd been Allen County State's Attorney. He'd been impulsive, a firebrand, and she'd been analytically intuitive. She'd guess suspects' motivations. If they blew smoke, she'd sense it. Then,

298

point by point, she'd think it all through. And if she and Tip disagreed—he'd learned this, she knew—Cooper usually turned out to be right.

"Yeah, so I won't Taser the jerk," LaPerle said now. "But?"

Cooper remembered they'd gone to see Rawston's apartment, and Jack Abbott showed up with the key, then refused to answer questions. Before he stormed off, though, he'd hinted that if he ever talked to anyone, it would be Mike Bolknor. That puzzled Cooper, since it was Bolknor who'd decked Abbott in front of her house. Gent's rules, she supposed. You want my respect? Then knock my block off.

No need to tell Tip that Abbott preferred to talk with Bolknor. He'd see it as another stomp on his foot from the big-city cop.

"Let us do Abbott," Cooper said. "Nessie Greffier, too—another one buzzing around that schoolhouse, and let's not forget, Sonny Rawston paid her a visit."

"All right," LaPerle said. "Dill PD'll keep on hunting Rawston, plus that gray-haired biker—Rawston's hired man, I bet."

He sat scowling.

"Well, let's go kick butt," he said.

Cooper made the thumbs-up sign.

"Yea Team," she said.

One-thirty-two Starke Lane.

Cooper sat in her Volvo, looking at the Cape-Cod style cottage, its clapboards brown, built in the 1920s, but

299

periodically repainted and reshingled, with updates, like heat-saving windows. It matched this neighborhood's other houses, respectable and comfortable and not large.

Over the telephone, Nessie had snapped: "I haven't got time."

Cooper told her: "Your choice—it'll be me parking out front, or the Dill PD."

Now, in her car, Cooper sat looking at the lilacs flanking Nessie's brick walkway, just black branches and twigs, late-October skeletons.

She'd arrived three minutes early. So she waited. She meant to ring the bell precisely on time, at eleven, giving Nessie one less reason for umbrage.

Nessie's animosity annoyed Cooper. She'd never done anything to Nessie. Her old classmate hated her, it seemed, simply for who she was.

"Nothing to do about it!"

For once, Cooper agreed with her mother's admonishment.

She got out of the car, retrieving her cane from the rear seat. She leaned on it, relishing what might be autumn's last mild morning, but then she glanced at her wristwatch and limped up the brick pathway, her leg aching more than usual. Drew Saunders had said it wasn't worn-out shoe inserts that hurt. It was polio's aftermath.

For that, too, she supposed, there really was "nothing to do about it," except take OxyContin, which she wouldn't. Or she could ignore it, which she would. She always had.

Odd, she thought. A woman who craves alcohol, yet abhors drugs.

She rang the bell.

She waited, longer than seemed necessary, Nessie making some kind of point. Finally the door opened.

"So what's this supposed to be about?" Nessie said.

"Murder," Cooper said, and Nessie's sneer faltered.

In the living room, where Nessie sat staring at her, now sullen, Cooper made no attempt at small talk.

"Our student got shot," Cooper said. "We're investigating, Campus Security and Dill police."

"What's it got to do with me?" Nessie said.

"I'm here to find out," Cooper said. "Let's start with Sonny Rawston."

Nessie looked puzzled. Genuinely, it seemed to Cooper.

"Rawston's a prime suspect," Cooper said. "Not for pulling the trigger, maybe, but for criminal involvement, and now he's hiding, so that's doubly suspicious."

She watched Nessie's face, looking for any guilty wince or blink. Nessie just looked irritated.

"Do you know Sonny?" Cooper said.

"We played bridge with his parents," Nessie said. "Me and the jackass, currently my jackass ex—so what?"

"Sonny Rawston was seen visiting here, recently," Cooper said.

Nessie's eyes widened.

"He got off his motorcycle," Cooper said. "He walked up to your front door, carrying an envelope, rang the bell, and then went inside with you."

Nessie's eyes widened more, and it looked to Cooper like anger.

"After about ten minutes, he came back out, without the envelope," Cooper said. "He drove away on his motorcycle."

Nessie's mouth curled down.

"This is crap!" she said.

Cooper looked at her, waiting.

"So who's your little spy, peeping at my house?"

Cooper sat expressionless, still waiting.

"You've got nothing better to do?" Nessie said.

Cooper said nothing.

"My old motorcycle trailer, okay?" Nessie said. "I had it in storage, and I put a for-sale ad in the newspaper—big deal."

Cooper hadn't known motorcycles could pull trailers. Something small, she assumed.

"I had it for camping trips, with the motorcycle club, okay?" Nessie said. "To carry my tent and stuff— now I just do day trips, so I got rid of the thing, and I desperately hope you don't mind."

Cooper ignored the sarcasm and considered.

Nessie's probably not lying, she decided. It's too easily verified, like that newspaper ad. On the other hand, this should answer key questions, but the timeline's wrong.

"So, that day with the envelope, that's when Sonny got the trailer?" Cooper asked.

"No."

Cooper waited. Nessie looked stubborn, clearly wishing Cooper would go away, but finally, as the silence grew, she explained, grudgingly.

"Test drive, okay?" she said. "I let him get it from the storage unit, use it a few days, I can't remember, maybe a week, whatever, and then he showed up with the six-hundred dollars."

"Cash?" Cooper asked.

"Yeah, in the envelope," Nessie said. "So I'm under arrest, for selling a trailer?"

She presented her wrists for the cuffs.

Cooper ignored it, mentally ticking off old questions.

Henry, snatched from her yard—how do you carry a crated dog through town on a motorcycle?

And how do you vacate your apartment, and haul away everything you own on a bike?

Nessie's trailer.

That, however, raised new questions, like where jobless Sonny Rawston got six-hundred dollars in cash. And where did he keep the trailer? Tip had officers watching Rawston's apartment house, and they'd seen his bike parked out front, but never a trailer.

Cooper ignored Nessie's glare, and eyed her speculatively. When she'd mentioned Rawston's name, Nessie's eyes didn't shift. She'd just looked mystified.

"We may need to check your bank statements," Cooper said. "For a six-hundred-dollar deposit."

"Oh, be my guest," Nessie said. "You can gloat, how much more money you've got."

No hesitation or evasion. So the deposit must be there, Cooper decided. Nessie wasn't lying. She did get the payment from Rawston.

Cooper ignored Nessie's irritated glare, considering. She'd once thought it possible that Nessie the sharpshooter was….

She asked: "Do you have a .30-06 rifle?"

Nessie turned up her eyes.

"Jeesum," she said. "That's for hunting, and I don't go tramping around in the woods killing furry things—I shoot targets, and if you'd like to come look at my gun collection right now...."

Cooper said: "Maybe another time."

Clearly no .30-06 currently in her arsenal, or she wouldn't have invited Cooper to go look. And, if she'd had one, then got rid of it after that nighttime shot at Cooper, she couldn't keep it secret. Other target shooters, like Beverly Abbott, would know she'd had it. So probably she told the truth about the gun, too, and hadn't fired that first shot, on the rainy night.

One possibility: Jack Abbott did it, maybe to scare her into selling her house, or maybe to get her dead before she willed it to her nephew or the college.

More likely: the gray-bearded biker. He'd shot at Cooper in the park. He shot Stacey. So he probably took that first potshot, too. And, eighteen years ago, that same gray-beard visited Mildred Langley.

"Moving on," Cooper said. "Over in Hart's Corners, eighteen years back, a teacher got murdered— what was your connection?"

Nessie's mouth dropped open. It looked to Cooper like a combination of shock and outrage.

"What on earth...."

"Answer the question," Cooper said.

Nessie looked stupefied.

"You were seen back then, several times, talking to Mildred Langley at the school," Cooper said. "Not nicely."

Nessie sputtered: "This is...."

304

Cooper waited.

Nessie had turned brick red.

"Always the bully!"

That's ironic, Cooper thought.

And she waited.

"Always cutting me down!" Nessie shouted.

She slammed her fist on her chair's arm and lurched to her feet.

"There she sits, her Ladyship, High and Mighty, the Duchess of North!"

Cooper regarded her without expression, a courtroom skill.

Nessie's eyes seemed ready to pop out.

"Like in Mrs. Grogan's class!"

Cooper almost laughed.

We're back in elementary school?

"I studied, every damned night, way late, until my head pounded!"

Cooper wasn't sure she cared.

"Finally I did it, every answer right, just like you—and who still got the number-one seat?"

Mrs. Grogan sat them in order of their test scores. Cooper always won the number-one seat. Probably, if Cooper and Nessie both had perfect scores, that one time, she put Cooper in the first seat out of habit.

Cooper thought: this matters now?

"Doted on!" Nessie shouted, face now looking like an over-inflated balloon, set to burst. "Fancy-pants family, buddies with the almighty Dills, that big brick house—and, boy, did you love sticking it to a girl whose father fixed cars!"

Cooper didn't remember sticking anything to Nessie. What she did remember, all through school, was Nessie Greffier, pretty and popular, and Cooper North, neither.

"Even in French class," Nessie hissed.

So she'd moved through the years to high school now.

"You got the A's, and I was lucky to get a C-plus, and my whole damned family spoke French, for God's sake!"

Cooper maintained her trial face, expressionless. Don't give anything away.

Again she heard her mother's third-grade admonishment: "Cooper, if they're nasty, it's on them, so pay no attention."

She had paid attention, though.

Week after week, they'd milled around her in girls' gym class, mocking her tallness and her thinness and her gaunt cheekbones. And, every morning, at the lockers, they'd whispered insults, like "bookworm" and "giraffe."

Nessie had led them. Her voice the loudest, and nastiest.

And, finally, Cooper had enough.

She consulted with her younger brother. He gleefully coached her, showed her moves.

And the next time they ganged up, Cooper smiled at her biggest tormenter, an Amazonian girl named Claudette, and lashed out, a hard straight right. Bloody nose. Bawling. And for Cooper, a week in detention.

It hadn't bothered her. She had homework to do, and books to read.

After that, fearing another punch, the gang of nasties left her alone, overtly. Underneath, though, the animosity bubbled, kept alive by Nessie. It came out whenever Cooper spoke in class, covert titters.

And now Nessie hissed again.

"You got every damned thing!"

She glared at Cooper, looking ready to spit.

"You got praise, and success, and money, all on an ivy-league platter—and I got the jackass!"

Nessie suddenly looked as if she'd been struck.

"And those parents."

Her voice had fallen to a whisper.

"You went home to them after school, and I...."

Slowly, now, her glare faded, like a fire going out, its fuel exhausted. She looked down and wouldn't raise her eyes.

Cooper thought: you peaked in high school. You were the golden girl. Then we graduated and it all turned to tin. You made your choices. Not my fault. And whatever happened in your home, that certainly wasn't my fault.

She let the silence build.

"Are you done?" Cooper finally said.

No answer, except the downcast eyes, and she let Nessie marinate, a while, in what she'd revealed about herself.

Nessie finally raised her head, but looked aside, still not meeting Cooper's gaze.

"Here's some professional advice," Cooper said. "Cooperate."

Nessie, still looking away, faintly nodded.

"Tell me about Hart's Corners," Cooper said.

Nessie sighed.

"Jack Abbott came to me," she said, her voice subdued. "I was starting my real-estate agency, and…."

Eighteen years ago, Cooper thought, Jack Abbott would have been about twenty-seven, just getting traction, starting his rise.

"He wanted to buy three Hart's Corners farms," Nessie said. "All abutting."

They'd all quit farming and sold their herds, but Jack Abbott planned to repurpose the properties.

Agri-tourism, he told Nessie. Vermont's future!

City people would pay big, he'd said. To show their kids real sheep. Or for a romantic Green Mountains getaway. Smell the clover and timothy. Shuck corn. Milk Holsteins.

Abbott planned to transform the old farms into an agricultural Epcot Center, turning the farmhouses into rustic inns, with token cows and chickens and hogs and sheep, and draft horses, and hay-wagon rides, and a museum of old-time farming. Two of the landowners agreed to his offers, but to make it work he also needed the big farm in the middle, the Langley farm. Erna Langley, widowed, and too old and sick to bother, turned the issue over to her daughter, and Mildred wouldn't sell.

"We went up to the school and argued with Mildred about it," Nessie said. "She just wouldn't sell, and Jack went nuclear—you know how he can be."

"What happened?" Cooper said.

"Jack went at her a few more times, I guess, on his own—he was about ready to blow—but he couldn't browbeat Mildred into it," Nessie said. "And then she got killed, so the whole Hart's Corners deal fell through."

Cooper gazed at her, and Nessie averted her eyes. They sat that way a moment longer, both silent.

"All right," Cooper finally said.

She got up and started toward the door, thumping her cane on the hardwood floorboards.

Nessie, behind her, whispered "Cooper…."

A plaintive tone.

Cooper ignored her. She pushed opened the door and went out and shut it behind her.

Later, in her office, Cooper ate an organic-fried-eggplant sandwich, from the Sweet Kumquat, along with a mango smoothie. Crumbs fell on her desk. She sloshed pureed mango onto the floor. Her office was a perpetual pigsty.

Henry used to scarf up the scattered food bits.

She stared glumly at the floor.

Janitors will clean in here, she thought. Eventually.

On a pad she kept on her desk, she'd scribbled "Jack Abbott—Bolknor?" She sat staring at it, until someone knocked, and the door burst open.

Chip Stack and Nikki Winkel and Jerry Shapiro crowded in. Chip had his usual deer-in-the-headlights stare, except he kept blinking. Jerry affected hipster hands-in-pockets insouciance, but practically twitched, wanting to talk. Nikki just looked intense.

"Last night we all drove over to Montpelier," Nikki said.

"There's this indy band," Jerry said. "Irradiated Rodents, and they've got a lead singer…."

Nikki interrupted.

"We saw Sonny Rawston," she said.

Then they all spoke at once.

"After the concert, we stopped for gas…."

"You know, that convenience store, just across the bridge, on Route 2?"

"Anyway, there was a bike parked there, with a trailer, and…."

"We noticed, because it's odd, you know? Driving a motorcycle this late in the year?"

"Anyway, out of the store comes the biker, with his helmet on, carrying bags of stuff, which he dumped into the trailer."

"Then he got on the bike and drove off, and we suddenly realized who it was."

"We tried to follow, but the nozzle was still in the gas tank, and…."

"Anyway, we saw one thing he bought."

"Yeah, a bag of Alpo!"

Cooper sank back in her chair, eyes shut.

Dogfood.

"Good work, guys," she said, eyes still shut.

They stood silent, looking at Cooper, waiting for her to say something else.

"We called you on Nikki's cell, but you didn't answer."

"Then we called Campus Security, but Mr. Bolknor wasn't in, and a work-study student answered, and said all the guys were out because of a car smash."

"When we got back, we stopped by your house, but your lights were out."

"Then this morning you weren't around, and we tried to tell Mr. Bolknor...."

"He didn't seem to be listening, sort of in a fog...."

"So that's why we didn't get to you until now."

Cooper didn't open her eyes.

She'd never fed him Alpo. She hoped he liked it.

"Thank you," she said, eyes still shut. "Go do something—I've got to think."

She thought, and then she rode the elevator down to the first floor, to Campus Security headquarters, where Chip Stack sat at his desk, heaped with textbooks and essay papers. It occurred to Cooper that Chip now did his class work here, and virtually lived here.

"Mike Bolknor in?" she asked him.

He looked pointedly at Bolknor's closed office door and nodded. He continued to gaze at the door, looking puzzled. Cooper started to ask him about it, then changed her mind and walked to Bolknor's door and knocked.

No response, so she knocked again. Still no response.

Cooper, impatient, opened the door and said, "Mike?"

He sat at his desk, looking too big for it, and for the chair. On the desk lay a calendar, and Cooper saw he'd circled the day after tomorrow, in red. Also on the desk lay his Glock 22, and three .40-caliber rounds, but he'd snapped in the clip, so the rounds were extras and the Glock was loaded.

"Mike?" Cooper said.

He didn't respond, sitting inert, staring at the calendar, so Cooper spoke again.

"Mike?"

He slowly turned in his chair, to face her. His eyes looked dead.

"Hmm?" he said.

"I need to talk with you about Jack Abbott," she said. "And the students spotted Sonny Rawston."

He stared at her, blearily, as if he didn't clearly see her, as if she were only a blurred ghost.

"Mike?" she said.

Slowly his eyes came back alive, but incompletely. Underneath, the deadness remained.

"Yes?" he said.

Cooper felt heaviness, as if the room's air weighed too much. She wanted to ask, Mike, for God's sake, what? No, she thought. Don't transgress boundaries. Yet, this office's gloom disturbed her.

She wanted to tell him about the Alpo. About her relief, knowing Henry still lived. She even wanted to say how much the dog mattered to her, even though he'd lived so few days in her home.

His eyes looked dead, though.

She suddenly missed Mona Dill Saunders, and not for the first time. She could discuss such things with Mona. She thought about Berry Randolph.

So much younger than she. Yet....

Cooper glanced again at the marked date on Bolknor's calendar. What would be happening the day after tomorrow?

He continued to look at her, deadness in his eyes.

312

"We have to grill Abbott," Cooper said. "And you have to do it."

Back in her office, she telephoned Jack Abbott to arrange a meeting. He snarled, but she reminded him there'd been a murder, and he'd damned well better talk to them. One o'clock, he said. My office. Then he slammed down the phone.

Almost immediately Cooper's own phone buzzed, Tip LaPerle calling. He wanted her to know the Montpelier police had spotted a motorcycle last night, heading out of town, towing a trailer, and they'd remembered the APB on Sonny Rawston. They'd tried to catch him, but the bike outran their cruiser and they lost him. He'd seemed heading back toward Dill.

Cooper suddenly realized the students never called Tip last night, that it hadn't even occurred to them. They were college centered, but what was her own excuse? She felt vaguely guilty for not calling him as soon as the students left her office.

"Rawston must still be hiding around here," she said.

"Yeah, but where?" Tip said.

She told him about the Alpo.

"So my dog's still alive," she said.

"Yeah, good," Tip said. "When you visit Abbott, don't be nice."

She put down the phone feeling vaguely blank. Once again, she wished Mona had not gone to Spain, and she considered calling Berry Randolph.

Jack Abbott had his office upstairs in a Main Street building he owned. He leased the ground floor to The Apothecarium, formerly the Dill Pharmacy, but now under new management with a new name and a hip new carved-wood sign featuring flasks and test tubes. A central glass door opened into the pharmacy. A second door, varnished wood, off to the brick building's side, inconspicuous, bore a small brass plaque: "Abbott Enterprises."

It always puzzled Cooper that Jack Abbott, so bellicose and aggressive, kept his business premises discreet, even tasteful. She supposed it was because mostly he bought properties and sold them, and collected rents, and did development deals, with little public contact. No need for a showy headquarters. Not that he innately leaned toward modesty. Certainly the edifice in which he and Beverly lived had nothing modest about it, a sprawling mini-Versailles on thirty-two hillside acres, with a view across the Ira River to Tenement Row, where Jack Abbott started in life.

Cooper climbed the stairs to Abbott's office, while Mike Bolknor waited below. She ascended painfully, step by step, using her cane.

When she got to the top, she saw Bolknor still at the bottom, leaning against the wall, lost in mental murk.

"Mike?" she said.

He looked up, and she had the strange sensation of being on a ship, looking over the rail at a man far below, in the water, drowning. He followed her up, big shoes clumping on the treads.

At the head of the stairs, they faced a second door, with another small brass plaque: "Abbott Enterprises." Cooper knocked, and they heard Abbott's gravelly voice: "Yeah, it's open."

They walked into a large room, one wall all window, overlooking Main Street. No curtains. In a corner stood a desk for Abbott's accountant and assistant of many years, gray-haired Angie Dupre, currently absent, probably because Abbott sent her home whenever her rheumatoid arthritis flared. She'd clearly had no hand in decorating the office, because there were no decorations. A door to one side led to a restroom. Metal filing cabinets lined one wall. On another wall hung a large map of Dill, dotted with red and yellow tacks, indicating the Abbott empire's residential and commercial properties. On a small table rested a Keurig coffee machine and a stainless-steel carousel holding plastic coffee pods in various flavors. Otherwise, there were just a few lightweight chairs for visitors and Abbott's massive oak desk, a nineteenth-century relic, time blackened.

Jack Abbott sat behind the desk, glowering at them.

"Well," he demanded. "What the hell now?"

Cooper sat in Angie's chair, in her corner, trying to look invisible. They'd arranged that Mike Bolknor would do the talking. He pulled a chair around to one side of Abbott's desk and sat in it, close up to Abbott, without the big desk between them. Abbott seemed about to complain, about Bolknor taking that liberty, but then didn't, and he sat waiting, with his arms crossed.

315

Bolknor stared at the wall, silent, and Cooper thought it must be a ploy, to get the suspect off balance, but then she saw his eyes had gone dead again.

"Mike?" she said.

Whatever demons tortured him, Cooper saw, he willed aside. His eyes sharpened, a cop's eyes again, and he kept them on Abbott, considering.

"It's like this," Bolknor said. "You're a suspect in two murders, and this is your chance to clear yourself."

Abbott said, "What the hell?"

He stared at Bolknor, outraged, and shocked.

"What's your connection to Sonny Rawston?" Bolknor said.

"What's this damned crap about murders?"

"Answer the question," Bolknor said. "What's your connection to Rawston?"

"No connection," Abbott said.

"Yes there is," Bolknor said. "You were seen on Main Street, arguing with Rawston."

"Who the hell said that?" Abbott demanded.

"Your wife," Bolknor said. "At a Mona Saunders luncheon."

Abbott glared across the room at Cooper, that information's obvious source, but she kept her face impassive.

"Also, there's Rawston's rent," Bolknor said. "You won't say how much, and that's suspicious."

Abbott reddened, angry. Cooper wondered if he'd ever had an emotion that wasn't some shade of anger. He thudded a fist onto his desk and sat staring down at it. For a long time, they all sat silent.

316

"Tell us about the rent," Bolknor finally said. "If you won't, we'll get warrants."

Another long silence.

"We'll go through your financial records," Bolknor said.

Abbott sighed. His face sagged, and he sank back in his chair. He seemed smaller.

"Everybody thinks I'm on Easy Street," he said, addressing his two clenched fists, resting on his desk.

After that, another silence. Bolknor finally spoke.

"What was the rent?"

"Nothing," Abbott told his hands.

Bolknor and Cooper waited.

"I didn't charge him rent," Abbott said.

Bolknor and Cooper both stared, surprised.

"Why not?" Bolknor finally asked.

Abbott made fists again, and stared down at them.

"Let's just say I felt sorry for him," he said. "Young guy, made a mistake, fresh out of jail…."

"Let's not say that," Bolknor said. "Why'd you actually do it—let's say that."

Abbott loudly exhaled, as if he'd been holding his breath a long time, and finally decided to breathe again.

"Hell, time's passed, you can't do anything," he said.

He stared at the two of them, in turn, defiant. Neither spoke, both waiting.

"Statute of limitations," Abbott said. "I looked it up."

Another silence.

"Three years, that's it," he said. "And it's been a lot longer than three damned years."

317

They waited.

"All right," Abbott said. "It's my pin-head son."

They waited again, while Abbott seemed to watch some internal movie, frowning and shaking his head. Finally he looked at them.

"Promise not to spread this all over town."

"We can't promise anything," Bolknor said. "But we're not in the gossip business—we're trying to solve two murders."

"Everyone thinks I'm a low-life bastard," Abbott said. "Well, to hell with them, but I've got a business, and if whispering starts, that we're shady…."

He stared angrily at his fists, then stared at Bolknor.

"My daughter's got an MBA, for God's sake— she's in Boston, big investment company, she's only twenty-eight, and they send her everywhere, Singapore right now—but Robby? He couldn't find his own ass!"

Abbott had his eyes fixed on Bolknor now, fierce, as if to force Bolknor to understand. And Cooper thought: it's not just that Bolknor beat him in a fight. That's not the only reason he'll talk to him. No, it's because Bolknor's a former New York cop. He isn't from Dill.

"Garbage pit's where I started," Abbott said. "Fought my way out, starting with my meat-head father, and then I fought my way up, just these hands."

He displayed his big hands.

"And Beverly, by God, those farmers worked her like a mule—but Robby? That kid can't even spell 'work.'"

After his son graduated from high school, Abbott said, he mainly chased girls. He roared around Allen County on his motorcycle, a roadhouse regular. It wasn't until later they found out about the drugs.

"Rawston!" Abbott said.

It was Sonny Rawston, he said, who got Robby Abbott smoking marijuana. Rawston then graduated him to cocaine. Finally heroin.

Abbott glared at his fists.

"Your son's in the Navy now," Bolknor said. "Is he okay?"

"Drug rehab, in California," Abbott said. "That finally fixed him."

They'd sent him as far from Dill as they could. He came home sober.

"That's when I personally hauled his butt to the enlistment office," Abbott said. "Get him out of this town."

"Drug addiction's everywhere now," Bolknor said. "It can't have been so…."

"It was worse than you think," Abbott said.

Rawston got Robby addicted, Abbott said, but that was just setting his hook. Next, in exchange for fixes, he forced Robby Abbott to carry drugs for him, on his motorcycle, to New York and Boston. And then he got Robby into pushing.

Abbott sat staring at his fists again.

Cooper thought: Sonny Rawston didn't need Robby Abbott's help. It just amused Rawston, turning this rich boy into his puppet.

Abbott sighed.

"One kid, over in a Montpelier trailer park, who my genius son supplied, over-dosed, wound up dead," he said.

He shook his head.

"That's when we shipped Robby to California rehab," he said. "And that dead kid's mother, what a piece of trash—no daddy around—but I hushed her, and right now she's rich trash."

They sat in silence, while Abbott stared at his hands.

"Anything more about Rawston?" Bolknor said.

"Yeah," Abbott said.

Fresh out of prison, Sonny Rawston showed up here in Abbott's office, saying they needed to make a deal. Abbott sent Angie Dupre home for the afternoon.

Rawston's deal was simple: Robby Abbott—drug pusher. Jack Abbott—abetting the crime. And he, Sonny Rawston, would spread the news.

Unless....

It started with the rent-free apartment. Then it escalated to regular demands for cash.

"Thousands," Abbott said. "And I'd already practically bankrupted us buying off that trailer-park woman."

He frowned at the opposite wall, with the map of his properties.

"Business's been bad," he said. "That recession, I got hit there, and then a couple of deals that...."

Cooper almost sympathized. His money bin emptied, desperate for a cash infusion. So he fixated on the old North house, she thought, my house, abutting the campus, perfect site for the college's and Dill Industries' new artificial-intelligence lab. They'd pay him millions for it.

Pugnacious, bellicose Jack Abbott. Nearly broke. And all the while, Sonny Rawston had him by the neck.

"Where's Rawston now?" Bolknor asked.

Abbott snorted.

"In hell, I hope," he said.

That's the truth, Cooper decided. He really doesn't know where Rawston's hiding.

A realization came to her: it wasn't just to harass me. That's not why Sonny came back to Dill. That was a sideshow. He got out of jail broke, but with a plan. He came back to Dill to bleed Jack Abbott.

Bolknor nodded to Cooper, indicating he, too, believed Abbott. Wherever Rawston hid, Abbott didn't know.

"All right," Bolknor said. "Let's talk about Mildred Langley."

Abbott looked confused.

"That damned farm?" he finally said. "She wouldn't sell it to me."

"And then she got murdered," Bolknor said.

Abbott stared, realizing where this was going.

"Now, eighteen years later, our student gets shot," Bolknor said.

He waited, but Abbott didn't react.

"Stacey Gillibrand was investigating that old murder," Bolknor said. "And immediately after the newspaper reported it, she got shot."

Abbott's eyes widened.

"You actually think…."

"Eighteen years ago, you were seen at the Hart's Corners school, several times," Bolknor said. "You argued with Mildred Langley, you yelled at her."

Abbott slammed his fist onto his desk.

"Because she screwed up my deal," he said. "Just like…."

He glared at Cooper, then quickly looked away, realizing the implication.

"Yes, and Cooper also wouldn't sell to you," Bolknor said. "Did that make you angry enough to shoot at her?"

Abbott shook his head.

"Is that your pattern?" Bolknor asked. "Demand, get refused, explode?"

"Langley didn't need that damned farm!" Abbott said.

"Did you get so angry you hit her with an axe?" Bolknor asked.

Abbott threw up his hands, then slammed his fists down onto his desk.

"No, damn it!" he said.

Cooper, watching from the corner, suddenly remembered Johnny Fandozzi, the janitor at the Hart's Corner school, pining for his lost love, Marie Cappobianco. He'd told them he'd feel terrible if she'd thrown him over for another guy. Even so, he said, he'd never hurt Marie. But if he actually did go bozo….

What then, they'd asked.

"It'd be disaster city in here," he'd told them. "Paint cans all over the floor, tools thrown around, and that axe would've whopped everything, like this bed and

322

the table and the boiler—like an H-bomb going off in here."

Cooper saw Bolknor, about to resume questioning, glance at her. She shook her head, subtly.

"Mike," she said. "Let me ask a final question here."

Bolknor looked surprised, then shrugged, waiting for her to speak.

Cooper addressed herself to Abbott.

"Jack, when you were at that school, arguing with Mildred Langley, did you ever see a man with shoulder-length gray hair and a gray beard?"

Abbott made a disgusted expression and spread his hands.

"No, just kids," he said. "And teachers—it was an elementary school, for God's sake."

He sat slouched in his chair.

"Nessie Greffier," he said.

They waited.

"I had her with me sometimes," he said. "Real estate, you know? I thought, a woman, part of the deal, maybe that'd soften Langley up."

Cooper and Bolknor got up and started toward the door. Behind them, Abbott made a disgusted grunt.

"Just that snake, Rawston," he muttered.

Cooper and Bolknor both turned. They eyed Abbott, slouched in his chair, still staring at his hands. He sensed their gaze and looked up.

"I saw him a couple of times, talking with the Langley woman," he said. "I didn't pay attention—he was just out of college, still a snot-nosed kid, so who cared?"

Cooper and Bolknor exchanged a look, then headed for the door.

Behind them, Jack Abbott still sat his desk, staring at his fists.

On the street, in front of the Abbott Enterprises door, Bolknor fished his cell phone out of his jacket pocket and called the Dill PD, arranging to stop in, so he could report to Tip LaPerle on their meeting with Jack Abbott.

Good move, Cooper thought, listening. Politic. She only hoped Bolknor wouldn't go dead-eyed somewhere on Main Street, though, and drive the Campus Security Prius into a hydrant.

"Here's my thinking," she told him. "Let's say Jack Abbott killed Mildred Langley—it'd be because she defied him, cost him his big deal. So he'd explode, right? H-bomb?"

Bolknor stared at her, face expressionless. After a moment he nodded.

"Yes," he said. "But it wasn't like that—no explosion, just Mildred Langley dead, everything else in the basement untouched."

"So it wasn't a slaughter, what you'd expect from an enraged Abbott," Cooper said. "It was an execution."

"That axe was handy," Bolknor said. "So maybe the murder just happened, not preplanned...."

"Or maybe it was," Cooper said. "Precisely preplanned, gloves, the axe...."

Bolknor nodded.

"To frame Nub Duckins," he said.

324

"So who has a mind like that?" Cooper asked.

She drove home in her Volvo, and parked in her driveway. It occurred to her that Campus Security still kept watch on her house at night, and she decided to tell them to stop it. No reason now for someone to shoot her. And it felt creepy, needing bodyguards.

She got her mail out of the box, just bills and advertising circulars and a letter from her nephew, now in Brussels, probably wanting to know, among other things, how Henry was doing. She sighed.

Later, she thought. When I've got the strength.

Otherwise, there was only a business-sized envelope with no return address, but a Burlington postmark. She had no idea what that might be.

Inside, she dropped the mail onto the kitchen table and flung her parka over a chair. She started to brew a cup of coffee, then changed her mind and switched to green-mint tea. Then she changed her mind again and started a cup of cocoa brewing, in honor of oncoming November and the nippy afternoon.

As she sipped the cocoa, still too hot to drink outright, thinking about Mike Bolknor's depression, worried about it, she idly used a kitchen knife to open the mystery letter. It contained a snapshot photograph, taken with a cell phone, probably, and she sat staring at it, stupefied.

Henry looked out of the photograph. He lay on his stomach, squeezed into a wire-mesh crate. His fur looked unkempt. His eyes radiated misery. They seemed to beseech her. Beside the crate, carefully placed for visibility, lay a rifle.

A .30-06, Cooper guessed.

Still staring at the photograph, she fumbled inside the envelope with the fingers of her left hand and felt a slip of folded paper and pulled it out and opened it, a hand-printed note.

"Stop your harassment, North," she read. "Montpelier the other night—cops chasing me."

"Call them off, North. You started years ago, harassing me and ruining my life, and you're still at it. So call off your cops. I'll drive out of here and be gone. Otherwise, this little doggie of yours gets shot in the head.

"You've got a few days, and then I'm starting away, taking your little doggie with me—if no cops hassle me, I'll leave him at some Humane Society shelter. Somewhere. I'll give them your address, so they can call you to pick him up. If cops harass me, count on it: this little doggie gets a bullet."

Cooper laid down the note and stared at the wall.

After a while, she picked up the photograph and studied it.

Henry's crate rested on a wide-plank floor. Not sanded and varnished planks. These boards looked unfinished and worn. And they fitted together roughly, not like seamless residential flooring. She made out some knotholes. Maybe industrial flooring, or a warehouse. Certainly not in a home.

What else?

The rifle.

Cooper knew little about guns, but she thought this one seemed old. For instance, the stock looked worn, not shiny. Not an antique, though, just a weapon that had seen service, probably in deer camps. Tip might make something of it. Or Mike Bolknor, although she doubted hunting rifles popped up much in NYPD cases.

Otherwise, the snapshot showed little. By design, she supposed.

In Tip LaPerle's office, they'd interviewed the scoutmaster, she remembered now. His troop had distributed Sonny Rawston's fliers, aimed at forcing Cooper to humiliate herself. He'd spoken with Rawston on the telephone, he'd said. And, in the background, he'd heard "a sort of grinding sound, kind of far off," Cooper remembered. "Or maybe," he'd said, "it was more like a whooshing."

Cooper squinted at the photograph again. It wasn't a place she recognized, not in particular. In general, though, she felt she'd been in such a place, with a rough board floor, scattered with debris.

In the photograph, she couldn't make out the debris. Snippets of string?

She grabbed the photograph and note and hobbled through the kitchen and dining room, then down the hall, to her home office. From her desk drawer she pulled a magnifying glass, which she'd used for decades to read the fine print in legal documents, and she held it over the photograph, peering at the floorboards.

She saw dust. And she saw scattered slender strands, some shorter, some longer, some straight, some bent.

What were they, though?

Nothing else in the photograph. Just Henry, his eyes unbearably sad.

She looked again at the note.

He asked her to "call off" the cops, as if she could do that. This man was wanted in connection with a murder. At least one murder. Maybe two. Every officer in Vermont and in neighboring states was on the lookout for a red-headed motorcyclist. And they couldn't miss him. It was nearly November, in northern New England. Few bikers would be out in this cold. Just him, desperate to get away.

She supposed he'd driven his motorcycle all the way to Burlington to mail his note, to make it impossible to trace to him. Probably he'd gone late at night, when he'd be least likely to be spotted. She imagined him driving that motorcycle west on I-89 at two in the morning, on a late-autumn night in Vermont, bundled up, but cold to the bone.

He's desperate, Cooper thought. A desperate man wrote this note. Wherever he is, he can't stay there forever, making stealthy runs into neighboring towns to buy food. He's no longer in control. And what might he do to regain control, at least in his own mind?

Kill my dog, Cooper thought.

Or maybe, to feel in control, he'd drive here in the night, with that rifle, and shoot me.

More likely, he'd shoot Henry.

Still, she decided not to call off her nighttime bodyguards just yet.

She slumped back in her chair and stared at the photograph.

Everyone had died—her father, mother, brother. How many years had she lived alone in this house, after she moved back here to care for her ailing, widowed mother, so old? She'd lived alone, but she'd had friends and work, and she was tough. Then, just days ago, Henry came. She supposed it should embarrass her, tough old Cooper North, because he was just a dog, an animal. Maybe. But she loved this corgi. This intelligent dog. So aware. Staring at her now, out of this photograph.

His eyes seemed to speak: "Why did you let this happen to me? Why can't you help me?"

Scotch. Vodka.

It felt like a punch, this need, this urge.

It made her hands shake.

She didn't want this again. She didn't want to feel this. No matter what.

She willed it away, hating it, straining against it so hard she scrunched up her face.

Even if something did happen to Henry.

"Nothing to do about it."

Or maybe she'd think of something.

Not with her brain numbed, though. Not drunk. She'd think of nothing. She'd be useless.

"Go to hell," she thought.

CHAPTER THIRTY-ONE

At seven that evening, Cooper laid down the *Dill Chronicle* on the lamp table, and she slouched in her armchair, sourly eyeing the Palladian window's drawn drapes. She knew a Campus Security officer watched outside—she'd brought him a thermos of coffee—and she felt cowardly for drawing the curtains, like a child afraid to see the darkness.

Her telephone rang.

She checked the Caller ID: Germany.

Her nephew, she decided. Probably traveling in Europe, calling from a hotel on his smartphone, to check on Henry.

She sighed. She didn't want to have this conversation, but she picked up the handset, and said, "Hello."

She glanced at her wristwatch—in Western Europe, it would be one a.m.

"Professor North?"

A woman's voice.

"Yes."

"I'm calling about Mike Bolknor."

Silence on both ends of the line. Finally, the woman spoke again.

"Are you his friend?"

"Who is this?" Cooper said.

"I called the campus, and they said Mike worked with you."

"Who is this?" Cooper repeated.

"If you'd worked with him, I thought, maybe you'd become friendly."

"I need to know who you are," Cooper said.

"I'm sorry," the woman said. "I'm upset, not communicating well."

Silence.

Cooper waited.

"This is Kirstie," the woman said. "Kirstie Bolknor."

Cooper stayed silent, waiting for more explanation. On the other end, she sensed the woman also waiting. Finally the caller spoke.

"I guess he hasn't mentioned me," she said.

Cooper waited.

"Has he talked at all about Rachel?"

"No," Cooper said.

"Frank?" she said. "Abigail?"

"No," Cooper said.

"Oh, God," the woman said. "He's still keeping it all in."

She sounded worried, and miserable.

"This is confusing," Cooper said. "You gave me your name, Kirstie, but I don't understand who you are."

"I'm Mike's sister," she said.

"You're German?" Cooper asked.

"What? Oh, no—I'm over here in the Army," the woman said. "I'm a captain in the military police."

"I see," Cooper said. "And why are you calling?"

"Mike won't answer his telephone," the woman said. "Not since he moved up there, to Vermont, and I'm worried sick about him, and I thought, if he's made some friends…."

"Can you tell me what's troubling you?" Cooper said.

On the other end of the line, an intake of breath.

Silence.

Then: "I can't."

Cooper waited.

"If he doesn't want to talk about it, then it's wrong for me to…."

Cooper waited through a silence, until the woman finally spoke again.

"I shouldn't have called," she said. "I'm terribly sorry to bother you, Professor North, but I've been sitting here, thinking that it's been a year, coming up, and…."

Cooper waited.

"I'm sorry I've bothered you."

A click at the other end, across the ocean, and then a dial tone.

Cooper held the handset away from her and stared at it. Then, gently, she put it back in its cradle.

Kirstie Bolknor obviously worried about her brother. So did Cooper. Heaviness hung on him, as if thick lead filled his shoes and lined his clothing. Her worry had cranked up earlier today, seeing him in his

332

office with dulled eyes, the day after tomorrow circled on his calendar, and his pistol lying on his desk, loaded. She didn't know why, exactly, but she felt panic.

"Are you his friend?" his sister had asked.

Cooper, alone in her living room, nodded.

I am.

What should I do?

And then the telephone rang.

"It's me again, Kirstie Bolknor," the woman said. "You must think I'm nuts."

"Actually, I think you're worried about Mike," Cooper said. "So am I, and I'd like to help, but I'm in the dark."

"I've decided to tell you, trust you to help him, actually, but I don't know where to start."

"At the beginning, Kirstie—start there."

"Well, he met Rachel when they were both at the university, and…."

"University?"

"So he hasn't even told you that much," Kirstie said, and she sighed.

Silence.

"Okay," she finally said. "Wolf Bolknor, that's our grandfather—cop. Mitch Bolknor, our father—cop. So that's Mitch's Law, choose any work you want, as long as it's NYPD, and I'm sure you get the picture."

"Yes," Cooper said.

"Mike sort of rebelled," Kirstie said. "He enlisted in the Army, and wound up in the MPs, which is what I did, too, when it was my turn, so family karma, right?"

Afterwards, she said, under the GI bill, her brother enrolled at Fordham University, which ticked off

333

their father—a son, trying to outdo his father, that's how he saw it.

"Hey, Schoolboy," he'd say. "Too smart to be a dumb cop?"

Mike Bolknor fought it. He stayed at Fordham. He'd always been a reader, and he wanted to teach English in high school.

"Big lug like him," Kirstie said. "High-school football, then an Army heavy-weight boxing contender, and I don't think it occurred to him he might scare the jeans off students."

He met Rachel Golden at Fordham. She also aimed to teach English. By then Mike's mother had died, of breast cancer, and Mitch Bolknor, still fighting the you've-gotta-be-a-cop war, wouldn't speak to his son, so Rachel and Mike got married in a minimal ceremony, just Kirstie and Rachel's immediate family. That was midway through Mike's final semester at Fordham. And a few weeks after the wedding, in the Bronx, quelling a gang fight, Mitch Bolknor got knifed.

"We sat with him in the hospital," Kirstie said. "Dad rolled his head over to stare at Mike, and he spoke to him, whispered, actually, but we could make out what he said."

"Why wouldn't you make me proud?"

Two days later, their father died, Kirstie said. That same day, Mike dropped out of Fordham. And the day after that he offered himself to the NYPD.

"Obligation, that's what drives him," Kirstie said. "Duty, all that kind of stuff."

It had worked out. Bolknor had his Army MP background, and rose fast in the police force. And, truthfully, Kirstie said, he felt comfortable, being a detective. He saw it as protecting society against bad guys, worthy work.

"Probably he wouldn't have been a great English teacher anyway," Kirstie said. "He's never been a talker."

Rachel, meanwhile, taught at a Manhattan high school for high-achieving kids, with time-outs to give birth to Abigail, and then Frank. Mike enjoyed his work, and Rachel enjoyed hers, and they loved each other, and the kids.

"Sounds sappy, I guess, but that was the truth," Kirstie said. "I'd go over there for dinner all the time, and you could see it, not like our mother and father, always at each other, and that's how it was until coming up on a year ago."

They'd decided to fly down to Tampa, to help Rachel's mother, now widowed, to move into an assisted-living facility. At the last minute, though, Mike got assigned to a major racketeering investigation. He felt he had to pursue it aggressively, couldn't take a break, so they decided just Rachel and the kids would fly down.

"We know what happened because people saw it," Kirstie said. "People on the sidewalks, other drivers...."

Rachel had rented a car at the airport, and they were driving through Tampa to her mother's facility, in heavy traffic, when a silver Lexus RC sports car—the driver with his eyes down, on his smartphone, texting—abruptly swerved in front of a red Ford F-150 pickup. That angered the truck's driver, so he blared his horn and smacked his pickup's front bumper into the back of the Lexus.

Road rage erupted—shouting through opened windows, weaving through traffic.

Rachel's rental car got sandwiched, the pickup in the lane to her left, the Lexus to her right. A Mack truck tailgated her, so she couldn't hit the brakes, to get behind the two yelling contenders, now giving each other the finger.

Then it escalated: both drew handguns.

"Rachel got caught in the crossfire," Kirstie said. "It was bumper to bumper traffic and she couldn't go anywhere—one bullet hit her in the head."

She died instantly. Her car swerved into the Lexus. In the smashup, the Lexus's driver died. So did Abigail and Frank. According to the pickup's driver, he'd had to "stand his ground," and under Florida law that justified his shooting at the Lexus driver, who wasn't around to give his side of the story. So the pickup driver got off.

"All through the investigation, and funerals, and the burials, Mike only said one thing, 'I should have been there.'"

As far as Kirstie could tell, he'd gone back to work and never told his NYPD colleagues what had happened. He'd just plugged away. As time went on, he'd barely talk even with Kirstie.

"It wasn't because he'd turned against me," she told Cooper. "I knew that—he just didn't want it to come up, couldn't talk about it."

Something of a family trait, she said. At least among Bolknor men. Keep it to yourself.

Almost a year passed like that, Kirstie said. Mike going into work like a zombie. Then, as the one-year anniversary loomed, he abruptly quit the NYPD and took the job at Mt. Augustus College. Since then, he hadn't responded to his sister's telephone calls.

"I'm really worried," she told Cooper.

"So am I," Cooper said. "You know him—any idea what I can do?"

"No," she said.

Silence, both thinking.

"If you talk to him about it directly, you'll lose him," Kirstie said.

Silence again, and then Kirstie spoke.

"He's like a guy in a black depression, standing on a forty-eighth-floor window ledge, looking down, you know?"

"Yes," Cooper said.

After a silence, Kirstie spoke again.

"It's like you have to find just the right words," she said.

When she woke up the next morning, Cooper still didn't know what to do. Once again she wished Mona Dill Saunders was in town. A friend to talk with.

"Get real," she thought.

Tact wasn't one of Mona's strengths. Neither was sensitivity. She'd have no suggestions for helping Mike Bolknor. No good ones, anyway.

Cooper sipped her morning coffee, hardly noticing she did it.

She thought: what he wants is to be left alone.

And she thought: sorry, Mike, that's not going to happen.

337

Except she still didn't know what to do about it. Or anything else.

She got out the photo Rawston sent her, Henry, in his crate, looking at her with beseeching eyes.

I left him alone in the yard, she thought.

I should have been there.

"Damn," she said.

She slid the photograph and Rawston's note into her briefcase. She put on her parka, while a fresh cup of coffee brewed. Then she took the cup with her, out to the car, careful not to spill any.

A gray autumn morning. Winter in the air. Somewhere, high up, ravens yelled.

Mike Bolknor sat at his desk. He glanced at Cooper, when she walked into his office and shut the door behind her. Then he looked away again.

No pistol visible now, but he'd taken the calendar down from the wall and laid it on his desk, with tomorrow's date circled in red.

Cooper sat in his visitor's chair and put down her coffee cup on his desk, vaguely proud she hadn't yet sloshed it. She eyed him speculatively. He stared vacantly at the wall.

"Your sister called me last night," Cooper said. "From Germany."

Bolknor turned his head and looked at her. His face seemed made of granite, unreadable.

"Kirstie—I liked her," Cooper said.

She waited for a response, but got none, except that Bolknor looked away again, and his body stiffened.

He knows what Kirstie told me, Cooper thought. He doesn't want it discussed.

"Mike, I need help," she said.

He looked at her again.

"Couple of things," Cooper said. "One is that boy out there."

She pointed at his office's closed door. On the other side of it, Chip Stack sat at a computer station, keyboarding in data.

"Last night I scared myself," Cooper said. "Talking with Kirstie, I got to thinking you might leave us, maybe go back to the NYPD, or something—I hope you stick with us."

He continued looking at her, and she took that as a good sign.

"Chip's father says he'll shame the family," Cooper said. "For not becoming a doctor."

Bolknor knew all that, but she wanted to remind him.

"You're the antidote, right?" she said. "Chip's lifeboat?"

Bolknor shrugged.

"I worry, if you weren't here, he'd sink," she said. "Breakdown."

She waited for a response. Bolknor continued looking at her, and she decided that would have to do.

"You're his coach," Cooper said. "Just by being here."

Bolknor turned his hands over on the desk, palms up. Cooper took that as agreement.

She waited, but he didn't say anything. Point made. Point taken? She didn't know.

"Then there's this," Cooper said.

She opened her briefcase, peered inside, then pulled out Rawston's note and the photograph. She laid them both on Bolknor's desk.

She watched him read the note and look at the photograph.

"What do you think?" she said.

He shrugged again.

"He wants a 'get-out-of-jail-free card,'" Bolknor said. "Can't be done."

His voice sounded heavy, as if he'd been climbing a mountain, with many uphill miles ahead.

"It's like getting punched, losing Henry," Cooper said. "It's...."

Bolknor looked about to say something, about loss, maybe, but then didn't.

"I don't know what to do," Cooper said.

Bolknor slumped in his chair and looked at his hands.

"Neither do I," he said, not looking up.

"Well, let's both be thinking about it," Cooper said.

She slid Henry's photograph and Rawston's note back into her briefcase and slung its strap over her shoulder. Then she stood and gingerly lifted her coffee cup and got hold of her cane and started out. At the door, she turned.

"It's not just Chip Stack," she said. "It's me, too—I need you here, for my own selfish sake."

She left without waiting for a response.

Noon at the Percolator.

Cooper chose a corner booth, away from the lunch-hour crowd's hubbub. She had questions to ask, but mostly she just wanted to talk.

So many knotted-up worries. She wanted to unmoor from them, to float free.

Without vodka.

She watched the front door, waiting for her companion to arrive.

Normally she'd have called Mona Dill Saunders, because Mona amused her, for one thing. Imperial, yes, but also intelligent and honest and well meaning, although with zero tact.

Mona, however, was still in Europe, gallery hopping. Cooper had just received a postcard from her, date-marked Barcelona, its message a single scrawled word: "Picasso!!!"

Leaning back, still watching the front door, Cooper eyed the crowd. Mostly familiar faces. She'd lived in Dill nearly seventy years, so she knew just about everyone, and liked most of them, but to varying degrees.

Beverly Abbott, for instance—she sat at a table across the room, with the new Episcopal priest, a peppy woman Cooper hadn't yet met. Cooper liked Beverly, felt warmly toward her, but she couldn't imagine an extended conversation with Beverly.

She thought about people not in the Percolator right now, like Tip LaPerle.

One of her best friends. He was three decades younger, a gender apart, not much schooling, a little rough, maybe, but even so, she'd enjoy having lunch with Tip. They'd worked together so long. With him she could

341

discuss almost anything, although not quite everything. Henry, for instance. If she confided her heartache over losing the dog, he'd be polite, but he'd think: "It's just a dog, Coop, an animal."

Mike Bolknor. She hoped he'd become a friend, too. Younger, yes, but aware. Very much so. You could talk about virtually anything with him, she thought, as long as you didn't expect him to offer a lot of words. And she sensed integrity, decency. His sister said so.

He'd walled himself in, but she'd lure him out.

Unless....

She shoved that thought aside. She'd come here to forget worries.

Cooper went back to eyeing the crowd. She felt friendly with most of them, but at a distance. As if she might wave to them, and smile, sincerely, but across a river. Not for the first time, she wondered, am I a snob?

She visualized Emerson Clough's supercilious eyebrows.

"Good Lord," she thought. "Please, not that!"

And then the Percolator's front door opened and in came Berry Randolph.

Everyone looked at her, couldn't help it.

Cooper thought: Ethiopian princess.

Cooper waved and Berry, seeing her, offered a dazzling smile and started to weave through the tables in her direction. Cooper suddenly felt concerned: the young veterinarian dragged her feet, almost as if walking underwater. And when she got to Cooper's booth she virtually collapsed into her seat, exhausted. She slouched a moment like that, hunched—Cooper could see her gathering strength—and then she sat up straighter and looked Cooper in the eye and smiled.

"I know it's about an investigation," Berry said. "But thanks for calling me—I could use a time out with somebody nice."

"All Creatures Clinic runs okay?" Cooper said. "When the vet's AWOL?"

"Tony Petracelli's in the cockpit," Berry said. "My husband, my Gibraltar, the man I dearly love."

She smiled ruefully.

"He's been flying solo for nearly a week," she said.

She pretended to pout.

"What, I'm unessential?" she said.

"You've been away?" Cooper asked.

"Sort of," Berry said, and fell silent.

Cooper could almost read her thoughts. Explain or not? Finally the question got resolved, because Berry shrugged.

"I've been in the hospital," she said. "One of my episodes."

Sickle cell, Cooper thought.

"It's all okay now," Berry said, giving Cooper a smile. "So hit me with your Dick Tracy questions."

Cooper reached across the table and, offering no explanation, patted Berry's hand. A kind of hug.

"Here's one," Cooper said. "Eighteen years ago, that gray-haired biker—remember any more about him, like his height?"

Berry made a thinking face.

"My husband's six foot," she said. "I'd guess he was about that."

343

"Did you ever hear him speak?" Cooper asked.

Again, the thinking face.

"I don't think so," she said. "He and Miss Langley whispered, and he only showed up in the classroom a few times."

"They seemed friendly?"

Berry looked searchingly at Cooper.

"Do you think…."

"He's a suspect," Cooper said.

Berry shivered.

"Miss Langley certainly seemed glad to see him," she said. "At least, that's how I remember it, and maybe she seemed worried a little, too, about a visitor during school hours, I guess."

June Winkel hurried up, pulled a pen from behind her ear and poised it over her order pad, waiting to hear what they wanted. Coffee and a tuna-salad sandwich for Cooper. Perrier and a chocolate sundae for Berry.

"That's lunch?" Cooper said.

Berry looked guilty.

"I'm not quite back to normal yet," she said. "That's about what I can get down."

For some reason, that made Cooper suddenly sad, almost forlorn. She sat a moment, staring at the table.

"I hope you're going to be alright," she said.

"Oh, sure," Berry said brightly. "It usually takes a few days, that's all—got more questions?"

"That red-headed fellow you saw," Cooper said. "Did he and the gray-bearded biker ever visit the school together?"

Berry thought again, then shook her head.

Jigsaw-puzzle pieces, Cooper thought. Try this one. Then that one. See what fits. Keep trying, and the puzzle's image begins to appear. It would be a face.

Or a spider, she suddenly thought.

"Well, that's it for now," Cooper said.

"Okay," Berry said. "How's my friend Henry?"

Cooper froze, momentarily unable to respond.

"Dognapped," she finally said. "We don't know where he is."

Berry stared at her, astonished.

"But the GPS…"

Cooper looked at her, uncomprehending.

"You got the top-end care plan," Berry said. "That included a tracking collar for Henry, so you could find him if he got lost, so didn't you…."

Cooper abruptly stood up and grabbed her cane. She fished her wallet out of her parka pocket and slapped bills onto the table, without counting, but enough to cover both their meals and a huge tip for June Winkel. Berry stared at her, perplexed.

"I'm sorry," Cooper said. "But what you just told me…."

She started away, then turned back.

"I'll call you, Berry," she said. "This is…."

She cut it off, no time to finish, and rushed to the door, bumping into tables, cane thumping.

Where had she put it?

Cooper tried the pantry off the kitchen and didn't find it, and then the hall closet and didn't find it. She cursed herself for being slovenly and rushed up the stairs, whacking the treads with her cane, and checked the bedroom closet, not finding it, then sat on the bed, staring in despair at the books and magazines and cartons and clothes she'd left strewn on the floor, and then she spotted it.

She'd brought it home and dropped it in a corner of the bedroom, figuring she'd find a place for it later, then forgot it. She fetched it now—Henry's kit from the All Creatures Clinic—and began pulling out the contents, peering at them, then hurling them onto the bedspread.

Drops to repel fleas and ticks.

A grooming brush.

Dog toothbrush and toothpaste.

First-aid instructions, for a medical emergency.

And—yes!—the owner's manual for Henry's tracking collar, still sealed into its plastic pouch, which wouldn't open no matter how much she pulled at it, even using her teeth, until she suddenly rushed into the bathroom, returned with fingernail scissors, and managed to cut the plastic open, and pull out the booklet.

She began reading, but couldn't make sense of it. Computer. Smartphone. CD disc. Do this incomprehensible thing, then that. She knew panic fogged her thinking, but she couldn't unfog.

"Damn!"

She grabbed the manual and thumped back downstairs and found her jacket where she'd left it, on the floor, having aimed for a dining room chair and missed. She got an arm and shoulder into the jacket, then lost patience and barged out the front door, with the parka half on. She got to the driveway, cursed, rushed back to the stoop, still pulling on the parka, locked the door. Then she thumped back to her Volvo, started it, and backed out of the driveway, door not yet shut.

She drove—too fast—onto the Mt. Augustus campus, then wheeled into the Campus Security lot and parked askew, front end in one slot, rear end in the adjacent slot, and half ran into the building.

"Where's Mike Bolknor?" she asked one of the officers, Jimmy Donahue, who was hurrying out just as she hurried in, so they had to both turn sideways in the doorway, making room for each other.

"Nobody's seen him," Donahue said. "Gotta run—tractor-trailer, out on the Interstate ramp, tipped, spilled toxic stuff, and we've all been called out, troopers, Dill PD, us…."

She saw it thrilled him, liberation from boring campus patrols, off to handle a big-deal emergency with the other cops, tv cameras sure to be whirring. Inside, the office looked empty. She feared everyone in Campus Security had gone to the exciting toxic spill.

"Hello!" she shouted, desperate. "Anybody here?"

A head appeared, looking around the doorway of a cubicle.

Chip Stack.

"Thank God," Cooper said.

"That's easy," Chip said, putting the manual down on his desk.

He extracted the CD disk from its back-of-the-manual sleeve, then inserted it into the computer. He reached for the computer's mouse.

Cooper, sitting in the chair beside his, stared at the screen, currently blank, willing something to appear.

"Could do this on your smartphone," Chip said. "Let's use the big screen, though."

He began pressing keys.

Messages appeared on the screen, nothing that meant anything to Cooper. She couldn't stand it and got up and walked to the cubicle's doorway and looked out at Campus Security's empty headquarters, suddenly convinced this couldn't possibly work.

Because it was magic.

Cyber fingers? Reaching out through the ether, to Henry?

"Take a look," Chip said.

A map filled the screen. Cooper saw Dill's streets, and the byways leading out of town. Along one of them, the Snowville Road, at a site a few miles south of town, a tiny dog icon blinked.

Cooper stared at the map, and the blinking icon.

She dropped back into her chair, still staring.

"I almost know where that is," she said.

"Yeah?" Chip said. "Let's see."

He pressed keys and the screen went back to the desktop. He fiddled with the mouse, and Cooper saw the cursor dart to an icon, like a blue-and-white marble.

"Google Earth," Chip said, and clicked on it.

More clicks and mouse moves.

And it was exactly like magic: on the computer's big flat screen, Cooper cruised south on the Snowville Road, as if in her car, passing overgrown pastures, then an abandoned farmhouse, on the right, and—a little

348

farther, on the left—an old barn. Its unpainted vertical slat siding weathered to silvery brown.

"There you go," Chip said.

Cooper leaned forward in her seat to stare at the image. Scrubby pastures, no longer used for Holsteins, surrounded it, and the barbed wire fencing along the road had come loose in some places, the strands drooping down into the grass, the fence posts slanting.

In the field behind the barn, phalanxes of huge aerodynamic wind turbines stood frozen, but in real life, right now out on the Snowville Road, they'd be slowly turning, feeding kilowatts into the grid.

That scoutmaster—they'd interviewed him at the police station—what had he said? His troop distributed circulars, not knowing who'd hired them. Or that Sonny Rawston meant for the circulars to humiliate Cooper. It had been just a voice on the phone, the scoutmaster said. In the background, though, he'd heard a grinding. Or a whooshing.

Those windmills, Cooper thought.

Mona's windmills.

"So, you know this place?" Chip asked.

"My father boarded horses here," Cooper said.

In the photograph Sonny had sent her, of Henry in his cage, she'd seen odd strands lying on the board floors. They'd puzzled her, but now she realized they were bits of old hay.

Cooper got to her feet and impulsively rushed to Mike Bolknor's corner office, knowing he wasn't there, but hoping he'd left a clue where he'd gone. She knocked, then threw open the door.

On his desk lay his calendar, tomorrow's date circled in red. Cooper studied it, saw appointments and tasks listed for every day until yesterday. Nothing for today, though. And, after today, every square blank.

No Glock 22 lying on the desk. No extra .40-caliber rounds.

Chip Stack appeared in the doorway.

"He left, this morning, right after you talked with him, after he got some telephone calls and did some paperwork," Chip said. "He didn't say where he was going, so nobody knows where he is."

Cooper hurried to the building's door. She opened it, then turned and saw Chip still standing there, watching her, perplexed.

"If Mike comes back, tell him to call me, on my cell, right away," she told Chip.

She didn't wait for him to reply. She hurried out to the lot, got into her Volvo, started it, then shot off onto Mt. Augustus Avenue, the campus's central thoroughfare. She turned right onto Maple Street, then stopped abruptly in front of Number Twenty-Five, the salmon-colored Victorian with green trim where Bolknor rented an apartment.

Out of the car, she had to go back, because she'd left the door flung open. She slammed it, then hurried past the walk's guardian spruce, ignored the two mailboxes by the front door, stepped into the anteroom, and knocked on the dark oak door to her left, "Apartment One."

Beside the door, the metal holder for a name card remained empty.

She knocked again.

No response from inside, and her knock sounded hollow, an empty sound.

She tried the knob and it turned and the door cracked open. She paused, thinking what to do, then muttered under her breath.

"Oh, hell!"

She pushed open the door and walked inside.

A living room, with a big window looking out on Maple Street. A sofa. An armchair. A television. An end table with books, in a neat stack.

Off that room a kitchen. No dirty dishes. Everything neat.

Bedroom—neat, bed made.

A small study, with a desk and office chair. On the floor, placed neatly beside the desk, a modem and router. On the desk, otherwise clear, except for a laptop, lay a photograph—an attractive woman, slender, dark hair worn short, smiling. Beside her, a little girl, her miniature twin, also smiling. On the other side of her, a boy, even littler, who resembled Mike Bolknor, and stared seriously at the camera. Cooper noticed that the photograph lay perfectly centered on the desk. She supposed it had been taken several years earlier, when the children were younger.

She backed out of the study, stopped in the apartment's doorway, and leaned against the frame, deciding what to do. She finally shut the apartment's door, carefully.

"Damn!" she said.

She hurried out the front door, back to her Volvo, and got into the driver's seat. She started the car, but then sat thinking. After a moment, she pulled her cellphone

351

out of her parka's pocket and glanced at the list of stored numbers, found Bolknor's cellphone number, and punched it in.

"Service not available."

She punched in Tip LaPerle's cell number.

"Service not available."

From memory, she punched in another number, and someone picked up, a familiar voice.

"Dill Police Department."

Margaret Prescott, a dispatcher.

"This is Cooper North—I need to speak with Tip, right away."

"Coop, I'm sorry, but Chief LaPerle's off to a meeting, and he didn't say what it was or when he'd be back or anything."

Cooper sighed.

"I'll try his radio," Margaret said.

Cooper waited.

Margaret spoke on the phone again.

"Nope," she said. "He's not picking up—must be out of the car, and his shoulder receiver isn't on."

"Well, give me any of the other officers," Cooper said. "I need someone to go with me—one of our suspects might be there."

"Gee, all the guys are out at the Interstate ramp, where that tractor-trailer tipped over, and...."

"If Tip gets in, please tell him to call me at this number, fast."

"Sure, but are you...."

Cooper clicked off her phone, breaking the connection.

She sat staring out the windshield, at Maple Street's well-kept houses and leafless trees, holding her cellphone. Both of them, LaPerle and Bolknor, had gotten to places with no cell-phone service. Easily done in mountainous Vermont.

"God damn it!" she said aloud.

With the dog, at least, she could do something.

She punched in another number on her cell phone, from memory, waited through a few rings, and then heard a voice.

"Her Majesty's off in Iberia, gobbling art, so— Darn!—there's only me."

"Cut the crap, Drew," she said. "I need help."

"Sweetcakes!" he said. "I saw it was you on caller ID and…."

"That barn of Mona's, out on the Snowville Road—what's going on with that?"

"Windpower!" Drew said. "Power through meteorology!"

"I mean the barn itself," Cooper said. "Sonny Rawston's got my dog in there."

Silence.

She imagined Drew staring at his telephone, stunned. Finally he spoke.

"Coop, that jerk just might have a key."

"To the barn?"

"We used to get hay from there, for flowerbed mulch," Drew said. "Sonny did our lawn work, back then, and we gave him a barn key, to go fetch hay."

Cooper remembered confronting Rawston at his apartment, when Henry first disappeared. She'd searched the place. In his bedroom, atop a chest of drawers, she'd seen a chipped cereal bowl. It held a skeleton key.

"I'm going out there," Cooper said. "You've got another key?"

"Yes, I'm sure we do, but...."

"I'm coming to get it," Cooper said, and pushed the phone's "end" button.

On the way, she stopped at her house to get a canister of pepper spray. She'd never used it. She couldn't remember where she'd put it. She couldn't find it. Anyway, she didn't know how she'd use it, so she left the house again without it.

As she locked the front door, Chip Stack's battered Honda Civic pulled up at the curb. Doors flew open, front and back, and Chip, Nikki Winkel, and Jerry Shapiro got out. All three jogged up the driveway, looking determined.

"No way you're going out there alone," Nikki said.

"Yeah," Jerry said. "Remember—Stacey Gillibrand!"

They wanted to be her backup. It pleased her.

She shook her head.

"There's a better job for you," she said.

She couldn't endanger students. Besides, it was her dog.

"Track down Bolknor, or LaPerle," she said. "Get one of them out to that barn."

Stubborn faces.

"No, we need badges out there," she said. "So, please!"

Now they looked unsure.

"I need you to do this," Cooper said.

Continued blank looks. They stirred, glancing at each other, until Chip finally spoke.

"Where do we start?"

Cooper shut her eyes, thinking.

"Work-study students," she said. "Whoever handled Campus Security's telephones this morning."

She opened her eyes.

"Who called Mike Bolknor—find out," she said. "Same thing with the Dill PD dispatchers—who'd Tip talk with?"

She thought more.

"Maybe go out to the Interstate ramp, see if any of the Dill cops out there know where Tip went."

Jerry Shapiro pretended to salute.

"We're on it, Chief," he said.

Cooper watched them jog back to Chip's battered Civic. She thought of ducklings, and wanly smiled.

Jerry and Chip already had their smartphones out. Nikki didn't, and it occurred to Cooper that Nikki didn't have one, couldn't afford the service. She used a cheap clamshell phone, no contract, and probably could barely afford that.

Doors slammed on the Honda. Cooper watched the car U-turn, then head back toward the campus.

A moment later, in her own car, she drove east on Hill Street, past one house, another, and then she pulled into the driveway of Mona and Drew Saunders' edifice and parked under the portico. As she started up the front stoop's steps, the door opened, and Drew stepped out.

For once, he had no twinkly eyed, let's kid around look. He looked concerned.

He held up a key.

"Don't go alone, Coop," he said. "Let's get Tip LaPerle, or one of his cops, to go out there with you. What about that big guy you've got running Campus Security?"

Cooper, plucking the key from his fingers, shook her head.

"Nobody's around," she said. "What's in that barn?"

He frowned, thinking.

"It's just stuff," he finally said. "We used it for storage, like an old camping cot."

He fell silent, thinking.

"Actually, it's mostly my stuff," he said. "Like when Mona banned motorcycles?—Remember that?—So my red Honda's out there, steed of my youth."

He looked momentarily amused.

"I've got Dill Theater Guild props stored out there, too," he said. "And then we had the imperial no-hunting edict, so my old rifle's out there...."

"Was that a .30-06?" Cooper said.

Drew's gaze, which had drifted off into reverie, suddenly sharpened.

"Coop, don't go alone, please," he said. "Get a police guy, for God's sake!"

"That bastard means to shoot my dog," she said. "Probably with that old .30-06 of yours."

She hurried down the steps, climbed into her Volvo, and started the engine. She saw Drew watching her from the stoop, grimacing with worry. It warmed her, a little, to be worried about, but she stamped on the accelerator and shot the car out from under the portico, then down the driveway. In the rear-view mirror, she saw Drew, still staring after her, abruptly spin around and disappear into the house.

Cooper turned left, onto Hill Street. Now she focused on the road ahead.

Speeding through Abner Park, she glanced up at the bare branches, an automatic response, but saw no movement. Migratory species would be gone, she thought. There'd be crows, though, and jays and chickadees. That seemed reassuring, for no logical reason. Nuthatches, downy woodpeckers, slate-colored juncos, they'd be stockpiling seeds, she hoped, to see them through the winter.

Up ahead, Dill Industries' glass-and-steel headquarters loomed, but just before she reached the corporate campus she swerved right, down Slope Drive. At the bottom, she turned right again, onto Main Street, accelerating west.

Pedestrians on the sidewalks looked up from their smartphones as the Volvo roared by. She guessed she looked like the Grim Reaper at the wheel.

After she passed the Dill National Bank, she turned left onto Snowville Street. Across the Ira River Bridge, it changed names, becoming the Snowville Road.

Her black Volvo sped south, rollercoastering up and down hills. She passed Jack and Beverly Abbott's mini-Versailles, on her left, then other newer houses, built on hilltops with across-the-river views of Dill and the mountain range north of town. Quickly, though, the newer houses dwindled away, and now old farms flashed by, their pastures gone to weeds and brush.

A somber landscape. Nearly November now. Roadside maples, leafless, looked skeletal, their branches like black bones. Crows, in a ragged line, flapped across the gray sky.

She felt alone.

CHAPTER THIRTY-TWO

A narrow weedy patch separated the barn from the road, and Cooper pulled in there. She turned off the engine and peered through her Volvo's windshield at the barn's story-high doors.

One door swung left, the other right, so tractors could pull hay wagons through, but the doors had weathered into decrepitude. They sagged on rusted hinges. A padlock secured them, but it didn't matter. Their bottom edges had long ago sunk into the ground.

Cooper got out to check the padlock.

Rusted through. Petrified.

No point trying the key.

She leaned on her cane, listening—in the meadow out back, Mona's windmills slowly turned their huge blades, seeming to whisper.

Cooper grimaced.

Henry's tracking collar had failed.

She craved alcohol, a powerful urge, sudden, and looked at the ground, settling for blankness. It lasted a few moments. Then, gradually, she registered what she saw: at her feet, a faint trail ran through the weeds.

It started at the road, a line of flattened stems. It flanked the barn, then swerved around back. It looked as if a python had slithered through.

Motorcycle.

Cooper started along the trail, carefully, fearing a twisted ankle, but then faster, finally rushing, dried goldenrod and hawkweeds crunching under her Nikes, thistles scratching at her jeans. Her cane kept snagging in the tangled dead plants, and she impatiently jerked it free.

She rounded the barn and saw another set of story-high doors, matching the doors out front, and equally decrepit. Decades ago, tractors coming from the hayfields pulled laden wagons through this rear doorway. Inside, workers unloaded the bales. Then the tractors pulled the emptied wagons straight ahead, out the front doors. No need to back up. Now, though, these rear doors had also sunk into the ground, and could never open.

There was another door, off to the side.

It was newer, slightly larger than an ordinary house door, wide enough for a garden tractor to squeeze through. Or a motorcycle.

This was where the path through the weeds led.

Balsams clustered around that corner of the barn. On one branch, a red squirrel crouched, glaring at Cooper. Abruptly, it stood up tall. It chittered and chuffed, shaking its bushy tail.

Cooper touched the door's keyhole, and her finger came away oily. She tested the hinges, and they, too, had been recently oiled.

She tried the doorknob, but it wouldn't twist. Locked.

She pulled the key from her pocket and tried to insert it into the keyhole, but her hand shook, from tension, and a little from fear. She stood a moment, staring at the keyhole and listening to the irritated squirrel. Finally she steadied her right hand with her left and got the key into the keyhole and turned it.

A click.

She twisted the knob again and the door swung open, and the barn exhaled an aroma of old dried hay.

High windows let in some daylight, but she'd just come from outdoors, and she stopped a few steps in, letting her eyes adjust to the dimmer light.

"Henry?"

Her voice sounded weak in the cavernous space.

Now she saw a cot, off to her left, a rumpled sleeping bag strewn on it. Beside it rested a suitcase, its top up, like an open mouth, displaying folded clothes. Nearby, on the floorboards, stood a small Primus camp stove, with a pot alongside, and a can opener, and stacked cans of baked beans, tuna, sardines, corn, peas.

A black motorcycle leaned on its kickstand, giving off a whiff of gasoline. Behind it, a small trailer stood ready for the motorcycle to tow. Nessie Greffier's old trailer, sold to Sonny Rawston. He'd used it to transport his belongings here, when he went on the run. Before that, he'd used it to carry away the corgi.

"Henry?"

Her voice faded into the barn's silence.

361

Rawston wasn't in the barn, but his motorcycle was here. So he couldn't be far away. Maybe he'd gone for a walk in the meadow.

Just a few days to November, nights ever colder. Cooper thought: he can't hide much longer in this unheated barn. He must be desperate.

Behind the motorcycle and the trailer lay heaps of the Saunders' discards—old vinyl records, Beatles, Rolling Stones, The Grateful Dead, and folded-up blankets and faded bedspreads and tablecloths, two portable beach chairs....

A scratching sound.

"Henry?"

Silence. Then more scratching.

"Henry?"

She thought she heard a bark.

She froze, listening.

Another faint bark.

"Henry!"

She lurched toward the sound, thumping her cane onto the floor planks, past more of Mona's and Drew's castoffs, past a few remnant hay bales stacked up, and then past a long swath of empty floorboards, everything dim in the gray light from the high windows, until she got near the barn's far end, toward the road, and she made out a wire-mesh crate on the floor.

A dark shape inside.

Another weak bark.

She got down on her knees, pushing aside an empty food bowl and a partly coiled leash and a half-empty water bowl, spilling water onto her fingers and onto the floor, and got her fingers onto the crate's latch,

362

but couldn't work it. Inside the crate Henry lay looking at her with confused eyes, as if he'd lapsed into a partial coma, and been that way a long while, and only now, slowly, was awakening.

She finally fumbled open the latch, pulled open the door. Henry still lay prone, the crate too small for him to stand, so Cooper reached in and got her hands on him—his fur felt warm—and pulled. For a moment, he resisted, as if he'd been pulled out of here before, by hands he didn't like, but suddenly, maybe finally registering her familiar scent, he barked and scrabbled toward her as she pulled, claws scratching on the wire mesh. Then he was out, looking at her, kneeling before him, and his eyes came alive.

He barked, and vaulted forward, stood up on his short hind legs, pressing himself against her chest, and she held him with her arms, while he continued to bark, as if with many pent-up things to say.

She stood, after a while, and he leaned against her leg, pressing against her. She reached down for the leash, so she wouldn't lose him again, and snapped it onto his collar. She'd never bothered to look at that collar, not once since Berry Randolph put it on him, and only now did she notice its attached tracking device, a compact package. She berated herself: I should've paid more attention. I'd have found him sooner.

"Let's go detect," she told him. "Okay, Henry?"

She walked to the pile on the floor, haltingly, because Henry still insisted on cleaving to her leg, and she began looking through the Saunders' rejects, obsolete percolators and battered skis and ski boots and ice skates, a typewriter, a grimy power lawn mower, dried grass clippings stuck to it, a floor lamp....

Cooper worked her way along the pile, finding nothing of interest, until she got back to the indoor camping site, near the back of the barn, with its cot and camp stove, and the parked motorcycle. Her eyes, now fully adjusted to the dimness, saw what she'd missed before—on the floorboards, beside the motorcycle, lay a rifle.

Drew Saunders' old .30-06 hunting rifle. She had no doubt. Single shot, bolt action. She guessed he'd stowed it out here, after Mona's imperial anti-hunting decree. Cooper would get state technicians to go over it. They'd match it to the two bullets fired at her, and to the bullet that killed Stacey Gillibrand. They'd also check for prints.

Outside, the squirrel had resumed chuffing.

She needed badges out here.

Fast, she decided.

She jabbed a hand into her jacket pocket, fished out her smartphone, punched in the Dill PD number, from memory, but it didn't ring.

No bars.

Rural Vermont. No service.

She cursed.

Leave, she told herself. Now.

Get into the car, with Henry. Drive straight to the Dill Police Station. Or maybe back to the campus, to see if Mike Bolknor came in—worries about him flooded back, but nothing to do about that right now.

She started for the door, Henry still pressing against her leg. Almost immediately, she stopped, staring at the motorcycle's rear fender. A red spot.

Blood?

She bent down to peer at it.

Paint.

A thrown-up stone had chipped the bike's black over-coat, letting the original red paint show through. She could see it, now that she looked closely—this motorcycle came from the factory cherry red. Someone had used a hardware-store spray can to repaint it black, but this was surely Drew Saunders' old Honda, the red motorcycle on which he'd arrived in Dill, so many decades ago.

So—Sonny Rawston got into this barn, using the key Mona and Drew gave him, when he'd been their lawn boy. He'd appropriated the Honda, repainted it black.

That much seemed likely.

What else to see, before she left? Trailer, empty. Behind it, though, on the floor, lay a spear and a Roman shield. Cooper hefted them. Almost weightless. Plastic props, she remembered now, from a Dill Theater Guild production. She couldn't remember the play, except that she'd gone with Mona, and that Drew played a tribune, strikingly handsome in his kilt and plastic armor. Maybe she couldn't remember because she'd been drunk. Twelve years ago?

Next to the spear lay a cowboy Stetson. And chaps. She remembered that one, *Oklahoma*.

And, lying nearby on the floor, a wig.

Gray hair, shoulder length.

She lifted it, using two fingers, as if it were the dried carcass of a long-dead animal. Underneath lay a fake gray beard.

"Hell," she muttered.

A memory, from decades ago: the Dill Theater Guild's production of *The Wizard of Oz*. Drew—still young then—had played the wizard, costumed as an old man. Cooper stared at the wig in her hand, and mental gears meshed, Rawston, sneaking into this barn, hiding out here, finding these things....

Outside, the squirrel chittered again, high-pitched and angry.

Henry growled.

A man had stepped into the barn, and now stood still, looking at her.

"Well, well."

Average height, but stocky, blocking her only way out. She didn't immediately recognize him because his red hair had grown shaggy. And he had a red beard now, unkempt.

They stared at each other.

"How about that!" he finally said. "There's your little doggie!"

"You bastard," Cooper said.

"Please, no hysterics," he said, holding up a hand. "Just a game, find-the-dog—can't take a joke?"

Outside, the squirrel had gone silent, but Henry still growled, a low noise in his chest.

"It's over, Sonny," she said. "You can ride into town with me."

He snickered.

"It really is over," Cooper said.

366

He snickered again.

"I'll tell you what's over," he said. "Using that meadow for a bathroom, that's over."

He glared at her now.

"And that creek, washing up in ice water," he said. "Give me your car keys."

"You're insane," Cooper said.

"Really?" he said. "Says the old-lady state's attorney, fanatic about screwing up my life?"

"I just did my job," she said. "What about Hart's Corners, that school teacher?"

"What teacher?" he said.

"Mildred Langley, the one you killed," Cooper said. "Eighteen years ago."

Sonny stared at her, then laughed. Abruptly, he lurched toward her, and when she backed away, pulling the growling corgi with her, he smirked. He stooped to snatch up the rifle, one hand on the barrel, the other on the stock, then laughed again, seeing the fear she tried to hide.

He pointed the rifle over her head and said, "Bang!"

"Why'd you kill Mildred Langley?" Cooper asked.

Sonny now pointed the rifle at her.

"Actually, I do remember that teacher," he said, squinting through the sights, making a show of it. "She sold me a car."

Cooper shook her head.

"Bull," she said.

"Yes she did, my first car, right out of college," he said. "An old blue 1986 Dodge Colt, sounded like a lawn mower, guzzled oil like Cooper North gulping scotch, or is it vodka now?"

"Why'd you kill her?" Cooper asked.

"Saw her ad in the paper, and I hitchhiked over there, couple of times, until she finally lowered the junker's price down into the sane range."

"Fought over the car price?" Cooper said. "Lost your temper?"

"Don't be stupid," Rawston said. "I never shot anyone—except maybe right now."

He aimed the rifle at Cooper's forehead.

He didn't have a finger on the trigger. And the rifle held just one cartridge. If he missed his first shot, there'd be no more bullets.

Rush him, before he could shoot? Or weave, so he'd miss—he held the rifle awkwardly—then jab the cane's tip into his stomach, or whack it up between his legs?

No, he'd get his finger on the trigger before she ever got to him. And he wouldn't miss, not at this distance. She couldn't run out the door, either. She'd get the bullet in her back.

"Why'd you shoot Stacey Gillibrand?" she said. "Because she found out you'd killed that teacher?"

He glared at her, still pointing the rifle.

"Yeah, I knew you'd pin the Gillibrand thing on me," he said. "That's why I'm stuck in this rotten barn—death penalty for you?"

Cooper thought about unhitching Henry from his leash, so at least he could scamper out the door to safety. He wouldn't run, though. He continually growled, low, barely audible. This was the man who'd snatched him, imprisoned him. Unleashed, he'd charge. Sonny would shoot him.

Maybe that would be better, Cooper thought. Without me, what would happen to Henry?

Nikki Winkel, she thought. Nikki would do something. Or Mona. When she got back from Spain.

"Sonny, it really is over," she said.

Outside, the squirrel chuffed.

Rawston moved the rifle, now pointing it at her heart.

"I need your car, North," he said. "You'll be locked in here, see how you like it."

Outside, the squirrel loudly chittered, working itself into a rage.

Subtly, the light changed.

They both looked at the doorway—a silhouette filled it, a man, tall and slim.

"Hey, Sweetcakes," he said. "Couldn't let you come here all alone."

For once, it didn't irritate her, being called "Sweetcakes."

Rawston resumed peering through the rifle's sights at Cooper.

"Get your nose out of this, Saunders," he said.

Drew stepped into the barn, hands behind him. Showing he's not a threat, Cooper thought. Smart. He took a step toward Rawston.

"You shooting people?" Drew said. "That's not nice."

Another step toward Rawston.

"Cut the garbage, Drew," Rawston said. "Or else!"

Drew stopped, then moved again, another half step toward Rawston.

He means to grab that gun, Cooper thought. Sonny's shorter, but he's younger, and built heftier. If Drew grabbed for the gun, she decided, while Rawston was distracted, she'd rush him, aim her cane's tip at an eye.

"Ye gods and little fishes!" Drew said. "You should just roar off on that bike there...."

"Have you gone bananas?" Sonny yelled.

He jerked the rifle around and pointed it at Drew, who froze.

"Whatever game you're playing, Saunders, watch out," Rawston said. "You better...."

Cooper had started toward him, aiming her cane, and everything became slow motion—Rawston jerking the rifle back, pointing at Cooper's forehead, grim faced, holding the rifle awkwardly, but steady.

A frozen moment.

Then a crack, like a snapped stick.

A rosebud blossomed on Sonny Rawston's forehead.

He stared at Cooper, but his eyes had no sight in them. He still stood, but the rifle slipped from his hands and clattered onto the floor, and he crumpled, to his knees, then sprawled, his forehead thudding onto the floorboards, and his body lay inert.

Drew, still clenching the pistol he'd held behind his back, stared down at the dead man, his mouth open in shock, eyes wide.

"Good Lord," he whispered.

Cooper, in her long career, had seen many shooting victims, but she'd never watched someone being shot.

She limped to the cot and plopped down on it, her eyes on the prone body on the floorboards, a heap of rags, except Sonny's head twisted aside and his red beard splayed out, like flames. After a moment the cot sagged, Drew sitting beside her, and she felt his arm around her shoulders.

"You all right, Coop?" he said.

He still had shock in his voice.

He lifted the pistol, clenched in his leather driving glove, and held it before his eyes and stared at it.

"God, he meant to shoot you, Sweetcakes," he said. "Using my own damned rifle."

Cooper said nothing, her mind jammed, fixated on that rosebud, blossoming on Rawston's forehead. She almost swooned with gratitude—for still being alive, and for stalwart friends, and because it was over. Finally, after all these weeks. Henry, too, back safe. Tonight, in her living room, she'd read, maybe a Jane Austen novel, with Henry lying beside her chair, glancing up at her, sometimes, to reassure himself. She'd have peppermint tea.

Right now, though, inchoate thoughts stampeded through her head, like animals fleeing a forest fire.

Drew, sitting beside her, moaned.

"He never did seem right, even as a kid, mowing our lawn," he said. "But who'd think he'd go shoot that college girl!"

Cooper shrugged.

"He was a psychopath," she said, staring at the body.

She got up.

"Extremely manipulative," she said. "And he had no empathy—other people were just tables, chairs."

Almost in a trance, she walked to where Rawston lay.

"No responsibility for what he did," she said. "It was always somebody else's fault."

She knelt to peer at the rifle lying beside the body. She pulled a Kleenex from her jacket pocket and used it to keep off her prints, as she twisted up the bolt handle, unlocking the bolt. She pulled it back and stared into the opened cartridge chamber.

Empty.

"He never had a bullet in this gun," she said.

"Good Lord," Drew said. "I thought…."

"No way to know," Cooper said, staring down at the body.

"That's just a single-shot," Drew said. "I got it that way, hunter's honor, you know? Because if you can't get your buck with one shot, then you don't deserve it—I used to think like that, when I was young."

He stared at the pistol in his gloved hand, as if he held a rattlesnake.

"You had no way to know," Cooper said.

Had Rawston known the rifle wasn't loaded? He held it so awkwardly….

"It's strange," Cooper said, thinking aloud.

All those years, dealing drugs, but no record of violence. Rawston hadn't even killed Henry….

372

In her mind, jigsaw pieces juggled themselves, fitting together, the picture coming almost into focus....

"I've got to go," she said, and her voice sounded faint.

"You bet, Sweetcakes," Drew said.

He walked ahead of her and stood in the doorway. She stopped.

"Why would Sonny paint that motorcycle black?" Cooper said. "He had no need."

Drew, now leaning against the doorframe, thought a moment, then shook his head, rueful.

"Actually, I did it, way back," he said. "Mona tabooed my bike—remember?—but I still wanted to tool around some, so a little spray paint...."

Cooper stared at him.

"Sonny got title to that Honda," she said. "He had to have title, because he had it registered and licensed in his name."

Drew looked perplexed.

"Why, how'd he ever do that?" he said.

Cooper felt herself going into shock.

"You gave him the motorcycle," she said.

She felt sick.

"You gave him this barn's key, too," she said. "After he got out of prison."

Drew cocked his head to one side and looked at her, amused, the shock he'd shown at the killing now shrugged off, like a masquerade party mask, no longer needed.

"Why'd I ever do such things?" he said.

Cooper looked at him, this man she'd known so long. He'd fooled her. Fooled them all. Fooled Mona.

373

Actor.

"Goodness, you're supposed to be the smart one," Drew said, grinning now. "So whatever's going on here, Sweetcakes?"

"Stop calling me that," Cooper said.

"Yes, Ma'am," he said. "Sugarplum."

Drew stood in the doorway, blocking her way out. And, in her head, the puzzle pieces moved, rapidly now, fitting together, as memories flashed through her mind.

That college surveillance video.

It showed Stacey Gillibrand's killer. He wore the fake gray beard and the gray wig—a tall, slim man. Rawston was stocky, average height.

And eighteen years ago, when the gray-haired biker visited the teacher in Hart's Corners, and finally killed her, Rawston had no access to that wig and beard. He'd had no motorcycle back then, either.

He handled the rifle awkwardly, too. She'd just seen that. He didn't really know how to hold it. So it wasn't Sonny Rawston who'd twice fired that rifle at her. And when she accused him of killing Mildred Langley, he protested he'd never shot anyone, clearly unaware she hadn't been shot. She'd been axed to death.

So he didn't kill Mildred Langley. And if Stacey Gillibrand reopened that old case, that meant nothing to him.

He'd come back to Dill solely to blackmail Jack Abbott, bleed him. Others, too, maybe. And he had a secondary mission: make life miserable for Cooper North. She'd prosecuted him, jailed him, ruined his drug business. It was all her fault.

So a psychopath.

374

But not a killer.

Drew leaned against the doorframe, grinning, eyes on Cooper.

"Stumped?" he said.

"Why'd you kill Mildred Langley?" Cooper asked.

Drew laughed and shook his head.

"What a story that is," he said. "You'd best sit down."

He waved the pistol in his gloved hand to indicate the cot. It wasn't a friendly suggestion. Cooper hesitated, then walked over and sat. Henry sat leaning against her leg, looking at the man in the doorway, puzzled. Something about this stranger seemed wrong to Henry.

Drew left the doorway and stood in front of Cooper, still blocking her only way out.

He positioned himself, she noticed, just out of reach of her cane. A tactical choice.

"Act One," he said, wryly. "A tale of Old Charleston."

He shook his head, indicating a rueful memory.

"Scene One—evening in the Deep South, and home comes Daddy, after another hundred-degree day hammering shingles," Drew said. "He's dirty and tired and whupped, and Momma comes home from the assembly line, looking like dirty laundry—little Drew certainly doesn't want that for himself."

In high school, grown tall and handsome, Drew performed in school plays. He liked the pretense—what you see ain't what you really got! It felt powerful.

Movie career? He'd need lightning to strike, and he knew it.

"I was such a practical lad," he said.

His after-school job was tending a wealthy old widow's yard, and running errands for her. She lived alone in her big house, with columns in front. He'd charmed her. He'd always charmed everyone. Such a smart boy, too. She couldn't let so much ability go to waste. So she paid his way through the state university. A charity. And right after graduation, before getting on with his own life, he'd returned to help his benefactor with household problems, because she'd grown a bit feeble. He arranged for plumbing work. And supervised repaving the long drive. He even prepared some meals for her. And he called in an exterminator, because there were rats....

"All alone in the world, that old lady," Drew told Cooper. "With that fortune—wouldn't you think she'd will it to her protégé?"

And the exterminator left behind a box of rat poison.

"Thing is, she was half dead anyway," Drew said. "So who'd ever suspect she died of anything besides just rust?"

He'd been right about that. He'd been wrong about the will. She left it all to a charity for African orphans.

"Bump in the road," Drew said, looking theatrically sad.

"On the other hand," he said, brightly, "if they ever tested for poisons, nobody could say I had motive for doing in the old bat."

Still, he'd brushed against the electric chair. No more of that, he vowed. He'd get the fortune he craved some safer way.

Immediately, though, he needed money to support himself, while he hunted that windfall, so he appropriated valuables from the empty mansion, before it was auctioned off, jewelry and artworks. He'd decided on podiatry, less taxing than regular medical school, he supposed, especially if you get that degree on a Caribbean island.

He started out as the junior partner of a podiatrist in Stowe, Vermont, chosen for the skiing and for the concentration of wealthy people, who just might cotton to a charming young man, with movie-star looks, and South Carolina sugar in his voice.

Sure enough, along came Mona Dill, fresh out of Skidmore.

Cooper felt sick.

"No, it's okay!" Drew said, amused by her expression. "We did just dandy, because she got herself a Greek statue, that being me, and I got access to the Dill bullion—and that 'Taming of the Drew' stuff, what'd I care?"

He'd strayed now and then. Of course. Women did throw themselves at him.

"I'm just a guy who can't say no," he said.

Cooper remembered little Berry Randolph and friends, sitting in a row on the fence, waiting for their boondocks film idol to emerge from old Erna Langley's farmhouse.

"You met Mildred Langley at her mother's house," Cooper said. "And that led to...."

"I told her, plain," Drew said. "Just for fun."

"She didn't go along," Cooper said.

Drew frowned and shook his head, exasperated.

377

"Deluded," he said. "She thought I'd give up everything for a love-starved hick school teacher."

He shook his head again.

"She finally threatened to telephone Mona," he said. "Tell her about us—so she gave me no choice, did she?"

He scowled.

"You killed her in a rage," Cooper said.

He looked at Cooper, astonished. Then shook his head.

"You insult me," he said. "You don't understand—that's why I'm telling you all this."

He studied the pistol in his gloved hand, seeming to pout.

No escape, she thought. He'd already demonstrated that. A crack shot.

It didn't matter. She couldn't get by him. She was sixty-nine, with a bad leg, and a woman.

"I want you to grasp the genius of all this," Drew now said, frowning at Cooper, as if she were a pupil and he the disappointed teacher.

All these years, she thought. Never once did I have a glimmer. Never noticed the mask. Never sensed what hid behind it, that intelligence like ice.

He'd planned it precisely—the old, mildly retarded janitor in the Hart's Corners Elementary School's basement. That axe for chopping firewood, the janitor's fingerprints all over it....

"Of course, I wore gloves," Drew said, as if he expected Cooper to nod approval.

Drew stood thinking, and then he laughed.

"That idiot, Emerson Clough...."

He gazed at Cooper, grinning.

"I'm an artist, you know," he said.

"Actually, you're nuts," Cooper said. "Just another psychopath, like Sonny Rawston."

Anger contorted his face. Just for a moment, he looked ugly. Then he looked serene again, in control.

"Sonny?" he said, disgusted. "Just a piker, that boy, a third-rate psychopath, but right now you're looking at the real deal!"

He suddenly grinned.

"I'm the DaVinci of psychopaths!"

He studied her, amused.

"Listen up, Sugarplum," he said. "Be awed."

Framing the old janitor had been easy. Still, eighteen years later, the *Dill Chronicle* reported that Cooper North meant to have her class reopen that old case.

"See what you made me do?" he said. "Sugarplum?"

Just when that worrisome *Chronicle* story appeared, Sonny Rawston got out of prison.

"Well, years before, I did make a little slip," Drew said. "Oops."

One of his two-minute romances craved cocaine, so he bought her some, from Sonny. And now Sonny, back in Dill after jail, demanded money not to tell.

Drew frowned, looking inward, and Cooper started to get up from the cot, meaning to rush to the door, but he saw her and indicated, with an irritable wave of his pistol, for her to keep sitting.

"Sonny thought he had me," Drew said.

He smirked.

"Of course, it was me who had him."

He began grooming Sonny, framing him for Cooper's upcoming murder. He told him Cooper had switched from drinking scotch to vodka martinis.

"Little things like that," he said. "Make him more threatening."

Drew wore his gray wig and fake beard to shoot at Cooper in the night, and then again at the park. After that, he turned over the motorcycle to Sonny, inventing a fake company, Specialty Sales, to make the handover.

"He thought he'd scored quite a coup," Drew said.

Cooper could see him looking, to see if she appreciated the cleverness—biker takes shots, and suddenly there's Sonny Rawston, with a bike.

Then a second report in the *Chronicle* corrected the previous story—Cooper North and her class had no interest in the old Hart's Corners murder. It was just Stacey Gillibrand investigating it, on her own.

"That was a relief, Sugarplum," he said. "I didn't have to shoot you after all."

In some weird way, Cooper thought, he actually meant it.

Now it was Stacey Gillibrand who had to die.

Drew gave Sonny a suggestion: "Really want to irk Cooper? Start co-opting her students."

And he pointed out, helpfully, that one of those students—Drew had already checked it out—lived next door.

"What a tangled web we weave," Cooper quoted.

Drew laughed.

"Watch this!" he said.

He knelt beside Sonny's body, still eyeing Cooper, and laid his pistol across the forehead, carefully aiming it out the barn's open door.

At the shot, Cooper jerked back, startled.

Drew, still wearing his leather driving gloves, pressed the dead man's fingers against the pistol's handle and trigger.

He stood, looking calmly down at the body.

"Too bad about poor Sonny, shooting himself, out of guilt," he said. "They'll find that powder mark on his temple."

"Everybody knows that Mustang of yours," Cooper said. "Somebody'll have seen it parked out front."

"No they won't," he said.

An old tractor road ran alongside Mona's meadow and wound around back, now used by technicians servicing the windmill turbines. Drew had parked back there.

"See?" he said. "Every little detail!"

He looked as if he expected Cooper to cheer.

"Thing is, I've really enjoyed you," he said. "Good brain, fun to play with."

As Sonny had done, with the unloaded rifle, he aimed the pistol at Cooper's forehead. This time, though, the chamber held a cartridge.

Escape plans blossomed in Cooper's mind, and immediately died. Hopeless. Like an eland facing a lion. It would feel like this. Numbed by fear. So it wouldn't feel the teeth.

She did feel horror—her best friend, Mona Dill Saunders, would go on living with this monster. She'd never know. There'd be nobody to warn her.

Henry, too. Abandoned. A stray. She pushed the thought away.

Somebody would take him in. Nikki. Mona.

"Do you appreciate this?" Drew said. "Sonny shot himself—they'll find this gun by his dead hand."

He gazed at her, pistol aimed.

"His prints will be on it," he said.

She saw him thinking.

"Interesting detail," he said. "I'd thought of hinting to you, I really did, that Sonny hid out here, but you got here all on your own."

He smiled.

"Do you see it?" he said. "How I could goad him? Planned it? Make it look like I just had to shoot him? And you my witness?"

He kept the gun pointed, but looked quizzical.

"You wouldn't buy it, though," he said. "Just wouldn't."

He made a sad face.

"Look what you're making me do."

Chittering and chuffing from outside.

"By-by, Sugarplum," Drew said. "I'll miss you, truly."

He squinted through the sights.

Cooper shut her eyes.

"Hey!"

A shot, loud, the sharp sound of it filling the barn.

A heavy thud. Then nothing.

Cooper opened her eyes.

Drew lay sprawled beside Sonny Rawston, on his back, a large bloody patch on his chest's left side.

382

Just inside the doorway, Mike Bolknor stood, legs apart, holding out that big Glock 22 of his, two handed, still aimed where Drew Saunders had stood.

CHAPTER THIRTY-THREE

A few minutes later, out front of the barn, away from the two dead men inside, Cooper felt oddly serene, even disconnected.

Mike Bolknor sat in his parked Prius, with the door open, one foot outside, talking on the radio with the Dill PD dispatcher. Chip Stack had squeezed his battered Civic between the Campus Security Prius and Cooper's Volvo, and he and Jerry Shapiro and Nikki Winkel leaned against it, talking to Cooper, excited. She could hear them, but as if they spoke from a distance.

"...so then we asked the dispatcher, and she said Chief LaPerle's wife managed the granite company's office, so we drove over there...."

"...and Mrs. LaPerle told us, if the Chief needed a don't-bother-me place, to seriously talk with someone, he'd use his uncle's deer-hunting camp, and she told us how to get there, so...."

They'd found them both at the camp, and Bolknor took right off for this barn. They'd mentioned the toxic spill at the Interstate ramp, news to LaPerle, and he'd rushed to check on it, and send officers to the barn.

Cooper listened, hearing, but distantly, with Henry leaning against her leg. Mike Bolknor walked up and studied her face, which seemed strange thing to do.

She fished in her jeans pocket and got out her car keys.

Bolknor frowned and shook his head.

"Cooper, we need to get downtown, give our statements," he said. "Why don't you ride with me, let these kids drive your car home?"

She thought: he believes I'm in shock and shouldn't drive.

Okay.

She handed her keys to Jerry Shapiro and got into the Prius on the passenger side, laying her cane between the seats. Henry scrabbled into the car and then climbed onto her lap and sighed.

Jane Austen tonight, she thought. Peppermint tea.

As they drove north toward Dill, neither of them speaking, the engine soundless, she sat serenely watching the autumnal landscape slip by. Thoughts and emotions swam slowly through her mind.

A Dill PD cruiser passed them, going the other way, headed for the barn, blue lights flashing, siren wailing. Then another. Soon the forensics van would speed along here, coming from Waterbury.

Cooper felt as if a lump of lead sat in her chest. Slowly, she understood why: she mourned for Drew Saunders.

Not the monster. She'd just met him. She despised him. No, it was her old friend she missed, that charming fellow, such amusing company. Her imaginary friend.

She started to tell Mike Bolknor about that odd sort of mourning, as he drove. She stopped herself. Kept silent. This man truly mourned. One year ago, in a stupid incident of road rage, a man killed his wife and children.

Was he handling it? She feared to ask. Not right now.

They topped a hill and before them lay the Ira River, a gray ribbon under the gray sky, and on the other side Dill climbed its hills, with the Green Mountains billowing beyond. It looked from here like a model-railroad's city, its houses and business buildings and steepled churches all tiny.

No spider's web strands spread through the town now.

Nobody needs to park outside my house all night, Cooper thought.

It was over.

Except for one more hard thing to do, the hardest.

They waited for Tip LaPerle to come back from the front desk, where he'd gone for a radio talk with his officers at the barn. Henry no longer felt compelled to press against Cooper's leg. He explored the office, sniffing, and she could see his natural cockiness coming back.

Mike Bolknor sat with both large shoes planted on the floor, looking ahead, saying nothing.

"How's everything going, Mike?" Cooper asked.

He didn't look at her, or respond.

Just then Tip LaPerle came back into the office and sat behind his desk, shaking his head.

"Jeezum Crow," he said. "Who'd believe it—Drew Saunders!"

Cooper looked down and sighed.

"I called my sister, in Germany," Mike suddenly said.

Cooper looked up, saw him still staring straight ahead.

"Kirstie said she'd like to meet you," he told Cooper, still looking ahead.

Tip glanced from one of them to the other, sensing this conversation was in code.

"I invited her here for Christmas," Mike said. "She'll get leave—hope that'll be good with you."

"That'll be wonderful," Cooper said.

Cooper felt relief.

He'd invited Kirstie for a visit. It meant the crisis had passed. He wanted her to know.

"Christmas," Cooper said. "I'm looking forward to it."

"Yeah, *Jingle Bells* all around," Tip said. "Cooper—we've been out at the hunting camp, Mike and me, because we had something to thrash out."

Cooper thought: like who's got the bigger antlers? Who kicks hardest?

"Dill PD, we've got budget problems, right?" Tip said. "If we need a detective, we have to go begging to the troopers."

That wasn't news to Cooper.

"They're understaffed, getting tighter all the time," Tip said.

He sat back in his chair and exhaled, as if this was difficult to say.

"I talked with Mike about working with us, when we need him, moonlighting, but more like a volunteer," he said. "Dill PD'll pay back by helping out on the campus—like with patrols—so what do you think?"

Cooper almost laughed, but stopped herself.

What did she think? Peace! Country Mouse vs. City Mouse, the war over.

"Well, I'll have to run this by the administration, of course," Cooper said.

She pretended to think.

"I expect it'll be arranged," she said.

Tip leaned back in his chair, looking relieved.

"Mike?" Cooper said. "Would you give us a lift home, Henry and me?"

What she had to do now she dreaded.

At home, she took off her jacket, and put out water and food for Henry, while he barked, demanding accelerated service.

"Got our swagger back, have we?" she asked him.

She sank into an armchair, shut her eyes, and didn't move.

After a while, she sighed.

She opened her eyes and stared at the telephone on the chair-side stand.

Finally she reached for it and lifted it from its cradle.

She tapped in a long number.

Barcelona.

Three days later Cooper sat in Mona Saunders' living room, watching Mona drink a gin martini. She drank a Perrier herself, all she wanted.

She'd just brought Mona home from the Burlington airport, and Mona's two Gucci suitcases lay on the carpet, only one opened.

Mona peered at the olive in her glass. Then took another sip.

"Mm, mm, good," she said.

"How are you?" Cooper said.

Mona looked at her, over her cocktail glass's rim, balefully.

"Hunky-dory," she said.

She raised the glass high, a toast.

"Here's to your security guy's Glock."

She sipped, thinking.

She raised the glass again.

"Ding-dong—the wizard's dead!"

"Seriously," Cooper said.

"Horrible," she said. "The murderer part."

"You never suspected?" Cooper said.

"That he was a psychopathic killer, that son of a bitch?" Mona said. "No—just the philandering cracker part, and those weren't only suspicions."

Cooper raised her eyebrows, a question.

"I've got spies," Mona said.

She gestured with her glass, northeast, toward Hart's Corners.

"Even at the world's edge—so, yeah, I knew about that tarty teacher."

She stared into her martini glass, as if it were a crystal ball.

"What's disgusting is I did know, so he didn't even need to kill her," Mona said. "I didn't want him killing deer—never thought of school marms."

They both sat silently, thinking.

"You know what's funny?" Mona said. "It wasn't a bad marriage, in its weird way."

She shook her head.

"We had amusement, you know? And I got beauty and he got gold."

Cooper waited, watching her friend think.

"Good sex," Mona said. "Too much information?"

Cooper said nothing, letting Mona think and talk.

"I'm an aesthetics addict," Mona said. "Paintings, music...Drew."

With her forefinger she irritably wiped away a tear.

"Something wasn't there..." she said.

Cooper thought: connection? Love?

Mona drained her cocktail glass and got up and disappeared into the kitchen, for a refill. She returned and stared out the big window, at Hill Street, her back to Cooper.

"I've had a lover," she said.

Cooper said nothing, looking at Mona's back.

"All along," she said. "In Spain."

Cooper kept silent.

"Gabriela's an actress," Mona said. "In the Spanish movies."

Cooper remained silent.

"Gorgeous," Mona said. "She loves me."

She spun around and stared fiercely at Cooper.

"Have I shocked you?" she said. "Revolted you?"

Cooper considered.

"A little shocked, I guess," she said. "That's all."

"I've got legal things," Mona said. "Then I'm going back to Barcelona, hide out with Gabriela."

"For a while?" Cooper asked.

"Just for a while," Mona said.

Cooper got up and walked over and put her arms around Mona, who also was weeping, just a little.

Later that evening, in her own living room, Cooper sat in her favorite armchair. Henry lay beside her, glancing at her every so often, reassuring himself that all was back as it should be.

Cooper had a book in her lap—*Sense and Sensibility*—but she'd stopped reading a while ago and sat with her head back, thinking. She shook her head once. Faintly, she smiled, sadly.

On the table beside her chair rested a cup of peppermint tea.

She'd left her front window's curtains open. No parked Campus Security cruiser hid out under the maples, in the moonlight. Nobody kept watch.

No need.

THE END